ANGELUS

By Sabrina Benulis

THE BOOKS OF RAZIEL

ARCHON

COVENANT

ANGELUS

THE BOOKS OF RAZIEL

SABRINA BENULIS

HARPER Voyager

An Imprint of HarperCollins*Publishers*

ANGELUS. Copyright © 2016 by Sabrina Benulis. All rights reserved. Printed in the United States of America. No part of this book may be used or reproduced in any manner whatsoever without written permission except in the case of brief quotations embodied in critical articles and reviews. For information address HarperCollins Publishers, 195 Broadway, New York, NY 10007.

HarperCollins books may be purchased for educational, business, or sales promotional use. For information please e-mail the Special Markets Department at SPsales@harpercollins.com.

First Harper Voyager trade paperback edition published 2016.

Harper Voyager and design is a trademark of HarperCollins Publishers L.L.C.

Designed by Paula Russell Szafranski

Library of Congress Cataloging-in-Publication Data has been applied for.

ISBN 978-0-06-206942-9

16 17 18 19 20   OV/RRD   10 9 8 7 6 5 4 3 2 1

FOR MY DAUGHTER,
WHO IS ALL THE INSPIRATION I NEED

Acknowledgments

Five years ago, when I sat down to write the acknowledgments for *Archon,* the first installment in the Books of Raziel trilogy, the day when I'd sit to write them again for the final novel in the series seemed like a speck on the horizon of life.

Yet here I am.

I've spent a literal decade in Angela Mathers's world. In that time, I've learned so much about myself as a person and as a writer that in many ways, I can say these novels are a part of me. It is a surreal feeling to leave these characters behind. But like all turning points in life, this stage was inevitable. These acknowledgments are a fond farewell from me to a world I've created, but they're also an embrace of the future and all those who've made it possible.

So I sincerely thank my husband, my precious daughter, my parents, my family, my close friends, and all the fans of this trilogy for their encouragement, faith, and pride in my work. No words can ever express how much that has meant to me throughout this journey.

I also sincerely thank my agent, Ann Behar, my editor,

Kelly O'Connor, copy editor Laurie McGee, cover artist Nekro, and the team at Harper Voyager who worked to turn this book into a concrete reality. Thank you for all you've done to help make my dreams come true.

My dear cockatiel, Caesar, thank you for always chirping your enthusiasm over the years.

And God, who makes all things possible, thank You for carrying me through them.

Until next time, everyone!

ANGELUS

Genesis ∽ The Story So Far

Before the beginning of all things, there was a Mother who sang and carried the stars within her.

Worry consumed her because often the stars near her heart burned and jostled, as if fighting one another. Then the unthinkable happened, and she gave birth to twins long before the appointed time. These children were meant to be equal in every way, but from the start one twin decided to claim dominion over our universe. He attacked his sibling, murdering him, and from then on a fragile balance weighed toward the side of shadows.

The Mother who had carried these gods fell into the deepest despair and took her punishment to the depths of the eternal Abyss.

Innumerable cycles of time passed before an angel named Raziel found her again.

Raziel was one of three powerful sibling angels, and they had also been told their purpose was to share equal rule over the universe. Yet the jealousy and rivalry between two of them, Israfel and Lucifel, grew to a feverish pitch, and upon returning to his home in Heaven, Raziel found his sister, Lucifel, instigating the infamous War that would divide the angels forever into two opposing kingdoms.

It was a dreadful time of blood and feathers falling like the snow.

Raziel was the last to fall. Horrified and determined to end the bloodshed, he had confronted God and begged for intervention to stop Lucifel's rebellion. Instead, he plummeted to his death in full view of his siblings, one of whom loved him more than life itself.

The glorious time of Israfel's rule as Archangel in Heaven was over.

Lucifel too had failed to claim the crown she so desperately desired, and she fled to her new kingdom of Hell. But the Throne of Hell was little more than a prison, and Lucifel found herself swiftly jailed by the angels who had once worshipped her. They called themselves demons, and though their kingdom remained forever dark and dismal, they never forgot the glories of long ago.

This truce between angels and demons could not last. Instead, Lucifel's influence grew from the darkness, and her twisted ideals seeped throughout the universe. Seeking the mysterious power contained in Raziel's Book, one of his greatest treasures, it is claimed she means to destroy the universe that mocks her suffering.

The last hope for a crumbling world is a being called the Archon, also known as Angela Mathers. Angela is human, but her unique soul is protected by the spirit of Raziel. She alone can successfully oppose Lucifel and open Raziel's Book for the power of good rather than evil. However, the Book is not a thing but a person, and Angela knows that to open the Book would mean murdering her best friend,

Sophia. She has refused to do so, seemingly sentencing the universe to a fate of silence worse than death, because it would be one without resurrection.

Angela Mathers firmly believed that even Hell could not separate her from her friend. She suffered, and bled, and fought in a twisted demonic maze to save the Book from destruction, only to unwittingly allow Lucifel to escape back to Heaven.

Now Angela sits on the Throne of Hell, fulfilling a prophecy of Ruin. But Ruin does not always mean destruction. Sometimes it means Revolution. Crowns pass from one person to the next, yet it takes a special soul to heal the burdens of all.

The Mother's song no longer echoes throughout the universe, and new notes wait to be revealed. Now, the moment of change has finally arrived. The end of a cycle of pain has begun.

For though souls have hurt, and bled, and cried, the light ever returns in a rushing, relentless tide.

Zero

Father Schrader clutched the parchment in his hands and stared up at the scaffolding climbing the side of St. Matthias Church. He'd been careful to erase each of his footprints as he'd advanced through the heavy snow, leaning down to fill them back in before anyone noticed. Perhaps that would all be for nothing. Surely, the scaffolding would rattle the second he set foot on it.

He didn't have much choice. The church doors were probably locked.

He glanced around, observing the nearby buildings. Most of them were in a state of heavy decay. Only one or two probably had any inhabitants. Faintly, down a long cobbled alley, he could see flickering candles set in one of the windows. As if the people inside sensed they were being watched, the candles suddenly snuffed out.

Father Schrader looked up at the dark sky. He listened for the telltale sound of heavy wingbeats.

Nothing. Now was his chance.

He folded the paper into fourths and set his numb hands

on the metal scaffold. The first two sections used ladders rather than stairs, and a layer of glassy ice slicked the rails. He bit his lip, trying to ignore the painful chill already leaching into his palms. His teeth chattered despite his heavy coat. "I'm getting too old for this," he muttered to no one in particular, and his voice sounded hollow in the lonely air.

He really should have sent one of the novices on this mission. But Nina Willis had insisted that it was best he go himself.

With painful slowness, he ascended the scaffold. It didn't rattle after all. Perhaps it was too cold, as if the church also had a skeleton and bones that could freeze solid.

His foot slipped once, twice. Adrenaline raced through him like fire, and his heartbeat galloped. Then, at last, he reached a platform next to one of the broken windows. It had once held a sparkling picture of the Annunciation. Now it was a busted menagerie of color. The angel's face in the picture had shattered, leaving behind a headless figure with white wings. Father Schrader settled down beside the hole in the angel's face. His hands shivering with cold, he pulled out the parchment and reread it. The writing looked hasty, more scratches than letters.

Father Schrader,

Some of the members of the Vermilion Order have been meeting secretly at St. Matthias Church. Fury says they often arrive at midnight, but it's too dangerous for her to enter the church herself, and besides, the angels are shooting down too many crows for sport. None remain at that location, and so my presence would be suspect too. I have a bad feeling about what's going on there. We'll do our part to scour Luz and find Gloriana's mirror tonight—and

take it before anyone notices. If we don't hear from
you by morning, Juno will come looking.
  Best of luck,
  Nina Willis

Father Schrader hesitated for a moment. Then, his mind set, he tore the parchment into minuscule pieces and shoved them into his pocket. If he was killed, let his murderers think he'd acted alone.

The silence gnawed at him. His heart still racing, he turned and looked out over the western side of Luz.

The grander mansions owned by the Vatican still shone with an ironically optimistic golden light. If he focused, Father Schrader could discern the steeple of St. Mary's Cathedral, and surrounding it, many of Westwood Academy's tallest buildings. Beyond them lay the poorer divisions of the island city, and then the landscape sloped downward, and most of the houses descended with it, until one stood at the edge of an eerily calm ocean. Ordinarily, the view from where he sat would have been even more spectacular. Glorious lights had probably kissed every window in the city only a few months ago, during the festive Christmas season. Amazing, the shadows that fear brought.

Because in the sky overloaded with stars, another city revolved. It seemed large as a galaxy, and its multicolored brilliance emanated power and majesty. From its sparkling depths, angels flew and entered Luz, and its light shone like a moon in Luz's perpetual night. The beauty of the angelic city almost matched the terror it induced.

Worlds that should never have contact with each other were on the brink of colliding.

Father Schrader startled. Voices had started to echo inside

the church. Carefully, he turned, leaned close to the hole in the window, and peered inside. A suffocating darkness filled the space, but his eyes eventually adjusted. Slivers of light from the angelic city penetrated even here.

There was nothing to see at first. Just rotten pews and snow.

He searched in the direction of the altar. Shadows moved and conversed anxiously with one another. It was clear that some of them wore the long black coats of novices. Others were priests he recognized from conclaves in Luz. Others wore ordinary clothes, but their stance and louder voices suggested people in authority. The jumble of voices made it impossible to glean anything from their conversation.

Then, every voice silenced. A few candles were lit, and the faces above them searched the ramparts of the church for spies. One of those faces focused in on the Annunciation window.

Father Schrader ducked. Despite the cold, sweat beaded his forehead.

But nothing happened. He must not have been seen.

Inch by inch, he dared to rise and look through the hole again. There were more lights now, and he recognized a few individuals with absolute certainty. Two of them were female: a novice under his direction named Lizbeth and a young girl from the elementary grades. He didn't know her name, but she'd been to him for confession multiple times. Her blond hair caught the light and seemed to shine. Many of those in the church spoke to her with a reverence almost as shocking as her presence.

Then she turned aside to speak to Lizbeth, and her eyes flashed an ominous shade of crimson.

It couldn't be.

Father Schrader held his breath, struggling to hear. The young girl's voice floated toward him like an echo.

". . . I will not tolerate anyone standing in my way. Besides, I respect you enough to see you as less than absolute fools. Neither the Archon nor Her supporters will win this battle. So make certain that if you join my mother's cause, you have no intention of turning back. She tolerates betrayal even less than myself . . ."

"How do we know that *you* won't betray *us*?" a bombastic voice said. "Do you think we allowed you to take those souls from Memorial Cemetery without suffering for it? Even now—and forgive me—but it almost feels like a mistake. You're unlike the other angels, after all. You must understand our concern . . ."

Father Schrader recognized that voice. It was Bishop Kline, the mayor of Luz in all but actual title.

The priest shivered more. How fortunate he'd decided not to be open with any of his superiors.

"Do you mean you're suffering from a guilty conscience?" the girl asked. Her eyes glowed softly. "That is none of my concern, priest. Besides, consider the great good you're doing in exchange. My mother, Lucifel, will reward you for your service. Trust me, unlike how she has been portrayed throughout history, she tends to keep her promises."

"But if you would just tell us what you intend to do with them—"

"Does it matter?" the girl said. "In your beliefs they are beyond pain. That should be enough to console you for now."

Bishop Kline's hesitant stance suggested he wasn't quite sure of his beliefs anymore.

Father Schrader struggled to control his ragged breaths. He'd encountered this strange angel before. Her name was

Mikel, and, stunningly enough, she'd just revealed herself to be the Devil's daughter. But why were the angels stealing human souls? The frightening hunger behind Mikel's burning eyes could mean all sorts of things. Though there was sadness too. Its oppressive weight seemed to tighten the world around them all.

Even so, he couldn't understand. Why would angels obey Lucifel? She ruled over Hell.

Unless—

Had she infiltrated Heaven again somehow?

Now a young male novice stepped forward. The gold cross at his neck gleamed brightly. "Enough of this fearmongering," he said bravely, inching toward Mikel.

His left hand fidgeted behind his back with something else that caught the light. A dagger.

He searched his companions nervously, but none dared to move with him or back him up. "What can your kind possibly do for us?" the novice continued, his voice trembling. "You're nothing but winged monsters. And you—you're the most monstrous of all. I know what will happen. Whether with the Archon's help or without it, we're doomed. Lucifel will destroy us when she tires of our existence. You're probably taking those souls to devour them, or to use them for some hellish purpose. I remember what that demon did in St. Mary's. So then, *this is for my dead sister*," he shouted.

He lunged at Mikel with the dagger.

A few individuals rushed to hold him back. Cries of anger and fear reverberated through the church.

Instantly, the little girl dropped unconscious to the ground and the novice began to scream.

His screams ceased as abruptly as they began. The little girl stirred in her sleep and a priest swiftly knelt by her side, lifting her up into a sitting position. "She's alive," he said sharply to the others who'd gathered around them. A collective sigh of relief went through everyone.

But the novice who'd dared to attack Mikel now stood with his eyes glowing red.

"Would anyone else like to try something stupid?" the angel said through him.

Everyone turned and stared at him, wide-eyed. No one said a word. Mikel had jumped from one body to another in the space of a thought.

"This should convince you," she said softly, "that the Archon's power can't match my mother's or mine. And if you think the Supernal Israfel will save you, consider that he's imprisoned by Lucifel now as well. If Lucifel's new reign is about to begin, make the intelligent decision about whose side to be on. The universe's last hourglass has turned over, and God no longer holds it. It is us or Angela Mathers. And I doubt she'll feel very merciful toward the humans who made her life so miserable."

So that was it. Despite whatever was going on with the human souls taken from Memorial Cemetery, Mikel's intention was for Angela Mathers—the Archon—to die if she returned to Luz. It was pure insanity—Angela could certainly choose to end the world, but she could also choose to save it. Lucifel, on the other hand . . . no human really knew her goals, but they couldn't be good.

Yet it made little sense. Nina had told Father Schrader that Mikel had been helpful previously.

The angel probably had her own motivations. Her oppressive sorrow might be a clue. But regardless of everything, that meant once they'd brought Angela back from Hell, she would have to be protected. No one could afford her death.

The Book of Raziel had to be opened and the final choice to ultimately save or destroy the universe made, and before it crumbled apart or—just as terribly—the dimensions collided together.

He could only wonder what was keeping Angela from making that choice already.

Father Schrader shifted his weight to his knees.

An echoing creak shuddered through the scaffold. A piece of the platform snapped.

Mikel whipped around to look up at the hole in the window. She saw him. Her red eyes narrowed angrily.

The others in the church shouted in confusion. Father Schrader sensed rather than saw that Mikel was coming after him. Trembling violently, he scrambled backward and began to half climb and half slide down the first ladder back to the ground. If he slipped, he'd certainly either die or at least break bones.

He was halfway there already. He might make it.

Glass smashed above him. It flew past him in chunks to the snow. One piece caught his cheek, slicing into it like solid fire.

He looked above him. Mikel—or more accurately, the novice she was possessing—had flown through the window and snagged the platform where he'd been standing. The novice's face and hands bled with cuts from the glass. Then she half flipped over the side of the platform, racing down the ladder toward Father Schrader. Perhaps she'd rethought pushing the novice's body with another flight. It wasn't necessary anyway. She was preternaturally fast.

She was gaining on him too quickly. He had no choice but to jump now.

He let go of the last ladder, plummeting ungracefully into

the snow below. Father Schrader sank, crying out as his body hit the frozen ground beneath. An immense pain overtook him, threatening to shut down his heart and brain. He struggled for breath, fighting off the urge to sink into unconsciousness. His legs screamed out they were broken, and they refused to move as a strange warmth crept through him.

"*Exorcizo te,*" he shouted, waiting to feel Mikel's hands wrap around his neck any second. *I exorcize you . . .*

His voice died away. Nothing happened. He opened his eyes, startled to find the novice Mikel had possessed lying in the snow a few feet away. The young man's ankle looked broken. Many of the cuts bled profusely.

Father Schrader fought with his fear, but then he speedily reached over and felt for a pulse.

The novice was alive.

And—Father Schrader looked down at his own body in surprise—he must not have injured his legs badly, after all.

Voices sounded from outside near the front of the church. Those inside were probably exiting to find him and Mikel. He stole one last glance at the novice crumpled on the ground, muttered a prayer of healing, and then shot away toward a narrow alley at the church's rear. Though Nina had said no more crows lived near the church, he burst through a few of them strutting around a storm grate in the alley. They launched away from him, screeching madly, and wild with fear, he continued to run and didn't stop until he found shelter inside an abandoned fortune-telling shop.

Gasping for breath, he slid to the ground.

Time passed. He hadn't been followed, but Father Schrader still felt it wise to lie low for a bit longer. Absently, he fingered a few of the discarded items strewn across the floor. One of them was a gilded hand mirror. He picked it up, studying the ornate carvings on its back. Heavens, his head ached. He was lucky to be alive after a shock like that.

He flipped the mirror over. Father Schrader's face betrayed his years, and his white hair had matted with melted snow.

He focused on his weary features. The headache was already consuming him. Had he suffered a concussion of some kind from his fall? Slowly, his vision wavered. He couldn't be that tired, surely. A new fear overtook him, and the worst possible scenario erupted into his mind.

He thought frantically of Nina Willis and the others while the world disappeared. The mirror clattered from his hands, but not before he'd already seen it.

There—in his irises—a flash of red.

PART ONE

Reawakening

Thirty-Five Days until the Great Silence

Because all memories are but grains of sand,
fallen through the hourglass of dreams.

One

The sky had cleared in Luz.

The endless snowfall of months past had ceased, and now most of the city lay frozen in layers of whiteness.

Wind no longer blew. As ever, the sun refused to show itself, but now the clouds and moon had also vanished. Only millions of stars shone overhead, somehow much too bright and far too close. In the glassy ocean surrounding the isolated city, dead fish floated to the surface day after day, and a strange gleam on the horizon birthed constant rumors of the sea icing over. No wonder there were no more waves. Soon, everyone knew, that ice would finally reach Luz and freeze it solid.

Did the world outside know or care? Did it suffer in the same way? Nobody really knew.

For months on end, Luz had been cut off from mainland America. It was a tiny island city owned by the Vatican, governing itself, steeped in its unique miasma of gothic decadence. Luz answered to no one and opened its doors to few.

Most of those few made up the population of the Vatican's Westwood Academy, and even more of those students were "blood heads"—the feared embodiment of a prophecy of Ruin. That Ruin was an occult woman called the Archon—someone whom many priests and theologians considered to be the reincarnation of the dead angel Raziel. Her defining feature was thought to be Her blood-red hair, a trait shared with the angel. The Archon would soon make a choice: either to save the universe or ultimately take the route of the Devil and let it fall to pieces.

By the look of things, Nina Willis understood most people assumed the latter had already happened. They believed that no matter what the Vatican had done to sniff out and erase the Archon's existence, She'd entered the Academy, survived its intrigues, and gone on to choose destruction for the humanity that had made Her life so wretched.

Then again, most people didn't know Angela Mathers like Nina did. Because without any doubt whatsoever, Nina knew that they were wrong.

She sighed and stared out at the angelic city of Malakhim revolving against the western horizon, infinitely high above the broken human city of Luz.

Malakhim had appeared a few weeks ago, like a galaxy set where the sun should have been. Gradually, each day it seemed a little larger and brighter. Occasionally, an angel would be spotted here or there in the star-speckled sky, soaring from its glory. Yet no matter what the priests said, they could no longer console people into being optimistic. Most citizens of Luz hid in their homes, holed up in icy terror. A desperate few had taken rowboats to sea. Better to take their chances there, they'd hoped.

The Realms were threatening to merge.

Dimensions would collide before crumbling forever. And then . . .

The sound of wingbeats met Nina's ears. She turned, startled for only a second.

The tree branch beside her creaked and snapped beneath a heavy weight. The woods surrounding them lay blanketed in ice and snow, and anything that broke the peace sounded alarmingly loud. The naked branches glistened like diamonds in the glow of gas lamps sprinkled throughout Memorial Cemetery. More ice crackled as the visitor shifted weight.

Have you found what you were looking for? A girlish voice echoed in Nina's head.

I think so, Nina responded. *But I still can't believe it . . .*

She knelt down beside a tiny sapling growing in the half-frozen soil. Its crown had actually punched through a layer of ice. Mysteriously, its branches were in bud.

Very close by, a large hole with half-frozen clods of dirt tossed out of it gaped next to a great tree trunk. They were the last remnants of an ancient oak, split and burned by lightning.

The branches above Nina creaked and groaned with the weight resting on them again. A crow's guttural croak shivered through the air, announcing the enormous bird that flew out of the shadows and landed on another branch to Nina's right. A different pair of owlish yellow eyes gleamed back at Nina from the darkness of the canopy where the bird had escaped and the ice crackled.

Their owner stared at the little sapling with burning interest, and then chose to speak out loud. "That's a baby tree? How can they start so small?"

Nina laughed. "Just like you did. Everyone starts small, and then grows. That's just the way of things."

"Yes," the voice said sadly. "Just like how everyone dies?" A soft hiss of regret ended the sentence.

"Well, that is true," Nina agreed. "But sometimes," she whispered, "there are exceptions."

She was one of them.

Nina had been a normal human girl once, and a very ordinary one except for a crucial detail: she'd been able to speak to the souls of the dead. That talent had earned her a place at Westwood Academy, but it hadn't earned her any real friends. Until Angela Mathers came along. Then the wheels of Nina's fate had been set in motion. She often wondered if there was anyone who had died as many times as she herself had. First, she'd died because of a demon. Then, she'd died trying to save the Jinn Troy and her niece Juno from another demon. Juno had explained it was that act of sacrifice that had allowed Nina to resurrect. Nina's soul had then been placed in the body of a crow—just like Fury's.

Nina glanced up again at the large black bird watching her from the treetops. Fury clacked her beak and preened nervously at a few feathers.

Yet a crucial difference already lay between them. Nina could change her shape. She only had to be a crow when she found it useful.

It was unprecedented. No Jinn familiar had that kind of talent.

If you're satisfied, Fury's sweet girlish voice interrupted Nina's thoughts again, *we should leave. We don't have much time to infiltrate the Tower. I didn't risk my life finding that mirror for nothing.*

The large crow flapped its wings in emphasis.

"She's right," the other voice in the trees added. "I'm sure the longer we wait here, the sooner an angel might spot us."

Nina peeked worriedly at the starry sky. That was true. But—and she looked back down at the baby oak tree—she was glad she'd risked coming back so soon. Seeing the sapling confirmed everything for her. Even though the world was literally falling apart, there was also another change slowly but surely taking place and fighting the destruction. At last, a Revolution had begun. Was Angela responsible?

If only Nina could ask the souls buried around them.

But they were gone. They'd already been harvested by the angels who'd stealthily infiltrated Luz. The last souls on Earth who could help the Archon were locked away somewhere, silenced. Tonight, if she could, Nina would find out exactly where, and soon she would free them. No matter what it took. That's what she was here for, after all. She sighed with relief remembering how Father Schrader had offered to help her and Juno. Hopefully, he was all right scouting at St. Matthias Church alone. Nina had a feeling about tonight, and when she had a feeling, nothing good usually happened. But they couldn't just sit back and do nothing, either.

"If only Auntie could help us," the voice in the trees said, sighing with regret. "She would know what to do next."

"I know," Nina said, sighing with her. "But the only thing we can do now is to think like Troy would think. Father Schrader said we have to get the mirror, and that it might be in the Tower. Fury confirmed it's there. We'll have to worry about where all those souls might be and how to free them later. This might be our only chance to get that mirror back."

A great *whoosh* of air erupted high above them.

Nina threw herself against a tree trunk, breathing hard.

Fury and the little Jinn high up in the trees stiffened like statues.

Slowly, like a dream, an angel winged his way through

the everlasting night. He flew so gracefully, the spectacle threatened to still Nina's heart for good again. She recognized in his slender hands the arrows that terrified Fury so much. They gleamed faintly with energy. Fury had almost been shot down by one a few days ago, shortly after they'd all entered the cemetery through the Netherworld Gate again.

The cemetery had once been inundated with crows. Now, most had at last left Luz to its fate.

In seconds, the angel was gone. "That was close," Nina whispered.

You're ready, then? Fury glided down from the canopy and croaked impatiently. *Follow me—I found a safer route toward that part of the city last night. We shouldn't be seen.*

"What about her?" Nina said, pointing up at the little Jinn still hiding in the trees.

Before Fury could answer, the Jinn's tone changed to one of deadly purpose. Her small but lethally sharp nails split the wood beneath them, and the cracking sound echoed. "I'll manage," she hissed.

Nina closed her eyes and concentrated. Instantly, it began. She sensed herself molding and shaping into a lighter body. Exhilarated, she flapped her bird wings the moment they formed and soared after Fury into the clear sky toward the Academy. The still air broke icily against her feathered body.

She stole one last glance at the sapling before the cemetery tightened to a circle of naked trees beneath them.

Nina was the first to land at the Bell Tower.

Her crow's feet scraped one of many windowsills, scrabbling for purchase on slick ice. Fury landed beside her, much more gracefully. She cocked her head at Nina in amusement before soaring up one more level onto a large veranda.

Nina followed and landed beside her, stifling the urge to knock Fury with her beak.

Instead, she hopped toward the glass pane of a great set of gabled windows and peered inside. Rags fluttered beneath a mysterious breeze. The Tower had so many fissures and cracks, they might have to war with the rats that had set up residence. Nina tapped on the glass with her beak, and she was certain she saw a huge rat scuttle away under a pile of boxes.

Where was the mirror? Where was it?

Nina remembered the mirror from Mother Cassel's fortune shop. It didn't look like much—just a brassy antique that desperately needed repairs. Even so, Gloriana Cassel had warned her to never gaze too long at it.

Father Schrader had said that was because the mirror functioned like a miniature portal to the other Realms. A rarity, such artifacts were usually hunted down by the Vatican and destroyed. Somehow, this one had survived.

With it, there was a chance, however slim, that they could contact Angela. Or maybe even bring her and Sophia back to Luz.

But first, the mirror needed to be stolen back from the authorities who'd confiscated it and locked it away in the Academy's infamous Bell Tower. Nina should have caught on to that sooner. The structure was too high and too guarded for any human to infiltrate.

Nina smiled inwardly. She wasn't just any old human anymore.

Over there, Fury said sharply. *Look at the right corner of the room. There it is.*

Nina focused and, yes, she could see it. The mirror's reflective glass briefly caught the lights of the city, and then a fluttering rag smothered it again. *All right,* she said to Fury. *Time to go in. Do you see a broken window anywhere?*

A loud crash and the sound of glass smashing answered her question.

Nina winced. Cursing inwardly, she broke away from the veranda and followed Fury to a smaller window with a giant hole now punched through the glass. More pieces of glass dangled from the break before dropping to the ground. The wind whipped and gusted into the musty room. Juno, Troy's niece, sat in a pile of broken glass looking completely bewildered. She blinked and hissed at the pain of the shards cutting into her feet.

Nina touched down beside her and shifted to her human form again. She knelt near the young Jinn and tried not to shout. They'd be lucky if no one heard that. But Nina wasn't really in a position to yell at her Jinn master, and she bit her lip hard.

She shook her head and quickly plucked some glass from the sole of Juno's foot. Juno held back the pain admirably.

Like her aunt, the new Jinn Queen was a lethal but lovely vision of chalk-white skin, sickle-shaped black wings, and flexing pointed ears. Her large yellow eyes sometimes glowed with a phosphorescent sheen. Unlike her aunt, Juno typically lacked any kind of gracefulness and finesse. Rarely did she look the part of the perfect hunter. Her chain earring— usually adorned with a metal crow's foot like her aunt's— had now broken, adding to her disheveled look. The iron pendant was missing, perhaps lost somewhere in the gutters of Luz.

Juno sat on her haunches and licked away the rest of the blood.

She breathed hard, staring at the window like it had betrayed her. Also unlike Troy, she had little experience with glass—something Luz had in abundance.

Fury touched down near them and shook her crow's head in irritation. *The little one is becoming a liability,* she croaked.

Nina shot her a nasty look. *Watch what you say. You know how Troy would respond if she were here.*

The Vapor ignored Nina, flapped her black wings, and glided over to the mirror. She landed on top of its gilded frame and tugged at the rag, dropping it to the floor. The mirror's reflective surface gleamed and glistened.

Juno gazed at it pensively. Nina watched as she approached the mirror and stared at her reflection. A network of fine blue veins laced beneath Juno's ghostly white skin, and her eyes threw back all the light of the room like a cat's. Her azure-tinted lips parted in wonder as she touched the glass. Juno drew back her hand at the noise of her black nails scraping its surface. Her ears flicked thoughtfully.

"Will you be able to carry that heavy thing such a distance?" Nina whispered to her.

Juno adopted a superior attitude. She stood, stretching her wings. Her ears pressed against her skull in annoyance. "Are you kidding? I could carry this in my sleep."

Nina chose not to press the issue any further. They didn't have many options. "All right," she continued. "But make sure you stick to the darkest paths possible. We can't have anyone seeing—"

There was the muffled sound of wingbeats and feet touching the floor of the veranda.

She paused. Fury stiffened. Juno hunkered close to the ground and seemed to regress into the shadows. Soon, she'd melted into them so skillfully her presence could have been a dream. Her eyes narrowed to glowing slits and then blinked out.

Swiftly, Nina shifted back to her crow shape and crouched beside Fury.

Together, they watched a tall, angelic silhouette pace the veranda. At last, the angel paused and fiddled with the great set of windows. They swung open noiselessly. He strode into the room, letting in a gust of icy air, his great wings arched impressively above his back. He was dressed like a soldier of some kind, with glittering cuffs along the bones of his pinions. The bow and arrow at his side glittered with the lights of Luz. Slowly, his large blue eyes scanned the darkness. He was perfect, as all angels were, and in the most unnerving way. Nina would guess his senses were almost as keen as Juno's or Troy's.

He strode toward the mirror, gazing at it in curiosity.

It was clear he wasn't leaving anytime soon. He circled and paced for what felt like an eternity. Eventually, his back turned to Nina and Fury. The angel's mahogany-colored wings and hair were familiar—he must have been the same angel patrolling the skies near Memorial Cemetery.

Nina, Juno's thoughts whispered into her mind, *on my signal—attack him. I'll do the rest.*

Are you sure? Juno, he's dangerous—

I'm sure. Trust me.

That was hard to do when Juno was still little more than a chick. But Nina had few choices when it came to obeying her master. She tried to calm herself, taking deep breaths. Time seemed to slow.

Juno's eyes glowed back at her briefly from a corner of the room and then blinked out again.

The angel spun on his heel, suspicious. Another odd but howling gust of wind penetrated the tower.

NOW! Juno's voice rang.

Two

Nina had no time to rethink what came next. The fear would have stifled her. She burst from the darkness, Fury behind her, both of their talons aiming for the angel's eyes.

He turned, tossing a crackling wave of energy in their direction.

It fanned at Nina like blue lightning.

Fury screeched and dropped to the ground quickly. But Nina found her mark, slicing the angel across the face with her nails. He whipped out his bow and arrow almost too fast to see. His perfect teeth gritted together, and his chin bled. The arrow glowed fatally and shot in her direction.

Nina let herself plummet to the floor. The arrow whistled past, striking the wall with a vicious burst of light.

Despite the painful brilliance, Juno exploded from her hiding place and slammed into the angel. Her weight pitched him to the floor on his back.

BOOM.

Juno bit his hand before he could reach for another arrow. The sharp smell of more blood hit Nina. But the angel only screamed once before Juno's nails threatened to cut off his air for good. This was an incredible opportunity. If Juno acted right, they could find out so much important information, or better still, they could learn where Angela might be. Nina could only watch eagerly, her avian heart thrumming like a bee's wings.

"Talk," Juno snarled. A deadly light brightened her eyes more. Now she looked much more like her aunt.

"A Jinn chick?" the angel whispered hoarsely. "Little feathered rat!" He tried to spit in her face. Juno clamped down harder on his throat.

"Talk. I won't say it again," she snapped at him. Only Nina and Fury knew how afraid she probably was right now. Her subtly shaking wings gave her away. "Why are you in Luz?"

"I could say . . . the same about you . . ." the angel wheezed. When Juno's lips lifted, revealing her sharp teeth, he managed to stammer a better answer. "Reconnaissance. The Realms are colliding slowly. Archangel Zion sent us to investigate before his abdication. The human priests have been cooperating with us to flush out any evil creatures in their city before we leave it to its fate."

At the word *abdication* Juno looked confused.

The angel continued with obvious reluctance. "Now the crown of Heaven has been passed to another."

"To who?" Juno said.

The angel's lips sealed tightly this time. Obviously, he wasn't going to offer anything further.

"To the Archon?" Juno offered.

The angel smirked. "She doesn't need the crown of Heaven. She already has one in Hell."

Nina had to keep herself from gasping. Angela was still in

Hell—but on Lucifel's Throne. Then where was Lucifel? Was it she who now ruled Heaven?

A deep chill worked its way through Nina's soul.

Juno tilted her head, seeming to think. Carefully, she reached down and broke first the angel's bow and then each adamant arrow. Finally, she leaned in very close to his face. The angel breathed hard and fast as Juno sniffed the cut on his chin. Hunger was written all over her face. Earth wasn't hospitable to Jinn, angels, or demons. In the human Realm they often suffered the longer they stayed, and after a few days, Juno's hunger must have been immense. Rats might not have been enough for her anymore.

Nina watched in tense silence. Fury limped to her side, also silent.

Slowly, Juno licked the blood from the angel's chin. She closed her eyes, as if savoring the taste. The angel stared up at her, both transfixed and terrified.

Her hand struck him powerfully across the face again.

The angel screamed before falling unconscious, his head thumping back against the stone floor.

"That's for letting my people starve for millennia," she muttered. "I'm not like you, angel. Things have to change—in a good way."

Juno climbed off his chest and shook out the feathers of her wings. She truly resembled an indignant queen, even if a small one.

Nina and Fury looked at each other.

They both let out a sigh of relief that sounded like a croak.

Juno arched her wings proudly and turned, nodding at the mirror. Her hunger and the angel were already forgotten. The fear that had made her wings tremble had also misted over her bright eyes, but she seemed to be recovering fast.

"What are we waiting for?" she said brightly to Nina. "I guess it's time to leave."

Nina strutted over to the angel and examined his pale face. There was no telling how long he'd be unconscious. And now, their presence would be known.

Reconnaissance? She looked to Fury. That didn't explain why all the human souls had disappeared.

Fury hadn't bought the angel's explanation either. She stared off into the distance, seeming disturbed.

Nina's mind raced. Her bad feeling was becoming worse. Somehow, it didn't seem beyond some of the officials in Luz to try bargaining with these angels to save their skins. She could only wonder what the price happened to be for their help. Probably nothing good.

Her thoughts switched over again to the human spirits trapped in the cemetery and harvested by angels. What did they possibly need them for?

Nina hadn't prayed in a long time. Even so, she hoped her feelings could find their way to Angela through so much distance and danger. She glanced at the angelic city on the horizon, and another shiver worked through her body that was born from something other than the icy chill. Despite its beauty and grandeur, Heaven didn't seem quite so heavenly right now.

Angela, we need you. Open the Book of Raziel quickly, before it's too late. I don't understand—what are you waiting for? What's happened to you?

Faintly, like the farthest echo imaginable, she could have sworn an answer reached her.

Nina wasn't sure she liked what she heard.

Three

Deadly tension filled the Council chamber as the imprisoned angel was brought forward.

He was tall like the demons but boasted blond hair and wings. Shining metal cuffs—the mark of a soldier—protected his wing bones and a few decorous gems glittered near his shoulders. Of course his weapons had been taken some time ago, and his hands had been secured by adamant, energy-repelling manacles.

Kim watched with the others in stark silence as the demons flung the prisoner before Angela. A dull echo rang throughout the chamber as his knees hit the stone. Two sharp tridents jabbed immediately afterward for the angel's neck. "You will kneel before the Prince of Hell," one of the demons said maliciously.

The angel obeyed but stared ahead. The demons who'd poked him continued to stand guard anyway. Side by side, their shared heritage with the angel was more obvious than ever before. These guards were from the younger generation of demons, and though their skin was a dark copper color, and their eyelids glowed with phosphorescent paint, their features and the angel's were close to identical.

Angela shifted position on her onyx throne, crossing her legs. Half of her face lit up in the dim bloody light of Lucifel's former Altar.

The angel's wings trembled, and even the guards beside him drew back for a second.

The obsidian walls gleamed around Kim and the presiding demons of the Council like dark mirrors. In them, Angela on her great throne appeared to reflect a thousand times over, looming over every demon present. Her face had always been rather lean, and though now it appeared even more sharp and resolute, her large eyes—one blue and one a deep emerald green—and her knee-length, blood-red hair softened her features, reminding everyone that she was still human and young. Yet Angela was the Archon, and that remained the crucial difference. Now, she wore the heavy obsidian crown and the authority to prove it. Her dominating gaze said everything.

Kim wondered if this was how Lucifel behaved before she'd been caged.

Angela continued to stare at the angel with a look that might incinerate rock.

What was she thinking?

He glanced briefly at Sophia for answers, but she was pretending not to notice him. As usual she stood in the shadows behind Angela's great throne, her thick curled hair and silver dress drenched in the darkness. But her storm-gray eyes and pale skin still somehow gleamed, catching whatever light remained to her. A necklace with a white jewel pendant sparkled like a star set on her chest.

The acidic air stung Kim's throat. He turned aside,

coughing into his hand. Beside him, the Great Demon Lilith turned and shot him an irritated glare.

She'd been smiling at the impending drama, gently stroking a giant glistening spider that sat on her knee like a cat. Kim shuddered and turned away just as quickly. He could hear the spider chittering in contentment.

"There, there," Lilith whispered. She sat back deeper into her ornate chair, giving the spider's legs longer strokes. Finally it had enough and scuttled up her arm to perch on her shoulder, at last coming to rest far too close to Kim for comfort. "It will all be over soon," Lilith said, her silken voice dripping with anticipation.

The demon turned and looked pointedly at Kim.

He had no choice but to look back. Lilith was always striking, but tonight she was even more so than usual. Her dark skin blended almost seamlessly with her ebony dress, and her orange eyes seemed to burn with a fascinating inner fire. Someone had braided her inky hair. He doubted Lilith had done it. She wasn't the type to lift a finger for herself.

"Uncomfortable?" Lilith suggested, her voice high with amusement.

"Not at all," Kim whispered.

Lilith smiled. "Well, forgive me, but your shaking hands say otherwise. You should have told me you hated spiders. What a shame, yes," she said, turning to the spider and cooing at it. "He hates you, and you haven't done a thing to him." Then she added darkly, "*Yet.*"

Kim struggled to appear unconcerned. "I'm surprised you decided to come to this Council," he said, aware that his words sounded even more suspicious than he felt.

"I never miss a good show," Lilith murmured. "Especially when the Archon is starring."

Should he press his luck? He had to try to find out the truth for Angela's sake. He knew she was suffering, even if she couldn't tell him anymore.

"Perhaps it wasn't wise for you to come," Kim began.

Lilith peered at him sharply. "What do you mean? What nonsense are you about to annoy me with?"

"Well, there are rumors that you're controlling the Archon. That She's little more than a puppet ruler with you pulling the strings. That makes you a target for Lucifel's remaining worshippers, and—"

"And?" Her voice burned like her eyes.

"It's common knowledge your son, Python, desires the Throne of Hell. No one would be surprised if you're doing what you can to keep him off it. Who can really blame you?"

Lilith said nothing. Her sensual lips sealed into a tight line. "I knew I shouldn't have started a conversation with you," she finally said, sighing. "You're as ignorant as the rest of your race. Ah, wait, I'd forgotten. You're the only half-Jinn unfortunate enough to be alive." She narrowed her eyes at him, as if trying to pierce him with her words. "I wonder what it's like to be in love with a woman who barely remembers who you are? If you've decided to become Angela Mathers's knight in shining armor now, you might as well put an end to the dream today. I think it's painfully clear you're about as useful to her as a common fly."

The spider on Lilith's shoulder chittered again. Surely, it couldn't understand the word *fly*? Then again, Kim wouldn't have been surprised if that spider had once been human itself.

"Yes, I suppose you're right," Kim said, but not meaning it in the slightest. He'd never give up on Angela. Neither would Sophia.

And at last he was certain he'd struck on a solution.

Months ago, when Lilith had forced Angela to drink angel blood to peer into her mind, Kim had feared there'd be lingering aftereffects. He'd not only been right, but the worst had happened: Angela lost most of her memories. She no longer remembered chunks of her former life on Earth in the city of Luz, or much of her hellish journey to rescue Sophia from Python's clutches. In Angela's mind, she had been the Prince of Hell for a while, and it was a lie Lilith intended to nurture. Lilith was transparent enough. She wanted prosperity for Hell. She wanted control of that prosperity. And she didn't need anyone to know about it.

The only flaw in her plans was that Angela didn't seem to know how to open the Book of Raziel anymore, and Sophia could feign ignorance forever. No one was stupid enough to harm the Book—the universe's last chance of salvation—or the Archon who could open her.

But time was running out. The disintegration was rapidly affecting Hell, and Kim couldn't imagine what was going on in Luz.

Lilith's growing nastiness was a sure sign of her worries.

She tapped her bare foot against the stone floor, suddenly impatient with Angela's fearfully regal attitude.

At last, Angela was ready to speak.

Sophia stepped forward, emerging into the red light of the glowing pentagrams so that her dress shimmered. Her thick curls resembled a dark storm cloud, and her fathomless gaze scanned the assembled demons, lingering on certain individuals with interest—or suspicion. She lingered longest on Lilith. Her glance at Kim was briefer than he'd hoped, but for the best. She'd surely received his message. Now all she had to do was give him the sign that their meeting would take place tonight.

"This angel was found on the Silent Plain before the Gates of Babylon," one of the demonic guards explained in answer to a quiet question from Sophia. "We have every reason to believe he is a spy sent to infiltrate the city."

Angela stood and examined the angel carefully.

Immediately, the ranks of demons thronging the chairs set around the throne stood from their seats and knelt before her. Lilith gave a heavy sigh, but tossed the fan in her lap at a servant and knelt with the others.

High above Angela, Lucifel's former chains swayed and clinked together gently in the quiet. There, the great angel had hung in the eternal gloom of Hell, so admired and feared by her worshippers that none dared to free her. There, her mind had wandered from darkness into what Kim knew to be insanity. It was a madness he'd never allow to touch Angela as long as he lived.

The pentagrams around them pulsed with a dull bloody light. The beasts carved into the throne warped their shapes in the shadows.

"A spy?" Angela reiterated. Her voice rang, shivering Lucifel's manacles and chains again. Kim's heart raced. The sound of Angela's voice sent tremors through his soul. "That's ludicrous," she said softly. "The portals to the other Realms have all been destroyed as the dimensions are collapsing. He must have arrived here by mistake. Sit down," she said, gesturing at the kneeling demons.

They piled back into their seats. No one voiced their relief louder than Lilith. Seeming to have lost all sense of decorum, she brushed dirt from her dress and slid back into her chair, sighing loudly again.

Now the Council was open for discussion, though Angela of course had the final say in everything, and very few dared to voice an opinion despite her lack of cruelty. Angela couldn't kill with a touch or manipulate her own shadow like Lucifel, but there was something about her presence that overpowered every other. Fearful mystery reflected in that emerald green eye of hers, and it tended to silence a room. Only Kim, Sophia, Lilith, and Python acted relatively at ease around her. Perhaps because they were the few individuals who knew she wasn't like the Devil at all. But the general populace of Hell trembled before its new ruler, and Kim had nearly lost his own wits the few times Angela glared at him sideways. Did she know that if it weren't for the protective power of the Grail, she'd be hanging from the same chains that had imprisoned the Devil who'd ruled before her?

Just another reason to bring the old Angela back.

"He arrived here by mistake?" one of the Council demons reiterated to Angela. "So this is all just a big coincidence?"

Angela looked at him sharply. The tension in the chamber grew by leaps and bounds. "Maybe. Let's ask him."

She stepped directly in front of the angel, her boots clacking against the stone. He continued to stare blankly at her waist. His wings shook like leaves in a gale. Certainly he knew his life was in danger.

"How did you get here?" Angela said. Her voice echoed. No answer.

Muttering filled the room. Angela glared at him. "Do you understand what kind of danger you're in right now? Tell me how you came to Babylon and why."

Nothing. The angel could have been made of the same stone surrounding them.

One of the demons flanking the angel's side twisted his trident on the curve of the angel's neck. He flinched as a spot of blood welled from the cut. "Speak, you arrogant crow," the demon hissed. "The Prince of Hell commands you."

The dull noise in the room expanded, taking up every spare inch of space. Kim's vision swam. Angela wasn't going to execute the angel—so he hoped—but even she would sense the angel's pride wasn't making her look like much of a leader, either. Angela breathed hard and glanced around, finally settling her gaze on Kim. They both knew she couldn't afford to lose the fear that kept her subjects in awe of her. Her expression was almost asking permission of him to behave more forcefully.

Kim shook his head in denial.

Now Sophia gave him the sign he'd been waiting for. She retrieved two silver barrettes from her thick hair.

So she'd agreed to meet him as he'd asked. He offered Sophia a nod in reply.

Thankfully, Angela didn't notice. She seemed to think, at war with herself. Angela's memories of Kim were somewhat unchanged, and Kim knew she trusted him and Sophia above everyone. Her feelings had stayed intact, despite her inability to remember many of their past moments together, and Kim was grateful. But a sick feeling tied his stomach into knots when he thought of how returning her memories to her might change all that. Angela didn't need him, she just thought she did, and for Kim it was an illusion worth sustaining. He certainly couldn't rely solely on his appearance to justify his place by her side.

The obsidian reflected his pale face an even chalkier hue than usual. Being trapped in Hell alongside Angela wasn't to his advantage, despite his heritage as a half-Jinn. Tiredness glazed his amber eyes. His black hair had grown out ragged and uneven, and the red streak in his bangs had faded away to a splash of color above his nose. With no sun to mark the passage of time, he'd been sharing in Angela's nearly sleepless nights.

All he wanted was to thrust all of Hell aside and embrace her forever. Instead, he had to survive by Angela's side as an anxious shadow.

Even for him, that was no longer good enough. The Book of Raziel had to be opened. Waiting was no longer an option for anyone.

Kim pressed a hand against his pocket. Inside, the metal crow's foot talisman warmed his thigh. He wasn't sure if accepting any demon's help, especially *this* demon's, in returning Angela's memories was smart, but there was little choice left. Besides, Kim couldn't stand watching her suffer anymore. Angela had nightmares and waking visions almost every day. She spoke of being torn apart in her dreams, of the pieces of her body being flung throughout the stars. Fear plucked at him every time she spoke like that.

Was Lucifel's Grail—the emerald green Eye now a living part of Angela—responsible for such visions?

And whose eye had it been in the first place?

Perhaps that question best remained unanswered for now.

Uncharacteristic shouts erupted throughout the chamber. The more vocal demons had started to openly clamor for the angel's death. Right when the arguments reached a feverish pitch, Angela stooped down and leaned in close to the terrified angel's ear.

The angel gave a start at whatever he heard. He raised his face to Angela's, observing her with keen fascination. Had he expected her to be someone else? Maybe Lucifel? Obviously, he'd expected to die instead of being mercifully spared. Angela would never execute anyone. Kim could only ponder what she might have said to the angel that finally goaded him into speaking.

"I'm not a spy," the angel said slowly.

The escalating furor of the room died as if a switch had been flipped. Silence descended once more. Braziers set in the rock flickered.

Lilith sat up with renewed interest.

The angel glanced around before turning to Angela again. "I'm not a spy," he repeated louder, perhaps hoping that every last demon in Babylon would get the message. "I was sent on a harvesting mission to Earth and accidentally entered a new portal. You believe there are no more ways to travel between the Realms? You're wrong. Heaven and Earth are now permanently connected at the linchpin of Luz, and one city stares at the other across a divide that lessens by the hour. Hell will join them soon. The Realms are on a collision course. What hasn't crumbled is about to collide with what also remains. And then . . ."

No one spoke. Kim sensed there hadn't been such silence in Hell since it had rested empty before Lucifel's reign.

A harvesting mission? What could that mean? A chill ran up his spine.

Kim's pulse beat like a drum in his ears. If this angel spoke the truth, he, Sophia, and Angela were much closer to Luz than they'd probably ever thought possible. Angela did her best to appear unruffled by the news, though the mention of Luz in particular seemed to cause her true concern. Her brow furrowed. Perhaps she was trying to remember something crucial.

"Lies," she ended up saying, certainly aiming to poke the angel into explaining further. She turned her back to him. "Why would such a thing happen so suddenly?"

"Lucifel's breach into Heaven clearly instigated it," the angel retorted. "When she took the Throne of Heaven, the dimensional destruction accelerated."

Lucifel sat on Heaven's Throne?

Now Angela turned back around, a clear expression of alarm and worry tightening her features. Even Lilith sucked in a sharp breath. The spider on her shoulder scuttled anxiously to her other arm.

The Council devolved immediately into a fury. Voices clamored. Angela was seemingly too lost in her thoughts to demand order with either her aura or her voice. Kim could read her thoughts plainly now. If that was the case, and Lucifel ruled Heaven, then what had happened to Israfel, Heaven's former Archangel who'd followed his sister back home? Was he dead? Imprisoned? Anything could be going on. Ever since Angela took Lucifel's place in Hell, she'd been searching for an escape. She just didn't know it. Getting out of Hell and stopping Lucifel had appeared impossible to Kim, and he'd never bothered mentioning it, and he'd obsessively sought ways to open the Book of Raziel, and without accidentally destroying Sophia, before the worst happened.

Perhaps they were all too late.

Sophia often spoke to Kim of how she and Angela had raced after Lucifel on the great plain that spread throughout Hell. Her description was so vivid, Kim could always feel the Kirin beneath him as if he rode it himself, and Sophia's arms gripping his waist. He could hear Angela's scream of frustration and defeat as the portal closed with a clap and a tremendous explosion of light. Lucifel and Israfel had entered that light, returning to Heaven. Back to the angelic city that had revolved before Hell like a wheel of fire and stars.

Angela pressed a hand to her green eye, struggling to hide what Kim knew to be pain. If she wasn't careful, the visions would take her. He struggled to stay seated while a cold sweat chilled his forehead.

The angel already looked at Angela suspiciously.

"Do you speak the truth?" Angela demanded of the angel, displaying her emerald eye again. It was a struggle to keep the pain out of her voice, but she was accomplishing it admirably.

The angel examined her, obviously trying to gauge the trustworthiness of what must have been Angela's promise to spare his life. "You're the Archon, aren't you?" he whispered back, his voice steady with awe.

Angela nodded.

"The Devil herself is indeed in Heaven," the angel said quietly. "That, the collapsing dimensions, and the equal surprise of Prince Israfel's return caused a grievous divide. Then our nightmare began. Archangel Zion abdicated and Lucifel's worshippers rose swiftly to power, taking advantage of fear to imprison Israfel and set Lucifel on the throne. Of course, most angels do not wish Lucifel to rule. But we are all running out of time, and desperate souls make desperate choices. Both family and friendships crumble as everyone turns on one another in their panic. If you are the Archon, why do you let the chaos continue? If you haven't chosen to let the universe die, why not accomplish what you must to save it?"

Angela stared at him.

What could she say? She no longer knew how to open the Book, and even if she remembered, Kim knew something else held Angela back. Whenever she regarded Sophia, Angela seemed sorrowful. Her tone always became more gentle, and her stance around Sophia was always more protective. Deep down inside, her spirit certainly remembered a terrible truth. He couldn't imagine what it might be.

Most of the demons believed the Book of Raziel could not be opened at all.

Kim refused to accept that. But regardless of how the deed could be accomplished, and where the Lock and Key to open Sophia might be found, Angela alone could accomplish it. The great angel Raziel had arranged everything that way, after all. But that didn't mean Sophia was exempt from suffering. Immortal in a unique way, she could not die like a human despite the worst tortures. Often, the more rebellious demons examined her with calculating, hungry eyes.

Kim shuddered. He couldn't imagine how it would feel to exist in pieces after desperate demons tore you apart.

"The harvesting mission to Earth that you mentioned," Angela reminded the angel. "Explain to me what that's about."

But the calm of the room had given way to renewed discussion, arguments, and turmoil, and it drowned the angel's voice. Kim could barely hear himself think, and it was now clear Angela had to voice her decision about the angel's fate for everyone to hear before a riot broke out.

"Silence," Angela proclaimed, her voice echoing. "I've heard the prisoner's full confession. And this is my judgment as Prince of Hell."

Some of the noise died down.

She stole brief peeks at Kim and Sophia. If Sophia appeared fearful and abnormally pale, Kim was certain he looked the same.

"As it stands right now," Angela continued, "I do not find him guilty of conspiracy against the Realm of Hell. It is my judgment that he remain in our prison near the onyx mines, and that after ten days he will be released to return home if he can, and without any opposition whatsoever. If his life is taken on the great plain by a Hound, then fate will have given us our justice. It is so ordered."

The angel let out a relieved sigh. But the demons' collective irritation erupted like a volcano.

Lilith stood this time. She gave Angela one long, forced smile before she escaped Kim's side, walked into the throngs, and vanished, her servants trailing behind her. Her disdain for Angela's decision was evident, and it appeared to spark even more discontent. Immediately, a general consensus was reached by the demons of the Council.

The Book of Raziel *must* be opened. A tumult of voices demanded answers from Angela.

Angela sat back on her chair, rigid as a statue. Even if she trembled inside, Kim couldn't help but marvel at how she kept her voice calm and steady. "There is no way to open the Book," Angela replied for the thousandth time, repeating it over and over.

"Archon!" the angel shouted, and he shot Angela a desperate look as he was escorted from the chamber. "Do what you must! Or as you well know, all of us are doomed to death—"

His words finally faded away, as his distance and the noise in the chamber increased.

Sophia stared at Kim, her eyes taking on a deep and fathomless darkness.

Her delicate hand grasped the jewel pendant resting on her chest.

They nodded at each other now as the turmoil in the room showed no signs of dying down. Yes, it was time to act.

Four

Cold air wafted up through the tunnel leading back to Babylon. To Kim's right, the Styx River foamed and bubbled powerfully. Pentagrams pulsed the length of the passageway, hazing the fog to a strange purple shade. The Council was over, and Kim had had every opportunity to return to Angela's side in safety. Instead here he was, prepared to behave with incredible foolishness.

Well, this was something he *had* to do.

He'd deliberately stopped at a narrow passageway, not very far from where Lucifel's guardian Thrones used to rest. He actually wanted to run. The innermost depths of the Dead Tunnels always struck him with horror. But he'd decided to steel himself. Taking a deep breath, he looked around for anyone who might be watching.

No one. He was alone.

Kim entered. Pitch-black shadows threatened to swallow everything.

Carefully, he navigated down a deep and much narrower passageway of smoothly carved stone. Demonic hieroglyphs spattered the walls in haphazard patterns, glowing weakly. Kim understood enough of the language to make out the words *danger* and *punishment,* and it took all the courage within him to continue moving. A strange sensation of watchfulness oppressed him. The air tasted stale.

Dim flickering embers hid in the uppermost recesses of the rocks near the ceiling. Kim followed them, careful not to lose sight of the path they marked.

This was the hidden and more dreadful path to and from Lucifel's Altar, but also the quickest one. Even so, most demons never used it. The last time Kim had walked through was months ago when Python had forced Angela into a slow march to free Lucifel from her prison.

Kim had strolled a mere hundred feet when the worst began. Bodies of angels and demons had been melded into the walls. Most were alive, but they remained eternal statues. Arms and wings jutted out of the stone at odd angles. Hair hung ragged and dusty. Skin had taken on the deathly color of white marble.

Their eyes followed Kim in the darkness.

The hair rose on the back of his neck. Despite the deep silence, he seemed to hear thousands of voices calling his name and questioning his presence. He glanced around, but the whispers faded from his mind like half-forgotten dreams.

"Don't worry," he heard himself say. "She'll free you . . . somehow. Someday."

Angela often spoke to him about how she longed to find a way to rescue these poor souls. Yet she feared that dislodging them might kill them even faster.

This could have been that angel's fate if Angela had spurned being merciful.

To live like this—no one deserved such a Hell. Kim paused

in front of an angel who looked much like the one Angela had pardoned. With a shaking hand, he brushed some hair from the angel's marble white chin.

The angel's wings twitched and his eyes snapped open.

Kim jumped back, gasping for breath. He steadied himself with a hand, waiting awhile to summon his bravery again. At last he continued on until he found what he'd been looking for.

He stared up at a demon imprisoned in the stone. The demon appeared fast asleep, his black hair hanging in his face. Tears blurred Kim's vision and ran hotly down his cheeks. He turned aside, squeezing his eyes shut and allowing himself the time to sob quietly. He refused to move, even as a set of footsteps broke the eerie quiet. It was Lilith again, and she paused beside Kim to also stare up at Mastema, the imprisoned demon who had been his foster father.

Mastema had been second only to Lucifel before she'd escaped, and he'd been one of the strongest supporters of her insane ideals. Kim had feared Mastema and the power he wielded as much as he adored him.

Kim's soul felt like it had been stabbed.

"Was I too hard on you at the Council?" Lilith said almost too softly to Kim. There may have been a note of true regret in her voice. But it was unlikely. "Perhaps my words were a bit harsh. Calling you ignorant and so on. Believe it or not, it hurts me to see you so sad. I may be a demon, but more than anyone, I know what it is to grieve."

"What do you want?" Kim said. Wasn't the pain in his voice enough for her?

Lilith sighed. "I knew I would find you here. Whether you're a half-breed or not, we're both on the same side, aren't we? What I want is what you want, and that's what's best for the Archon. Why must we always be at odds, Kim? I shouldn't have said you were useless to the Archon. So sorry. Can't you overlook that?"

Kim bit his lip. Wanting what was best for Angela had nothing to do with locking away her memories. And it was hard to accept an apology from a demon, especially an obviously insincere one.

Best to stay silent for the moment.

Lilith crossed her arms and continued to stare up at Mastema, who never stirred in his eternal jail. "But can you deny what a relief it is to have him here at last?" she ventured. "Finally, one more threat to the Archon has been extinguished. And Mastema's light was always a flame too easily snuffed out. If it weren't for his supporters, I would have done away with him long ago."

Kim closed his eyes. He rubbed at his face. She only spoke the truth. "Now that I see him like this, it's hard to believe I feared him so much," Kim whispered.

"Oh," Lilith said, "you weren't alone in your fear. Mastema was a shadow, after all. Lucifel's. In the end, however, like all shadows he disappeared with the rise of a new sun, and that is the Archon's."

"Even so," Kim said. He stifled another sob. "He was like a father to me. My real father was a devil, a Jinn who deserved to die for the torment he caused my mother and me. Mastema was the one who gave me the courage to get rid of him once and for all . . ."

"But only to use you like a pawn," Lilith rejoined quickly. "Mastema's love was always a conditional one. His first and last obsession was Lucifel. He knew that only a half-Jinn like yourself, someone who was neither angel, nor demon, nor full-blooded Jinn, could unlock Lucifel's adamant chains. If it weren't for that, he would have let you die in poverty like a dog. And for murdering your blood father, now you have a Jinn relative hunting you who will never stop until you go the same route. Troy, I believe her name is? That was Mastema's legacy to you. Only death. He deserves his fate, here in the final darkness."

"He would have wanted me to kill Angela," Kim said. He shook his head. "He saw her as a threat to Lucifel."

It was his only justification for allowing this to happen.

"So I did what was necessary," Lilith said softly. "And you're foolish to regret it. The Archon must reign unopposed. And I will get rid of whoever stands in Her way, by whatever means necessary. Mastema was only the first of many . . . if need be."

Kim shivered. He should have been grateful for Lilith's protection. But now he knew for certain that it was she who wished to live unopposed. Angela was nothing but a convenient excuse.

Kim was the one who cared, and he would suffer even more for Angela, and lose everything important to him if it came to that. Whatever it took for her to survive. If Lilith knew what he'd planned—and with whom—she'd seal Kim in these walls just like she had his foster father.

Luckily for him, Lilith's pride continued to blind her. She didn't seem to have a clue. Maybe it was because what he was about to do was so insane, it hadn't even entered her thoughts as a possibility.

"As I said," Lilith continued, "the Archon's sun has now risen. The old order is finally passing. You've noticed Her restlessness, haven't you? She wants change. But She's young, and still inept at being forceful and commandeering like Lucifel, and so Her life is constantly in danger." Lilith stood closer to Mastema, as if sharing the news with him. "And now that a new revolt in Heaven has taken place, I wonder what will happen? Lucifel made her next move. Now it's Angela's turn, for better or for worse."

The dam walling up Kim's heart burst suddenly. The words were out of his lips before he could stop himself. "And where is my place in all of that change and glory?" he whispered. "That's what I'm afraid of. What's the purpose of my life, now that Lucifel is free?"

"You're a romantic," Lilith said, laughing softly. "You should be able to see the answer in the Archon's eyes when She looks at you."

Kim hung his head. "Angela has the Book—Sophia. And she barely remembers her past moments with me."

Lilith looked at Kim meaningfully, as if suspicious. As if he had no right to be unhappy that Angela had been forced to lose half of her past. As if he might actually do something about it. Then her face changed. Her smile suddenly looked strange and all too warm on her cold face. "So this all comes down to loneliness?" Lilith said. "Why didn't you say so earlier?" Lilith slid a dark arm around Kim, drawing him close. She spoke seductively in his ear. "I must admit, you're quite the enigma. I never seem to have you figured out. But learning about a person goes both ways. For instance, you never did tell me how you got this precious little human name of yours . . . Kim . . . enlighten me."

"My mother wanted me to be a girl," Kim said flatly.

"Well, I'm glad she was wrong," Lilith said, and her eyes flashed at him intensely. She ran her fingers through his tangle of hair. "If you're still feeling depressed tonight, feel free to come to my mansion. The Archon doesn't have to know. And believe me, in one hour I can make you forget the entire world."

Kim barely heard what she said.

He nodded but continued to examine Mastema sorrowfully as Lilith slunk away. He wasn't sure how much more time had passed. Kim's ears still buzzed with her lies and false promises. Lilith knew he was up to something. She just couldn't figure out exactly what. That invitation to her mansion was just a way to keep him in check. He took a deep breath and stepped away, intent on leaving. Sophia was waiting for him, after all. But a flicker of movement caught the corner of his eye.

As if congealing from the shadows of the wall, a black snake appeared next to Mastema and peered down at Kim with bright orange eyes.

Kim froze. His pulse roared in his ears.

"You're keeping me in suspense?" The snake's mouth opened, revealing curved, needle-sharp fangs. "Because that," the snake said, slithering around Mastema's neck and stretching out to meet Kim, "wouldn't be a wise thing to do, I'm afraid."

"I won't change my mind," Kim said. He curled his hands into fists. "Angela needs her memories back."

"Good . . ." the snake said. It gazed at him more intensely. "Just make sure you hold up your end of the bargain."

"I'm not a liar," Kim muttered. "And neither is Sophia."

Though Sophia hadn't agreed to anything just yet.

Kim stiffened as the snake stretched toward his shoulder and slithered around his neck. Its cool voice echoed inside of his ear, and its tongue flicked against his skin. "Of course not. You can't afford to be," the snake said.

It laughed, and the noise rang through the tunnel like a terrible bell as its reptilian body turned to ash, crumbling from Kim's shoulders to the ground.

Five

Kim guided his Kirin swiftly through Babylon, knowing that the night would pass all too quickly, that their time was running out. The snake's cold laughter echoed in his brain, timed to the burning image of Lilith's piercing eyes.

One wrong move with either demon, and Angela might never be healed.

Sophia followed close behind on a steed of her own, but the beast didn't have the same stealth as Kim's. Its heavy paws thumped against the stone and earth as if they were boulders striking flint. Kim's breaths erupted ragged and tired already. But neither he nor Sophia could slacken the pace until they were at least outside of the city, and right now its lights still shone like cold yellow stars on their backs.

He'd never become accustomed to riding these creatures. The Kirin resembled horses from Earth, but they were more like Hellish unicorns with a lethally sharp ribbed horn rising from the middle of their head, glowing eyes, and bodies that flickered with phosphorescent blue light.

Kim held the reins tight but winced at the pain in his

hands. This Kirin had bitten him in his haste to release it from its paddock beneath Angela's personal mansion.

Its flanks rippled with the light that signified distress. He and Sophia would be lucky to make it through the city unnoticed.

But so far, so good.

Many of the streets at this hour were deserted. Most demons knew enough not to wander on their own in the more lawless hours of the night. Kim and Sophia weaved through alleys and desolate wastes, they galloped over a bridge spanning the foaming Styx River, and then they were plunging into the lower levels of the city.

Kim glanced up at some guards patrolling the bridge. They noted his passage but didn't make a move to stop him. Their silhouettes reappeared and disappeared behind grim spikes of obsidian as they casually strolled the bridge's expanse. The fine mist above them responded to the increasingly chill air, tumbling in little crystals that glittered like diamond dust. Most of the guards weren't used to any unannounced visitors into the lower levels at this hour, and certainly wiser souls knew enough never to visit at all.

Every demon in Hell knew what to expect here and what to fear.

Sophia and Kim were nearing one of the most gruesome vestiges of Babylon's customs during Lucifel's reign.

Kim stared straight ahead and refused to look to either side as the fog began to close in on them. Whenever the mists parted, it was only to reveal mounds upon mounds of skeletons. Some of them were demon skeletons, mostly children Kim assumed were born less than perfect. Others were dead Kirin or other terrible creatures from Hell that—for him at least—would always remain nameless.

Setting his jaw, Kim tried as hard as he could not to concentrate on what surrounded him. The sight of the dead children, or "chicks" as the demons called them, tore at his insides.

The angels hadn't behaved any better in their past. From the heights of Heaven, deformed or less than desirable offspring had been thrown into Hell to fend for themselves or die. From the few survivors, the Jinn race had evolved. Kim was half-Jinn and he thought he looked normal enough.

That kind of exactness and cruelty had always torn at his soul. Angels and demons considered themselves superior to all other creatures. No, he'd never understand it.

Kim forced himself to keep riding. He and Sophia had almost arrived.

Finally, they entered a tunnel in the deepest reaches of the city.

The silence became absolute, except for the gentle paw strikes of the Kirin. Kim's Kirin champed nervously as they navigated the narrow strip of stone bordering the Styx, and he had to use a few well-timed caresses to goad the beast into moving forward. They were down to a slow trot. Beside them, the water churned.

Even the Kirin knew that to accidentally step into the Styx meant at the very least losing a limb to the acidic water.

Yet that wasn't the only reason he and Sophia had little to fear from spies.

Every living thing sensed the demon who lorded over this part of Babylon. The very smell of the place usually kept any creature from entering. Finally, the Kirin refused to go ahead any farther. Kim slid off his mount and Sophia copied him.

Together, they walked forward into the darkness, following the hieroglyphs marking the stone. Carved serpents and stern warnings glowed along their path. Ignoring both, they continued to march down, and down, and down. Behind them, the Kirin reared but didn't bolt. They also must have thought their masters would change their minds.

Sophia walked stiffly, barely looking at Kim. The Kirin's frightened neighing echoed in the background.

"Are you certain he knows we're coming?" she said to Kim.

Kim's reply nearly drowned in the Styx now roaring past them. "Yes," he said firmly.

Sophia paused for a moment, a haunted expression on her face. Maybe she was rethinking everything. Kim had to admit, he'd been astonished at how swiftly she'd agreed to this plan. He'd barely needed to coax her into her Kirin's saddle.

The Styx boiled only a step away from them. Sophia glanced at the water, her eyes glazed and unreadable.

One wrong move and they might fall in, helpless as the acidic water dissolved their bodies and bones to smoke. Kim wrinkled his nose. The vinegary air cut into his throat whenever he breathed. He had to focus to see the arching gateway that marked the end of the tunnel through the thick fog. He strode toward it, offering a guiding hand to Sophia.

She shook her head politely, but stayed close by his side. Somehow the silence between them acted as a chain linking them together.

Fear could be a powerful instigator of new friendships.

Then they at last exited through the gateway and emerged on the eastern border of Babylon, its sky illuminated by faint orange globes. Their eerie light illuminated the far eastern crags of the unthinkably immense cavern cradling the city. Kim and Sophia stood on a tall hill, and a path cut steeply down its sides, rising back up among the stone again to end at the mansion of a Great Demon.

Sophia stared at it, her mouth tightly pursed. But she was the first to take another step forward.

Kim looked at her in surprise. He steeled himself and followed, never taking his gaze off what awaited.

Python's private mansion sat alone. There were no other dwellings or signs of life near it, but perhaps there didn't need to be. The building had enough personality to make up for that tenfold. Whereas Lilith's and Angela's mansions were cut with smooth elegance, Python's reared up into Babylon's fog with reams of jagged pyramid-shaped spires. Obelisks covered in hieroglyphs and grim mosaics flanked its enormous onyx doors. Statues of Hounds and feathered serpents, carved with terrible precision, sat above eaves and windows.

The gothic city of Luz, ensconced on Earth as if in its own little corner of the universe, had held only a shadow of such dark beauty.

Soon, Kim and Sophia stood at the mansion's entrance, both of them focused on the glittering eyes of a feathered serpent statue near the door. Kim glanced at Sophia. She raised an eyebrow questioningly. There were no guards, or even beasts to warn of someone's arrival.

Kim swallowed nervously.

"This place is enormous," Sophia whispered. It sounded like she had to search to find her words. "You've never been here before at all?" She turned to Kim for answers again.

He shook his head. "Never. Python hated Mastema. Even when I was a child, it was understood to keep me far away from Python and anything he happened to claim as his own."

"So I suppose now Python's making up for the years lost between you two?"

Kim had nothing to say to that. He looked back up at the mansion rearing in front of them, wishing he could see through it. "Trust me, we wouldn't be here if there was another way to help Angela. But there isn't."

"I know," Sophia said. She closed her eyes and took a deep breath. She opened them again and her smooth brow furrowed. "I don't see signs of anyone inside."

"You won't. Python keeps his entertainments as secret as possible. All the better for him to do what he likes without arousing suspicion. As if anyone trusts him any longer." He ended with a laugh. "He judges his mother for her parties, but in the end he's no better than she is. They simply miss what they lost in Heaven."

Sophia approached the doors. They were the opposite of the door in Luz that Python had used to lure Angela into his deadly maze months ago. That door had been covered in grotesque carvings of hellish creatures, and its knob had been shaped like a snake. These doors were plain stone and had no knobs or handles. Two twining snakes rested atop the lintel, but that was all.

"Sophia," Kim whispered in warning.

But Sophia didn't budge. She examined the doors top to bottom.

Then she touched them.

Six

The doors creaked open so lightly they could have been made of air. Gently, Kim pushed Sophia to the side and peered into the noiseless shadows within the mansion. The building appeared deserted, but they both knew better than that.

Kim beckoned, urging Sophia to follow him.

They stepped into the building carefully. The place truly appeared abandoned. Webs of fine dust littered the furniture that had been left behind. More dust filtered through the air and choked off Kim's breath. Most of the furniture pieces looked like faded relics, and their construction was too odd and opulent to be made by demons. Kim walked down the long hall with Sophia strolling cautiously behind; he was unable to keep from feeling that most of what he saw had been taken from Heaven as a remembrance of days past, long, long ago.

It felt like journeying through a cathedral. The hall seemed endless, the ceiling was far too vast and shadowy, and there were too many stairs and doors.

Finally, they paused in a circular room that connected to at least five other doorways.

"What is this nonsense?" Kim said bitterly. He wanted to scream. Did Python agree to this deal or not? Why would he waste time toying with them like this?

"Hold on," Sophia said, stepping toward one of the doors. "Listen! Can you hear that?"

Kim sidled next to her.

Sophia nodded. "It sounds like . . . chanting. But I can't make out what they're saying."

Kim's lips parted. His face blanched as he listened. He stepped back and stared at his feet, questioning what he'd thought he'd heard. Surely, he was wrong. But he found himself setting his hand against the door anyway and, despite his better judgment, pushing it open.

Sophia clasped his arm with an iron grip. Kim knew they both expected the same thing to greet them—an immense crowd of chanting demons.

The door swung wide with a powerful creak.

A long hallway met them. Its arched ceiling appeared as distant as the sky, and large crystal pendants hung along its length, casting a dull red light everywhere.

There was dead silence. No crowd. Kim and Sophia stepped onto the red velvet carpet that stretched along the floor toward a dais and a chair on the far side of the room. The onyx chair was smaller than Angela's, but somehow more menacing, carved with serpents and shadowy beasts with rubies for eyes. Upon it, the demon Python sat sideways with his legs slung over one armrest and his head tipped back lazily against the other. He appeared to be sleeping, and his pale face appeared almost peaceful. His thick black and violet hair hid his fearsome reptilian eyes.

Sophia seemed unable to let go of Kim's arm.

He turned and examined her carefully. She nodded at him.

Together, they strode side by side up to Python and his throne. Kim felt like he was dragging his feet through quicksand. Each step became harder than the last. Finally, they were at the foot of the stairs leading up to Python's chair.

The demon opened one scarred eye, his snakelike gaze focusing on Kim in particular. A smile spread slowly on Python's handsome face. He swung his feet to the floor and settled back in his seat again with his legs crossed. The jewels studding his dark coat glittered in the dim light. Even from this distance, Kim could see the scales on Python's eyelids and bare feet. A chill shuddered through him.

"Well, well, well," Python said in his suave voice. "Look who kept his part of the bargain, after all. I was beginning to worry about you, half-breed. The hour is late. I almost fell asleep waiting."

That was clearly a lie. Demons like Python never slept at all. They schemed.

"We're here, and that's all that matters," Kim said. "So, now what? You said you can restore Angela's memories, but you didn't say how. Or what you want in return."

At the sound of Kim's voice a strange hissing noise echoed throughout the hall. It sounded like a gigantic animal.

That sound was familiar. It echoed in Kim's nightmares constantly.

"What is that?" he whispered, more to himself than anyone else.

Python smirked. "Never you mind," he said. He stood and sauntered down the stairs to meet them, appearing to glide more than walk. "What I want? Oh, I'm a demon of simple needs, Kim. Some might even call me transparent. No matter, I think we can both agree it's refreshing to wear one's heart on one's sleeve. How else would I have known to approach you?

Even a blind man could see how much you love the Archon. How much it hurts you to see Her suffer. It hurts me as well. It's hard to see the ruler of Hell so infuriatingly *weak*."

Python snapped his fingers, producing a crystal decanter with a red liquid inside. He tipped back his head and took a long drink, licking some ruby droplets from his mouth with a forked tongue. Then with a sudden vicious glare he tossed the decanter at Kim's head.

Sophia screamed.

The decanter disappeared in a flash of bright purple light. It reappeared and dropped to the ground behind Kim, smashing into pieces.

"That was for making me wait," Python said coolly. "You should be grateful. I changed my mind about embedding the shards in your forehead, boy. Now," he said, examining his dark nails. He slowly turned his gaze back to Kim and Sophia. "Where, pray tell, is the Archon?"

Kim stared back at the demon unflinchingly, trying to regain his bravery as Python's eyes burned down to his soul. "There was no way to persuade Angela into leaving her mansion tonight. Besides, she would have never agreed to meet you. Your reputation—"

"Isn't a pleasant one?" Python said. "Perhaps I should have shown my face at the Councils since Lucifel escaped Hell. It sounds like the Archon has the wrong idea about me. I hope you haven't said anything incriminating?"

Kim held his tongue. *Wrong idea?* If Angela remembered even half of what Python had put her through, she would have rode a Kirin to his mansion to cage him herself.

Sophia took another deep breath. Her delicate hand played nervously with her jeweled pendant. A long silence fell, and once again the chilling hiss that met their ears earlier seemed to echo from everywhere at once. Sophia's eyes widened, but she still said nothing. Her gaze fixed on Python and remained riveted there, as if the moment she looked askance he would disappear in a cloud of violet smoke.

"Well, we don't need Angela Mathers's physical presence . . . yet," Python said. He looked pointedly at Kim, and his words softened. "All we need is something important that links one of you to her." He examined the pendant at Sophia's chest.

She stepped backward, gasping.

"Is that still such an important necklace to you, dear?" Python leaned in closer and whispered in her ear.

Sophia wrapped her hand around the pendant even more tightly.

"Because I know the Archon wears one just like it. How very quaint and sweet. Two friends who share a special bond decided to exchange matching necklaces. That will do nicely. In fact, it's just too perfect. Lend it to me. I promise you'll get your trinket back in one piece." Python held out his hand. The scales on his fingers glistened.

Sophia hesitated.

Kim would never know what memories the pendant symbolized, but for Sophia to be unsure even now about parting with it certainly meant something special. He turned aside, feeling the sudden pain in his heart like a lance. He'd admit it—he was jealous.

"Love," Python whispered.

Kim looked up at the demon again. "What?"

Python held Sophia's white sapphire pendant so that it swung on its chain, clasped between his fingers. "Everyone wants love, but so few attain it. I mean that unconditional love that crosses every boundary of space and time. Do you know what I think?" Python smiled at Kim. "I think that was what drove Lucifel mad. She couldn't escape her feelings, and they devoured her soul. Now, she seeks to silence all feeling. Now, she wants to open Raziel's Book, to take the power within, to end the lives that mock her despair. It's such a grand, tragic thing—love. Sometimes, it's so grand, it can clip even the greatest angel's wings."

The demon threw the necklace in the air and snatched it back with a hand.

"Now we can get to work."

Python walked back up the stairs. He clapped his hands once and the throne he'd been seated upon vanished in a purplish mist, only to reappear as a long, flat, onyx altar. Ominous carvings of Hounds and serpents twisted around its pillar-shaped legs. Python slid a hand against its dark stone. "Now, listen carefully, boy. With this necklace, I can summon Angela Mathers here, body and soul. But that's the easy part. Returning someone's memories requires more of a connection. Memories are a part of someone's spirit. Losing them is like a death, no matter how small. And there are very few ways to bring the dead back to life . . . successfully." Python finally lost his false smile. "Angela Mathers's life force must connect to another's forever."

As Python allowed those words to sink in, Kim watched the demon pull another decanter, a bag of red sand, and an hourglass from the ether.

Python set the objects down on the altar and stretched, supporting himself with both hands spread against the stone.

"What's the catch?" Kim said.

Python cocked his head. "Catch?"

"I mean, what do you get out of this? Why even bother to help?"

"It really doesn't matter what I ultimately get out of it," Python said coolly. "Because I'm all you have right now. Correct? Besides, I'm not a fool. Even I know the Book of Raziel needs to be opened. The Archon will have to remember how to do it quickly."

Sophia gripped Kim's hand hard. She looked into his eyes, breathing fast. "Wait," she whispered.

He turned to her, peering at her sharply. "What? Are you changing your mind?" he whispered back.

"I just need to talk to you first."

"Can you give us a moment . . . alone?" Kim turned away and said to Python.

"You get a moment," Python said. "You don't get it alone. Make your little chat quick."

Kim and Sophia edged to the shadows of the long hall. "You know he's up to something," she said.

"Of course Python's up to something. But does it really matter anymore?"

"Going behind Angela's back like this isn't right!"

"And would she agree to come here on her own?"

Sophia went silent. She sighed.

"Exactly."

"Kim, he knows that you're the only person here who can connect your life force with Angela's. I can't—I . . ."

She didn't need to explain. Though she looked human, Sophia was not alive in the sense that Kim was alive. Perhaps she didn't even have an aura at all. Troy's past comments suggested as much.

Kim let out a shuddering sigh as he thought of his Jinn cousin.

He could feel his hands shaking as he pushed the hair from his eyes.

"I don't want you to do this, Kim," Sophia said. She looked at him with eyes glazed by tears. "We'll find another way to help Angela."

"No. We won't. I've made up my mind. If it's for her, it's worth whatever happens to me next."

"Kim, wait—"

He had to walk away from Sophia, otherwise he just might rethink everything. Still, he could feel her anguish like it was wrapping around his chest, squeezing the breath out of him. "I'll volunteer," Kim said, returning before the altar to Python. He heard his voice crack painfully.

Python didn't laugh, but the sound hid within the shadows of his words. "Of course you will."

Python dangled the necklace above the altar.

Kim and Sophia stood by his side, wordless. Sophia especially looked distraught. Her face was ghastly and pale. Kim swallowed hard, trying to concentrate as Python had requested. Then, a blazing purple light flashed all around them before condensing back to a single point below the necklace's swinging pendant. Kim almost forgot to breathe as Angela's shadow appeared, and slowly her sleeping form materialized from a heavy purplish mist.

In seconds she lay on the altar, her entire body limp, and her mouth slack.

She looked dead, but her chest still rose and fell with her breaths. Kim breathed with her again, his heart thrumming. She was so beautiful. The pendant that matched Sophia's glittered on the pale skin below her neck. Even with Angela's arms and legs blotched where her cruel-looking burn scars were exposed, she'd never seemed lovelier. The minuscule jewels on her black satin gown shimmered like stars.

Her practiced regality as the Archon seemed like a dream as Kim stared at her face.

For once, it seemed she wasn't having one of her terrible and confusing visions.

It felt like a sin to break that peace. Python was the first to have the courage to do so. Slowly, he began to circle Angela's body, tracing along its contours with his fingers, muttering softly. A strange, admiring expression lit up his face.

Kim set his jaw.

He tried to push Python's hand aside, knowing it was a stupid thing to do, but unable to hold back.

The demon offered a nasty glare. "Do the smart thing and stay out of my way," Python whispered. "I don't have to do a thing for her, you know."

Sophia said nothing. She only stared down at Angela with tearful eyes. Once, she looked up at Kim again and searched his face as if hoping against hope that he might change his mind, and a miracle would happen, and Angela would awaken on her own with her memories fully restored. And because they both knew the truth, she looked away just as quickly and stroked Angela's cheek.

All too swiftly, Python was done with his ritual. He straightened and tousled his mop of hair. "There. She'll remain asleep as long as the ritual lasts, and possibly for another night. But her spirit is unusually resistant to any kind of mental barrier being broken; the typical spells aren't going to work." He looked askance at Sophia. "It seems the time has come for you to be helpful again. I need the Angelus."

Another long silence.

"How do you know about that?" Sophia said, her voice shaking.

Kim swallowed hard. A thick tension filled the echoing

air of the room. For the first time in a while, he felt another presence in the hall. A familiar iciness crept through his entire body. Someone else was watching what took place.

"Every ancient angel knows the Angelus melody," Python said. "The Supernal Israfel was the first to sing it. Supposedly, he learned it from God. I say, perhaps he learned it from you. That was Lucifel's theory. And despite how I grew to loathe her, I'll admit she was always right."

"I can't sing that here," Sophia said firmly. "I won't. Besides, only Israfel can manipulate matter with the power of his voice. He's the Creator Supernal. Not me."

"That's right. You're not him," Python said. "You're someone much more special, Sophia. Your true power might remain under lock and key, but I can see it behind your eyes, swirling like a storm. The choice is yours, of course. You can help Angela, or you can continue to watch both her and the universe waste away."

"What is the Angelus?" Kim asked her.

"The song of creation," Sophia said, still staring back at Python. "But it's not to be used lightly. It has great, no, *immense* power."

"Why would it be important now?"

"Because," Python chimed in, "it is ultimately a song of Binding. Its notes hold the universe together, and so they would also contain the power to connect your soul with the Archon's to break down the walls of Her mind, to bring back Her memories. Think hard—for the dimensions to be disintegrating, the notes of the song must have faltered. It would seem someone has stopped singing." The demon looked around them, as if addressing an omnipresent person they couldn't see. "And by someone, I mean God."

Kim opened his mouth to speak but couldn't find words anymore. Sophia's lips sealed to a tightly knit line.

"Now," Python said softly, "I wonder how that happened? Did He grow weary at last? Is He perhaps dead—"

"I'll do it," Sophia said. Her eyes shone with indignation.

Python stepped back, his arms folded. Kim watched her, waiting with the demon. He wanted to fall on his knees and beg her to sing if that was what Python needed. Yet Sophia's face had taken on a frightful superiority. For a second, it would be the height of idiocy to take one step closer to her.

Sophia took a deep breath, closing her eyes. Kim let out a soft sigh of relief. Then, a hot fear arose in him again. Patterns began to flicker on Sophia's skin. They were words, written in the hieroglyphic angel writing Merkebah. Faintly, he heard her singing, and sounds that seemed at first unintelligible formed into beautiful words kissing his ears. He pressed a hand against the altar to steady himself.

> *Were you there in the Garden of Shadows?*
> *Were you near when the Father took wing?*
> *Did you sigh when the starlight outpoured us?*
> *When the silver bright water could sing . . .*

"Then, if you're decided . . ." Python said. He suddenly stood next to Kim, offering the decanter as Sophia's pure voice rose and fell. "The final step is for you to drink this. I'll take care of the rest."

"What is it?" Kim said, taking the bottle and instinctively sniffing the contents.

Python sighed. "Does it really matter?"

No, it didn't. Kim looked at Angela. She moaned in her

sleep, her face pale with suffering. Kim pressed the bottle to his lips and, tipping his head back, began to drink. The liquid tasted sour and went down thick. When he was done, he wiped his lips and rubbed more hair away from his sweaty forehead. Already, he felt a bit out of sorts. His vision blurred slightly, but he kept his attention on Angela. She looked like a beautiful black-and-red mirage.

"Stand here," Python said curtly, dragging Kim to a spot in front of the altar.

Python began to whisper in Theban, the language of the demons. Kim noted the words when he could as they mixed with and complemented Sophia's song, but he was riveted on the dull glow that began to surround Angela. The glow steadily increased in brightness. Soon, it became bright as a sun. Kim's eyes pulsed with pain, and then the song reached its end, and before he thought his brain might ignite from the fire and brilliance at last, the light faded.

Now the room was as silent and dark as before. His skin felt hot to the touch.

The presence in the room, the source of the terrible hissing noise, was suddenly gone. Perhaps the light had been too much for whatever had been observing them.

Sophia opened her eyes as if breaking from a trance. The words faded from her skin, and she ran to Kim's side, supporting him as he swayed next to the altar.

He turned to her, suddenly so very tired. "Is that song . . . is that the power hidden inside of you?" he whispered. "Inside the Book of Raziel?"

"Yes," Sophia said. "And no. The last stanzas have been sealed away. I don't remember them. Only Raziel knew, and he locked them away so that the Archon alone can obtain them or wield them."

"What are you really?" Kim said, staring at her.

They remained like that for a moment longer. Sophia's features masked over with pain.

BOOM. Python slammed the hourglass down on the altar next to them. Its insides were now filled with crimson sand pulsing with dull light. The demon then flipped the hourglass. A few grains sprinkled to its bottom.

"Here is your life force," Python said. He gazed into the hourglass almost hungrily. "You have until the last grain falls to the bottom. After that, well—"

He snapped his fingers and a necklace with a small hourglass pendant swung from Kim's neck. As if it were an afterthought, the demon tossed back the sapphire necklace suspended in the air to Sophia. She caught it expertly, but that couldn't erase the fury emanating from her like smoke. "What did you do?" she demanded of Python.

Yes, what did *he do?* Kim swallowed. It felt like his soul was bottoming out inside of him. He grasped the pendant and forced himself to breathe.

"I didn't *do* anything," Python said. "We're all simply prisoners to the laws of the universe. And I'm sad to bring you this news if you're unaware, but when one person's life force Binds with another's, the helping individual is drained. Slowly, but always surely. Your time, Kim, will eventually be up." Python reached into the bag of crimson sand and slowly let some grains slip through his fingers. "Time is merely the hourglass of God. The only difference is that in this case, I'm the one who flipped that hourglass into action. And it was all thanks to Sophia's divine little song."

Sophia trembled. Her steely grip was now stopping the flow of blood in his arms. Kim wanted to be enraged. He had every right to be. But something had broken within him.

Looking at Angela, knowing he was doing what he could to help her, he had no regrets. The old hardness within him was dying.

And he loved her for it.

Kim never took his eyes off her. It was like he couldn't anymore. "When the last grains fall to the hourglass's bottom, what will happen next?" he murmured. He already knew the answer.

Python grew deeply serious. The very air seemed to hang on his words. "Well, then, you're mine," he said softly.

Now Sophia let loose. "You devious *snake*," she screamed at Python.

Kim lowered his head and leaned against the table. If someone had punched him, the effect couldn't have been worse. He stared at Angela, brushing aside her hair. Tears filled his eyes and trickled hotly down his face.

"Kim," Sophia shouted, "he has no right to claim your soul. You can't be Python's slave."

Kim had nothing to say.

"Don't you understand what this means?" Sophia screamed at him.

He nodded, his mind and soul already lost in a strange fog. "I do. And I know that I have no regrets. For the first time, only I could help Angela." He gripped one of Angela's hands impulsively. "Besides, what do I have left now, anyway? I'm a man without purpose. I'm a soul walking in a haze. Maybe this is what it was all for—this moment. Maybe every moment of my life led me not to Lucifel's Altar, but here."

Sophia became speechless. She probably felt both guilty and grieved, but it was too late. It was all too late.

Python stepped closer to Kim and examined the hourglass pendant, lifting it with his fingers. "A perfect minia-ture," he said. "It will match the hourglass I keep here. You see, Kim, I'm a gentleman at heart. I always find it polite to let a soul I favor know just how much time it has left. And even though I tended to despise you by turns, I'll admit your bravery earned a special place in my heart today."

Kim grasped the pendant, sickness welling within him in a flood. "Promise me one thing," he said weakly. He meant the words for everyone. "Don't tell Angela what I've done."

Sophia's gentle sobbing cut him to the heart.

A great weariness overtook Kim. He barely protested as Python stroked Angela's cheek and she sighed, her face relaxed, her suffering starting to diminish.

But although the demon's words were reassuring, his smile was not.

"Oh, don't worry," Python said, staring down at Angela. "I doubt she'll ever find out."

Seven

Angela Mathers opened her eyes to pitch blackness, and a sweet warmth embracing her. She was floating, and a gentle pulse thrummed rhythmically through her entire body. A beautiful song she already knew but couldn't quite remember soothed her like a lullaby. That was when Angela knew the nightmare had returned.

Her heart hammered with anticipation. Fear and fire crept through her.

But she was locked in the vision and could do nothing to stop it. Angela had little choice but to lie in the warm, still darkness, vaguely aware of someone else resting beside her. Their presence was far from reassuring. Dread twisted at her insides. A stifling sense of being watched and despised plucked at her nerves.

Her left eye burned painfully.

Then, the terror began.

A muffled sound broke the silence around her. The warmth dissipated, and she emerged from a jagged hole into a bleak, shockingly cold darkness. Clusters of light dotted the icy void. They were innumerable stars sprinkled throughout space like *jewels on velvet. They shivered with the silent screams of Angela's dying mother.*

She never had a chance to cry out herself.

In an instant it was upon her. It was neither male nor female, but something that combined all the features of both into a perfect and terrible beauty. She had a brief glimpse of long dark hair, dozens of wings, a marble face striped with bluish veins like a tiger's, and green eyes that burned into her soul. It was the being that called itself the Father, the very creature she had watched murder the angel Raziel in the shared memories of his past. Now, it was murdering her.

Where was Angela's mother? Was she already dead? Why couldn't she stop this from happening?

The sudden pain drowned out every other thought and question. Her opponent's onslaught was furious and merciless. Angela's flesh sliced to ribbons. Her wings broke like glass. The stars disappeared, replaced by the Father's face as he tore her apart and flung piece after piece to the Abyss. Her left eye, though, continued to stare at him.

He'd kept that much of her, anyway, clutching it like a treasured gem.

And that Eye continued to watch him, even as Angela's consciousness vanished, and she began an eternity hidden in the void of the Abyss. When awareness briefly returned, she stared back into a different face. This one was much like the Father's, but distinctly female. It was an angel with ashen hair and wings. She wore a black crown and her crimson eyes glittered like garnets. She looked into Angela's Eye and smiled.

It was the Devil—Lucifel.

The Grail, the Eye of God, was now hers.

∽

A long and terrible scream forced Angela to awaken.

She jerked upright in her chair, flinching as it skidded backward across the floor. But this wasn't the stone floor of Hell. Westwood Academy's Latin classroom with its brick walls and broken tiles instantly came into focus. The city of Luz gleamed through the windows next to Angela's student seat, and beyond them the clear star-filled sky beckoned, and the ocean lay unruffled as a plate of glass. She stared outside, still seeing Lucifel's eyes in the reddish flickering lights that dotted the island city. A familiar angel statue with long hair and high arching wings perched on a balustrade nearby. Then Angela noticed the immense reflection in the glass of something behind her.

It was the faces of her fellow students in the room—every single one of them either concerned or irritated. They'd all turned toward Angela.

Angela spun around, breathing hard.

What in the world is going on? Am I really back in Luz?

She glanced around the room, a strange panic overwhelming her moment by moment.

Where's Sophia?

"Are you quite done, Miss Mathers?" a voice said from the head of the classroom.

It was a Vatican novice with glasses and foppish hair. He lowered the glasses and peered at her intently.

"I—" Angela started to say.

She grabbed her throat. It actually felt raw inside. That must have been *her* screaming. "I—I . . . yes. I'm sorry." Angela grabbed her chair and sat down again.

The novice turned back to his book. The other students murmured, but all of them eventually returned to the work on their desks. Angela looked down at the large book sitting open on her desk. She couldn't remember its title, but there was something strangely impressive about it. Was it the bright red color of the leather binding? Or perhaps the gold leaf in the pages? Slowly, she began to turn them.

So many words. And pictures. These were familiar scenes of people and things. Angela instantly recognized Sophia with her doll-like beauty and thick curling hair. Kim appeared next, with his penetrating gaze. Then there was an angel—and she couldn't quite remember his name—but he was beautiful beyond anything she'd seen, a picture of silvery glory. On the other page was a strange female devil with sickle-shaped wings and pointed ears, and though her image sent a shudder up Angela's spine, she too was fascinating to look at.

Angela stopped at the picture of a tall angel dressed in a clingy black bodysuit. It was hard to tell if the angel was male or female. He or she had ashen gray hair and crimson eyes and six intimidating gray wings. A pendant with a great emerald green eye hung around the angel's neck.

Angela paused. *Lucifel . . .*

She stared at the Eye that was the pendant and her own left eye began to burn.

Her vision swam and blurred over. Her heartbeat thrummed in her chest. The world started to spin, and she heard music and words. Pain streaked through her left eye, deep into her head, radiating like fire throughout her entire body.

But before she could scream again, it was all over. Angela's sight returned to normal. Her hearing no longer buzzed. Her body lost its unnatural warmth. She continued to sit at her desk, flipping through pages of the book, wondering at the characters and story inside. They were all so beautiful, and terrible, and completely beyond her. The novice signaled the class's end, and Angela reluctantly slapped the book shut. Like all the other students, she stood from her seat and filed out of the classroom.

Her feet carried her mindlessly down the building's dark hallway among a throng of students of all ages.

Maybe it's all been a dream. All of it. Sophia . . . Kim . . . even Lucifel. They're nothing more than characters in a long, strange story. How could I have fallen asleep in class like that?

The sun shone brightly outside. Angela paused and lifted a hand to block the light from her eyes. Her long hair blew in the warm ocean breeze.

The sun?

A nagging sense of unease tugged at her. She stood like that a moment longer, allowing the wind to tease more of her brown hair.

That's right. It was a dull mousy color. Angela flipped the strands from her mouth and eyes. She stood gazing at the thick white clouds scudding across the sky, and then she walked down a long cobbled street, headed for her dormitory. A friend joined her shortly afterward, and they walked together. The girl looked nothing like Sophia, but she was pleasant enough. She was normal. Angela didn't feel a need to protect her, or any unearthly sense of magic strolling by her side, yet in its own way that was somehow refreshing.

Yes, a soft voice said in her head. *This is what you've always wanted, isn't it?*

Angela continued walking. She smiled at her friend's joke. Her mind wandered, lingering on tomorrow's test and the upcoming Spring Festival.

This is what it is to be normal. Here, you don't have a dark past. Here, you're free to blend in with the crowd.

Whose voice was this? It was so familiar . . .

Everything else was only a long dream. This is reality. And you're happy to be in it.

Angela parted with her friend at the door to her dormitory. Silently, she strolled up the stone staircase, unlocked the heavy wooden doors, and slipped inside. A group of cheerful faces met her, smiling and saying hello. Angela smiled back, ready to join her friends. They gathered in the dining room, sat down for dinner together, and started to chat loudly amid a table loaded down with food, drinks, and festive spring decorations. The heady scent of lilies wafted throughout the dining room. Gilded eggs adorned the table. Angela sat back, done with conversation for a while, but still laughing at a joke she'd just heard.

That was when she saw it. An hourglass.

It sat at the middle of the table, strangely unnoticed. It glittered amid the candlelight, and the sand inside had been dyed blood red. Black embellished metal cradled its glass form. Angela stared at it entranced. How had no one else seen it yet?

Angela reached out to grab it.

A warm hand wrapped around her wrist, jerking it away. She found herself looking at a dark but dazzlingly beautiful woman with preternatural orange eyes. The woman smiled at Angela, and when she spoke, her voice was the same as the one in Angela's mind—smooth as honey and heavy as gold.

"You don't have to do that, dear. That's what I'm here for. Trust me, you don't want to awaken from this dream."

A spider scuttled from the woman's wrist to Angela's.

In a brilliant flash, the room changed. Instead of a warm dining hall filled with friends and candlelight, Angela sat on a hard chair, at a dark table, surrounded by people just as beautiful and terrible as the woman gripping her wrist. Angela wore a long black dress, and her head pounded again with the weight of the crown set upon it. Mocking and superior faces regarded her coldly. Before her sat a heavy goblet filled with red liquid. Her reflection shimmered back at her, her left eye burning a brilliant green.

With another flash the dark scene disappeared. Angela was once again in the cheerful dining hall. The dark woman next to her smiled. *"This is a far better world to live in,"* she said in her satiny voice. *"And you can stay in it forever. I'll take care of everything else. The crown is far too heavy for you to wear alone."*

Everything the woman said sounded so reasonable. The spider crawling back to her wrist shone in the light like a living piece of onyx.

But Angela couldn't stop staring at the hourglass. She couldn't help wondering what would happen if she disobeyed.

Her mind raced. *There's something not quite right about all this. There's something very important that I'm forgetting.*

Another flash overtook her.

Angela suddenly stood on a balcony jutting out into the cold fog over an immense, dark city. Pyramids and sprawling mansions littered the ground in every direction, for as far as she could see. Glowing orange globes shone through the thick clouds like faraway suns. Below her, between a file of onyx obelisks, an innumerable throng of winged beings stood waiting for her orders. Great horselike beasts with flanks shimmering in phosphorescent blue held black-clad riders with menacing tridents. Pennants fluttered in a dull breeze. Angela's blood-red hair whipped against her face. The crown resting atop her head felt heavy as iron this time.

In seconds, the vision panned away, returning to being a mysterious reflection in the hourglass.

"*You don't want to touch it,*" the female voice said to her anxiously. "*Think of all the peace you would give up. You don't need memories. The past should stay locked away. That's what you've always tried to accomplish.*"

Angela agreed, yet a different part of her couldn't help stretching out her hand again.

"*You'll regret it. You're better off staying here . . . forgetting everything,*" the woman said, and her tone became sinister. "*It's not too late to stop yourself . . .*"

The woman's dark-skinned hand grasped Angela's again, but Angela struggled and the fingers locked around her wrist spasmed before crumbling to ash. The woman shouted in frustration, her voice chilling and cruel.

Angela's heart pounded. Her head ached again. Warmth filled her body, and a soft buzzing noise erupted in her ears. Slowly she grasped the hourglass and flipped it upside down.

Crimson grains started sprinkling through its narrow neck to the bottom.

Angela watched them, transfixed. The more she focused, the more every grain became a moment in her life. First came her bleak childhood—the horrific period in her life when she received so many scars inside and outside from a human family intent on hating her. Next her first days in Luz arrived, and her first meeting with Sophia as Angela stood on the dormitory rooftop. There was Westwood Academy's fearsome witch, Stephanie Walsh, and the oak Fae named Tileaf, and the first time Kim had ever touched her and sent a tingle of excitement through her skin. Then, Lucifel's crimson eyes were burning into Angela's brain. A door with a snake-shaped knob appeared next, and Angela once again descended a shadowed stairway, searching for Sophia, the Book of Raziel. Angela encountered Hell. She nearly perished in it in her madness to rescue her friend. She'd been forced to drink angel blood to see the Supernal Raziel's past, and her memories had vanished little by little. That explained her vision of sitting with a cup of red liquid before her. Every day since then she'd been manipulated into drinking more.

Now she remembered everything.

It had all come back to her. Every last second of joy and pain. Every face. Every terror.

Slowly, Angela dug her fingers into the tablecloth in front of her. The dinner party felt so real, yet it was all just an illusion. The real world was the bleakness of Hell, and the crown she now wore as its ruler. The reality before her was that Lucifel was now in Heaven, and the Book of Raziel remained unopened, because worst of all, Angela remembered that for the Book to be opened, Sophia had to die by Angela's own hand.

The demon by Angela's side—Lilith—gasped. "So that's the answer," she said softly.

She turned and regarded Angela. A dangerous smile spread across her face.

Lilith must have also seen all Angela's past and memories. She now knew how to open Sophia.

Before Angela could even think of what to do next, the illusion finally ended, thrusting the world back into darkness.

Eight

Were you there in the Garden of Shadows . . .

Angela awoke to those words, sung as if by a mirage in an unearthly, feminine voice.

Her eyes opened blearily and she took in the world around her. For a while, she lay where she was, too fearful to move. Perhaps this was just another illusion. Her bed was long and hard, and above her a great chandelier flickered in a pool of darkness. Beyond its light she could make out mosaics. One of them displayed the image of a feathered serpent twined around a tree laden heavily with red fruit. Another showed a dark gray angel she knew to be Lucifel. The Grail—the emerald Eye—seemed to glitter where it hung against Lucifel's chest.

Where am I? This isn't my own room.

Her chest tightened with fear. Suddenly, Angela realized sweat beaded her forehead and cheeks. She listened intently to the familiar song as it continued.

> *Were you near when the Father took wing?*
> *Did you sigh when the starlight outpoured us?*
> *When the silver bright water could sing . . .*

Have you drunk from a river of amber?
Or eaten the nectar of dreams?
Where thoughts linger determining eons,
And time stretches apart at the seams . . .

The terrible vision she'd lived through yet again flickered and finally died away. Her head throbbed and her temples ached. It felt like someone had pulled out her brain and stuffed it back into her skull. Even the familiar song echoing throughout the chamber made it hurt. Angela breathed softly, still too cautious to get up. The song stopped. Footsteps clattered to her side.

Quickly, Angela swung her legs over the side of the table she lay upon and grabbed her attacker, pinning the person's arms behind her back at the same second her own feet hit the ground.

"Angela!" a soft voice said. Curls smelling of incense fluffed against Angela's chin. More of the cloying scent wafted through the room.

"Sophia?" Angela whispered.

She let go, allowing Sophia to stumble and regain her balance.

For a second, they stared deep into each other's eyes. Sophia's normally placid face was drawn with anxiety. Fear tugged at all her delicate features. With a wild cry of happiness, Angela reached forward and clasped her tightly, unable to believe that they were looking at each other again just as meaningfully as in the past. Sophia held Angela against her chest, stroking her hair. "You're all right," Sophia said, letting out a long and shaky sigh. "So it worked, then."

"What worked?" Angela said, still in pain, but barely feeling it anymore.

Sophia shook her head. "Nothing. Never mind . . ." A haunted look flickered across her face. "All that matters is your memories should have returned completely. Kim and I suspected you were being secretly fed angel blood over time. Eventually, we knew for certain. But you're all right now."

Yes. I'm all right now. But—

"Where is Kim? Where are we?" Angela said.

"Promise me you won't go crazy, Angela."

Angela felt her entire body tighten. Sophia's new tone was alarming. "What? Why?"

"Just promise me. You have to."

"Fine, I promise."

"Like you mean it."

Angela took a deep breath. She spoke slowly. "I promise I won't do or say anything stupid."

Sophia squeezed her eyes shut, opened them again, and, seeming to find the courage to speak again, began to explain. "We're in Python's mansion. Kim has—well, I don't know where he is anymore—" She must have seen how shocked and upset Angela looked, because here Sophia paused and grasped Angela by the wrists. "Angela, calm down. It will be all right."

This time, Angela knew she stared at her like they'd never seen each other before.

"It was the only way to restore your memories," Sophia added hastily. Her voice cracked with pain. "Please understand. I went along with this only for your sake. It was Kim's idea, and I agreed to it of my own free will. Neither of us could stand seeing you suffer anymore. Your visions—I know they're frightening and terrible—"

"How could you know that?" Angela whispered. She slumped against the cold table that had been her bed, trying to take everything in. Python had been the cause of all her misery mere months ago. He'd been responsible for luring Angela into Hell in the first place. And Sophia and Kim had bargained with him?

"I know," Sophia said, tears rolling down her pink cheeks once again. "All you need to do is believe me. Just like every other time. Please do that for me . . . Angela."

Sophia gently touched her arm.

Angela bit her lip. She sighed and glanced at their surroundings. The gilded room was little more than a glittering prison cell. There were no windows. The velvet-draped furniture lay in heavy shadows, and the serpent mosaics on the ceiling played with her eyes this time. They watered as more incense drifted by. She spotted the doors on the far side of the room. Perhaps they were unlocked.

Angela's eyes widened.

"Lilith. She knows how to open you, Sophia. We have to get out of here!"

She ran to the doors and yanked on them hard. They didn't even budge. Locked, just as she'd feared. They were trapped.

"Do you know a way to get out of here?" Angela said. "Come on! Come on!" she shouted, stumbling as her grip slipped on the ornate door handles. "Help me open these doors. If we pull together—"

"That won't work," Sophia said. "Python has a strong seal on the doors. Besides, he'll know if you break them and get out."

"So that's it then?" Angela said. She glanced around the room frantically.

"Well—there is one way out. But it's not ideal."

"Anything," Angela said. "Just show me what to do."

Sophia sucked in a deep breath. She looked around the room, as if suspecting eavesdroppers. Then she motioned Angela toward its center. Now Angela noticed that a slab of carved onyx lay flat in the middle of the room. It was large enough to be suspicious, but small enough to escape notice without proper attention. A coiled serpent with glittering garnet eyes had been carved on the surface. "Help me push," Sophia said, and she knelt down, already starting to edge the slab to the left.

Angela knelt and helped her. The onyx scraped and screeched against the stones where it rested. As it moved, a thin strip of darkness appeared. A dank musky odor drifted up from the hole they were gradually uncovering. Finally, they'd pushed the slab completely to the side, exposing a circular hole resembling the mouth of a stone well. Angela stared down into the inky blackness that greeted them. "How in the world did you know this was here?" she said, turning to Sophia again.

Sophia continued staring into the hole. "I suspected this was a sacrificial chamber. Python probably sends prisoners here for sport. There were many demons like him in the old days. Lucifel eradicated most of them—they were wild, rebellious, truly dangerous types that even she found repugnant. Python, though, had his mother, Lilith, to protect him." Sophia shook her head sadly, as if mourning for so many unnamed victims. "Typically, this hole would be uncovered. Despite the decadence and luxury of the room, eventually anyone would go mad from being confined for so long, especially without food. Once they can't bear anymore, the prisoner has no choice but to escape using this hole."

Angela felt all the blood drain from her face. "And? Then what?"

Sophia looked back up at her. "Well—that's what we're going to find out, I suppose."

Angela stared back down into the hole. She couldn't see a thing, and the Grail that was her left Eye wasn't helping or making a difference.

The incense in the room continued to nearly suffocate her. She'd hated smoke ever since her family had perished in a fire. Now, with those visions that had been assaulting her day and night, she'd grown to hate darkness as well.

Angela's vision began to swim again. "*Angela!*"

Angela jumped as Sophia's fingers brushed her cheek, revealing all her inner torment and concern.

Angela held Sophia's chilly fingers, and as she looked down, she saw that the white sapphire pendant she'd given Sophia no longer sparkled. "What happened to the stone in your necklace?" she asked weakly.

Sophia dropped her gaze to the floor. "Its fire has gone out," she said. "Perhaps because we've been down in Hell for so long. Everything eventually changes in this awful place."

Angela pawed her own chest, rubbing the gem of her matching necklace with her thumb. Even with her memories temporarily erased, her reasons for cherishing the symbolic gem had somehow never vanished. "Well," Angela said. "We haven't changed. We're still together, right? We always lean on each other for the most important things, right? That means much more than a gemstone."

"Yes, we do share everything with each other," Sophia whispered. But her smile was faint and sorrowful.

"Then I think it's about time you told me," Angela finally said.

Sophia paused. She peered carefully at Angela, clearly startled. "Tell you what?"

"What that lullaby you sing really means. Israfel sang it, using it to guide me to him the first time we met in Luz." *Yes,* Angela thought, *on that long, long ago day in Luz.* "And you told me it was a lullaby. And that even he, the great angel that he was, doesn't know what the lyrics really mean. Because it's your song. So tell me what they mean, and how in the world Israfel's song can be your song at all."

Sophia's eyes went glassy. Her face masked over with distress.

"Well?" Angela said insistently, unable to stop. "Where have you been for so long that Israfel learned a lullaby from you, Sophia? How did you survive in the Abyss so that Raziel could find you?"

They should have left by now, but Angela couldn't help thinking about her vision whenever she looked at Sophia. As if the answers were right in front of her. But nothing about it really made sense. Even though Lucifel had remarked on Angela's likeness to the Father more than once, Angela was a human being, not a god. Her soul was said to be mysterious, but Raziel had chosen her to be the Archon because it was the best choice available to him at the time.

She wasn't special. Or maybe she just didn't want to be. Angela wasn't sure she even knew anymore.

Sophia's lips parted. She looked at Angela and back to the black hole in the floor, as if tempted to jump inside to avoid the question. Then she shook her head. "No. You wouldn't understand. Not yet."

"*That's* what I don't get. How could I not understand? I've understood everything else about you, haven't I? I think I'm more than ready to grasp the rest. Why are you trying to evade the question?"

"Because you're not ready to know everything about me,"

Sophia said softly. "That's why." She sighed painfully. "It's time for us to leave, Angela—"

"No. I've had it. Enough secrets." Angela held her tightly by the hands. "What was the punishment you suffered, Sophia, that was so great? What could you have done to merit being in darkness that deep? When I look at you, all I see is kindness, and compassion, and beauty. You're not a murderer or a thief. So what did you do and how could you be so impossibly ancient?"

"I told you I died in childbirth," Sophia whispered. "And that wasn't a lie. And that's why I'm what you see before you now. I'm just a soul trapped in a body made from scraps of my original one."

"Fine, scraps then. But what does that mean? I hate these riddles!"

Sophia set a finger on Angela's lips to silence her. "See? There's no way you can understand right now. But trust me when I say you'll know everything, and you will understand, soon enough."

"And then?"

Sophia stared deep into Angela's eyes. She pushed away some blood-red hair from Angela's cheeks and then cradled her face with both hands.

"You're so sad again," Angela said softly. "Why are you always looking at me like that?"

Sophia kissed her on the forehead. Angela's eyes watered and she looked down at her feet.

"You've come such a long way," Sophia said to her. "From that self-loathing girl I met at Westwood Academy not so long ago. That young woman couldn't separate dreams from reality. She'd been abused by parents who'd labeled her as a freak and a murderous monster even before she was born. So she shut herself off and shut people out. Because she thought it was better to be alone forever than to feel the pain of a broken heart. So what happened? Well, once she saw that even angels aren't perfect, she learned to forgive herself. She stood taller every day and grew prouder of how she'd survived so much pain. Finally, she walked tall and I could only walk feebly by her side, admiring what she'd become. That was the young woman who braved Hell and the Devil to save me from death—or what she thought would be my death. That was the person who said she couldn't murder me to save the world, because she'd learned there is light in that world and hope. Angela, you asked why Raziel chose your soul to be the Archon's. You asked why he chose *you* to make the ultimate decision to save the universe or silence it like Lucifel wishes to.

"Have you ever stopped to consider, it's because of the person you are?"

Sophia caressed the matching pendant resting on Angela's chest. "I never knew how, I never knew when, but in the end, I always, always believed you would set things right."

She's speaking in the past tense. How could she know I would set anything right if we never knew each other back then?

Angela shook her head. She didn't want to just drop the topic, but the time to escape was slipping by quickly. Without another word, she squeezed Sophia's hand and looked back at the dreadful hole in the floor.

"Are you ready?" she said.

The heavy incense in the room smelled as sacrificial and ominous as Sophia had suggested. It was starting to choke off air as much as it screened light.

"I'm not fond of entering potentially bottomless pits."

Sophia sighed. "Unfortunately, I know my answer has to be yes."

Angela commiserated with a frown. She knelt down and felt along the inside rim of the hole. Her fingers brushed metal rungs. "There's some kind of ladder. Thank God." She took a deep breath. "I'll go first," she said, trying to be noble and brave, but feeling less courageous the more she pondered what might be waiting at the bottom.

Carefully, she maneuvered herself onto the first set of shockingly cold rungs. Angela had to force herself to hold on to them as her palms began to numb. Slowly, she used the sole of her shoes to feel below for the next rungs, one at a time. A dank breeze wafted beneath her black nightgown. Of course she was stuck wearing the worst possible outfit for whatever happened next.

Angela was already in utter darkness when she heard the rustle of Sophia's dress as she followed, both of them plunging deep into the shadows to survive.

Angela couldn't imagine how Troy, despite being a Jinn adapted to darkness and tunnels, could live like this for so many centuries. The thought of her made a cold knife of guilt twist in Angela's soul.

Is Troy even alive? She saved my life when we first entered Hell, but I never found out if she and her niece Juno escaped. And then I lost my memories. I wonder if she thinks I betrayed her? I wonder where she could be? More than ever, we could use her help.

Angela knew that last thought was foolish.

Certainly, wherever Troy was, she was far, far away.

"Sophia," Angela dared to whisper. Her voice echoed against the stone walls of the hole anyway. "Do you know what happened to Troy? Is she alive?"

Sophia paused suddenly on the rungs above Angela. She stayed silent for a while, as if she didn't quite know how to respond. "She's alive," Sophia finally said.

"How do you know?" Angela pressed.

Another long pause. Angela could sense that Sophia's mind was working. When Sophia spoke again, her voice sounded almost frantic, as if she'd forgotten something crucial. "Quickly," she whispered. "We need to keep moving. There isn't much time."

Angela knew that already. So Sophia must have been referring to something else that might happen soon. Without trying to pry any further, Angela forced herself to descend faster.

She remembered that Sophia didn't know where Kim had been taken.

Maybe we can find him down here.

Or perhaps someone else will find him first.

Nine

Troy squeezed her eyes shut. The lights of the room, however dim for her, cut into her brain like claws. After weeks of being forced to fight for her life in Python's noisy Arena, the sudden silence stifled her, and her eyes throbbed painfully.

The demon hadn't been kind enough to blindfold her this time, but he'd of course remembered to muzzle her. She licked her lips, wishing for a way to chew out of her prison. Manacles had also been clamped around her wrists, and a collar with a leaden chain attached her to her iron cage. She'd stopped trying to slip her wrists out of the manacles hours ago, but remained saturated in the stench of her own blood.

She was certain she'd heard Sariel—her half-Jinn cousin known to others as Kim—and the Book of Raziel speaking to Python. She'd even dared to hiss at the sound of his voice.

Now, she knew that perhaps it had all been a dream.

She was too hungry and so confined that the world was escaping her. If only she could see through the velvet drapery thrown over her cage. For months she'd been jailed like this, forced to fight for her life for the demons' amusement, the thought of her niece Juno traveling alone through the plain near Babylon torturing her at every other moment.

Footsteps paused nearby. Python's distinctive scent wafted through the drapery to her like a poison.

Troy couldn't stop a growl of rage from bubbling inside of her. The fabric lifted from her cage and she narrowed her eyes to slits. The demon stood right next to her, leaning over the upper bars.

She turned on him, glaring from the darkest corner of her little prison. Python was decadently dressed in a black overcoat studded with red gems. A serpent brooch glittered below his neck. He paused, probably alarmed by the predatory hatred shining behind Troy's eyes. But Python's fascination soon overcame his fear. He knelt down to what they both knew was a dangerously close position. Behind him, the dull haze of the chamber cast a reddish glow onto his hair and back.

"The High Assassin of the Jinn," he whispered proudly. "But thanks to me, no better than a flightless bird in a cage. Do you think you can keep winning your battles with only one wing? I'll admit it's certainly entertaining to watch. I see that the wound has healed over nicely—" His hand reached for a few feathers sticking out between the bars.

Troy lunged.

Python snatched his fingers away, but he smacked them accidentally against the bars, cursing.

"It will heal even better," Troy hissed, "when I medicate it with your blood."

"Always so feisty," Python said, winking at her. He examined her fearlessly, shaking the pain from his hand. Troy stared right back at him, wishing he could see her teeth more clearly and feel her nails ripping into him all over again.

The scar over his left eye always sent a thrill of satisfaction through her. That deserved wound had been Troy's handiwork, after all. "It makes me wonder how you'll behave," he continued, "when you see who your next opponent will be—and how much you'll owe me the satisfaction of making him suffer."

"It will be another Jinn," Troy snapped at him. "You're too boring to try anything else. And once again, I refuse to kill one of my own race."

"I just love your confidence," Python whispered. He gritted his teeth. "The simple fact that you're wrong makes me so warm and tingly inside." He ran a hand through his hair. "Tell me, Troy, what's it like to be little more than a mangy beast? Of course you're more attractive than most of your race—dare I say it, even beautiful. I could have made a lovely scarf for myself with those feathers of yours. Oh, and those piercing golden eyes. So enchanting. I can see how you hypnotize your prey so easily. Everything about you is dainty, and elegant, and lethal. I almost admire it. Almost, because—"

He dared to lean in close and whisper into her flicking ear.

"—because, of course, you're in the cage and I'm not. Tell me, then, who is the better hunter? All those little victory bones and teeth tied into your ragged mess of hair, but you've only ended up another rat in a trap, haven't you? Well, it's high time I added to my own trophy collection." His voice lowered meaningfully. "I expect you'll go on doing your best to continue entertaining me. It's your duty to enthrall on demand. It's because of me that you're the new Jinn Queen, after all."

He pounded the bars and laughed.

Troy's head rang. She would have grabbed his wrist in that

split second and broken it, but her own hands were manacled and so she could only lurk, and wait, and continue to nurture the deadly promise of utter destruction she'd made to Python those few months ago when he first captured her.

"Don't worry," he said. "Just a few more minutes and you'll be free for the short time I grant to you. But if you'll excuse me, I'm going to release you from a safe location. I just can't trust that bloodthirsty instinct of yours."

A purplish mist rose from the ground and covered his body until Python disappeared.

Now, if you'll be sweet enough to give me a moment. Python's voice remained, echoing in the dank, musty room that was more a dungeon than any actual kind of chamber. Embers flickered on the onyx walls. Grotesque creatures had been carved in the stone. Troy recognized only a few of them. She tended to concentrate more on the wards written in demonic Theban meant to help cage her if she ever escaped from these iron bars.

Even as she watched, they began to fade from the walls.

What was Python doing? He wasn't dragging her to the Arena this time?

I'm sure you heard your half-breed cousin conversing with me not so long ago, Python said. His voice seemed to echo from everywhere at once. *He's alive, Troy. I have him in a prison here. The game is that you need only to find which one.*

Troy stiffened. Her hair stood on end as sparks of crimson light broke the muzzle on her face and snapped the manacles on her wrist and neck. Slowly, the gate of her cage opened.

See how kind of a master I am, pet? I'm allowing you to have your revenge on him at last. Now you can make him suffer for murdering your uncle. Pay close attention here—he can suffer. *But you can't kill him. I won't allow that. And be sure to stay within the boundaries because I will know if you overreach them.*

Surely, Python was lying. But Troy knew Sariel was indeed in Hell. Whether or not he'd ever contacted Angela had been open to guesses.

Either way, Troy was free to scamper through Python's dungeon. At the very least, she could probably find a way to free herself. Tentatively, she crawled out of the cage, smarting at the feel of chill stone against her palms. Her nails scraped the rock as she stood, examining the heavy door blocking her exit from the jail.

It was now wide open.

Through the acidic fog, a familiar, though very faint scent, worked its way to Troy.

As if in a trance, she began to follow it. For once, this demon hadn't lied.

Ten

The second Angela's feet finally brushed the ground, she froze. Sophia paused, still stuck in the tunnel above her. They'd ended their descent in a long stone tunnel dripping with water that steamed as it met the stone. To their right, in the direction of a strange reddish glow, strange animalistic noises drifted toward them. But they were only audible because of the echoing effect of the stone.

Other odd noises resounded from above. Angela couldn't tell if she was hearing voices or a constant roar. It almost sounded like an enormous crowd hid nearby, just out of sight.

Slowly, Sophia set her dainty slippers on the stone floor beside Angela as she dropped at last from their hole.

Her face blanched.

"What is that roaring sound?" Angela whispered to her. "It sounds almost like chanting voices."

Sophia looked up at the ceiling worriedly. Angela felt the same. The hole in the room where they'd been trapped had dropped them into another tunnel, which forced them to walk east or west. Angela had chosen east and then they'd been forced to enter the hole from which they'd just emerged. Perhaps they weren't underneath Python's mansion anymore. Certainly they might be underneath the portion of Babylon directly outside it.

"Do you know what this noise is?" Angela said, unable to stop listening to it.

Sophia shook her head. "We should keep moving."

Angela nodded and grabbed her hand. She turned to the right and then the left. Neither choice was the best. They still had no clue where they were going. "There's light in this direction," Angela said, facing the reddish glow. The animalistic noises sounded slightly familiar. Then a long braying screech echoed back to them.

Angela gasped. Kirin had been stabled down there. These must have been the underground paddocks where Python kept his beasts.

"All right, hurry," Angela said. She grabbed Sophia and forced her to run behind her.

Sophia had already caught on. "They're Python's animals, Angela. They might not let us ride without his permission."

"Oh, they'll let us ride," Angela said. She glanced back at Sophia meaningfully, finding it more and more difficult to speak as they ran. "Trust me."

Hieroglyphs on the walls pulsed with red light. They quickly encroached upon a huge gate with two serpents twined above, their necks hooked together in a reciprocal *S* shape. Cautiously, Angela and Sophia crept close enough to the gate to see inside. Angela could make out the long rows of individual paddocks. Troughs carved with dragons and serpents held colorless vegetation from the plains surrounding Babylon, and a smooth wall of rock displayed silver pegs, each holding a bridle studded with gems. There were no signs of saddles anywhere.

Angela reached out to shove the gates open.

The twin snakes instantly lunged and hissed at her. Their jaws snapped for her hands.

Sophia screamed.

Angela backed away. The Kirin began snorting in alarm. They'd probably been spooked by her unfamiliar smell. Angela had certainly ridden enough Kirin now in Hell to understand their behavior. But even though she had her own stables as Hell's Prince, Angela had never found any Kirin willing to bond with her. It was as if they could sense she was from another world.

Think, Angela. Think! This is the perfect way to escape, especially if there are other creatures down in these tunnels. But these snakes—this gate—

If only she could summon the Glaive. But doing so would mean that she'd suffer great pain, maybe even go temporarily blind. The Glaive was a pole-arm of crystallized blue blood from Lucifel's Grail. To summon the weapon, she'd need to stab her new green Eye to make it bleed. The very thought worked shivers through her entire body.

She'd have to take her chances with the snakes for now.

"*Angela, wait—*" Sophia shouted.

Angela grasped the lock on the gate, fumbled with it, and refused to let go, even as the serpents twined down the iron bars and sank their fangs deep into the flesh of her hands.

Sophia latched on to them, shouting as she tried to pull them off.

"Sophia, let go," Angela gasped through the pain. "*Let— go—*"

Sophia only pulled harder.

Angela groaned, biting her lip hard to hold back screams. The reptiles chewed deeper into her skin. Blue blood trickled down her wrists.

Sophia froze, her hands still locked around the serpents' necks. Angela ignored her pain for a moment, watching with her mind turning in panicked circles as the blue blood dripped, and dripped, and dripped.

I bleed this color now? Just like the Grail? WHY?

Sophia staggered, letting go abruptly. She must have been able to sense what Angela was about to do. Almost instinctively, Angela willed the blood in her palms to pool together and crystallize. Radiant light illuminated the inside of the stables and the tunnel behind Angela and Sophia as the Glaive materialized in Angela's hands. As the haft took shape, the snakes hissed madly and crumbled to black ash. The blade appeared in a wicked scimitar of blue.

"Stand back!" Angela shouted.

She swiped at the bars of the gate.

They smashed like glass, chunks of metal sprinkling to the ground around them. Angela's hands throbbed painfully, but she held on to the weapon tightly. She ducked through the hole in the gate, turned back to offer a free hand and help Sophia step inside, and then motioned for her to stay still as Angela glanced around for danger. The Kirin continued to bray and screech. They'd been pushed to panic by the Glaive's light.

Which paddock do I open? I guess it doesn't matter. Any Kirin will do.

A terrible *WHUMP* sounded throughout the stable, echoing off the walls. Instantly, the other Kirin hushed. They nickered in their paddocks, their large paws scuffing at the stone floor. The sound had come from the largest paddock, directly across from Angela. She turned to look up at the barred hole set in its door. From inside, a great yellow eye gleamed back at her. A snort of hot breath left the nostrils of the Kirin inside. Angela had never seen one so large.

"It's enormous," Sophia whispered by her side. "It must be a male."

Angela took a step forward. She and the beast gazed at each other steadily. Time slowed. The creature's intelligent eyes locked on Angela's green eye, the Grail, and the power within it ignited like a fire between them and held the animal fast.

Angela walked up to the door of the paddock. As quietly as possible, she snapped the lock open with the Glaive. She then willed the weapon to collapse.

Blue blood splashed to the ground. The Kirin inside neighed and tensed.

Angela stared a second longer. Then she grabbed Sophia and ran with her to the other side of the room.

They'd dashed out of the way just in time.

The winged Kirin exploded from its stable and galloped directly in front of Angela and Sophia, rearing above them with its horn nearly scraping the cavern ceiling. It returned to the earth with a resounding crash of its paws against the ground. The vibration shuddered powerfully up through Angela's legs and chest. The other Kirin surrounding them had now gone completely still and silent.

Sophia gripped Angela by the shoulder. They sat on the ground with the beast looming over them.

The Kirin's entire body gleamed dark ebony, and beautiful bluish-green stripes of light rippled up and down its flanks. Its eyes fixed on Angela and pierced her. Enormous reptilian wings flapped powerfully against its sides, throwing out gusts of air. It was completely different from any Kirin she'd ever seen in Hell. Three times larger, winged, and with a noble bearing. No wonder Python had shut it up underneath his mansion, away from prying eyes.

"Angela," Sophia whispered in warning.

The Kirin lowered its neck invitingly and then went still.

Had the power of the Eye subdued it like Angela had planned? Yet even as she reached out as if in a dream to stroke the animal's long muzzle, she couldn't help feeling that this creature was somehow hers. It allowed itself to be petted for a minute, then arched its neck again and began to nicker nervously. Now was their chance.

"Come on! Hurry!" Angela said, hoisting Sophia up with her from the ground. Sophia panted for breath but didn't protest as Angela helped her carefully climb onto the Kirin's broad back. Angela followed, ducking as the Kirin's leathery wings tested the air again. She held fast to the Kirin's mane, tightening her grip as Sophia locked her arms around Angela's waist.

Swiftly, she tugged so that the Kirin turned back toward the gate.

"All right," she said to Sophia. "Whatever you do—don't let go."

The winged Kirin reared before sprinting, and its long screech set its fellow herd members into a frenzy again. Angela winced as the beast jumped over the pieces of the gate blocking its way. The impact shuddered up through her bones and chattered her teeth as it landed again.

Then they galloped fast, with nothing to stop them.

They had no choice except to travel in the opposite direction from which they'd come.

Angela gritted her teeth. She dared to shut her eyes, relishing the sensation of the chilly air working its way through her hair. Sophia pressed against her back, head buried in her shoulder. The odd noise they'd heard in the tunnel became louder the more they galloped. There could have been a waterfall nearby, though Angela knew that was impossible. They were miles from the Styx River right now.

A deeper chill worked its way through her. It was the same one she'd felt when she and Sophia rode after Lucifel before her escape from Hell—and before Angela was trapped in it forever.

Without warning the winged Kirin slowed its pace.

Soon, they were down to a trot. Sophia's weight lifted from against Angela's back. "What's going on?" she said, shouting above the roar surrounding them on all sides.

"I don't know," Angela shouted back.

Worry lanced through her like a shard of ice. She could have sworn the roar was actually the sound of a million voices. But they had to continue forward. There was no other exit.

A dull light had appeared ahead of them. Mysterious furrows had been etched through the rock walls, slicing the hieroglyphs there into halves. They looked like claw marks.

Angela kicked the Kirin's sides with her heels, forcing the creature to speed up again. Reluctantly, it began to move. This time, its wings beat with its movements, propelling it forward even faster, as if the beast glided on ice. The light and the sound grew both brighter and noisier.

They could have been entering a thundercloud. The noise shivered through Angela's entire body and set her bones aching.

Angela felt Sophia's fingers tighten painfully into her waist. "*It can't be,*" Sophia shouted.

But it was too late to stop. The Kirin burst out of the tunnel.

Light blinded them. Innumerable voices chanted in the native language of the demons. Angela didn't have the time to concentrate on what was being said. She was too busy trying to keep her and Sophia alive. The Kirin reared higher than before, threatening to dump them both onto the ground. Angela and Sophia screamed together.

As the Kirin returned to the earth again, Angela looked around wildly, trying to understand.

They were now outside, standing in the bottom center of a great arena swarming with chanting excited demons of every age and rank. Angela's mouth opened, but no sound came out of it. Her eyes watered from the brilliance of far too many braziers and lights.

Ice crystals drifted slowly to the ground from the heavy clouds, dusting the bare skin of her arms.

It was beyond Angela's imagination how Python disguised this place and hid it from the general view of Hell, but she suspected more than one of his dark mischievous powers behind it all. The Arena was too large not to be seen from the ground unless it was deliberately hidden somehow. It was bigger than more than a few of Babylon's city blocks put together and constructed entirely of black onyx with cruel-looking obsidian spires. Pennants with an orange snake fluttered from intimidating turrets.

The chanting grew louder, signifying that something was about to happen. The demons grew even more excited, hundreds of them standing to get a better view of what was taking place.

Angela could barely breathe.

"The Arena . . ." Sophia shouted behind her fearfully.

Angela clasped the pendant at her chest, tightening her hand around it into a fist.

"I thought it no longer existed," Sophia stammered.

"What do you mean?" Angela shouted back.

"Millennia ago, the Great Demons would host games here in Lucifel's name. Usually, captured angels were pitted against a demon who'd committed a crime against Lucifel's law, or worse, Jinn would be pitted against one another. Finally, Lucifel demanded the Arena be shut down and destroyed. No one knows why. But no one had the courage to say no to her, and it was slowly, piece by piece, dismantled. Or so most demons thought." Sophia took in a shaky breath. "Python must have either had it rebuilt or salvaged enough to commission repairs for what remained. I'd guess that now only demons of his choosing have any idea it exists. And I imagine that he makes them keep the secret on pain of death."

"How would he know if they talked about it?" Angela said. Dizziness began to overtake her as the winged Kirin turned in panicked circles.

"He has ways," Sophia said. "You of all people should know that by now."

A sudden breeze whipped out of nowhere, throwing up Angela's hair like a blood-red curtain.

Suddenly, most of the demons stood and looked directly at her, cheering wildly.

"They know it's you," Sophia said with horror.

Angela scanned the crowds, at last focusing on a great balcony where most of the pennants fluttered. Python was there, sitting on an enormous chair. Somehow, the Eye's gaze tightened the space between them so that Angela could examine every last detail. He wore an extravagant coat of black velvet and purple thread, and blood-red gems glittered against his brow. He'd been looking down at a mirror held between his hands. Now he set it aside and leaned forward, staring back at her. His snake's gaze lingered on Angela's.

You wouldn't dare, she said to him with her thoughts.

In answer, a satisfied smile broke on his thin lips.

Python stood and a deep silence fell throughout the Arena. He waved his hands, gesturing down at Angela and Sophia—or at something beyond them.

A sudden flash of reddish light and a wall of flickering energy spread up around the center of the Arena floor, meeting high on all sides in the sky to form a kind of dome. Python was making sure the winged Kirin couldn't fly them to safety.

Angela pictured the claw marks in the stone tunnel and her chest tightened.

She glanced around the Arena, searching desperately for another exit. There were two, each as large as the tunnel through which they'd entered. Without warning, the Kirin champed and spun in the other direction, facing the tunnel with the claw marks.

It lowered its head, its front legs stiffening defensively as it displayed its spiraling horn.

The earth itself seemed to growl and shudder. The crowd of demons remained deathly silent. Angela looked back at Python. He stood at the edge of his balcony, examining her with a cold smile. He'd been drinking from a goblet in the meantime, which he now pitched casually over the side to the ground.

Welcome to my Arena, Archon, his voice whispered in Angela's mind. *I'd like to thank you in advance for providing such unexpected entertainment.* Python leaned against the balcony railing. *In fact, you're just in time. I've obtained a very rare prize for this next show. One that cost me as much blood and sweat to obtain as that winged Kirin you've stolen.*

Angela could feel her rage heating her entire body. She struggled to keep the Kirin steady. *You know it's foolish to kill me. With me dead it's impossible to open the Book.*

Oh, that's quite all right. First, I'll watch you suffer. Then we can discuss how best to slice Sophia to ribbons with the Glaive.

"Angela," Sophia whispered fearfully. "It's coming. Whatever it is—it's coming!"

But Angela's world had stopped. All she could digest was that now both Lilith and her son, Python, knew how to open Sophia. But Python was playing it smart. He'd never force Angela to kill Sophia in front of so many demons. He'd want to keep a secret of that magnitude to himself. *How had he found out? Who could have possibly told him?* Certainly not Lilith. It wasn't like her to entrust her power-hungry son with such valuable information herself. Had he somehow pried into Angela's mind? Perhaps when she was unconscious?

"Angela, hurry! Do something!" Sophia dared to shout.

Python's voice interrupted Angela's thoughts like a bullet smashing through glass. *You'd better act fast, Archon. There's no one coming to the rescue this time.*

"*Angela!*" Sophia screamed.

Now the demonic crowd burst into a deafening roar of excitement. A creature covered in black fur slunk on all fours out of the tunnel, and the claws on its humanlike hands and feet scraped at the stone. Its growl reverberated through the Arena, echoing like distant thunder. Its three heads resembled the perfection of an angel's, yet also had bestial manes of black hair and fences of enormous glittering teeth. The creature's great green eyes burned like ghostly lanterns. It was a three-headed Hound. Even in their normal aspect, Hounds were Hell's most dreadful creatures. They were descendants of Cherubim that had fallen to Hell and bred in the lowest darkness.

The sound of the Hound's great wings opening and closing again swept through the Arena.

So—this was the monster that Python allowed to roam those lower tunnels and eat the captives of his choice.

The Hound had already spotted them. The beast prowled closer, and a sulfurous stench saturated the air.

The Glaive! Angela thought to herself.

But even as she willed it to materialize from her still raw and bleeding hands, nothing happened. Sophia's grip tightened on Angela's arms, as if she had already sensed the problem.

"The dome," Sophia shouted. "It's blocking you from using the ether!"

They didn't stand a chance on their own. Angela grasped the Kirin's mane tightly. It seemed to disobey her as the Hound approached, ignoring Angela's tugs and the kick of her heels. The crowd continued to roar and chant.

Angela's breath stopped.

Her body rocked forward and she slammed into the Kirin's neck, clutching desperately at its mane. Sophia screamed behind her. The wind shrieked as they charged together to attack the Hound, and then the Kirin leaped, air whistling beneath its paws.

A heavy *thump* reverberated from the Kirin through Angela's body. Blood sprayed back on her and Sophia. The Kirin's horn must have struck.

The Hound dashed to the side, its left flank streaming red.

Jaws instantly snapped for Angela's face. Then another of its heads turned on her, the creature's teeth inches from her shoulder, its hot breath scorching her cheek.

The Kirin kicked viciously with its front paws as its leathery wings flapped powerfully. Angela stared back into the Hound's enormous fiery eyes. The world around her was now just a blur of color, a storm of incessant noise. A painful inferno filled every inch of her body, and she knew it was fear.

Despite the hope within her, she wondered if Python knew something she didn't. Perhaps he didn't need Angela to open Sophia. Perhaps all he needed was her hands, or her Eye, or her blood.

Perhaps there was no way to win.

As the Hound's jaws snapped for her head again, Angela squeezed her eyes shut, praying for the first time since she'd climbed onto the Throne of Hell.

Then it happened, as if a bolt of lightning split the air. Something had changed. The Kirin dropped to the ground again, stamping its paws anxiously. The three-headed Hound lifted its many muzzles to the air and sniffed as a keen and hungry glaze stole over each head's burning eyes.

The beast turned around, snarling. Its growls rumbled through Angela's entire frame, shivering her bones.

More cheers erupted around them. Fists pounded rhythmically against stone. Trumpets blared.

"What's going on?" Sophia shouted behind Angela between gasps for breath.

"I don't know. But it can't be good!" Angela forced the Kirin to turn.

Python still sat in his chair, but the new goblet he'd raised to his lips had paused there, as if time had stopped. He seemed unable to believe his eyes. Slowly, he lowered the glass and slipped out of his chair, striding again to the edge of the balcony. Worry had tightened his mouth. He gripped the rails in front of him, and when an attending demon approached to whisper in his ear, Python shoved the demon aside like he was little more than a rag fluttering in front of Python's face. He was focused on something entering the Arena.

Angela tried to see through the hazy air. She coughed as the acidic air stung her lungs.

A figure with black rags clinging to its slender limbs had crept onto the battleground. The intruder crouched on its haunches for a moment and glanced around the Arena, as if searching for someone.

It was a female Jinn.

Her hair was a ragged black mess, and her chalky skin appeared marbled with scars. Her pointed ears pressed back against her skull as she cautiously stood up. A collar with a heavy chain dangling below it clung to her neck.

Odd. She only had one wing.

She struggled to open her eyes more against the light that for any Jinn must have been painfully blinding. Little by little, she scanned the crowds, the skies, and each and every balcony.

Her gaze at last rested on Angela.

It was Troy, the High Assassin of the Jinn, the terror of Hell and her race's Underworld, who was Bound to Angela for eternity. The last time Angela had seen her, Troy and her young niece Juno had fought vicious Hounds to save Angela and her friend from certain death in Python's cruel maze. Angela felt as if Troy's gaze were an arrow lodged in her chest.

Sophia was right. She isn't dead!

Angela's prayer had reached someone, after all—the devil that was Bound to her soul.

Eleven

Angela heard nothing for what felt like forever. Sophia shouted something behind her, but every word vanished within the haze clouding her mind. There were only Troy's great eyes burning through her. What could they say to each other, after all? Did Troy know that Angela was now the ruler of Hell in Lucifel's place?

Troy flicked her ears and crouched with her hair bristled by fear and anger. She bravely growled back at the three-headed beast between them. Angela knew Troy had reason to be worried. This Hound was insane with rage. Python must have starved it, hoping for a greater spectacle. Well, he was getting one.

The demons began to chant again. Angela tried to listen to the words, waiting for the demonic speech to form into language she could understand, but the clamor of so many warring voices only confused her further. The Kirin beneath her threatened to bolt to the left. Its wings flapped, sending rocks and pebbles tumbling away from its paws. The thick muscles of its back felt harder and more unforgiving than ever. Angela could whisk herself and Sophia to safety now. The path was clear. But she refused.

I'm no coward. And I'll never let myself be a coward. This is what Python didn't count on. Friends help friends.

She looked at him pointedly, allowing all her triumph to brighten her face.

Feeling nervous now? she whispered silently to him.

Python never flinched. Instead, he watched her with a face that could have been chiseled from ice.

Then the earth began to shake again. The three-headed Hound was galloping straight for Troy, its open jaws glistening with saliva. Troy's eyes widened. Her single wing flapped weakly. She couldn't fly, but she could at least run. She did neither, and pounced onto the Hound's back, clinging to its neck, digging in her nails as ferociously as possible.

In moments Troy dropped to the ground again, but not before her nails raked across some of the Hound's eyes.

The Hound screeched, and the chilling sound echoed throughout the Arena, overpowering the frenzied cheers of the demonic audience. Quickly, the monster twisted its necks and rounded on Troy, gnashing its teeth at her wing. The Jinn dodged at the last second, but it was clear that in her weakened state, she wouldn't last long.

"Angela," Sophia panted behind her, "wait—"

Angela spurred the Kirin toward Troy anyway. Sophia's breath and words cut off sharply.

Angela used the Eye to get Troy's attention as she passed.

We'll have to work together, Angela said to Troy in her mind. *Otherwise, neither of us will win.*

In the split second that Troy sprinted past Angela, Troy's eyes locked on her.

She'd heard.

Troy paused, seemingly calculating her next steps, and then she took off in the opposite direction, returning to the Hound.

She kept out of its way as much as possible but was clearly drawing it toward the wall of the Arena. The monster already had its back to Angela, and its sole focus was now its attempts to smack Troy to the ground with one of its cruel hands.

We can trap it there!

"Hold on tight," Angela shouted to Sophia. She kicked the Kirin's sides with her heels.

It galloped, its great wings propelling them faster and faster as they raced for the Hound. The Kirin instinctively lowered its horn. Sophia's fingers pierced into Angela's sides like knives.

Some groans of dismay rippled through the crowd, but they were drowned out soon by maniacal cheers.

The Kirin's horn connected with the Hound's back. The monster screamed and rounded on Angela, its mouth frothing. Its angelic eyes burned with pure hatred. Then Troy took her chance and bit the middle head's neck.

Angela balked at the blood splashing back on her bare legs. But Troy never let go, and she had almost severed the middle head entirely as the Hound crashed to the ground, twitching, its hands and feet grasping at nothing. Blood poured out like a river, and gradually the monster began to still.

Troy backed away from the corpse, panting. She looked to Angela. "Well done, Archon," Troy whispered hoarsely. She spat blood onto the ground.

The battle was over. Python's precious three-headed monstrosity was either dead or very close to it. Its green eyes turned glassy one by one. Angela searched the balcony for him, but Python was gone. "Something's not right," Sophia whispered in her ear.

Troy stood beside them, still breathing hard as she scanned the crowds.

The dome surrounding them began to flicker before dissipating entirely from the ground up, as if a curtain were being lifted. A new silence filled the Arena. Soon, many of the demons in the crowds slid from their seats onto their knees. Angela followed their collective attention to a spot high in the sky.

Lilith was descending from above. Her dark beauty seemed to disappear beside the vision of her immense and horrible wings. The acidic air had worn them to little more than bone and ragged flesh, with metal struts supporting what remained. Then she landed before Angela with the grace of a swan alighting in a lake, first her ebony-colored feet, and then her entire body. Her black dress fluttered around her in the echoing breeze.

"Hello, Angela," Lilith said softly. "I'd been wondering where you'd been these past few hours. Come—I'm here to take you home."

Wherever Angela was going, it wasn't back to her mansion. Lilith regarded Sophia almost hungrily, and Angela knew exactly what would happen the moment Lilith had them both under her power again.

"I'm not returning," Angela said, her voice shaking in spite of herself.

Lilith tilted her head as if she hadn't heard correctly. "Oh? And why not? Where is Hell's Prince going to go if not back to Her Throne?"

"Wherever She pleases, crow," Troy snapped.

Lilith turned to Troy, her elegant face twisting with disgust. "I told my son he was a fool to toy with you, you feathered rat. At least have the decency to know your place and be silent before your betters."

Troy's eyes half closed to lethal slits. Her fingers clenched and unclenched. Angela knew Troy was only holding back because she had little choice.

"You won't speak to her that way," Angela said. "And that's an order from your Prince. Go back to your own nest, Lilith. My affairs are none of your concern tonight."

Lilith laughed, and shook her head as if savoring the moment. "Yes, but that's where you're wrong, my dear Angela. Let's face facts—if it weren't for me, you'd have been strung up in chains like Lucifel long ago. You're only speaking and conscious because I've decided to be kind. Do we really need the demons to know you're Prince in name only? Imagine what that would mean—imagine what they might do to you." Her voice became lower and more dangerous than ever. "We both know that when it comes down to it, you're just a human. You're just a mortal girl whose shell hides Raziel's soul along with yours, odd though it might be. Trust me, the best course of action is to let go of all this brave foolhardiness and see things sensibly." Lilith's features iced over with emphasis.

Sophia's trembling fingers locked tighter on Angela's waist.

Troy tensed, as if waiting for Angela's word to rip Lilith's throat open.

"Where's Python?" Angela muttered.

Lilith arched an eyebrow. "Oh . . . I didn't think you were so interested in him, Angela. But if you really must know, he's being punished. My son's deserved more than a slap on the wrist for a while, after all. This time I just can't overlook the trouble he's caused me."

"You're insane if you think I'm going to just climb onto the Throne and let you erase half of my brain again," Angela finally said.

Lilith sighed. She wiped a bead of sweat from her smooth forehead and waved her hand. A dull rumbling sound approached the Arena. It sounded like thousands of hands clapping, or the rhythmic stamp of thousands of feet. Angela knew that noise from her time watching the demons assemble on the plains of Babylon.

It was an army. Lilith had sent her entire personal retinue after Angela to drag her home. And once there, Sophia's certain doom would be finalized.

"Leave not a single one of this rabble that claims allegiance to my son alive," Lilith said, and Angela knew she was speaking somehow to her army's commander.

A tumult of ear-piercing screeches broke suddenly over the Arena.

Hellish birds with leathery wings spiraled up from the turrets surrounding Python's Arena, panicked at the approaching danger. Already, arrows streaked like red lightning and methodically shot them down.

Whump. One fell to a twitching lump near the winged Kirin's paws. The Kirin trotted to the side, whinnying fearfully.

Angela kept a tight grip on its mane.

There was no way she could make the beast fly without it being shot down.

The noise grew deafening, even worse than the cheers and shouts that had filled the Arena. Demons screamed. Others moaned in sheer terror as Lilith's army broke through a pair of iron gates and poured inside like a flood. Troy looked to Angela, motioning to follow her to one of the only exits from the Arena, another tunnel on the far side. Angela spurred the Kirin to turn from Lilith and follow. The beast jumped over the dead Hound's body and galloped after Troy. Troy was already a few paces ahead, sprinting on all fours with a feline grace.

Wrong way, Lilith whispered in Angela's mind, her voice working its way down to the soul.

The screams followed them, swelling until Angela's own ears rang with pain and threatened to bleed. Then they entered the tunnel and blackness descended on every side. The horror suddenly sounded and seemed far away, but Angela knew Lilith at least would be in hot pursuit.

All they had was the eerie light of Troy's eyes to guide them.

Show me what kind of a hunter you are, Troy. Find a way out of here.

Troy didn't bother answering and her blistering pace never slackened. She took them right, then left, rounding one sharp corner after the next, and then they weren't ascending but descending, farther and farther. Angela couldn't help fearing they'd be trapped again. Worse yet, what if other creatures more vicious than the three-headed Hound dwelled in this darkness? But there was no turning back now.

At last, Troy slowed a little, and it took all Angela's strength to tug on the Kirin's mane and make it obey, bringing them down to a trot.

Without any warning, Troy skidded to an abrupt halt.

The Kirin instinctively did the same.

An absolute silence crushed them all, as if everyone now stood in the middle of a great void. They'd run to a dead end and what could have been an enormous silver mirror lay on the ground, illuminated by pulsing hieroglyphs in the rock. One of the Kirin's paws brushed its edge and the mirror rippled slightly. It was a pool of some kind.

Troy stared at the water with an intense and horrified look.

"What . . . what is this?" Angela finally dared to say.

"It's a Mirror Pool," Sophia replied. Her voice sounded so far away, but it struck Angela like a slap. Sophia had been so quiet for so long, she could have disappeared. "Very few of them still exist. This might be one of the last."

"But what are they?" Angela whispered. A great reverence stilled her as she gazed at the water, if that's what it was. Angela couldn't say how she knew, but she was sure this mysterious pool was incredibly ancient.

Troy crept nearer to the water and sniffed. She looked up, flipping back her ears.

"There are many theories," Sophia said. Her words fell without echoes. The air weighed on them like a still, dead thing. "Those with the proper skills can use them as a way to see into the present. This was how Israfel probably found you. When he was imprisoned in Ialdaboth, he was certainly looking into one of these pools at some point and saw you, the Archon, alive. There was no other way he could have known you existed."

"But it's just water, right?" Angela whispered.

Sophia seemed about to speak again, but stopped. Her fingers still clenched Angela's waist tightly.

A soft whisper found them, as if sprung from dreams. Angela might not have even heard it if they all hadn't been so silent. It was coming from the pool, and it sounded like voices, calling her name.

Troy began to back away. Her eyes seemed wider than ever. The miniature bones and teeth tied into her hair rattled ominously.

Now Angela noticed she'd been prodding the Kirin into entering the water. Had she been in a trance? Why wasn't Sophia stopping her? Why wasn't Troy saying anything? Or maybe none of them could stop what was happening. Angela froze, battling with her fear. Perhaps this was a trap. But the Kirin had already allowed its paws to slip into the pool. It barely hesitated but walked in deeper, as if following the voices. Maybe it heard something just as enticing but entirely different.

Angela looked down at the water, shocked to see a reflection that wasn't her own. Instead they stood above lights and a city that could have been rocking on stilts above an eerily calm sea. Darkness cloaked its towers and buildings like a thick blanket, though on its horizon, something brilliant gleamed like an iridescent moon.

Then it struck her. This was Luz.

Now the voices escalated from whispers to roars. The water around the Kirin churned and frothed like a whirlpool. An incredible force grabbed Angela's soul and twisted, forcing her to descend.

A fiery pain cut through Angela's hands, and she cried out. It was Troy, reaching out a bony hand for Angela, but her nails had only succeeded in slicing Angela's palm, and the cuts hurt like living flames. Troy switched tactics and grabbed for the Kirin's mane.

Her efforts were useless.

Angela, and Sophia, and the Kirin were sinking into the Mirror Pool. It was acting as a portal, taking them away, and either the Kirin could no longer fly or it couldn't escape whatever enchantment it was under. Images flashed before Angela's eyes. She saw herself on the Throne of Hell. She saw the Father murdering the angel Raziel all over again. She saw Israfel's sea-blue eyes and heard Lucifel's laughter. Last of all, she saw Kim's face, and her stomach twisted into a painful knot as she realized she'd failed him. There was no rescuing him now. Angela heard herself scream Troy's name.

Then the water closed over Sophia's head, and over Angela's head, and took them to darkness.

Twelve

Kim worked at the lock that sealed his prison cell, using the metal crow's foot talisman to pick it as noiselessly as possible. He was getting nowhere, really. Python would certainly know the moment Kim broke free, and yet the demon hadn't bothered to put any kind of magical seal on the door. It was as if he wanted Kim to work desperately for his freedom.

Kim slumped back on the stone floor, wiping the perspiration from his forehead. His bangs hung heavily in his eyes, and he pushed them aside.

He took a deep breath, trying to ignore his overwhelming hunger and thirst.

Where were Angela and Sophia? That was what he wanted to know most of all. Perhaps it shouldn't have surprised him that Python had decided to toss Kim into a cell. This was only the beginning of Kim's slavery, after all.

He licked his dry lips and clutched the hourglass pendant at his chest. It was oddly warm.

He hated it already. It hung from his neck as if the chain were made of iron. Yet he'd wear it forever if that was what

Angela needed. Kim held the hourglass to the light of the embers set in the walls of his dank prison. The sand continued to drain slowly but surely. His heartbeat thundered in his ears as he worked quickly on the lock, jiggling it every now and then. Shadows filled the cavern and the acidic air tormented his lungs. Sometimes, Kim was certain he heard animal noises echoing down the pitch-black tunnels outside.

His finger slipped this time, and the metal crow's foot accidentally pierced his palm.

Kim cursed out loud, clutching at his hand. He sucked the blood away, rocking a little. He was working too fast, but damn it, it wasn't like he had a choice.

A hiss echoed back to him.

At least, that's what Kim thought he heard. He froze, barely able to breathe.

Water dripped slowly from small stalactites to the ground. Kim looked back at the glittering mosaic set in the wall behind him. It displayed an image of an angel being devoured by some hellish monster. Was it really so surprising Python found that a suitable image for a prison? A small cot took up the other side of the cell where the round bed hung from rusted chains. Even more chains had been set in the walls. Kim listened a little while longer and then turned from his gloomy surroundings back to the lock. He fumbled with the iron crow's foot again until it slipped from his bloody fingers to the ground.

Kim sighed, stooping down to find where it had fallen in the pebbles.

When he straightened again, Troy stood in front of him on the other side of the bars.

Kim stopped breathing.

Fear arrested his heartbeat, stole through every corner of

his brain. He heard a strange clicking sound and realized his teeth chattered.

Troy looked absolutely ravaged. Scars marbled her skin and she'd lost a wing. The one that remained had grown back its feathers but still appeared ragged and unkempt. Some of her long nails had snapped and her fingertips were bloody. Blood ringed her mouth and stained her lips. She must have either eaten or been fighting with another creature recently. But her great yellow eyes remained exactly as he'd always remembered them, and they sliced down to his soul, peeling back layers only she could see. Kim could only stare back at her, stunned like a mouse before a cat.

The why or the how of her presence wasn't important.

He was about to die.

Long ago, Kim had killed his Jinn father. The reason had been to protect himself and his mother from abuse and pain. But Troy didn't understand that. Even though Kim was only half-Jinn, he'd broken a sacred law of the Clans and murdered a relative. Troy's sister, the reigning Jinn Queen, had ordered his execution and had chosen Troy to carry out justice. The only thing that had saved Kim from her clutches was that he'd known Angela was most likely the Archon. And after the revelation was certain, he'd escaped into Hell before Troy could devour his soul.

"Do you feel like gloating?" Troy said to him now.

Kim's voice emerged from him as if out of a thick darkness, and it was rickety with fear. "No . . ."

"You might as well," Troy said with lethal softness. "As you can see, you've had your revenge to some degree. Even though it's *you* who deserves justice. It must please you so much to see me flightless. It must thrill you to the core to know that to our Clan, I may as well be dead."

Kim didn't say anything. He stared at her and felt like a man peering into the Abyss.

When he finally spoke again, his voice escaped as an even more cracked, weary thing. "Were those your hisses I heard in Python's great hall?" Kim said. "Do you know what happened to Angela?" He touched his hourglass pendant, suddenly feeling as if he were in some strange dream that might never end. "There's only one fate left for me, Troy, and it's worse than anything you can do. If you want to kill me, feel free. I won't stop you. Only, promise me this—get Angela and Sophia out of here. I know Python's hidden them in his mansion somewhere."

But Troy tipped back her head and laughed. "Oh yes," she scoffed. "As if you haven't already discovered a way to worm out of Hell again. As if you'd really put their well-being before your own."

Kim trembled like a leaf, unable to rip his eyes away from her awful gaze.

Troy flicked her ears. Perhaps she sensed his sincerity and it had made her pause.

Her bony hand reached through the bars like a blur, grabbed Kim by the collar, and smacked him against the metal.

He groaned as the pain ricocheted through his bones. Troy's breath blasted hot and evil on his face. Then she sniffed his pendant, and despite his best efforts Kim moaned in fear. He knew in Troy's eyes, he deserved to die. Yet would Python really allow her to kill him? That didn't make sense. But why else would she have been allowed to get this close?

Troy licked her teeth, examining him carefully. The moments passed with an eternal sluggishness until she sat back on her haunches.

With a nasty grunt, she let him go.

Kim flew back to the ground, all the wind knocked out of him. He leaned up on his elbows and gasped as Troy set her good nails to the padlock on the cell bars and twisted her wrist sharply.

The padlock snapped. Troy flung it aside and threw open the gate.

This was it. Kim squeezed his eyes shut, waiting for her teeth to sink into his neck. Instead, Troy grabbed him tightly by the wrist and dragged him out of the cell.

"You're—you're not going to kill me?" Kim muttered, in a daze.

"I *can't* kill you," Troy whispered. She looked around at the rock walls, appearing keenly suspicious.

"But why!"

"*Quiet,*" Troy snarled at him. She flung him aside by the hand, but not before seeing the crow's foot talisman he still clutched in his fingers. Troy's face blanched even whiter. She opened her mouth as if to speak again, but instead ripped the talisman from Kim and cradled it in the center of her palm. "Where did you get this?" she demanded, apparently forgetting that she'd wanted silence.

"I found it," Kim whispered.

"Liar! Someone gave it to you!"

"Perhaps they did, but I can't imagine who. I found it outside of my chamber in Lilith's mansion. It's the symbol of your—*our*—Clan, I know. But I'm sure it's just a coincidence. I know I'd never be pardoned for my offense. I do remember the old stories, though. Even for a Jinn, apparently forgiveness isn't unheard of."

Troy folded her hand over the talisman, hiding it from Kim's view. "I'm keeping this," she growled shortly. She appeared concerned about something—or maybe someone—but it would be foolish for Kim to press for more information. The most he could gather was that the iron crow's foot probably belonged to a Jinn Troy knew. If Kim was lucky, it would also be a Jinn Troy cared about. The fine workmanship of the talisman suggested someone with high rank and youth.

"Sariel," Troy said, turning to Kim. She was using his given Jinn name. Kim hadn't heard it in so long that a shiver ran through him at the sound. "Angela and Sophia are gone."

Kim didn't know what to say at first. They couldn't just be gone, yet his cousin had no reason to use tricks. "But how do you know—"

"Do I need to explain myself?" she snarled. "If I haven't torn your head off yet, isn't that enough reason to trust me?"

"Where did they go?" Kim whispered, seeing Troy's bloody nails and mouth in a whole new light now.

"Back to Luz," Troy said. Her lips quivered as she spoke. "Python has been keeping me as his pet in Babylon for months. I've been biding my time, of course. Much like I bided it with *you*. Day by day, hour by hour, I've watched him and studied all his habits and learned his routine. But even I was surprised when that snake told me you were here in this mansion, and I was free to make you suffer. He found the idea entertaining. Your agony was to be his delight."

Kim swallowed painfully. Of course he knew Python would be so cruel. Even so, he'd been hoping otherwise. That explained—at least in part—why Troy couldn't kill Kim. She wasn't allowed to overstep Python's bounds. For now.

"But he never knew," Troy continued, "that the Archon and I are Bound. I heard Her calling me from Python's Arena. And I helped Her escape. Then I returned for you."

"Why would you return?" Kim said heatedly. "Why not follow Her?"

Troy was instantly in his face again, seething like a rabid dog. "Because maybe I wanted to take that serpent up on his offer," she shouted at him. "Then I find that you have this"—she grabbed his hourglass pendant—"around your neck. And the very second we're safe again, you'll explain to me why it smells like Angela, you fool. What trouble have you gotten her into now? Because as it is she's far beyond your help. I would love to know what idiotic deal you made that left you in that demon's debt, forcing you to beg for death at my hands."

Kim lowered his head. He squeezed his eyes shut, reliving those terrible moments when he essentially traded his life for Angela's. "You wouldn't believe me if I told you," Kim said, and sighed. He was so tired of listening to how Troy had him all figured out. "So why bother? Besides, we have to be quiet, remember? You're right—Python must be watching us. He'll know if we leave. So why do you want to tempt fate by freeing me anyway?"

"Because I hate that snake and everything he stands for," Troy said. "So, yes, I'll go against my better instincts and set you free. Because in exchange you're going to help me destroy this regime, for my late sister's sake."

Kim laughed softly. "Of course. Yet there's nothing stopping you from killing me the moment we're out of Python's reach, right?"

Troy paused and examined him. An unreadable look crossed her face. "You really are an idiot," she finally said.

Turning, Troy began to melt into the shadows she'd emerged from, certain that Kim would follow. He wasn't stupid. His odds of survival beneath Python's mansion were much better with Troy by his side. And besides, perhaps it wasn't actually a good idea to ask Troy to kill him, after all. He was connected to Angela, and there was a chance that Kim's death could hurt her somehow.

A bitter taste filled his mouth. How stupid he'd been not to consider that earlier.

The darkness outside his cell pressed on him like a vise. Kim listened for Troy's familiar sounds as she scuffled ahead of him in the dark. A powerful sense of urgency pressed on him and he knew Troy could feel it too. Python would be after them soon, especially now that Angela was gone.

Kim's mind turned and worked on those awful moments with Python yet again. Then it hit him. He stopped abruptly. "Troy—wait."

Troy's yellow eyes flashed in his direction. "What?" she hissed with palpable annoyance.

"You must not have heard, but Python spoke to Sophia and I about something called the Angelus. Sophia explained that it's a song of great power, but its last two stanzas are missing. Apparently, the Angelus's notes and words constitute the power in the Book of Raziel that Lucifel seeks. Do you know anything about this song? Did Raziel say anything to the Jinn about such a thing before he died?"

The silence between them tightened.

"Well?" Kim asked.

"I'm trying to think," Troy snapped. "Be patient."

More silence passed, and he heard her sigh heavily.

"No . . . he didn't," Troy whispered. "At least as far as I've been told." He heard a noise suggesting she paced in the darkness of the tunnel. Her nails slid against the rock, and Kim shivered thinking of how they'd feel piercing his skin. "Is that really all you know?" she said.

Kim thought hard. "Sophia said the Angelus is the song of creation. A song of Binding, its notes hold the universe together. Python then mentioned that the song has faltered, and that's why the dimensions are crumbling. He went so far as to say God himself is now absent or dead, absurd as it sounds. Sophia said Raziel sealed the last stanzas away so that only the Archon can discover and wield them. I find it astonishing Lucifel doesn't remember the final stanzas herself. This all has to do with Angela . . . I can't understand her sometimes. I don't know who she really is, Troy, even after all this time and how close we are. She isn't Raziel, but her soul is special enough to have been chosen and protected by him. Clearly, she needs to open the Book—only she can do it. But . . ."

"But?" Troy said quietly.

"The Lock is Sophia's body. The Key that opens her is the Glaive. Angela refuses to kill her friend. We're at an impasse now. And with Angela out of our reach . . ."

Kim gasped. Troy's great eyes shone right next to him now. He could faintly see her sharp little teeth. Her face was tight with anger. "And that's why I always hated human sentimentality," she said. "I knew Angela would grow too attached to the Book."

"Sophia's a person, Troy, not a thing. Angela's feelings are natural."

"Sophia is our last chance to survive," Troy spat at him. "And now we have to die because Angela feels guilty? What kind of weakness is that? And here I'd grown to respect her."

"Exactly," Kim shot back. "Because you've grown attached to Angela, even though you don't want to admit it. You're friends, whether you realize it or not. She's a person to you now, she's not just the Archon. Have you even realized how you call her by her name now?"

Troy's eyes went wide. With a snarl she shoved Kim aside and started stalking down the ice-cold tunnel again.

"Running away won't change how you feel, Troy," Kim said after her.

"But it will keep me alive," she snapped back. "Now you'd better follow me in silence. I'm not averse to sewing your mouth shut if I have to. We've talked enough already."

"There's one way to help Angela," he whispered. Troy was right; it might be foolish to continue talking, but if Kim didn't speak now he knew it would be too late.

"I'm listening, then," Troy said, though her tone now said she wouldn't be for long.

"We need to talk to Raziel ourselves."

Another pressing silence. "Impossible," Troy said at last. Yet once again her breath stirred unsettlingly close to Kim's neck. "You would at least need to scry a Mirror Pool for that. You don't have the skill. You'd go insane just peering into the water."

"You're forgetting," Kim said. "I have this." He jangled the chain of his hourglass pendant. It still felt oddly warm. He wondered how much sand had drained away by now. Kim had been too afraid to look. "It connects me to Angela. It's a part of both of us now. I'm certain we could contact Raziel's spirit that way, though we can't do it alone. We need someone skilled in scrying like you said."

"There *is* someone . . ." Troy said. Did Kim hear fear in her voice? "But if I take you to her, here's the deal: in exchange for my help, you will help *me*."

"How?"

"I already told you," Troy said. Her voice boiled with revenge. "The demon and his mother will suffer for what they've put us through. My people haven't forgotten how my namesake city was destroyed thanks to Python. I wonder how he would feel if the same happened to his little nest? You're going to help me topple him and his mother from their already decaying pedestals."

"Python will find us eventually, Troy," Kim whispered. "No matter where we go. Even Luz will be connected to Hell again soon enough, before both Realms are destroyed."

"Good," Troy said. "I'd love to see him face-to-face again." There was the crack of her nails splitting a stone. Then her wing brushed past him, and Kim sensed she traveled in the opposite direction now.

"Where are we going?" he dared to ask one last time, spinning to follow her.

Troy's voice sounded reluctant, but Kim could imagine the determined look on her face. Even Troy's need for revenge would have to take a backseat to opening the Book of Raziel, or at least speaking to Raziel himself. "We're returning to Luz," Troy said, and her words fell heavily enough to suggest their frightening fate—whatever it might be—was sealed. "And for everyone's sake, its angel had better talk."

Thirteen

Though he was a great angel, Israfel knew what it was to be outmatched and overpowered.

Adamant cuffs, impervious to energy of any kind, connected his wrists and bit into his skin like fangs. His chains dragged behind him, clanking musically. Step by painful step, he slid his bare feet across the cold glass floor of his old throne room in Heaven, listening to the murmurs of an invisible crowd.

An excruciating headache throbbed in his temples, and even with the blindfold over his eyes he saw red.

"Force the prisoner to halt," a voice finally said. Its soft, familiar tone cut into him even more painfully than the manacles.

Firm hands grabbed Israfel and stopped him from moving forward. A tense silence swelled throughout the chamber. Perhaps the other angels could now hear Israfel's heartbeat, roaring in his own ears.

He could only imagine what they thought of his apparent ruin. In the jails, everywhere he'd turned, the smooth glass had reflected back his image in a tousled mirage of silvery hair and large but tired blue eyes. The adamant cuffs and chains kept him from unfurling his six wings, imposing even more of his natural majesty on his sister and her worshippers. But Israfel always made certain to never lose his dignified poise. Only the slight twist to his lips could possibly betray his feelings.

"Take off the blindfold," the voice continued. "He *will* speak."

Hands worked on the fabric tied behind Israfel's head. Then the sash slipped to the floor. Israfel blinked, his eyes watering. A red haze still tinted the world.

He searched the shadowy mirage that was his old throne room. Now that Lucifel had taken over, she'd dimmed the light of the glass and crystal walls to nearly nothing. But Israfel needed little more than blurs to recognize familiar fixtures. The chamber was gloriously large and composed almost entirely of crystal and glass that usually shimmered and shone. Pillars held up a high domed-glass ceiling and gave the illusion of supporting the galaxies pinwheeling in the ether far beyond them. Two more intricate pillars flanked the throne, and feathered serpents carved into the crystal coiled toward arches etched with hieroglyphs in the shapes of constellations. Stretching from either side of the throne, long benches and chairs holding hundreds of angels dipped into the shadows. Row upon row of seats surrounded Israfel, and the angels upon them stared down at him, blanched with anxiety at the sight of the Creator Supernal at his sister's mercy.

These were Lucifel's most devoted followers and supporters, but even they knew the power Israfel's cuffs barely restrained.

Their black coats rustled as they shifted back and forth, conversing with one another again. But Lucifel, the Devil herself, slouched not in the embrace of Israfel's old glass throne, but at its base on the floor, her arms hugging her tucked knees. She looked pensive, or perhaps asleep. She wore a form-fitting black suit and a fitted coat without any other adornment whatsoever and at first seemed little more than a shadow cast on the ground. Then she lifted her head and regarded Israfel. The gray storm of Lucifel's hair blended with the ashen shadows, yet her skin still gleamed. Her red eyes glittered like rubies set in the statuesque perfection of her face.

Lucifel regarded Israfel, and the tension in the room grew unbearable. At last, she spoke. "Do you have any idea why you aren't dead yet?" she whispered.

Israfel refused to give her the satisfaction of a reply just yet.

"Answer me," Lucifel said after a while.

"You're right, I have no idea why you're keeping me alive," he said softly.

His musical voice carried effortlessly throughout the room. Despite all Lucifel's attempts to subdue his power, energy thrummed around them. The other angels stirred anxiously. Some shouted in fear. Murmurs broke out. Whispers erupted everywhere. Israfel refused to leave his sister's gaze now. Their spirits burned into each other.

"Enough," Lucifel said, straightening.

All noise died instantly. The angels on the benches froze.

Lucifel strode toward Israfel until they would have stood face-to-face if he hadn't been forced to kneel. She loomed over him, her mouth set into a tight line. Then, with lightning speed, she slapped him hard across the face.

Israfel pitched to the side but caught his fall.

He looked at her again, licking slightly at the salty blood trickling from his lip. Gasps of barely stifled terror rippled through the room. A few angels stood, as if ready to run away.

"Your former subjects might fear you still," Lucifel said, bending down to whisper in his ear, "but we both know the chance you had to play Archangel has been over for quite a while. Perhaps all that time in the jails didn't get the message across to you well enough."

"You know suffering of that kind means nothing to me by now," Israfel muttered.

Lucifel pulled away and stared him down again. Her red eyes narrowed.

"So," Israfel continued, "go on, then. Why haven't you killed me by now, sister?"

A slow smile touched Lucifel's lips. Gently, she touched Israfel's stomach with her finger.

Israfel breathed hard. His pulse quickened.

"I know what's inside of you, Israfel," Lucifel continued. "I know what you are. I also know what you fear the most. I'm sure in your pride you never stopped to consider that even though you killed the Father, that doesn't mean I can't send you back to him. Just imagine—an eternity with his corpse by your side. Though I assume you'll eventually starve. The Father has only so much blood to give, and you've stolen quite enough of it already. Don't you agree?"

Israfel clenched his fingers.

"Isn't it depressing to know," she continued casually, "that you followed me back home for no good reason? Your history is such a mess, Israfel. You murdered your own Creator to escape your Heavenly cage. Perhaps you thought you were doing the universe a favor by finding the Archon, atoning for your sin in some backward way by joining with Her to rule over a re-created world—using the body of the abominable child inside you to do it. But look, you couldn't protect Angela Mathers from sitting on Hell's Throne in my place. Was following me back to Heaven meant to serve as another penance? How ironic, considering in the end it's you who'll be sent back to decay with the Creator who caused all your misery."

"You mean the Creator you loved?" Israfel whispered icily. "And still love—"

Lucifel grabbed Israfel's chin, forcing him to go almost nose to nose with her. Her fingers couldn't hurt him no matter how hard she pinched, but her words cut like daggers. "What I would love is to know what it's like to be you," she said. "You—both male and female. What is it to be the only creature like yourself in this universe, Israfel? What was it like to have the Father's heart like no other angel?"

Was she saying that just to hurt him, or was she genuinely curious? Her envy had always been an unfathomable thing.

Israfel gazed unflinchingly into his sister's eyes. "It's better than being a fraud of a ruler like yourself."

Lucifel thrust him away from her. She laughed, but the sound had no humor in it. "It's too bad the Father isn't alive to know that of all creatures in this universe, *I'll* have the honor of reuniting you with him once more. I wonder how he would have reacted knowing I'm about to open the Book of Raziel and silence this awful mess of a world?"

Israfel knew she wasn't looking for any real answer this time.

Her eyes still burning, Lucifel straightened away from him. The mad light that had brightened her face while speaking of the Father faded as she scanned the angelic faces surrounding and observing them. "You see," she said, "this is the end result of your misguided hopes, Israfel. Look at how many of your former subjects had grown disheartened waiting for your return. By the time I arrived, they knew whose side to join."

Israfel dared to get back on his feet. No one stopped him as he stood up and glared regally at the black-robed angels thronging around them. Lucifel wasn't speaking all of the truth, but it wouldn't surprise him that some of her worshippers had remained like woodworms in Heaven even after her Rebellion, thriving on secret darkness. Even so, how had she managed to rise to the pinnacle of power so quickly after returning to Heaven?

"Israfel," a whispery voice said.

He looked up sharply, and a male angel stepped down from the strange shadows behind Israfel's old throne. The angel's hair was silvery like Lucifel's, and one of his red eyes glowed brightly. His four gray wings fanned behind him, blending into the darkness. It was Zion—one of Lucifel's forbidden children, long thought to be dead, and the current ruling Archangel. But his eye . . . something was wrong.

Lucifel gestured for Zion to join her side.

Zion stepped toward his mother reluctantly, never taking his eyes off Israfel.

It hit Israfel all at once. "Mikel," he said icily. "What have you done to your brother?"

But Israfel already knew. Mikel's brother, Zion, was dead. Mikel—a spirit—was possessing his body. Or at least possessing it by halves. Only one of his eyes glowed, after all. As Israfel had long suspected, Mikel had the ability to possess two bodies with her spirit at the same time, though it certainly weakened her to divide her essence.

"You wouldn't understand my actions," Mikel said through her dead brother's voice and lips. "I couldn't forgive Zion for the suffering he caused me. From the start, he schemed with you to seal me away and laughed at my pain from this crystal throne. While the stars gleamed like jewels at his feet, I cried in my loneliness, and he was happy to keep me locked away in the shadows. Mother is the only creature who can free me from those shadows, and I won't let anyone stop her. It's over, Israfel. Angela Mathers can't win this battle. The Archon is trapped in Hell, and even if She leaves, I'll make sure She doesn't get far."

Israfel regarded Mikel sadly. Unlike her mother, Lucifel, Mikel was having difficulty staring him down. Like the other angels she cowered under Israfel's regal bearing.

"That's your fatal flaw, Mikel," Israfel said. "You'll never escape the shadows if you continue hiding in them. In your irrational pride, you've forgotten there's always a way. Besides, I know without a doubt that Angela Mathers *will* win this battle for life and souls. And when she does, you'll regret siding with your poisonous mother and justifying all my fears about you. Remember, Angela's soul is different from all others. Even my sister fears it. And if the Devil isn't certain of her victory, why are you?"

He glanced one last time at Lucifel.

Lucifel made a sweeping gesture at him, icy indifference all over her face. "Take him away," she spat. "And make sure you gag him this time."

Israfel examined the stars through the glass ceiling, barely struggling as rough hands cinched the blindfold around his eyes and thrust him into darkness again. More fabric pushed between his lips.

He could sense Mikel's guilt like a fire spreading through the chamber.

"Enjoy your last night in the prisons, Israfel," his sister murmured. "And when you see the Father again, tell him how much I miss him. Your death will be that much more meaningful for me."

Her words followed him like a curse.

Israfel's darkness continued for countless hours, not ceasing until he was forced out of his jail by his guards for the final time to march up the spiraling stairway to Ialdaboth—the same place where their brother, Raziel, had plummeted to his death. With every extra step, Israfel's heart threatened to stop beating. Then, he was finally on the threshold of the vortex whirling above him, abandoned to his fate. As it began to swallow him, and he took that first step into the Father's nest, the blindfold slipped from his eyes.

Israfel turned and looked down upon the angelic city of Malakhim.

It spun like a gigantic disc of iridescent fire, glittering with thousands of turrets and bridges. The dull screech of a feathered serpent shivered through the stairway he stood upon. On the horizon, the human city of Luz glistened like a mirage the size of a moon. The air rippled slightly, as if reality were bending. The Realms were about to merge.

Surely, Lucifel knew this.

Mikel knew it.

Now Israfel knew it, and he could no longer help. Only the Archon could save everyone now. Yet despite his ultimate faith in Her, something crucial indeed nagged at Israfel. Who was She really? The thought had bothered him for so long. From the start, Angela had seemed so familiar, but not just because her soul was protected by Raziel's spirit and resembled the dead angel superficially. There had always been something else.

Israfel thought of the Father, and his great green eyes, so much like the Eye known as the Grail. The Grail that only Angela could wield properly, as if it belonged solely to her. He thought of Angela's resemblance to the Father in the shape of her face and her long hair, and he thought most of all about her indefinable soul. Last, he pondered Raziel's strange death and the forbidden knowledge he'd obtained.

You and me and Lucifel are siblings, Raziel had said to him one day.

Later, Lucifel had spoken of the Father's lack of answers concerning their origins. *He says he created us, and we ask for no proof, Israfel. Can't you see how we've blindly accepted everything until now?*

Israfel could still picture the haunting coldness behind her eyes as she spoke.

Why, Lucifel had said, *are we so different from all the other angels?*

Then, Raziel had created Sophia, who always unnerved Israfel with her terrible all-knowing expressions. Since the day she'd first arrived in Heaven, Sophia hovered near Raziel, doting over him like a mother. She'd often said the Supernals were one, and soon afterward Lucifel chained herself to the idea in the most rebellious way. Once again, Israfel seemed to look into the past, seeing the proud anger all over Lucifel's face as she prepared to murder him. *We're equals to God,* she'd said to him. *And I deserve the crown of Heaven as much as you ever did. What right did the Father have to give it to you alone?*

In a moment of pure spite, Lucifel had stolen the Eye—Lucifel's Grail—from the Father himself.

Yet the Father's eyes were whole and untouched.

So whose Eye was it? Why could only the Archon's soul wield and manipulate it properly?

At last, an answer struck Israfel. For a moment, pieces of a strange and tragic puzzle fell into place.

Israfel froze as if a thunderbolt had thrust him into eternity.

He knew who Angela really was. He knew why Raziel had chosen her soul and not another's to be the Archon. Worst of all, Israfel knew better than ever who he was as well. He looked down at his hands as if seeing them for the first time. The guards below him on the stairway said nothing, but they looked puzzled by the mask of shock on his face.

This time, Israfel couldn't remember to hide his feelings behind a regal screen. He opened his mouth to shout. He tried to send his words to Angela, because time and distance meant nothing to an angel like himself.

It was too late.

The portal closed on Israfel, trapping him once more in the Realm of Ialdaboth, where only the past flourished and nearly every last light had died.

PART TWO

Reunited

Thirty-Two Days until the Great Silence

*Faced with the choice to hope or despair, the soul
finds its answer in friends.*

Fourteen

◇ LUZ ◇

Angela felt like her entire body had been crushed and stretched and then crushed again. Her brain throbbed and her skull threatened to split. She was still aware of her fingers clenched tightly in the winged Kirin's mane, and of Sophia's fingers digging like claws into her waist. Pain drummed at her senses, drowning out thought.

She couldn't see a thing, and the darkness coiled tightly around her spirit, stopping her breath.

A brilliant light flashed in front of her eyes. Angela screamed.

The sound of something brittle smashing to pieces ricocheted through her. Pain blew back against her and sparkled in the light like crystals beneath the sun. Shards like glass seemed to dangle in the air beside her, frozen in time. Without warning, the Kirin broke out of the darkness and into a naked forest layered heavily in snow. It was night, but the stars shining in the clear sky tormented Angela's eyes. She wasn't used to brilliance like this anymore.

What was going on? Were they actually in Luz?

The winged Kirin shrieked in alarm, its great paws pounding the snow as it reared and fell to the earth to rear again. It kicked its legs wildly, nearly bucking Angela and Sophia to the ground.

Pieces of glass thumped to the snow around them. They were mirror shards, but their reflective surfaces rippled like water. Angela stared at them, thinking of the Mirror Pool beneath Python's mansion. They were in Luz, after all! But who could have helped bring them here? As the Kirin turned, its great paws crunched against the gilded frame of the mirror that had helped transport them to Luz.

Fear twisted Angela's insides in a knot.

Voices erupted from the trees. Priests and novices in black robes dashed from the dark undergrowth while others knelt and cocked crossbows at Angela and Sophia.

"Angela—" Sophia shouted.

The crossbows engaged. Arrows trailing nets assaulted them from either side.

The Kirin's wings flapped powerfully. The nets fell, and then threatened to cinch as the beast tore at them maniacally with its horn. Angela hunched against the Kirin's neck and peered through the nets, searching their attackers. Maybe there would be a friendly face who could help. She breathed hard, and every lungful of air froze her heart all over again. Sophia's breaths felt searingly hot against Angela's back as they clung to the Kirin while it kicked and brayed.

Screams broke over the shouting and noise. "*Stop it! Let them go! Angela, you have to run away—*"

That voice—it was so familiar. Angela turned to see a young woman with a brown ponytail, dressed in Westwood Academy's uniform, being forcibly restrained. Another novice pushed her down to her knees as hands clamped over her mouth. Another woman was being restrained beside her, but she looked much older and her thick hair was a deep red. A heavy shawl had been draped around her shoulders.

Another male voice erupted over the echoing shouts of the novices. "I told you to kill her! Who decided to let these damned crows stay alive? We need to complete this before that Jinn returns!"

Jinn! But he couldn't be talking about Troy. She was still in Hell, wasn't she?

A flash of red light blinded everyone for a moment. Angela regained her vision in time to see the young woman who'd shouted to Angela vanish within the mist it left behind and reshape herself. She was now a crow. She broke from her captor's grip and soared for the trees.

"*Shoot her down!*" the male voice shouted.

Gunshots broke through the noise. More arrows whistled. "*Shoot her down, damn it!*"

The crow was gone.

The Kirin's horn had broken a gigantic hole through the netting, and it brayed threateningly. Now the priests and novices turned and regarded Angela with horrified faces. They surely hadn't been counting on this. They'd expected a young woman, not a fearsome rider astride an even more fearsome beast. She and Sophia would have to take their chances and make for the trees. If they tried to fly, they would run the risk of being shot down.

Angela didn't even warn Sophia this time. She kicked the Kirin's flanks hard and it exploded through the last of the netting, heading for the thick darkness in a copse of broken oaks. This was Memorial Cemetery—it had to be. The oak Fae named Tileaf had lived and died here in Luz's last spot of life and greenery, and the winged Kirin jumped over the remnants of her broken oak tree as they neared the under-growth.

Soon they moved so fast, the branches melted into a blur as she and Sophia entered the thicket. Bullets screamed past them and lodged into tree trunks. Another grazed Angela's ankle before vanishing in the darkness. She bit her lip, trying to stifle a scream of pain.

They headed in the direction the crow had flown.

The priests will follow us. Memorial Cemetery is only so big, after all. They'll find us eventually, and then, and then . . .

Shouts suddenly echoed back to her. The same voice that shouted for the crow's death began to order retreat.

Angela thought of the Jinn that had been mentioned and gritted her teeth, praying for the best. They needed more than one person on their side right now.

An hour must have passed, and now Angela's adrenaline rush began to subside into waves of utter exhaustion. At last, even the winged Kirin slowed to a trot. It folded its great wings and began to slip silently between the trees like a shadow. Then it stilled and lowered to the moldy earth in a small clearing, giving Angela and Sophia the opportunity to dismount.

Angela winced as she gingerly slid off the beast's back. Her muscles screamed, and she couldn't help flinching as her bare feet brushed the rocks and frozen soil. Her bloody ankle throbbed, and blue blood stained the snow and dirt like ink. She was deathly cold already. The air was too pure and icy, and she still wore little more than a nightgown.

"You look absolutely frozen," Sophia whispered with concern. She took Angela's hand and carefully slid from the Kirin's back. "Your fingers feel like icicles already!"

"I'll be all right," Angela whispered. "Frozen is better than dead any time."

"Freeze for long enough, and you will be dead. What just happened, though?" Sophia said. Her gray eyes narrowed with suspicion. She quickly knelt down and examined Angela's injured ankle. "It's clear that you were summoned through a mirror. I never thought any mirrors connected to the portals still existed on Earth. Most were destroyed."

Angela tried to think. "I'm sure that if the Vatican knew the mirror existed they *would* have destroyed it. But—"

"What now?" Sophia said for her. She closed her eyes. "I'm sure we're safe for a little while. But they'll return to find you."

For the first time, Angela noticed the bruise on Sophia's body and the cuts from the mirror shards. She grabbed Sophia by the hands and forced her to stand still as Angela looked for anything worse.

"I don't know what to do," Angela said. She broke away from Sophia and clenched her fists. God, she just wanted to scream for hours. "I don't know. You're right, we'll have to keep moving no matter what."

"Not just yet. You need rest. You're staying right here while I find you some warmer clothes. Besides, you shouldn't walk on that ankle right away, even if the bullet only grazed you."

"You can't go into Luz, Sophia, they'll capture you!"

"Do you think I can't disguise myself? I can pass for a child easily enough. Just stay here. I lived by Lucifel's side for centuries, Angela. If I've told you once, I've told you a thousand times, I can take care of myself."

Sophia turned to leave. Angela grasped her by the wrist, tugging her back.

"No, please understand. Sophia, I can't keep losing you."

Sophia played with the lifeless stone on her necklace. She sighed and then sat by Angela's side next to the Kirin. Its leathery wings had almost disappeared against the darkness of its body. The beast had dimmed the bioluminescent lights usually rippling on its fur, but its great eyes still glowed. It regarded Angela and Sophia in turn, and then opened its wings like a canopy. Angela and Sophia looked at the wings, and then at each other.

Angela was the first to scoot closer to the Kirin's body, feeding off its warmth. Sophia did the same. Soon Angela was so comfortable, she could have had her back to a bonfire.

There was silence for a long while.

Until a twig snapped. The tree branches scraped one another overhead.

Angela gripped Sophia's arm, motioning with her other hand for silence. She rose slowly to her feet and searched the leafless canopy.

A giant crow with shining golden eyes hopped from branch to branch. At last it sat directly above and then glided to Angela's feet. Another crow followed it moments later. Both birds stepped back for a moment, seemingly unnerved by the sight of Angela and the intimidating Kirin. Then one of the crows took a cautious step forward, its attention focused on Angela's face.

Angela. Its words echoed through Angela's mind like memories. *You . . . look different.*

Angela thought of Troy's crow familiar, Fury. The larger of the two crows certainly looked just like her. But who was the other one speaking to Angela? That familiar voice—it couldn't be!

"Nina?" Angela said softly.

The crow's head bobbed up and down excitedly.

"Nina," Angela gasped. She flung herself on her knees in front of both birds, insensible now to the freezing hard ground against her knees. "What happened back there? How are you a Vapor now? The last time I saw you—" Angela's voice choked away. The last time she'd seen Nina, they'd been separated in Python's hellish maze, and Nina's leg had been badly burned by acidic water. Thank God she'd survived! But how had she become like Fury? Too many questions entered Angela's mind, and she wasn't sure how many answers she wanted. "This is Fury, right?" Angela said, and gestured to the other crow.

Yes. Angela, it's a long story. But I can't lie. I never thought I'd see you again. Ever since we were separated in Hell, I wondered what had happened to you. Did you find out how to open the Book of Raziel? Do you know Lucifel escaped Hell?

Angela stilled. Something within her felt wild and anguished. This was too much too soon. Since she'd awakened in Python's mansion, everything had been a whirlwind of terror and now she felt dizzy from it all. She just needed a minute to get her bearings, to think. "Yes . . . I know about Lucifel."

She couldn't look at Sophia right now.

What about Sophia? Thank God you found her again! But why haven't you opened her—

"You wouldn't understand," Angela snapped.

Nina flinched. Fury cocked her head curiously and then started preening her feathers.

Angela dug her fingers against the soil. "I'm sorry. Like you said, it's a long story."

I see . . .

Angela squeezed her eyes shut. *No,* she thought, *this isn't right. I have to tell her what's going on. We owe each other so very much.* "Nina, would you mind changing back to a human again? I—I don't feel right talking to you as a bird. It's just strange."

Fury stopped her preening and stared at Angela with a wounded expression.

"No offense," Angela said to her.

But there must have been some, because Fury glided over to Sophia and began tugging playfully at Sophia's curls, refusing to look at Angela again.

"I don't get it," Angela whispered to Nina. "Fury was human once too. What did I say that was so bad?"

There was a flash of red light and a mist and then Nina's human form coalesced. She stood beside Angela and shrugged. "Fury's been a crow for so long, she doesn't really think of herself as human anymore, Angela."

That's exactly how I feel, Angela thought. *I've been the Archon now long enough to feel like someone else entirely.*

But was that the truth? Angela had lost her memories and that wasn't entirely her fault. But she also hadn't thought about Luz, or worried about the burn scars on her arms and legs, or painted a single picture while in Hell. She openly talked to people now. She trusted people when she felt they deserved it. She had hope for once and clung to it.

"I'm different, as you can see," Nina continued. "I'm the only Vapor who can shape-shift. At least that's what Juno told me."

"Juno's alive!" Angela said excitedly.

"Yes, she and Troy risked their lives to save me while in Hell. That was how I died again and became a Vapor. Python tricked Stephanie into entering Hell, he possessed her, and she attacked me as he tempted me to become his slave. To save Troy and Juno from being killed by him, I attacked Stephanie to stop her . . . but I didn't survive."

Angela grabbed Nina in a swift hug. She held her tightly, trying not to cry. "Nina, I'm so sorry. You've gone through too much suffering. Because of me! Oh, God . . ."

And then it all spilled out of her at once in a torrent. Angela started from the moment Lucifel escaped Hell and continued from there, explaining how Lilith had erased her memories and that she was now the ruler of Hell in Lucifel's place. She didn't leave out anything, not even what it really meant to open the Book of Raziel. When she explained that Sophia needed to die for that to happen, Nina's eyes widened and she looked curiously at Sophia, who sat by the Kirin's side, staring into the trees in utter silence. Angela ended with their recent escape from Lilith and Python's control, and the winged Kirin breaking through the mirror as she and Sophia returned to Luz. Nina's face became grave.

"What about this?" Nina said, pointing at Angela's green left eye.

Angela looked at the ground for a moment. She thought of her visions of being torn apart. "Lucifel wounded my eye badly before she left Hell. The Grail moved there to take its place."

"So that gem *is* an eye, after all," Nina said, her words saturated with suspicion. "Whose?"

Sophia turned and looked back at them now. She seemed about to say something but must have thought better of it. Instead she sighed and patted the Kirin's muzzle.

"I don't know," Angela said. And it was the truth, though for some reason the answer still sat uncomfortably with her. It still felt too much like a lie.

"Things haven't been much better back here in Luz," Nina continued in a quiet voice. "As you can see, there's an eerie stillness to the air. It's too cold, but there's no more snow, and we never see the sun despite the hours passing every day. And now there's a city in the sky among the stars. Angels arrive here after traveling from their city to ours. They've killed most of the crows and birds in Luz for sport, Angela. Fury and I can't travel openly anymore. Worse, they took all the human souls still in Luz with them back to Heaven. No one knows why, but Fury and Juno and I think the Vermilion Order are responsible, and that a few officials in Luz made some kind of black deal with the angels—or perhaps with Lucifel—in order to survive whatever comes next. I don't really want to know what the Devil plans to do with all those human souls, but our focus has been returning them somehow. Father Schrader was being very helpful for a while, but that's changed. He doesn't say much anymore. I wonder sometimes if he's been bribed into lying low. Or worse . . ."

Angela swallowed, trying to digest all the awful information. "So we don't have many friends on our side?"

Nina sighed heavily. "There's Juno—and according to Juno, there are also the Jinn who recognize her as Queen of the Underworld, as few as those Jinn might be. Other than that . . ."

"What about Israfel? Has anyone seen him at all? He went to Heaven too, and I was told he was possibly imprisoned."

Nina shook her head grimly.

Angela slumped back to the frozen ground. She needed to think, but her mind had blanked over. Faced with a situation like this in the past, Angela would have turned to ice much like the soil. She would have said that this was a problem too great to involve her. Luckily, the wiser Angela was in charge forever now.

This has to end. Maybe if we find where all those poor human souls have been taken, we'll also find a way to reach Lucifel.

And then what would Angela do?

I want and need to change everything. But until Sophia is opened . . .

"I understand," Nina said softly. Tears glistened at the corners of her eyes.

"What?" Angela said.

Nina sat down beside her. "I understand why you're hesitating, Angela. If what you told me about opening Sophia—I mean, the Book of Raziel—is true, then I know how you feel. It's not fair. I get it. And I'm sorry for you. But there must be a way out of all of this."

"The only way is by entering Luz," Angela said, shaking her head in frustration. "We can't hide in this cemetery forever. I'm sure in a day or two at the most, we'll be found. But at least in the heart of the city, we can hide and lay low as long as necessary while we figure things out. Or until we're caught. The hardest part will be figuring out a way to travel without being seen."

Nina seemed to think this over. "So . . . what you're saying is that we need to enter the city through a passage no one else uses or hopefully knows about?"

Angela looked at her keenly. "Nina, the priests and novices know this city inside and out. There can't be a path they haven't discovered by now."

"But there are areas of Luz they avoid or don't dare to use for everyday travel. The canals beneath the city, for instance."

Angela gave Nina a long questioning look. A strange shiver ran through her.

"There is someone who can help us. She'll know where to go next," Nina whispered.

And though Angela wanted to stay optimistic, perhaps the cold had reached too far within her for Nina's words to do anything but chill.

Fifteen

Angela hadn't enjoyed the idea of leaving Sophia and the winged Kirin alone, no matter how briefly she and Nina would be gone. The darkness of the trees was different from the darkness of Hell. There was more life in it, and Angela didn't trust a gloom that grew anymore.

She crept through the naked trunks, following Nina's lead and slapping aside branches and twigs as they traveled. Away from the protection of the Kirin's blazing-warm body, Angela now felt the cold like a knife piercing through every pore of her skin.

Sophia was right. It was madness for Angela to walk around slowly freezing to death. But there was no time to take dangerous detours for clothing, so Angela forced her numb feet forward, step by step until she was sure they were turning purple.

It was a relief to approach the light of a bonfire blazing in the middle of Memorial Cemetery.

The priests and novices who'd chased Angela had returned to burn branches and logs and keep vigil until morning, perhaps in the hope that she'd return. Even Angela knew no one would risk entering the trees while they feared a Jinn hunted outside the ring of the bonfire's protective light.

Angela crouched onto the soil, resting her hand on an icy rock.

Nina had taken the shape of a crow again and glided down from the branches to settle on her shoulder. *Wait here,* Nina's voice echoed in Angela's mind.

Feathers fluttered as she lifted from Angela and vanished into the darkness of the woods.

A few minutes later, she returned with a long scarf and a pair of shoes hanging by their laces from her beak. Angela whispered her thanks and took both, smothering her neck and mouth behind the scarf and quickly slipping on the shoes. She was only slightly warmer, but even that made a great difference. At least now she could walk without hurting her feet so badly. She searched the small camp again, trying to understand why Nina had brought her back here.

This way, Nina said to her, and she strutted into the trees.

Angela silently followed. They both paused before a clearing where a woman with thick red hair and heavy shawls sat on the frozen ground. She stared up at the stars, her arm wrapped around a little girl gathered to her chest. Nina flapped her wings, settling on the ground behind them. The little girl turned, saw Nina, and turned around again to tug on her mother's sleeve.

The woman stood, calling to a tall novice sitting close by. Their conversation was muffled, but the woman continued pointing at her daughter, making frustrated gestures with her arms. The little girl looked at the novice with a pitiful, tearstained face.

Finally, he nodded and pointed at the trees.

As the woman brought her daughter into the undergrowth, Angela recognized her. She'd been present when Angela, Sophia, and the Kirin had burst through the mirror. Except then she'd been on her knees, trying to scream as hands clapped over her mouth. She was much taller up close, and had an earthy beauty about her, with her clanking necklaces piled on top of one another, peeking above her heavy scarves. Her daughter's rosy cheeks were the only sign that either felt the cold.

This must be the woman Nina said could help us. She looks like a fortune-teller . . . and she's a blood head like me. How did she manage to evade the Vatican police for so many years?

Angela remembered that occult practitioners and fortune-tellers were outlawed in Luz.

She stood as the woman and her daughter came closer. The woman caught sight of Angela and gasped. Her hand instinctively grabbed for her daughter and dragged her backward, away from Angela. Her heavy-lidded eyes were now wide as dinner plates.

A flutter of wingbeats and a heavy weight on Angela's shoulder signaled Nina's return to her perch.

Angela, Nina said, *this is Gloriana Cassel and her daughter, Tress. I used to work for Gloriana part-time at her curiosity shop in Luz. She used to help me understand my dreams and psychic abilities . . . as much as she could, anyway. She owned the mirror that the priests used to bring you into Luz.*

"Hello," Angela whispered awkwardly.

Gloriana said nothing at first. She scanned Angela from top to bottom with her sultry eyes, focusing on Angela's green left eye in particular. Her face had paled considerably. "So—you're safe," she said at last.

Angela nodded. "We—that is, Nina and I—have come for your help. I need to enter Luz, but I can't be seen for reasons I'm assuming you understand."

Gloriana stared at Angela as though a ghost stood in front of her.

Angela cleared her throat nervously and continued. "Nina said that you know a way around the main paths leading into Luz."

"Why do you wish to even enter the city?" Gloriana said softly.

Angela paused. The answer seemed so obvious to her. "Our odds of survival here are worse."

"Do you think so?"

Gloriana allowed her words to linger ominously. She still examined Angela as if she could see through to her bones. At last Tress mumbled something and buried herself in her mother's skirt, her little arms and hands trembling. She was clearly afraid of Angela.

What about Angela was so different now? In her eyes, she looked the same as when she attended Westwood Academy in Luz. Yet everyone paused now and treated her with deference. Was it the way she walked or stood? Was it something in her voice? She couldn't see it or understand it, and that frightened her even more. Had Hell changed her that much?

Angela took a step closer, and Gloriana and her daughter just as quickly shuffled back. "Listen, are you going to help us or not?" Angela demanded. "I've made up my mind, so if you won't help—"

"Do you know the Netherworld?" Gloriana said. She must have noticed how her fear was confusing Angela. With difficulty, she took a step closer again, forcing Tress to follow her.

Yes, Angela remembered the terrible human Netherworld. There, with the angel Mikel's help, she'd encountered her dead parents for the last time. The angel Azrael had then attacked her before she'd freed the souls that had been imprisoned by him, which had nearly kept them from their prophesied role of fighting by Angela's side in the future. The memory of him was enough to set her teeth chattering again.

I wonder if that's why Lucifel sent angels to steal the souls left in Luz. That could even be the reason she's hoarding them away in Heaven. To keep them away from me!

Angela also found it hard to understand why Mikel—Lucifel's rebellious angelic daughter—had been so helpful at the time and then had suddenly disappeared from Angela's side when she was needed most.

Maybe she hadn't been much of a friend after all.

Yet it was hard to forget the pain in Mikel's face when she spoke of her dead angel father Raziel, and that was enough to temper at least some of the suspicion and disgust starting to boil within Angela. She hadn't seen evil behind Mikel's strange eyes. But she'd seen despair, and that could be terrible enough. Angela knew all too well what could happen to a soul that had lost hope. The more she considered past events, the more Mikel's face haunted her. In the end, Angela had never discovered who told the demons that she was in Luz, beginning an avalanche of misery for all concerned. And she'd never figured out how Python knew enough to lure her into Hell. Perhaps Mikel had been the informant. Perhaps she loved Lucifel and clung to her for a reason Angela might never understand.

It certainly makes sense. Look at how the Vermilion Order is suddenly hunting me down. Lucifel's shadow has entered Luz. Perhaps Mikel is only her herald.

"I can see by your face that you have experience with the Realm where the dead walked," Gloriana said, interrupting Angela's thoughts.

Angela looked back at her again. "Yes, I do. But the Netherworld has been emptied since I left it. If it even exists anymore."

"It doesn't," Gloriana said. "But listen carefully to what I'm about to tell you. Whereas Azrael, the angel of death, lorded over the Netherworld, his twin, Kheshmar, chose to reside in the outer darkness beneath Luz. She is the one who can help you reach Lucifel. Perhaps she can also help you with Raziel's Book. She used to be one of Raziel's guardian Thrones."

"Do the priests know she exists?" Angela said, realizing that she was now down to whispers. "They knew about the Fae Tileaf and used her cruelly."

"Yes and no," Gloriana said. "Those who were foolish enough to search for Kheshmar never returned to Luz's upper levels. The priests abandoned all thought of communicating with her after stern warnings from the angelic Realms."

"Then how do you know about her?"

Gloriana seemed taken aback for a moment. That was when Angela saw it—a glint of yellow light behind Gloriana's eyes. It was the same as the eerie light behind Kim's. *Gloriana was not only a blood head, she was half-Jinn.* No wonder she could communicate with creatures from the Realms so easily!

Now Angela was the speechless one.

"Have you figured out my secret?" Gloriana said gently. "It's true. My father was a human, and my mother was . . ."

Rustling erupted in the naked canopy overhead. Two eyes gleamed at Angela from the darkness.

Juno, Troy's niece, had arrived.

Angela returned to regarding Gloriana carefully. Gloriana's mother, then, was a Jinn like Troy and Juno. What had happened to her? Why had Gloriana survived and most other half-Jinn did not? Kim had been certain he was the only half-Jinn human in the world, and the demons had also confidently thought so, using his unique half-bred hands to free Lucifel from her cage in Hell. Angela could only imagine how this news that he wasn't alone in the world would change everything for him. The more Angela thought about him, the more her soul felt like caving in on itself.

She had been in such a panic to get Sophia to safety, she'd forgotten that he remained in Hell, waiting for her. What would he say to her when they saw each other again? Angela wanted him to be happy, first and foremost. Kim hadn't deserved the cruel life handed to him. He'd allowed his heart to turn entirely to Angela's welfare, even when it caused him great suffering. And now it would look like she'd abandoned him.

If only he were here right now. Somehow, everything wouldn't be so hard if I knew he was safe.

She could only hope that Troy wouldn't find him and follow through on her stalled assassination mission.

Angela?

Angela shook her head. Nina's voice had interrupted her thoughts and now she felt the tears running down her face.

Angela, why are you crying? Nina pressed, her voice tightened by concern.

Everything inside of Angela broke for a moment, and then it put itself together again. She shook her head, wiped away her tears, and looked at Gloriana sadly. It was better to ignore Nina's anxiety, before the guards keeping

Gloriana and her daughter captive grew suspicious. It was obvious they'd pretended Tress needed to relieve herself in the bushes. "Tell me, then, how I can find Kheshmar and enter the lower levels of Luz," Angela said. "Before it's too late."

Gloriana nodded. "Leave Memorial Cemetery by using the main gates. They'll be lightly guarded. Most of the priests believe you'll try to escape on that beast from Hell by entering Luz's skies. Be careful, however, that you stay out of sight of any angels. There are eyes everywhere now. Once out of the gates, go left, and down a long tunnel that empties into the uppermost of Luz's lower levels. You'll find a large storm grate there. Lift the hatch and enter the water. It will take you down to the canals." Gloriana looked Angela up and down again. "Of course, you'll need better clothes than what you're wearing now, but either way, you're bound to get soaked at first."

Nina croaked gently. *Angela, there's no way I can follow you into the water as I am now.*

I know, Angela said back to her in her thoughts. *Don't worry, we'll figure something out.*

She remembered Juno who sat still and silent in the trees, suddenly invisible. Angela took a deep breath.

"Eventually, you'll come to two statues," Gloriana continued. "Pass through them. After that . . ."

"Yes?" Angela said eagerly.

"Well, nobody knows," Gloriana ended. "As I mentioned, no one has ever returned from that point. But you're the Archon. Perhaps you will succeed where all others have failed. We can only pray. This leads me to a question I hope you'll answer for me. Why does the Book of Raziel remain unopened?"

Angela lowered her head. "It's complicated, but . . . it can't be opened right now."

Gloriana shook her head and sighed.

Nina flapped her wings, acting as if she wanted to say something more. Wisely, she ultimately stayed silent. She settled with them into the pressing quiet.

"Well," Angela whispered, "thank you for your help."

"I'm happy to help you," Gloriana said. "I always knew the Archon would choose to be our salvation, not our Ruin. Even if my entire life was lived solely for this moment . . ." She caressed her daughter, who peeked a little more bravely at Angela from behind her mother's skirt. "For my daughter's future, at the very least, it's worth every danger."

Shouts echoed in their direction. The novice guarding Gloriana and her daughter must have become suspicious by now.

"Good luck to you," Gloriana said. "We'll pray for your success, Angela Mathers."

She knows my name, Angela thought to herself. Then she thought of entering the freezing cold water beneath Luz, and the canals, and meeting Kheshmar and she understood her earlier shivers for what they were.

As if sensing Angela's growing distress, Tress burst suddenly from her mother's side and ran up to Angela. She held out a long snow-white feather that looked as delicate as paper-thin porcelain. Angela recognized its size and shape.

Immediately, she thought of Israfel.

"The angels will watch over you," Tress whispered to her. Her child's eyes seemed to absorb all the darkness of the surrounding trees. "Like they watch over me."

I suppose she's talking about "good" angels. I have yet to meet one, Nina said dryly.

Angela took the feather, stroking it with a finger. "Where did you get this?" she said to Tress.

"It doesn't matter," Tress said, smiling. "You need it more than me, anyway. You can give it back someday—when it won't help anymore."

"Now hurry, Archon," Gloriana said shortly. And then she grabbed her daughter by the shoulders and steered her back into the trees and in the direction of the clearing until they were no more than shadows.

Fatigue had plucked at Angela little by little since they'd arrived in Luz. Now it began to wash over her. Her thoughts wandered and melted together into a murky pool. Her steps became mechanical as she and Nina returned to Sophia. After a while, the world around her vanished and she seemed to walk in a great darkness littered with stars. Fear stifled her. Any moment now, she would feel herself being torn apart again.

Who am I? I'm Angela Marie Mathers, right? My parents were Erianna and Marcus, and I had a brother named Brendan. They died in a fire accidentally caused by me. That fire left me with scars. My entire past left me with scars.

Her vision swam. It was as if she could see her parents and brother walking ahead of her like ghosts instead of Nina.

No . . . I'm the Archon. The angel Raziel died long ago, and then he chose my soul to be the Archon's and he resided within my body, next to my own spirit, to protect me and guide me. Only I can open his Book and choose good or evil for the universe. Only I can stop Lucifel from silencing the universe . . .

Angela paused. The icy air she breathed sliced like a knife through her lungs. She hugged herself, gripping her shivering arms. A deep silence surrounded her. It was so much like the silence from her terrible visions.

That's who I am . . . so why do I feel like neither of those facts are the truth?

She looked up into the misty blackness. Her left eye burned and suddenly her vision seemed to pierce through the ether. Distance disappeared and she found herself flying in her mind toward something immense. A great face materialized. It was the Father's, and it was neither male nor female in human terms, and terribly beautiful. His great eyes had glassed over lifelessly and he lay in a darkness somehow deeper than the one she stood within. Blue blood seeped in a pool from his broken body.

A silvery winged figure knelt beside him.

The angel turned to look at Angela, as if recognizing that he was being watched. It was Israfel. The Father's blue blood stained his mouth. His own eyes cried red tears.

Feathers surrounded him in a thick pile, and as he shifted his wings, even more spiraled to the floor. His face had paled and thinned to something ghostly.

He opened his mouth to cry out to her.

Angela . . .

Was that his voice? It sounded so different somehow, and with every passing second it grew louder.

Angela! WATCH OUT!

What? Angela looked up again. The distance grew between her and Israfel and the Father, and they streaked backward into the ether as fast as a lightning bolt.

Something hard slammed into her, tossing her sideways to the earth.

Angela shrieked and clutched at her head. Pain ricocheted through her skull. Bursts of light exploded in front of her eyes and faded. She pushed up on her arms, her palms scraping into the frozen soil. Warm blood trickled to her wrists. A hand grabbed her by the back of her shawl and flipped her around.

Angela focused hard on the face above her. It was male and astonishingly perfect, with large brown eyes and brown hair. Great chestnut-colored wings beat the air around them. It took a moment for her to register that an angel had knocked her to the ground and was ready to choke her if he felt like it.

"Stop it—" she gasped beneath his crushing fingers. "Stop—"

"Every citizen of Luz knows this is a restricted area," the angel said softly. He dropped her to the ground again, and his voice grew even colder. "Even to those called blood heads." He moved so quickly, Angela had barely blinked before a shining crossbow lifted in front of her and a sharp arrow jabbed at her forehead.

Nina screeched with alarm from the trees. The angel narrowed his eyes and searched the darkness.

"A Vapor," he whispered. "I should have known you'd be a witch, blood head." He kicked at Angela's ribs.

"Don't kill me," Angela whispered.

The angel laughed, and his perfect smile was one shade away from a demon's. "Why not?"

Angela noticed yellow eyes burning in the darkness behind him. Courage stole over her and she stared at the angel, her left eye burning.

His face blanched with fear and his mouth opened, but it was too late.

Juno exploded from the trees, her wings beating as she pounced on the angel and brought him to the ground. He fought back, and Angela rolled out of their way as feathers exploded around her, and Juno's furious snarls echoed into the night. She was on top of the angel's chest, her sharp nails pressed to his throat, when he overturned her, pinning her beneath him. Energy snapped and fizzled around his hands.

Angela willed the blood to trickle away from her wrists and pool in her cut palms. The Glaive formed and she swung it hard, stopping inches from the angel's bare neck.

"Let her go," Angela said, still gasping for breath. She fought a sudden wave of dizziness. The weapon was draining her life force even more strongly than usual.

The angel did nothing.

Until Angela pressed enough to put a cut in his skin.

He held up his hands and stepped away from Juno. Juno sprang to her feet and scampered over to Angela. If this were Troy the angel had tangled with, he'd either have died or suffered immensely by now. Clearly, Juno was a different kind of Jinn. She glared at the angel and sat by Angela's side, sighing and licking at a cut on her arm. Her wings relaxed and she finished by licking the blood from her teeth. Her nails split through the rocks beneath her hands as she leaned forward again, sniffing the angel.

"Thank you," Juno said to Angela when she'd finished her inspection.

"Anything for a friend," Angela said softly. She held the weapon steady, though her legs already threatened to buckle. "But as for you," she said to the angel. "What's your problem? Why did you attack me?"

You won't get anything worthwhile out of him, Angela, Nina said. She glided down from the trees. *We've tried, trust me.*

Well, Angela thought back. *It's worth a shot.*

"You do realize I can hurt you if I want to?" Angela said to the angel.

The angel kept silent.

Angela looked him over. Finally, her gaze settled on the adamant cuffs on his wings. They glistened like platinum beneath the stars overhead, but a strange shape had been etched into their metal. It looked a lot like a fly. Angela thought of how Lucifel's shadow had taken the shape of a giant fly during their battle in Luz.

Then it's true—Lucifel has control of Heaven!

"Why bother with me?" the angel said gently. "You have much bigger problems right now, after all."

"What do you mean?" Angela said sharply, keeping her blade at his neck.

"You're the Archon, I suppose," the angel continued. "At least that's what I'm gathering from the weapon against my neck. Lucifel sends her regards. She's grateful for your return. And for the gift you brought back with you."

Fear rattled Angela's insides. Her heart froze, and her soul turned to ice. The air suddenly seemed suffocatingly warm in comparison. Even though she was allowing the angel to continue, his words sounded from a faraway place.

"I agreed it was a mistake for Lucifel to let the Book escape her hands so easily," the angel said. "But the balance of power will be restored soon. Whether I live or die, I accomplished my mission well enough. Let me live, and I'll be glad to inform the new Prince of Heaven you're on your way. Let me die, and she'll put two and two together herself."

Red-hot anger colored Angela's entire world. She should have listened to her instincts and never left Sophia alone.

"Where is the Book of Raziel?" Angela seethed. She gripped the Glaive so hard her palms blistered with pain. "Tell me, or I'll—"

"You'll what?" the angel said, scoffing. "You'll kill me?"

Angela hesitated. She didn't want things to go that far, but when it came to Sophia, she couldn't stand even the thought of her in danger anymore. Honestly, Angela didn't know what she would do if something happened to Sophia. Her blade at the angel's neck trembled with her hands.

"Lucifel doesn't need you, Archon," the angel continued. "She thought she needed you, and it's true that Raziel devised everything so that your blood alone can open the Book. But we'll have that shortly as well. How long can you run, I wonder? It hasn't taken much to convince most of the people in Luz that you're evil, that your blood is worth any price. And they'll take it from you by any means necessary by now. Stay here, and you'll be captured by the priests. Enter the city, and you'll be murdered."

The angel's eyes shone strangely.

"He's lying," Juno growled in the background, but her voice sounded hopeful, not certain.

He'd better be lying, Angela thought frantically. *Or everything is lost. But Lucifel can't open the Book without me. She needs the Glaive.*

The same Glaive now made with Angela's mysterious, new, blue blood. Angela's racing thoughts stalled.

She felt her eyes widen. A short gasp escaped her. As long as Lucifel had Angela's *blood,* she could open the Book herself without anyone to stop her. That was the key. In the past, Lucifel had wielded the Glaive, but Angela's soul wasn't connected to it yet. Now it was. Now Angela had changed inside somehow and that had also changed Lucifel's strategy.

Nina! Stop worrying about me, and go help Sophia! Angela thought frantically.

But, Angela—

Go!

Nina flew through the trees, branches snapping around her as she left.

"You're too late," the angel said. "I made sure of that."

One of the angel's eyes flashed a brilliant red and he dropped to the ground unconscious. So—he'd been possessed. But by whom? Lucifel's shadow had been destroyed by Angela.

That left her daughter, Mikel.

Without another thought Angela dashed through the trees, in the direction Nina had flown. She could only assume Juno followed behind her. The cold and the pain and her overwhelming tiredness meant nothing to her now. And then, she stumbled into the copse where she, and Sophia, and the Kirin had rested only a short while ago. No one was there. Fury was gone. So were Nina and the Kirin. And so was Sophia.

Angela considered shouting, but if she did, the priests and novices still in the cemetery would certainly hear her.

Juno landed by her side. Immediately, the Jinn prowled and searched the dirt and rocks. She lifted her head, gazing in the direction of the western side of the cemetery. "They're definitely gone," Juno said, "and I'm certain they've escaped into the city."

"No," Angela whispered to herself. "What about the Kirin? It can't have gotten far without—"

"It escaped somehow," Juno whispered. "The Earth Realm will affect it like it affects Auntie and me. Although, I often heard the winged Kirin have other abilities."

Angela gripped the pendant resting against her chest, squeezing her eyes shut. Then she realized she still held the Glaive in her other hand, and she willed it to collapse.

Instantly, a rush of energy flowed through her. She staggered, absently wiping the blood from her hands onto her nightgown.

"I have to follow Sophia and Nina," she said to Juno, and she set off toward the thicket.

Juno's pointed ears flicked back. Her left ear was still floppy, and it drooped after a second or so. "You can't," Juno said with confusion. She began stalking in Angela's direction and then paused, as if hoping Angela would stop before anything further happened.

Angela continued on, ready to march into the bushes.

Whump. Juno landed right in front of her. Her yellow eyes burned into Angela. "I said you can't."

"Who are you to order me around?" Angela said, trying not to shout.

"Think about what you're going to do," Juno retorted.

"I've done enough thinking. I'm not going to let Sophia and Nina just vanish into Luz where anything can happen to them."

"They can blend in with the other humans to some degree. You can't. You'll be noticed soon enough. And then what?"

Angela shook her head angrily. "I'm going, and that's final."

"I won't let you," Juno said, and she stood up as tall as possible, which wasn't quite the height of her aunt, but tall enough to be frightening. Her wings snapped open and her eyes glowed brighter. "It's my responsibility to stop you from doing anything stupid. And entering Luz when everyone is brainwashed into murdering you is stupid. I'm now the Queen of the Jinn, and Auntie would want me to do what's best for our people. Letting the Archon die is not what's best for the Jinn. So, please stop."

Juno flexed her sharp nails for added emphasis.

Angela breathed hard. She balled her hands into fists. It was destroying her inside not to charge into Luz after Sophia and Nina. But Juno did have a point. Perhaps Juno wasn't using the violence and nasty language Troy would use to get the message across, but Angela wasn't so sure she wanted to test Juno's words either. A dangerous aura surrounded her right now.

"All right, you win," Angela muttered. She stepped away from the bushes.

Juno relaxed her ears and wings, looking a million times less threatening. "I heard what Gloriana said about the canals beneath Luz. I can go with you to meet Azrael's twin."

Angela considered her options, and diving into Luz's underworld was all that remained. She glanced up at the sky, a shot of fear burning through her as she thought she saw a shadow pass overhead, briefly blocking out the stars. Was it an angel again? Where had the winged Kirin gone? Hopefully it hadn't taken to the skies out of fear. She examined the stars, realizing with alarm that the sky shone brighter. The angelic city must have been coming closer to Luz.

The cold was probably even worse this hour than the previous. Realms were about to collide. She didn't have any time to delay. Sophia had said more than once she could take care of herself. Angela would have to trust and pray that was the case, no matter how much it left her screaming inside.

Angela glanced at Juno.

As if reading Angela's thoughts, the Jinn nodded sagely. Then it was settled. It was time to enter Luz's darkest level, to find the angel lurking in the mists.

Sixteen

Angela pressed against the bricks next to the storm grate Gloriana had mentioned was their entrance into the canals. She watched the silvery water churning below and swallowed. Already, she could feel the ice cold water freezing her bones and sucking out her air. She wanted Juno—anyone—to jump into the water with her.

But she'd already decided—she couldn't just let Sophia hide in Luz alone.

Over and over, she'd been practicing how to explain herself to Juno. Angela peeked back and forth down the empty alley. She was sure people lived down here, yet there weren't any lights behind the shuttered windows, and most of them were boarded up completely.

The cold air picked at her skin and lungs, and her breath looked like smoke.

At last, a gentle *thump* touched the cobblestones behind her. Angela turned quickly.

She'd never become used to how Jinn eyes glowed so eerily.

"Is something wrong?" Juno said, her ears pricking forward. She was on alert already.

"No, I'm sorry. I'm just not used to . . . well, never mind. Thanks for getting me these clothes," Angela said. She plucked the pair of brown pants from Juno and then grabbed the form-fitting black shirt offered to her. It wasn't much, but it would at least keep her from freezing to death for fifteen minutes or so. Angela laid aside the scarves she'd been wearing. They would be too dangerous to bring into the water, wrapped around her neck.

This is insane.

"There's no way I'm allowing you to enter the canals alone," Juno said almost sweetly.

Angela choked on her next breath. She stared at Juno. "How did you—"

"I could see it in your eyes," Juno whispered. "Deep down in your soul, you want me to go after Sophia and watch over her. You're misunderstanding everything. She's safer than you at the moment."

Angela took a deep breath again. "You're only saying that to make me feel better."

"No. I know she and Nina and Fury are all right—for now. Nina is my Vapor. I can sense if she's in danger or not."

"What?" Angela said. "Then you can tell me where they are, right?"

Juno's wings stiffened almost defensively. "I can't. If I would, don't you think I'd say something?"

"That's true. Well, tell me if you sense anything wrong at any point."

"I will."

"Juno?"

"Yes?"

"Thank you . . . for all your help."

Juno bared her teeth, which for most Jinn passed as a smile, and then she leaned down, lifting the heavy grate separating them from the churning water beneath. Angela was already shivering. There was no way to know they wouldn't just get dumped right into the ocean, or worse. She stepped closer and then knelt down. If it was possible, the air beneath the grate actually seemed colder. But wasn't water always warmer than the surrounding air? She remembered that much from her schooling. Even so, it would be a small consolation.

"I'll be right behind you," Juno said.

Angela steeled herself. She didn't want to jump into the water. She almost couldn't. Then, without thinking, she took the next step and slid inside.

The current snagged her like a fish on a hook, dragging her into water so cold it stole her breath away. Angela spluttered, trying to keep her head up to see and breathe, but it was almost impossible. Salt water entered her mouth and ears. Foam surrounded her head. The water roared, and she felt her entire body being thrown forward, faster and faster with every passing second. The bricks of the tunnel seemed to fly by on either side, and soon everything was a blur. She tried to shout for Juno, but only succeeded in getting more water in her mouth. Her bones ached. Her organs were probably freezing.

Then, Angela felt herself lurch over a sudden drop.

Her body splashed into calmer water and she used the last ounce of her strength to swim for an ancient boat moored to a shore of slimy cobblestones. The roar of the water was still deafening. Angela grasped the boat and clung to it as hard as she could. Somehow, she pulled herself inside and curled up, trying to stay warm. She couldn't take off her sopping wet clothes, and her hair was plastered icily against her neck. She glanced up at the high arches of the stone ceiling above her. Icicles that looked more like silver daggers hung among the rock.

Juno crawled across the ceiling, weaving her way around the ice. She glided into the boat but didn't land gracefully. More water splashed inside, and Juno recoiled from the cold as she spread her wings, shaking off the moisture.

Angela might have complained if her teeth weren't chattering so violently.

Only by summoning all her strength could Angela uncurl herself and sit up to start rowing the boat.

She grasped the rotten oar and started to push, letting the current take them again.

Juno edged closer to her and wrapped her wings around Angela, trying to warm her as best she could.

Angela fought to stay conscious. Gloriana had said to watch for two statues, but all Angela saw was more brick, and more water, and suddenly her exhaustion caught up with her.

She was aware of Juno shouting in alarm. But Angela could do nothing as sleep sank its claws into her brain and, instead of letting go, fatally tightened its grip.

Angela awakened to what was initially utter darkness.

Soon her eyes adjusted, and she realized she lay in the bottom of a boat with water leaking through its wooden frame. But despite that, the air was oddly hot and stuffy, and she was no longer freezing but warm and almost entirely dry.

Now she noticed the boat wasn't rocking. They must have hit some kind of shore.

Slowly, Angela sat up and peered out into the quiet darkness. Juno stood in front of two statues flanking either side of a narrow path. Hundreds of similarly ragged boats lay on the shore. Perhaps these were all that remained of adventurers who entered the underbelly of Luz. But something about the walls was strange. Angela noticed there were many tunnels branching off in various directions, all radiating from this central pool. The arches above the entryways had been skillfully constructed and elaborately carved. And then, her eyes focused completely.

Death lined the walls.

Innumerable bones had been set in just as innumerable shelves in the rock.

The canals beneath Luz were catacombs. Angela and Juno had entered a giant, watery tomb.

Angela swallowed, searching the empty eye sockets of thousands of grinning skulls.

She felt afraid to move again.

At any moment, it seemed the skulls would come to life and speak. Instead, they stared at her as they had stared into the water.

Juno crawled away from the statues and scampered nearer to Angela. She seemed relieved Angela was awake, but she shook her head again as they both regarded the bones that now made up the world. "They've been dead a long, long time," Juno said. "I can smell it."

"Please tell me you didn't try to taste any of them," Angela said weakly.

Juno sighed. "There's no meat left in them," she said very seriously. "Ah, I'm so hungry, though . . ."

Angela remembered Troy telling her how staying in this dimension caused her to become insanely hungry. The High Assassin of the Jinn had been a terror in Luz for a short time, taking the sick or criminals or other unsavory individuals as her prey. She'd said there'd been no choice. It was either kill and devour her meals or starve to death.

Angela eyed Juno carefully.

Juno showed no sign that she noticed, but she licked her lips, and her eyes glazed over as she examined the bones again.

"These statues," Angela said. She pointed at the two enormous stone angels flanking the narrow path Juno had been inspecting. "They look just like statues I've seen on buildings in Luz built by the Vatican. They probably made these catacombs ages ago. No wonder most people were unaware they existed. Every stupid teenager in Luz would be down here to see these bones if word got out. But why would an angel live down here? And why wouldn't she let people who found her leave again?"

Juno sniffed the air. "I don't smell an angel," she said softly.

"Exactly. I bet it's more of a legend than anything else. The Vatican probably never really sent anyone down here to find her. They just sent guards to silence people who found the catacombs."

"So Gloriana lied to us?" Juno flapped her wings before folding them crisply against her back again. "Why?"

Juno raised an interesting point. Gloriana had been smart enough to hide her real self from the Vatican for so long. She surely knew what she was talking about when it came to angels.

Angela trembled again, but the cold wasn't an excuse anymore. Fear crept into every fiber of her being.

She walked up to the statues and glanced from one to the other. Except for their size, they looked ordinary enough. The lanterns they held aloft had lost their flames ages ago. So how could Angela see in such darkness?

Then it hit her. The walls were glowing.

She peered more closely at the skulls and bones around them. Bluish lights danced behind their empty eye sockets before disappearing again. Angela knew these delicate glowing spheres. The first time she'd encountered them was in the Netherworld ruled by Azrael. They were human souls.

Maybe Gloriana is right. Azrael hoarded human souls. Why wouldn't his twin do the same?

What awaited them beyond the statues? According to Gloriana, no one had ever returned to tell.

Before she could reconsider her foolishness, Angela stepped beyond the statues and onto the long path to nowhere.

Juno followed behind, slinking with catlike grace among the heavy shadows. More of the bluish spheres flew by them into the blackness, and a few danced around Angela's head as if trying to warn her away. But she steeled herself and continued, listening to the slow and ominous drip of water from the icicles on the ceiling. Eventually, her ears caught a song floating toward them. There were no words, just a melody that seemed woven from time and starlight. Every note was clean and pure like a crystal dropped in water.

Angela gasped as she recognized it. This was Sophia's lullaby. As always, the song took Angela to distant worlds and back into unreachable time, and it plucked at her heart, summoning both pain and bliss. Tears burned the corners of Angela's eyes.

She felt so far away from everyone right now. Hearing this song only made the feeling worse.

If the song affected Juno, she didn't show it. But she didn't seem about to turn back either.

They entered another cavern. Narrow stone bridges stretched and crisscrossed over one another in a thousand different directions. Far, far below the perilously narrow walkways, a pool of water gleamed. Barely a ripple touched its surface, and it was impossible to tell what stream fed it or how.

The music grew unendurably beautiful by the second.

Juno stepped out onto the middle of the walkway they'd used to enter, and Angela followed her. Even in Hell, she'd never seen anything quite like this. Angela glanced down at the water, and dizziness swept through her like a tornado. She looked at the walls around them, seeing thousands more skulls.

"I don't understand," Angela whispered through the music. It now seemed to come from every direction at once. "Why would any angel hide in a place like this?"

Juno stiffened. She crouched down on her hands and feet and her ears pressed against her hair. She bared her teeth, snarling nastily.

Now the song sounded too enchanting, sweet, and pure. It had lured them deeper inside.

Angela's vision spun.

"Someone's coming," Juno growled.

Angela couldn't see a thing. Was this angel invisible?

"They're here," Juno said, her large eyes narrowing. She arched her wings defensively.

Angela and Juno each faced opposite directions instinctively.

Where was this angel? Where! And *what* was Angela even looking for?

The music stopped. Angela held her breath. Then, like he was emerging from a pocket in the air and ether, Kim appeared.

Seventeen

The moment Troy said they were returning to Luz, a sense of dread had suffocated Kim. The idea of returning to that city frosted over his soul and gnawed at his insides. Nothing good could come from some mysterious angel locked up in Luz.

And Kim thought he'd known all there was to know about the Vatican's mysterious city.

Unfortunately, he'd been wrong.

As he followed Troy on whatever path she felt would return them to Earth, he couldn't help wondering. Who was this angel, and why did Troy seem so frightened of her? Was this really the right thing to do when he had such little time left to help Angela? Trading his soul to Python had left Kim clinging to every second like it was his last. He forced himself to think of Angela, and her warmth as she nestled in his arms.

He bit his lip and continued behind Troy in silence. Perhaps the darkness would never end. Perhaps they were trapped in a rat's maze that would dump them out at the very edge of the universe.

Thank goodness, he was wrong about that too. At last, they stopped in a circular cavern with pulsing hieroglyphs etched into the stone walls. Before them, a pool of water rested like a silver mirror.

Troy stepped to the water's edge and looked back at Kim, gesturing for him to come closer.

This wasn't an ordinary pool. A strange whispering filled the air.

Kim had to push himself to reach Troy's side.

Her ears were high and alert, and her breathing sounded ragged. So—she was afraid too. Troy glanced back nervously, as if Python might step out of the darkness any second.

"This is what Angela used to enter Luz," Troy said so softly, she could have hissed. "The water called to her, she entered, and then she and the Book and the Kirin disappeared."

"You didn't do anything to keep her out?" Kim snapped.

"Of course! I tried," Troy snarled back at him. "But the pull of the water was too strong."

"So you're suggesting that we enter the water and that's how we'll return to Luz?" he offered.

Troy continued examining the pool's deceptively peaceful surface. "It's the surest and quickest way. We don't have the time to climb into Memorial Cemetery through the Netherworld."

That was an excuse and they both knew it. It seemed Troy was deliberately ignoring the fact that if either of them were spotted by a rival Jinn Clan—or their own—they would probably be killed. Perhaps her new status as a fugitive like Kim was so odious to her, she couldn't even bear mentioning it more than necessary.

"You're right," Kim said, agreeing for the sake of avoiding another argument. "No time. So, we just walk into the pool?" he said again.

"Quiet, I'm trying to think," Troy growled at him. She closed her glowing eyes. Then she opened them again and slid one toe into the water. Her entire body tensed.

Nothing happened.

Troy waded directly into the middle of the pool, cautiously at first, then with a hastiness born from frustration. Her ears flipped back in anger. She flapped her remaining wing, flinging silver droplets into the air. "I don't understand."

"What? What's wrong?" Kim said. He knelt down and slipped a hand into the water. It was shockingly cold. He held up his hand again, watching the droplets slide down his pale fingers.

Troy growled under her breath. She examined the demonic hieroglyphs on the cavern walls. She seemed tempted to spit angrily in the water, but checked herself. "I should have known. Angela was summoned. Whoever brought her back to Luz waited until the right moment. Only a witch could know how to do that. They must have used a mirror somehow connected to these pools."

"So now what?" Kim said, a little too angrily himself.

Troy noticed his accusatory tone. She gave him a warning glare. "Patience, cousin. *Let me think.*"

"For God's sake! We don't have time to climb into the Netherworld and we sure as hell don't have time to think," Kim muttered, knowing she could hear him and not caring anymore. "Since when did you become such a detective anyway?"

"A what?" Troy said, bristling like he'd called her something hideous.

She clearly didn't know what that word meant.

"Never mind. Just hurry, damn it!"

Troy paced within the water. Then her eyes widened. She reached up to her hair and untied the iron crow's foot talisman she'd taken from Kim. She held it up to him, nodding. Then she waited a long moment before finally letting go, dropping it into the pool.

The crow's foot disappeared with barely a ripple. The whispering in the air grew louder, as if a million voices called to them at once. Troy instinctively backed away from a whirlpool forming in the pool's center and stood next to Kim again, water dripping from her hair, wing, and face. "I knew it," she said. "As long as we have a physical connection to the Realm where we wish to travel, the pool acts as a portal." She quieted again as the pool's outer edges reflected an odd image of bones and skulls. Troy licked her lips. "So, she's there. She's alive!" Troy said with a tenderness in her voice Kim never expected.

Kim didn't think she was talking about Angela right now.

"Who's alive?" he said, hoping to get some kind of information out of her.

Troy shook her head, breathing hard.

"Come on," she said, grasping him by the arm so tightly Kim thought his bones might break. "We're leaving now. Before we miss our chance."

She dragged him into the ice-cold water. Kim fought his instinct to splash back to shore, because the more Troy waded toward the pool's center, the more he felt they were doing something incredibly dangerous. The waves overtook them, and foamy water churned into his mouth. Then Troy lost her grip, and Kim's feet slipped, and he plunged into a frigid darkness that wrapped around his heart and filled every inch of his lungs.

No—this was a mistake. He'd done the most stupid thing imaginable and allowed Troy to kill him when Angela needed him most.

Suddenly a different darkness seeped through Kim's brain. He felt stretched inside and out and nothingness took over. Was this death?

If so, it took Kim so stealthily, he might have fallen asleep.

The darkness didn't last. Kim's awareness returned by degrees, and before he knew what was happening, he surfaced for air, gasping and splashing his arms to catch his grip on anything that could save him. Finding nothing, Kim worked against an overwhelming ache in all his muscles and swam as hard as he could. At last, he reached some kind of shore. He collapsed like he was dead, spluttering water from between his lips. Now he realized the water tasted saline, as if it came from the ocean.

He grasped the hourglass pendant at his chest, turning over on his back as he examined it. One-third of the grains were gone.

A shot of fear scorched through him. How could that have happened so quickly?

Coughs to his left startled Kim from his horrified trance. He turned and saw Troy collapse on her hands and knees beside him, her wing feathers and hair sodden with water. Amazingly, she uncurled one of her palms and—*clink*—the crow's foot talisman dropped to the stone ground.

She'd somehow recovered it in the whirlpool.

They looked at each other.

Troy broke away from Kim's gaze and stood shakily to her feet. She leaned down, coughing out more water. She wiped her mouth, her face scrunching with surprise. She must have noticed the water's saltiness too.

It seemed like they hadn't made any progress at all, yet they were clearly in another place, and that place was apparently somewhere in Luz. The hieroglyphs were gone, and instead thousands of skulls and bones gleamed at them from long carved rows in the rock. Bluish spheres appeared and disappeared, hiding within the skeletal remains. A lilting melody echoed in the background.

They were in catacombs, hidden below Luz.

Kim pushed up on his hands and knees and slowly rose to his feet, staring goggle-eyed at the sheer amount of bones. They seemed innumerable.

Without warning, Troy tensed and dropped to the ground again, her single wing raised high and stiff. She bared her teeth and her hair stood on end.

She was so terrifying, Kim could hardly look at her.

That was when he heard a low rhythmic noise. It echoed from above. He glanced up, searching the cavern's ceiling. Thin bridges of rock crisscrossed above them, though on the far side, they met at a ledge of black stone jutting from the wall. An immense creature sat upon it, with its four wings folded, and its glassy pure black eyes locked on them.

Kim couldn't move. He could barely breathe anymore.

The creature resembled a Hound, but its mane and body were pure white and its wings held a dazzling shine. Its humanlike hands rested on top of each other as it slouched like a regal lion, examining the mice who'd dared to enter its domain. Was this the angel Troy had been talking about?

The angel yawned, revealing teeth like daggers.

Troy didn't relax, even though the angel was making no

move to confront them. Worse, it was large enough not to care. Its hand was the size of Kim's entire body.

"You plunged us into a death trap," Kim whispered to Troy. "What is this thing?"

"A Cherubim," Troy said slowly. "She was once one of Raziel's Thrones. Or so she says."

"How would you know? You've never been here before!"

"Some of my ancestors made it here. Only a few returned . . ."

"What? Why didn't all of them come back?"

Troy glanced at the bones surrounding them. "I'd guess the angel was hungry, fool."

"Then what's to say she isn't hungry now?"

"*So you've arrived,*" a low female voice said. The angel's words ricocheted through Kim. He stood absolutely still, his brain screaming to run as the Cherubim dropped from her ledge to the ground directly in front of them. Her feet and hands met the stone with an immense thud, and she loomed over them, her jaws so immense and horrible that Kim's sanity threatened to melt. "*You've come about the Archon.*"

The angel knew why they were here?

Kim glanced at the Mirror Pool, now so glassy and still it was as if they'd never left its waters. This angel must have had the ability to scry the pool. Perhaps she saw them long before they ever arrived.

Kim stared back into the angel's onyx-hued eyes. They were somehow both vacant and absolutely penetrating, like staring into two black holes. But it didn't take much longer for him to realize they were also blind. The Cherubim followed Troy more with her ears than her gaze.

Troy was still on the defensive. "Yes, that's indeed why we've come," Troy said cautiously.

The Cherubim turned and examined her with a strange vacant expression. *"A Jinn? I haven't spoken to one of your race in over two hundred years."*

"How unlucky of you," Kim rejoined sarcastically.

He shot Troy an ironic look she didn't bother noticing.

"Now, please explain to me why you're here. Because if it isn't for a good purpose, I have no use for you. And besides . . . I am rather hungry. They don't bring the dead down here anymore."

Kim shuddered. He wanted to ask exactly why there was a Cherubim beneath Luz and why it fed off the dead. But he doubted his questions would be answered satisfactorily. It was bad enough to know that a monster like this lived and breathed beneath the city. It was a certainty she couldn't leave at will. How many of the priests knew about her? How many had died trying to reach her? That might forever be a mystery.

"I thought you knew why we've come," Troy answered the Cherubim testily.

"I do indeed," the Cherubim said. *"Yet—only to a certain degree. I cannot always rely on the visions I see in the pool. Sometimes they lie."* The Cherubim sighed. She gazed now at Kim, piercing through to his soul as she spoke. *"One tiny change—a bird's wing testing the air, for instance—can set off a chain reaction that turns the present and the future in another direction. Between the time I gazed and saw you, and the moment you arrived, much could have changed concerning our destinies."*

"When did you last look?" Kim said breathlessly. He stared at the water to his left. It was definitely a Mirror Pool like the one in Hell. But how could one have existed beneath Luz, untouched by the ocean? The ocean came first, and Sophia had hinted that the Mirror Pools were incredibly ancient.

Kim remembered how the water tasted salty. He couldn't understand. A crucial detail was eluding him.

"When did I last look?" the angel repeated solemnly. *"Oh, a long time ago. And only a minute ago. Time is a concept, of course. Humans, and half-humans, aren't usually intelligent enough to understand. I won't even bother trying. This is the outer darkness beneath Luz. That is all you need to know."*

"What is she talking about?" Kim leaned over and whispered hurriedly in Troy's ear.

Troy bristled at his closeness. "She means that this portion of the earthly Realm is somehow outside of time. It follows the river of time but is not bound by it. She can not only see the present, but the future."

"How can that be? Even the Supernals don't have that ability."

Troy ignored him for a moment. "There is a rumor that this angel foresaw Raziel's death, left him as his Throne, and chose to dwell here. This place existed before Luz."

Kim felt the shock like a thunderbolt.

"The Thrones are actually Cherubim, but their bodies were tampered with to be more pleasing to the eyes, more typically angelic." Troy's tone became nasty. "Those arrogant crows should have left well enough alone. Changing a creature's appearance can't change its soul. And so most Thrones kept their instincts. The deformities marked them from the start. But this one chose not to undergo the transformation."

"Why is she down here? As a punishment?"

Troy shook her head grimly. "I doubt it."

"*It is because I know the very hour, minute, and moment of my impending death,*" the Cherubim said. She had been listening the entire time. "*A death it is impossible to avoid. But, more important, it is so I can be here to help you.*"

What twisted logic was that? It was almost maddening. "Why not run away if you know you will die?" Kim shouted up at her.

"*You've just answered the question, half-Jinn,*" the angel said. "*Because it is both my choice and my fate to stay.*"

"Satisfied?" Troy said, smiling at him with evil sweetness.

"*If I don't help you, you are lost,*" the Cherubim said. "*How could I not stay here, then? Especially when you might arrive at any time?*"

Kim's head began to spin with the reasoning of that, but he chose not to say anything about it anymore. He'd only become more confused. He took a deep breath and held up his hourglass pendant. "So you know why we're here. Fine. Can you speak to your late master Raziel for us? This pendant links me to the Archon's soul. She knows how to open the Book of Raziel, but we need to find another way. We already know that the Angelus is the real power within the Book. Is there any way to obtain the song in its entirety without harming the Book itself?"

"*Yes,*" the Cherubim said. "*And no.*"

"That's not any kind of answer," Kim snapped, struggling to keep his cool. He looked again at the Cherubim's ferocious teeth to remind himself not to be too brave.

"*It is the truth, half-Jinn, and that is answer enough. But first, ask yourself: are you aware of who and what the Book of Raziel truly is? As you can see, she appears human. But I can tell you that her age surpasses my own and that of all*

Cherubim. She existed even before the Supernals, though in a slightly different form. What you see of her now is merely what remains."

The Cherubim looked down at the silvery water. On its smooth surface, a ghostly image of Sophia appeared.

She wore, of all things, a Westwood Academy uniform and appeared to be walking down a long shadowed hallway toward a door. Darker shadows in the background followed her. Two of them had the shape of crows. Another was frighteningly larger and seemed more mirage than creature.

It looked exactly like a Kirin with leathery wings, but then it vanished and Kim couldn't help wondering if his eyes played tricks on him.

Sophia was in Luz. She'd infiltrated the Academy again. But why?

"*The Archon cannot open the Book,*" the Cherubim continued, "*because She understands more than anyone else that the Book is a person. The being you call 'Sophia' has a soul and a past. This is something everyone else has chosen to ignore to their peril. If things had been different, then perhaps the Book would have found within herself the final notes of the Angelus. But as facts stand now, she is Bound by the laws as we all are. If the Archon does not open the Book, those final notes will remain lost forever.*"

"Yet you also hinted there is a way to obtain those final stanzas *without* opening the Book," Kim pressed. "How?"

The Cherubim stared at him with her sightless eyes. "*By creating new ones.*"

That hardly seemed possible. And it was a far cry from what Kim wanted to hear. "I need to speak to Raziel," he said after a long pause. He breathed hard, trying to contain his impatience.

The Cherubim showed no emotion whatsoever. "*As you wish,*" she whispered.

She stepped backward and vanished as if into a thick darkness. Troy and the pool vanished with her instantly. Kim was suddenly alone in absolute nothingness. Yet before he could shout or scream, footsteps sounded behind him.

He whirled around—only to find himself face-to-face with the angel Raziel, exactly as he'd wished and hoped.

Eighteen

Kim had nothing to say at first.

The Supernal Raziel was everything Kim had ever imagined him to be and more. Raziel's large eyes resembled bluish opals and his four great wings shimmered blood red. Two more wings on his ears sparkled with white jewels dotting their arches, and yet more jewels swept up his brow and vanished into his thick hair. He wore a midnight-blue coat that reminded Kim of a starry night sky. He was as majestic and breathtaking as his siblings, yet there was one marked difference: Raziel's eyes exuded kindness and gentleness. There was none of Israfel's haughtiness or Lucifel's chilling apathy.

What do you want of me? Raziel's kind face seemed to say. His eyes still held the same commanding force characteristic of the other Supernals, but they were tempered by an aura of compassion.

Kim opened his mouth, but nothing came out.

Was this really a ghost standing in front of him? If this was all an illusion, it was the most convincing one that Kim had ever encountered.

He noticed the hourglass pendant at his chest felt warm again. He held it and looked at the grains. An intense fire swept through him. They were now almost halfway gone. That quickly, his life was escaping him and would soon be Python's. But it was for Angela, so it was worth all he had to give in the end.

"I—I need to ask you something," Kim stammered.

What an understatement. Every creature in the universe wanted to ask Raziel something by now. So many mysteries clung to his legacy that the list might go on forever.

Kim continued, blushing at his own appalling awkward- ness. "I need to know how we can obtain the power inside the Book of Raziel without destroying it with the Glaive."

Raziel sighed heavily. Without speaking, he turned and seemed to look up into the darkness. A spot of blinding bright light appeared. Kim shouted and shielded his eyes as the light raced toward them, swallowing them in a brilliant wash of color and sound.

He staggered, feeling like he'd been thrust across a thresh- old of some kind, and then he suddenly stood on a brilliant crystal staircase. All around him, feathers and blood fell through the air. Angels screamed and fought one another brutally, and in the background immense feathered serpents snatched the casualties amid a shining city within the stars.

This was the Celestial Revolution.

Kim glanced up to see Raziel ascending a transparent staircase.

He followed breathlessly.

The screams and the blood seemed to have no end as Kim climbed up and up. Finally, he paused steps away from Raziel and directly beneath a menacing portal pulsing with darkness. With another flash of light they were both inside, surrounded by a deep blackness lit here and there by glowing hieroglyphs. A being of striking beauty stood in front of Raziel, looming over the Supernal angel. The being was neither male nor female, but its face struck Kim immediately. He almost forgot to breathe.

Its features were identical to Angela's.

It stared down at Raziel, fanning immense wings in varying shades of crimson, gray, and bronze. Ink-black hair fell across half of its face like an ebony curtain.

"*. . . you can put an end to all of this . . .*"

Raziel was pleading with the being.

"*. . . do what you know is right. Now that I've brought Sophia back, there is a second chance for all of us . . . I know what kind of pain you must be in. But nothing has to last forever . . .*"

The being's eyes widened at this news. It gritted its perfect teeth and clenched a fist.

Raziel paused, his face shining with hope.

The creature that could have been Angela's twin looked at Raziel tenderly. It stroked his cheek and trailed its hand down to his heart.

Alarm bells seemed to sound in Kim's brain. He reached out a hand to Raziel, screaming in warning, but he knew no one could hear him, and that it was all too late, and he was about to see how Raziel had really died. A second later, a painful and blinding light overtook them. Kim staggered as Raziel's ghost rushed through him, his red wings nearly shredded to rags and streaming blood everywhere.

Kim followed him, running madly, consumed by the same fear.

Before he could stop himself, he was tumbling with Raziel, out of the portal, past the crystal stairs, down, and down into death's embrace.

He nearly fell backward as the vision sucked away and regressed to the white light that vanished, leaving Kim and Raziel alone again.

Kim gasped for breath. He couldn't believe he was still alive. He also couldn't quite believe what he'd just witnessed. Raziel had been murdered by a creature whose face resembled Angela's? That made no sense at all, until his mind started working, focusing especially on the mysterious identity of Angela's soul, and just why she of all people had been chosen by Raziel to become the Archon. Was there a connection of some kind between her and that mysterious being?

Raziel nodded, as if answering Kim's mental question.

Now the angel pointed down at the invisible ground. Kim obediently looked, and he realized they stood in nothingness. Yet far, far below them he could see a body, lying prone and still. The more he looked, the more he felt like he was flying toward whatever he and Raziel were examining. Kim could discern white limbs and a strange silvery dress. Whatever they were approaching, it looked a lot like a human woman, but she had even more wings, and her great gray eyes stared vacantly into the Abyss.

She was dead. Her stomach looked like it had been torn open.

Kim clutched a hand over his mouth, trying not to retch. He glanced at Raziel, the distance between them tightened, and a terrible image of the woman dying amid the endless stars burned into his brain. Silvery light that looked like water poured out of her. It scattered everywhere, flowing to the farthest reaches of the universe. As it did so, Kim could hear music.

The image of the dying woman was now replaced with Sophia, her back to Kim as she stood before Lucifel in the darkness of Hell, all her beauty dimmed by the shadows surrounding Lucifel and her onyx throne. Lucifel's great wings fanned above them menacingly.

Sophia was singing that same song he'd heard in Python's mansion: the Angelus.

Kim listened, waiting and waiting for the final stanzas of the song.

They never came. Sophia's voice faltered as if she'd forgotten something. She clutched at her throat, and as Lucifel sat above her, the Devil's pale mouth tightened into a firm line of irritation.

At last, every image disappeared once more and Kim and Raziel stood face-to-face.

But how was this an answer to Kim's question? All they had established was Angela's eerie resemblance to Raziel's murderer, the existence of the Angelus, and the corpse of a strange being hidden somewhere in the Abyss.

"Is that all you can offer me?" Kim said, allowing a hint of despair to creep into his voice.

Raziel shook his head. He held up his hand as if telling Kim to wait. The Supernal took a graceful step backward and an image of Lucifel appeared to his left, and an image of an oddly bronze-haired Israfel appeared to his right. Without warning, the images of all three Supernals layered on top of one another.

Wait! The creature who had murdered Raziel—was that who Kim was now seeing as the images of the Supernals blended together?

He leaned forward, as if that could help him examine them better. His heart pounded like mad, because Kim knew he was on the verge of something immense. Now he saw that the winged deity's eyes were unlike the Supernals' and shone a brilliant green. Then one of the eyes glowed like a star. Kim remained riveted on it, unable to look away as it seemed to grow larger, and larger, swallowing his entire world and piercing into the farthest reaches of his mind.

It hovered for a moment before him, then everything disappeared and Raziel stood with Angela's image by his side.

Her left eye shone a brilliant green.

With a final deep sigh, Raziel took a step backward and vanished.

Instantly, Angela's hair lost its red color, and her blue eye went hazel. She now looked like her deceased brother Brendan Mathers. All that remained of her that could capture Kim's imagination and reveal her as anything more than ordinary was that brilliant green eye.

Frustration choked away Kim's breath and words. He felt so close to the answers to everything, yet he couldn't make absolute sense of what he'd just seen. He turned in the circle of darkness surrounding him. "And that's all, is it?" he shouted. "Now you're leaving us to discover everything on our own? You've shared this much with us—why not more? I don't understand you. You're protecting the spirit of a human girl because only she can open the Book. But she refuses. Did you know that? You must. So why are you staying silent? Why? *Answer me, damn it!*"

Raziel reappeared to Kim's left.

He jumped slightly backward, startled by their sudden closeness. Raziel's majesty up close was enough to stifle Kim's breaths.

You're correct, Raziel said sadly in a voice that shivered through Kim's brain all the way down into his bones. *You don't understand me. No one ever truly did. Perhaps Israfel was the single exception to that before the end of our glorious days together, but those times are lost in mists and ether, and there is no use summoning them anymore. If it were simply a matter of telling you what you need to know, I would have done so. Yet I can't, because what you see of me now is nothing but a memory brought to life. When I was truly alive, pleading with the Father and revealing the extent of what I'd learned ultimately led to my death. Now, Sophia is all that remains of my legacy.*

It is she who holds your answer. Ask her about what you've seen today. You're very close to the truth. Indeed, it's right in front of you.

"But why can't you tell me now?" Kim demanded.

Raziel glanced at the hourglass pendant resting near Kim's chest. His expression became concerned. *There are other ears listening, other eyes watching. Be on your guard, or you will lose your chance.*

With a flash of light, the angel disappeared, and the catacombs and their endless skulls and bones returned.

Kim slumped to the ground, gasping for breath as his knees knocked painfully into the hard rock. The Cherubim remained before him, seated like a sphinx. She regarded him coolly but said nothing.

"Well?" Troy snapped at him. She dashed in front of Kim and grabbed him hard by the shoulders, her nails piercing through his coat. She shook him like a leaf clutched in her fist. "What happened? Did you see Raziel? What did he say?"

Kim wasn't sure where to begin. Perhaps if he explained the visions to Troy, she could make better sense of them.

Yet he didn't dare open his mouth. He knew perfectly well what Raziel had been hinting at when it came to eavesdroppers, and the idea that Python had also seen everything sealed his lips shut. A dark sense of danger stole over him.

Kim's gaze darted wildly around, searching for shadows. What if that treacherous serpent had followed them into Luz? The more Kim thought about it, there was no way Lilith would stand sharing the now vacant Throne of Hell with her son. It would be in Python's best interests to crawl out of his den and find a new home. Most of the portals that connected the Realms were irreparably destroyed, so the Mirror Pools were one of the only escapes.

Just like the one that had been hidden beneath Python's mansion.

Had Python followed them, waiting for Troy and Kim to use the pool to return to Luz and then entering himself shortly afterward?

If events continued on their current course, Earth and Hell would vanish, followed shortly by Heaven if the Realms collided and disintegrated. But by now Python surely knew his best chances of survival lay wherever Sophia happened to be.

And if Angela and Sophia were now in Luz . . .

Kim's mind flashed to the Cherubim speaking about how she'd foreseen her death. The universe was on the verge of collapse and the angel hadn't died yet. So when was that going to happen? Now the suffocating sense of danger in the air choked him. He grabbed Troy by the wrists and flung her off him so hard, his cousin actually looked surprised.

"What is wrong with you?" she said impatiently. "*Speak!*"

"No. There's no time to speak anymore. We have to get out of here. Sophia and Angela are in immense danger, Troy." Kim searched frantically for an exit.

The Cherubim watched him. Her sightless eyes blinked

slowly. She seemed to be waiting for whatever came next and that terrified him even more.

"Of course they're in danger," Troy growled. *"That's why we came here.* To help Angela—"

Kim lost his calm completely. He stormed over to Troy and grabbed her so impulsively, she must not have thought of shoving him off this time. "Python followed us through the Mirror Pool," he hissed at her.

Troy's face blanked. Her ears flipped back in irritation. "How do you know that?"

"Because he's here right now," Kim seethed at her. "Or at the very least he's watching from a safe distance, so *be quiet.*"

Kim looked down at his pendant, clutched it, and nearly screamed. The entire time, he'd feared it was just one more way for Python to keep track of him. Kim wanted to toss it into the wall, but he needed it to see how much of his life was left at any given moment. That way, at least he would know when to hide from Angela so she wouldn't see the terrible fate that awaited him.

"How could he possibly have arrived here with us?" Troy snarled, ignoring Kim's request for silence. "He would have awakened after emerging from the Mirror Pool beside us. We would have seen him, you fool."

"No," Kim said, and he shook his head, pacing. Panic began to drown out his thoughts, but he tried to whisper again. "Not necessarily. Not if he arrived first. It's possible, isn't it? Python is a demon and his nature is more compatible with the pools. He can probably transport faster than us." Kim turned to the Cherubim, aware that he probably looked as angry as he sounded. "Did anyone else arrive here before us?"

The Cherubim stared at him vacantly. *"Of course, half-*

Jinn. There are many, many others who have arrived in this ancient place." She looked up and around at the bluish spheres ducking in and out of thousands of bones.

"You know what I'm talking about," Kim said, trying not to scream at her.

The Cherubim seemed to think. "*As I said, this place is outside of time. As I also said, my fate is unavoidable.*"

That was all he needed to hear.

"We have to get out of this place," Kim muttered heatedly.

"But did we find out what we came for?" Troy shot back.

Kim shook his head. "We're not going to get any more information than what I saw just now. We can talk about it later. At the moment, we *have* to get out of these catacombs. I suppose we'll head for Luz's surface."

Troy didn't seem ready to waste any more time. She turned with barely hidden disgust and after reaching the far wall began to scale the rocks so quickly she could have been sprinting. Kim ran after her to keep up, but something made him turn at the last second.

The Cherubim made no move to leave. Was she prepared to defend herself? There was little doubt she could with such intimidating size and teeth. Yet Kim couldn't shake his sense of danger. Maybe the shivers and foreboding he'd felt while still in Hell had more to do with whatever came next than the mysterious angel Troy had led them to visit.

Maybe entering Luz was going to be the real mistake. Kim thought again of Sophia walking some long hallway in the Westwood Academy uniform. She'd infiltrated the school once more. That meant Angela would probably be with her.

After what Raziel had shown him, Kim knew he had to speak with Angela, see her, clasp her tight. He was terrified for her.

"*Farewell, my final visitors,*" the angel said.

A strange mist began to fill the catacombs. The bluish spheres streaked through the air as if in a panic.

"Good-bye," Kim muttered.

And then he took his chance and sprinted, following his fears toward the exit Troy had undoubtedly found. It wasn't until they'd found two angel statues and passed between them, stumbling into a colder underground passage that Kim thought of looking at his hourglass pendant.

Somehow, almost all the grains had fallen to its bottom.

Nineteen

Angela felt riveted to the stone as Kim emerged from the mists of the catacombs they stood within. Her chest ached, and a painful fire shot through her. What could she say to him after leaving Hell under such horrible circumstances?

Her mind raced through all the terrible possibilities, lingering especially on how much she missed his touch, even his breath. Everything. His figure began to emerge more clearly. She could make out a long dark coat and the long hair near his neck.

She caught her breath.

At last the figure stepped into the bluish gleam of the souls lighting the darkness like fireflies.

It wasn't him. This was a different man wearing the long black coat of a novice—a priest in training. His hair was a deep brown and shorter than Kim's, and his eyes were also darker. He held a rosary in his left hand, and a faint azure aura outlined his body.

Angela froze. She instinctively moved to step backward but checked herself.

Juno stopped growling. She straightened and peered at the priest. "It's a human soul," she said to Angela.

So he was merely one of the numerous souls filling the catacombs. Angela balled her hands into fists. She knew there would be little time to act—he was coming closer—but something told her to not behave too rashly. A sour smell hit her now. Her stomach turned. A sense of danger swept over her, summoning a wave of nausea in its wake. Then the priest paused in front of her, staring straight into her eyes. The enchanting music around them was even more melodious.

Leave this place.

Angela focused harder. Those thoughts weren't her own. He was speaking to her in her mind.

Why? she demanded.

She wanted to explain it wasn't so simple. She and Juno had gone through a lot of trouble to find the angel supposedly living in this terrible place. Turning around and retracing their steps wasn't high on her list of priorities.

Because you are too late.

The priest pointed down at the pool of water beneath them. Angela hadn't looked at it since walking with Juno over the narrow rock bridge.

A pale shape could be seen at its bottom center. The corpse resembled a Hound but was pure white and absolutely immense. Its beautiful, well-shaped hands had curled in agony. Blood tainted the water around it, spreading like an inky cloud from its body. The angel's brilliant wings had been crushed. Angela couldn't look much longer. The being that was the sole reason she and Juno dared the canals now had the look of a winged mouse squeezed to death by a snake. She peered up at the stone bridges above them. What

Angela thought had been water dripping now was clearly blood. She fought another wave of nausea.

Someone had murdered Kheshmar, and her body had plummeted to the bottom of the pool.

Angela forced herself to speak. "When did this happen?" she asked the priest.

His face changed at her question. He didn't seem to understand.

Fear churned inside of her. She'd learned that Lucifel had been stealing human souls with the Vatican's permission. So why were so many sequestered beneath Luz? "Are you the souls that Lucifel took from Memorial Cemetery? Please answer me."

The priest shook his head. *No, we're different. We've been trapped here for centuries.*

"Why not leave now?"

His face became even graver. *The Devil will find us if we try to enter Luz . . . she will use us to destroy you . . . so . . . we cannot leave anymore. Please understand, time is different in this place. This is a point in existence that connects to every other Realm. It is Luz's firmest connection to the other worlds, and it existed before the city.*

But Angela didn't understand. How could this place exist before Luz? "Are you saying this place is like the Netherworld?" Because that had also been connected to Luz when it existed.

The priest held out his hand, as if pleading with her. *No. This place is deeper and yet also higher than the Realm of the Dead—it is what angels call an "outer darkness." A century ago, a few of my colleagues and I chose to come here to find the angel that had chosen to dwell in this timeless place. We shouldn't have been so proud and foolish. Now*

I can never return. Now I too am one of those swallowed by time. Because, you see, the Cherubim that lived here ate time. That is how all Cherubim exist. They feed off space and ether, not flesh and blood. They helped balance what remains of the universe. Then, some of them were taken by higher-ranking angels and turned into Thrones. This Cherubim was the only one of her kind to exist on Earth by her own choice. Her twin, Azrael, dwelled in the Netherworld. They once belonged to the Supernal Raziel before his death.

Now they belong to death itself.

Leave before it is too late. I stayed and spoke to the angel like too many before me. By the time we had finished talking to each other, too much time had passed on Earth and we could not return. The Cherubim then devoured what had been left of our life spans . . . now our bones are all that remains of us. But though she is gone, some of her aura remains, and time continues to move . . .

The implications of what he said punched Angela in the gut.

She'd sensed something odd about the twin angel statues marking the threshold of the Cherubim's domain. Now she knew that by crossing that invisible barrier, they'd crossed beyond time. There was no telling what Luz would be like when they returned. How much time had passed in this place while they stood here?

She glanced down in horror at the Cherubim's teeth glistening below the water. She tried to imagine the angel eating someone's time—and couldn't. She tried to fathom how any place could exist where a passing second equaled an hour elsewhere.

"All these bones . . ." she whispered.

. . . are the bones, the priest finished for her, *of every*

unfortunate who has wandered below Luz—or been thrown down here.

There were thousands. Men, women, and children. Too many to count.

"We have to go," Angela managed to say in a hoarse voice. Horror had destroyed her sense of purpose. The Cherubim was dead. They'd come all this way only for someone to beat them and arrive first. Who? Why? Angela stared at the Cherubim one last time, and a reflection seemed to cross the water. Within it, she saw the angel locked in a bloody struggle with a gigantic black and violet serpent.

Oh no, she thought. Angela's arms and legs shivered. *No . . . not Python. Please.*

"How do we get back to Luz? There's no way to go back to our time?" she frantically asked the priest.

That is why you must leave. You have a chance . . . the Cherubim is dead. It cannot forcibly steal your remaining time if it wishes. You are still alive . . .

Go!

"But where will we go?"

Back the way you came.

"Hurry," Angela said hoarsely to Juno. A sense of dread propelled her faster than she'd ever thought possible. Juno tried to call after her, but Angela didn't hear anything besides the song and her own heart slamming within the walls of her chest.

The souls were the source of the music. They chanted its sweet melody over and over, and Angela thought her brain would melt with it by the time she and Juno crossed over the threshold, and she stumbled past the angel statues and their uplifted lanterns. Angela skidded to a halt, nearly slipping on a half-thawed seam of ice in the floor.

Superficially, nothing had changed. The water churned and foamed at the shore. The boat they'd climbed out of back onto land waited, bobbing in the water.

Even so, Angela felt like her stomach had bottomed out.

"What's a good way out of here?" Angela turned to Juno.

Juno's ears flipped back into her hair. She sniffed the air and then listened. "This way," she said.

Angela followed her in a daze. What could have happened to Sophia? To Kim and Troy? To Nina, Fury, and Israfel? How much time could possibly have passed in those brief minutes they'd spent in the cavern?

"I should have never come here," Angela whispered to herself.

The answers she'd been searching for had eluded her in the end anyway. Or so it seemed at the moment. Angela had believed that her only chance at survival had been to enter the canals, far from people who wanted to kill her. But it appeared at least one of them had caught up with her already. Where was Python? The thought of him in Luz haunted her.

"We're going back to the surface," Angela said to Juno.

Juno didn't argue with her this time, but she didn't seem thrilled, either. Her ears flattened. "I don't think it's a good idea, but I understand why you want to return now," Juno said. The young Jinn paused and turned to look at Angela. Then they entered a long low tunnel that seemed to form part of Luz's sewers.

Rats chittered from holes in the walls, but the dampness was receding. They climbed higher in a strikingly short amount of time. At first, Angela had been too upset to note the path Juno led them on. Now she realized the air had grown colder again. Within the Cherubim's domain it had been so much warmer. Angela wrapped her arms around her chest, shivering. Her breath left her in frosty plumes.

She didn't even want to know how pathetic and disheveled she probably looked.

"Wait here," Juno said softly. She slunk ahead into the darkness and returned so speedily, Angela jumped with surprise. "There's something up here you should look at," the Jinn said breathlessly. Her eyes were like flashlights in the blackness.

Angela followed Juno until a square shape loomed before them. Its metal body gleamed beneath a strange shaft of light peeking through a grate in the ceiling.

"Is that . . ." Angela whispered to herself.

She approached the rusted body of a carriage car. She'd heard the Vatican had an underground system of transportation in Luz. By now it had been out of use for over a century, but they'd never bothered to dismantle the tracks or get rid of the old cars. Angela walked up to the carriage car and slid her hand against its ice-cold body. The paint had worn away long ago, and her fingers rubbed against a pockmarked surface.

The vehicle probably linked to another one in the darkness ahead of them, and after that yet another. She couldn't feel the tracks, but when Angela moved to the left her heel hit something hard sticking up from the ground. There they were.

The holes that used to be windows set in the carriage car's back stared at her like empty eye sockets.

Angela looked away quickly and then examined the strip of light in the ceiling again.

She and Juno must have been very close to the surface already.

"What do you think?" she said to Juno and pointed at the opening responsible for the light.

Juno's nails screeched across metal as she scrambled up the side of the car and stood on its roof, getting a better view. Her silhouette blended almost entirely into the shadows. She returned just as quickly.

"This is our best chance to leave," Juno whispered.

Angela noticed the Jinn's hushed tone. "Wait—what's wrong? Why are you talking like that?"

Juno folded her wings against her back. "I don't know. I can sense something is different, but . . . I'm not sure what." She licked her upper teeth nervously. "It might be best to speak quietly."

Angela took a deep breath. Her nerves felt frayed to threads. She had no idea what kind of Luz waited for them up there. Maybe too much time hadn't passed. They were all still in existence anyway. That meant the Realms hadn't collided yet like the angel in Hell had warned her. "Is that grate an opening into Luz?" Angela asked Juno.

"I would say so," Juno said. "Although it's hard to tell for certain."

"Why?"

"The light," the Jinn said with a cool hiss. Her wings shivered slightly. "It hurts my eyes."

That was odd. Luz had been wrapped in celestial darkness for so long, and Angela deeply doubted that a lantern of some kind would hurt Juno's eyes. Her insides began to tie into a fearful knot. Yet she also had to make a choice. "Let's go," she said.

Angela worked her way over to the metal car and began to slowly scale it to the roof, using pits and holes in the metal as footholds. Juno stayed where she sat, staring at their exit with an uncertain expression that didn't change the closer Angela came. Angela struggled a little more, and her hands recoiled at the contact of the icy metal. Her fingers had numbed over when she reached the roof. Yet her time spent in survival mode while in Hell had paid off and she was standing next to Juno quicker than she'd hoped. From her new vantage point, Angela could see the cracked and missing tiles set in the arched ceiling and the other carriage cars curving off into the dark distance of the rail track.

She looked up at the grate. It was more corroded than she had originally thought and there was a ledge beneath it. If Juno helped hoist her higher, Angela could definitely hunch on the ledge, and then kick or push the filigreed bars of the grate out and emerge onto the surface.

"Can you support my feet?" Angela said, remembering to whisper.

Juno nodded and her chalk-white hands held Angela's weight with surprising steadiness as Angela used them to launch herself toward the ledge. She barely caught it, almost losing her balance entirely. With adrenaline setting her heart to a gallop, she pressed against the cobblestones in the wall.

"All right, here goes nothing," Angela muttered.

She steeled herself and gave the grate a powerful kick. She winced and her leg ached like mad, but the already weak metal bent in the middle. Angela kicked harder, and then harder. She kicked so hard she had nearly given up from the pain when the grate exploded onto what must have been the street above them.

Angela squirmed out of the opening onto her hands and knees, her face almost dragging against the bricks set in the street. She smelled salt water—they must have been much closer to the ocean than she thought. This was probably one of Luz's lowest levels. Yet there was no sound of waves crashing against the supports far, far beneath them.

The air was shockingly cold, as if a million needles pierced her lungs.

Angela's teeth chattered as she surveyed her surroundings. She couldn't move. She was now face-to-face with the glassy sea.

She stood on a level of Luz with a street that wrapped around its farthest side like an enormous balcony. Behind her lay the grate and openings into a few small alleys layered with trash. Snow and ice hid the railing that could protect her from plummeting over the side into the sea. In front of her, the ocean glimmered like a silver plate spread in all directions, while the stars above reflected in the water with rainbow hues. But the light was what really took her breath away. A powerful glow had lightened the sky from black to a deep shade of marine blue. Angela whirled around, looking up past the towers and half-broken turrets of Luz.

The angelic city revolved menacingly in the sky, so close that Angela felt like she could reach out and touch it.

It was much, much closer than before. Enough to take up half of her view.

The silence suffocated her. She couldn't stop looking at the Realm where Raziel had met his death. It shimmered like a glorious galaxy, but all Angela could see were the feathers and blood that had filled her visions in the past.

Suddenly, voices echoed back to her. People were approaching.

Angela searched desperately for a place to hide. There was none. The only choice she had was to escape back into the grate, and the strangers were coming closer. Now she could make out long black robes. Voices shouted now—they saw her. She had so little time. But how could anyone know where she'd been and what opening she'd used to emerge again into the city?

Angela dashed back to the grate and began to slide inside. Too late.

Hands seized her. She struggled and screamed for Juno, but the voices were louder than hers. Something struck her hard on the head, her body slammed to the ground, and an image of Sophia and then Kim flashed before her eyes.

Had everything she'd suffered through and accomplished been for nothing?

With her last conscious thoughts, Angela knew she'd find out too soon.

Twenty

Angela awakened slowly.

She lay on a soft bed in a room that could have been lifted from the Emerald House she and Sophia used to share as a dormitory while in Westwood Academy. This was definitely another mansion owned by the Vatican officials who supervised the school. A large tapestry depicting angels with black-and-gold wings hung over the window to her right. Mahogany dressers took up the wall opposite and a flickering candelabra hung from the ceiling. Angela patted her legs and arms and realized she was still in the same stolen clothes she'd used to enter the canals.

Thank goodness, though, Sophia's pendant still rested against her chest.

Angela clutched it, swung her legs over the side of the bed, and slipped to the ground. Her shoes were gone, but at least now she wore warm knee-high socks.

She walked to the door and tested the brass knob. Locked.

Angela bit back a frown. She jiggled the knob harder and pounded on the heavy door with her fist. "Hello? Hello!"

Met with silence, she resigned herself to climbing back into bed. Exhaustion tugged at her again, and Angela's eyes started to close once more when she heard footsteps echo down a hallway outside.

Now the lock on her door turned and someone entered the room. Suddenly nervous, Angela chose to keep her eyes closed as the footfalls approached her bed. Weight pressed against the mattress by her side.

"Angela," a low and familiar voice whispered.

She couldn't believe what she was hearing.

Angela turned over slowly and opened her eyes to find Kim sitting on the edge of her bed. Like the days that seemed so long ago when they'd first met, he wore the long black coat of a Vatican novice and his hair had been cut shorter. His amber eyes glistened with the light of the candle he held in his hand. Angela was pretty certain this must be a dream. She blinked and rubbed her eyes, but he was still there.

"But how—" she began to say.

Kim cut off her words by drawing in close, pressing a warm hand against her cheek, and giving her a slow, sweet-tasting kiss. His lips slid soft and teasing against hers. She returned the kiss and he embraced her more, pressing her against his chest so that she could feel his heartbeat.

When he pulled away, Angela touched her lips. It was him. *This was real.*

She was just about to open her mouth again, when Kim stopped her.

He grabbed her wrist hard. "I've come to get you out of here. If I'm found out, it will be the end for us both. Don't say anything. Pretend that nothing is out of the ordinary."

"Why am I here?" Angela said. She took the clothes he now handed to her. It was her old Westwood Academy uniform. But instead of the boots she used to wear there were tights and a pair of black clogs. He must not have wanted anyone to see her telltale scars. Angela hastily jumped out of bed and started to undress.

Kim turned around, giving her privacy. "Do you know how much time has passed since we parted ways in Hell?"

His voice sounded anguished.

A piercing fear went through Angela's heart. Had days gone by since Angela walked in those catacombs beneath Luz? Perhaps—she could hardly dare to consider it—even weeks? But the Realms had already been on the verge of colliding. Angela tried to focus on Kim and ignore the terror working its way through her. Every passing second now felt like a breath she couldn't bear to take again until she knew.

They were all still alive, so that meant the end hadn't arrived yet. But they could be on the verge now, ready to tip into the Abyss at any moment.

Kim no longer waited for her to answer. "It's been a *month*. Since then the Vatican has been gathering all female blood heads in the city and sequestering them in mansions like this one. But it's all a ploy. Most of them are being killed. They're trying to find *you*, Angela. Your existence is common knowledge now and red-haired women are being killed one by one as a precaution. Their blood is being gathered in individual urns . . . for Lucifel."

Angela thought back to how the angel under Mikel's control said Lucifel now only needed Angela's blood to open Sophia.

An excruciating lump formed in her throat.

All these girls were dying for her sake. It was a systematic genocide, and all to find her special blood.

"But how did you get here?" she said, half tripping as she

pulled on her tights and shoved on her shoes. She touched his shoulder so that he turned around again.

"Troy and I used the Mirror Pool beneath Python's mansion, just like you did. Troy had struck on the idea to speak to the Cherubim hidden beneath Luz and encourage her to scry the pool and speak to Raziel. I wanted to find a way for you to open Sophia without the Glaive—or to find the last stanzas of the Angelus. They're the key to stopping Lucifel. It's what she is searching for, Angela, and it's the power hidden within the Book. But—" Kim looked angry. "In the end it was no help at all. Raziel showed me his death. He showed me the creature responsible. And he showed me you." Kim stroked Angela's face, his fingers lingering near her left eye. "But I also learned it's impossible to open Sophia without killing her. The only other option is to create a new ending to the Angelus, whatever that means."

"The Cherubim!" Angela gripped Kim's arms. "She's dead, Kim!"

His face drained of the rest of its color. "What!"

"Python killed it. But that was before I ever met it myself. When Sophia and I came to Luz, we were ambushed. Somehow the priests used a mirror connected to the pools to bring us back to Earth when they got an opportunity. We escaped into Memorial Cemetery and found Nina and Fury—"

"Nina's alive," Kim said breathlessly.

"Yes! She took me to see a woman named Gloriana who—" Angela paused. She longed to tell Kim that he wasn't alone in the world. That Gloriana was also half-Jinn. But something checked her tongue. Maybe it was the intense look in Kim's eyes, and the overwhelming sorrow in his voice. She felt that if she spoke at the wrong time, it might do more harm than good. "Gloriana knew how to reach the Cherubim by using the canals beneath Luz," Angela continued. "But by the time Juno and I reached the angel, she was dead. A soul trapped in that place explained that time flows differently where the Cherubim choose to dwell. I was afraid it was too late by the time she and I got back to the surface . . ."

"So Juno's alive too," Kim said. A grim look crossed his face. He looked both hurt and frightened.

Angela paused. "Didn't Troy tell you about her?"

"No," Kim whispered. He didn't look too pleased about it either. "Probably because Troy's trying to protect her from me. But I remember learning about her existence, and about how anxious the Sixth Clan was to shelter her back then. She's the former Jinn Queen's heir, after all. Her survival means a lot. Now that I'm still technically up for execution, my closeness to Juno would be a liability to her safety. But Troy didn't bargain on Juno pardoning me."

Angela felt the surprise all over her face. "When did she do that?"

"When we were still in Hell. You'd certainly forgotten her after a time, so Juno must not have dared to approach you. She gave me her iron crow's foot talisman to symbolize her forgiveness of my so-called crimes. But I didn't know that Juno herself had left it. All I knew was that it was a young Jinn with high rank who'd shown me an ounce of compassion. Later, when Troy spied the talisman, she confiscated it and started guarding it closely. Now, I can put all the pieces of the puzzle together. Now it all makes sense.

"Juno's forgiveness is something I thought foreign to the Jinn for so long. You have no idea, Angela, what her gesture ultimately means. Or maybe you do. You know Troy well enough by now to understand how difficult it is for their kind to overlook the past. Yet I can never thank Juno in person and likely never will. In fact, I've resigned myself to that already." Kim shook his head and sighed. Then he said slowly, "But enough about Juno and Troy. Do you know what's happened to Sophia since you returned to Luz?"

Angela sighed with him. Tears threatened to blur her vision, but she forced them away. "All I know is that she's in the city. Somewhere safe, I hope. I have to find her now . . ."

Angela trailed off. For the first time she noticed the necklace Kim wore. It had an hourglass pendant and all the red grains sat at its bottom. She flashed back to the hourglass in her vision that Lilith tried to stop her from touching. Angela took a step away from him. A cold anxiety tightened her chest.

"What's wrong?" Kim said quickly.

"Well—that necklace. Why are you wearing something like that? Wait . . . Sophia mentioned that you both went to Python to help return my memories. *Kim, what did you say to him? What happened?*" It was all coming back to Angela so fast, and the more it did, the more frightened she became.

Kim breathed hard. He rubbed his face with his hands. "Angela, I had no choice. Lilith was using you to rule over Hell. She was biding her time. I couldn't stand watching that, and the Book needed to be opened. You deserve more than I can give you, and the thought hurts me more every day. But now . . . I . . . ."

"What is it?" Angela whispered.

His expression broke her heart, it was so despairing. Angela forgot the danger she was in for the moment and cradled his face, kissing him softly again.

Kim seemed to savor the taste of her. Then he pulled back. "Angela. Right now the most important thing is getting you where you need to be next."

"No," she said. "Right now the most important thing is freeing whatever girls are trapped here and still alive. Then I can think of what to do next."

"Lucifel is searching for you," he said heatedly, sounding more desperate by the second.

"I'm not leaving without freeing those girls—and that's final," Angela said in her most dangerous tone.

Kim let go of her arms. "All right. If that's what you want, I understand how you must feel. But if anything happens to you, those girls won't just lose their lives, they'll lose their souls."

"I have to do what's right," Angela said. "Don't let your feelings for me blind you to who I really am, Kim."

"You have no idea who you really are."

"Do *you*?" Angela demanded, whirling on him.

Kim reluctantly lowered his gaze. "I don't know. What Raziel showed me was confusing. But I do know you look just like the creature that killed him. And that Sophia knows why. You're taking your frustrations out on me right now. But Sophia is the one who's been leading you on. Demand answers from her, Angela. Before it's too late."

Angela could only look at him, letting her mind work. The creature he was talking about was the Father. What, then, was Angela's connection to him?

"Like I said," Angela explained slowly. "I don't know where Sophia is anymore . . ."

"And you don't think that Troy or Nina will find her? She's here somewhere, Angela. I saw her. And she'll find you again, and if you're in the wrong place at the wrong time, even I won't be able to help you anymore. I've always wondered what my purpose was after mistakenly freeing Lucifel. Now I know it was to be by your side. Maybe you'll cast me off when it suits you again, but despite what you might think right now, I'm not trying to be selfish. I'm just trying to act with your best interests in mind. But you're free to act as you please. Only . . ."

Kim knelt down in front of her. He reached for Angela's hand and kissed it.

". . . I need you to know that I think of you constantly. No matter what happens, remember that I do in fact love you. And that if I ever say or do anything otherwise—it's not by choice."

Silence fell between them.

This was one of the few times Angela had heard anyone at all say that they loved her. Besides Kim, there had only been Sophia. And maybe . . . someone else. But her mind was foggy and when she thought back as far as she could, she came up empty-handed.

"Kim, is there something else you need to tell me?" she said, her voice cracking.

Kim opened his mouth as if to say something. Instead, he shuddered and clutched at his throat, sliding to his knees. "No," he said hoarsely, his eyes large with fear. "No. Nothing."

"Why are you talking like that?" Angela said. "What's wrong?"

Was someone stopping Kim from talking? Perhaps it was Python—it had to be!

Angela threw herself at Kim, embracing him. She ran her fingers through his ebony hair and buried her face in his neck.

"I'm so sorry," she whispered. "I'm so sorry. Kim, I love . . ."

She wanted to say she loved him too, yet something held Angela back as well. But she didn't have the excuse of a demon's hold on her soul. She was just afraid of somehow causing Kim more pain.

"I love you too," she finally said in the smallest voice.

Kim gripped her tightly.

An aura of incredible sadness surrounded him. He was like a defeated man—not at all the hard personality she'd first met in Luz. It was like a part of him had broken. Then wetness touched her cheek and she knew Kim was crying. His cries grew into deep sobs that shook Angela down to her soul, and there was nothing she could do except hold him in their lonely moment that, instead of moving time forward, made it pause as if for eternity.

They escaped into a long hall connected to a corridor outside of the room where Angela had been imprisoned. Whatever mansion she was in, it was absolutely huge. Black and white tiles checkered the hall's floor and mirrors gleamed from the walls at regular intervals. Stained-glass windows reached high up to a ceiling with stone angels perched on arches and columns. Large lamps hung from ledges jutting from the walls, and a strange bluish light emanated through their glass.

Angela stared at the lamps, comparing them to the light of the souls in the catacombs.

Her left eye burned, and she heard thousands of whispers assaulting her ears at once.

Kim continued to speak to her in hushed tones. They weren't the only people walking around. Angela broke from her trance.

She lowered her head as they passed a novice, then a priest, and then a group of students in heavy muffs who glared at her suspiciously. Kim often stopped to talk with one person or another. Thankfully, no one seemed to recognize him. Perhaps those few individuals who knew him had left Luz.

But everyone seemed to regard Angela with curiosity at the very least. Kim acted like Angela was in his custody, which was true to some extent.

They were halfway to the exit when a man in a dark suit stopped them. Angela peeked up at him. She recognized his face but couldn't quite place it.

"Taking her down to the lower levels of the building?" he said to Kim confidentially.

Kim nodded and murmured something Angela couldn't quite hear.

"Well, you wouldn't mind if I took a look at her myself, then? From the first instant I saw her, I thought to myself . . . I know that one. I'll just be a minute. How are you, dear?" the man quickly said to Angela before Kim could protest.

She kept her head down.

"They're all shy now," the man said, shaking his head. "Such a pity. I've been buying as many of them as I can. The young ones have been put up for auction. Hair like this will be such a rarity someday. I want to make an investment if we all get through whatever disaster comes next. There's no clear reason why they all have to die anyway."

Angela bit her lip. Hot rage boiled in her veins. Redheaded students were commodities now? *Things to be bought and sold?*

"Besides, you're far too lovely to expire at such a young age," the man said.

Angela bristled at his disgusting tone. She looked at Kim, who shook his head and mouthed the word *no*. This wasn't the time to insist on her dignity. Angela fought the urge to grab the man by the neck and throttle him.

"Look at me," the man said sharply. He grabbed Angela by the chin, forcing her to stare him right in the eyes.

He examined her face for a few moments. "No," he said sullenly. "You look much like a young blood head whose paintings I viewed shortly after she first came to the Academy. In fact, you could be her twin. But your eyes . . ."

He seemed unable to stare at her anymore. He relinquished his grip like she'd burned him.

"Well, good luck," he said, patting Kim on the shoulder. "I heard some of them give the bloodletters a hard time. This one looks a bit feisty if you ask me."

As he left, Angela lost her cool and nearly lunged at him before Kim grabbed her and held her back, giving her a poignant look.

"Bastard," Angela whispered.

"Luz is full of them now," Kim whispered back. "Especially now that Lucifel's influence has grown. Her cult is becoming more obvious than ever."

Angela was too angry to speak for a while. She smoothed down her black-and-red skirt and continued to walk by Kim's side. Very soon, she'd free most of those blood head students and then men like that monster would be sorry. "You mentioned that it's now a matter of either opening Sophia or creating new stanzas to the Angelus," Angela dared to murmur when the most recent group of people had passed them. "What is the Angelus, though? I've never heard it."

"Yes, you have," Kim replied just as softly. "It's the lullaby Sophia likes to sing."

Angela stopped in the middle of the hall. People side-stepped them and cast some irritated glances.

"What are you doing?" Kim hissed at her.

Angela wasn't listening. She thought of Sophia constantly evading Angela's questions about the meaning of the song. If the Angelus was the ultimate key to keeping the universe from disintegrating, it must have had a strong connection to the world, and creation.

That meant Sophia did too.

Angela recalled that moment when Sophia spoke of dying in childbirth. Instantly, her mind jumped to her nightmarish visions of being born to the stars and torn apart. She remembered someone singing to her.

And loving her.

Angela's heart raced. She felt on the verge of the truth. If she could just reach out and grasp it. Without thinking, she touched her left eye—the Grail. Whose eye was it really? Hers? Angela's eye before she was murdered, and her body torn to bits? But who would have done such a thing to her? If only—if only she could—

". . . Angela! Angela!"

Kim clasped her hand.

Angela gasped and looked deep into his eyes.

"Don't. Say. A word," he whispered in warning. He nodded his head and looked warily down the hall. Three angels marched toward them, side by side and in perfect unison. The other people in the building all stopped whatever they were doing and stared in wide-eyed terror.

The angels were of course taller than everyone and dazzlingly perfect. Their large heavily lined eyes scanned down to people's souls, and as they walked barefoot toward Angela she noticed the shimmering quality of their feet, as if they'd been powdered in glitter. The cuffs on their wing bones, though, were the same as the angel's who'd attacked her in Memorial Cemetery. As if they were of one mind, each angel zeroed in on Angela.

She stood still and felt very alone as they stopped a foot away and stared her down. One of the angels carried a thin crossbow at his back. The other wielded a crystal dagger at his hip. None of them looked kind or understanding. It was the angel boasting thick black hair and dark wings who stepped closer to her.

She gazed back at him fearlessly. He examined her openly, lingering with special interest on Angela's left eye.

Angela clenched her fists, trying to stop her arms and hands from shaking. She could hear Kim breathing behind her. His hand brushed her wrist, and it was obvious he wanted to hold her, to calm her or even protect her. But that would give everything away.

"What is your name?" the angel asked.

"Marie," Angela lied.

The angel seemed to sense she wasn't telling the truth. He stepped closer, his height and handsomeness even more intimidating. Israfel's presence oozed elegance and grace, and the sight of him had always made Angela hunger desperately for more. These angels, though, reflected a hardness in their expressions that spoke of Lucifel's influence. Now Angela noticed that one of them held something black and feathered by its wiry legs.

The angel thrust it in Angela's face.

Kim gasped softly behind her.

"Tell me, human," the angel said too quietly. "Does this creature look familiar to you?"

Angela stared at the bird. Its body hung unnaturally stiff and its wings refused to close. Its eyes held no fire at all, but she didn't sense it was dead. Though she was very sure it might be at any second.

A sensation of dread clamped down on her like a vise. Her eyes watered and the world blurred.

"This is a Vapor that we caught soaring around the

Academy last night. Interestingly, it arrived shortly before you were found climbing out of the canals beneath Luz. A strange detail and a strange coincidence, don't you agree?"

"It's not familiar to me," Angela croaked. But of course it was. Angela felt her knees weaken. Her breath threatened to vanish.

"That's interesting," the angel continued. "Because as we gazed into its soul, we clearly saw someone who looks exactly like you. Indeed, that's the reason we found you right now. The Vapor's soul is calling to you. It led us to this place."

Angela couldn't tear her gaze away from the crow. This had to be either Fury or Nina.

"You don't want to talk?" the angel said. He nodded at his companion with the crystal dagger.

The other angel pressed it to the crow's throat. Suddenly, the bird came to life, powerfully flapping its wings. The black-haired angel held on to its feet, but he gritted his teeth, obviously struggling.

Angela couldn't watch much longer. She could see the frustration in the angel's eyes. Finally, that frustration broke the surface as dangerously as she feared.

"Do away with the disgusting nuisance," the angel's other companion said. "It's trouble enough. We found what we were looking for—"

The dagger-wielding angel set his blade to the struggling bird again.

Angela broke away from Kim, grabbing for the crow. The angel with the dagger was still at work, and he slipped, fighting for a moment with Angela.

She shrieked as the blade cut across her arm and blue blood streamed down to her fingers. The crow exploded out of their grip. Now she saw the older, telltale rattiness of its feathers. It was Fury.

Escape while you can! Angela shouted to Fury mentally.

Fury screeched and flew for the doors at the far end of the hall. People screamed and some fell to the floor, covering their heads. The angel with the crossbow notched it and aimed at Fury, but Angela was just as quick.

Angela willed her blood into her hands, light washed over her, and she summoned most of the Glaive. Its wickedly curved blade absorbed the light in the room, throwing it back in an ethereal shade of blue. The souls trapped in their lanterns began to dance. Noise exploded around them, and song, just like in the catacombs.

Angela took down the angel with the crossbow first, ramming him hard in the back with the Glaive's haft.

He fell, and she turned on his companions. One lost a hand still clutching his dagger. Kim screamed for Angela as the black-haired angel grabbed for her.

She sliced half his wing off.

Blood splashed everywhere. The angel screamed in agony and slammed to the ground. Angela forced the Glaive to collapse and slipped on all the blood as she turned and ran with Kim. Dizziness swallowed her. She was still too weak to use the weapon to its full potential. Now they were vulnerable, and even though no one tried to stop them yet, Angela knew it was only a matter of time before they were caught.

But what choice did she have at the time? They were going to kill Fury.

I'm not worth more lives lost . . .

Angela clutched her bleeding wrist and ran for the double mahogany doors they'd used to enter the hall. They flew open, revealing an enormous group of priests, novices, Academy officials, and even a few angels, at the head of the throng.

Before Kim and Angela could take another step, the angels notched their bows and aimed arrows sparking with energy at her head.

A dead silence overcame everyone. Angela could only wonder: what might have happened if she'd allowed Fury to die? But she had no regrets. She refused to.

A sharp exchange of words passed between a few Vatican officials, including a man in a red robe and hat who Angela knew as Bishop Kline. They gestured in her direction. She looked at Kim as four priests walked toward them and tugged their hands behind their backs, cuffing them. Kim said nothing. His grave face could have been chiseled from marble. Was he, too, agonizing inside over their failed escape, their inability to save the other red-haired women now that they'd been caught?

Yet behind his eyes Angela saw what she undeniably felt: a fire that she'd be damned they could bleed out of her.

Twenty-one

Nina perched on an icy ledge below one of the Emerald House's gabled windows. She tapped furiously with her beak on the pane, praying Sophia would hear her and lift the sash. Snow lay heavily on the deserted streets, but angels were certainly patrolling the nearby turrets. Nina folded her wings and tried to wait patiently, the cold air biting her like fangs all the while.

Finally, the pane slid open.

Nina glided inside, maneuvering around Sophia. She landed in front of the warm glow of the fireplace and shook out her feathers, relishing the sensation of the velvet area rug beneath her frozen feet. The rest of the house sat in a gloomy darkness strewn with cobwebs. It was clear that no one had resided here since Sophia said she and Angela had entered Hell, and in that time the Academy had barricaded the mansion's doors for good.

That made it the perfect place for Nina, Sophia, and Fury to hide as they waited for some sign that Angela was safe and, they hoped, nearby. In the meantime, Sophia had tasked herself with taking in and protecting as many red-haired female students as possible. The bloodlettings in the Academy were an ill-kept secret by now all throughout Luz, but Sophia had been sure that as long as she, and Nina, and the others kept a low profile, none of the angels would suspect their presence for quite a while.

She'd been right so far. But their luck could run out at any time.

Now that Fury had been captured . . .

Nina shifted into her customary human shape, but she could only stare at Sophia and the more trustworthy members of the Vermilion Order gathered in the den. Her mouth opened and shut again. Why was it so hard to tell them what had happened? Was it because she felt like a failure?

If only she and Fury hadn't let their guard down at such a crucial moment. The good thing was that Nina had seen Angela. She was alive, thank God. But Angela was now also in the clutches of the Academy officials, and Fury had been captured by angels—a terrible turn of events that was sure to mean trouble for them all.

Nina could still feel one of the angel's arrows whistling by her, ruffling her feathers with its wind and dazzling her eyes with its light.

It was hard to believe it hadn't struck her right in the heart. The breathless chase afterward would have been enough to make it burst anyway if Nina hadn't managed to lose the angels in a tangle of leaning Academy towers.

Only now did she realize her chest hadn't lost a fraction of its terrified tightness.

She slid to her knees, suddenly feeling dizzy.

"Were you spotted?" a red-haired young man with glasses and a long coat said as he stepped forward.

He was just one of many more blood head students and Vatican novices sitting in the shadows. Some had claimed the velvet upholstered armchairs; a few took the mahogany dining chairs, or nestled on the brocade sofa; and then there were those who'd claimed the warmest spots at the foot of the fireplace. But Nina didn't see any of the female students they'd rescued so far. Perhaps they were still sleeping upstairs or recuperating from their horrible ordeal.

"Yes," Nina said softly, but her words felt so heavy. "I was spotted. And Fury was captured by angels."

Groans of dismay took over.

Sophia had followed Nina from the window and then seemed to disappear. She must have gone to the kitchen, because now she knelt down in front of Nina with a glass of water. Nina took it gratefully, savoring each drop. She squeezed her eyes shut and tried to stay sane as the next words left her mouth. "I also saw Angela."

Nina had been handing her glass back to Sophia.

Sophia gasped at the news. Her grip slipped and the glass smashed on the floor. Her eyes looked pitch-black in the flickering candlelight. "Don't tell me the bloodletters have her?" Sophia said. Her voice almost cracked with horror.

"They do," Nina managed to say.

Sophia's mouth tightened to a line. She stared into the golden fire, seeming to think. Questions flew at her from all directions, but Sophia said nothing, only turning back to everyone after a long while.

The noise died down. Every face turned to regard her.

None of them knew Sophia was the Book of Raziel. Even the novices had bought the story that Sophia was a Vapor like Nina and Fury, only more special. They knew she'd been a close familiar of Angela Mathers and that was all.

"We've reached the crucial moment," Sophia began. She looked at each face in turn. "Eventually we knew the angels would find us, though we hoped it would be at the world's end if it came down to it. Luckily, we've escaped notice until now. But mark my words, the angels will see into Fury's soul and be upon us soon. So we don't have much time."

"We can't just leave," a red-haired novice clasping a book in her hands said fearfully. "Where else will we go?"

"That's just it," Sophia said, turning to her. "We do have to leave. At least—some of us do." Her tone grew even more grave, and Nina felt her heart thrum and burn. "Angela is humanity's—the universe's—last hope for survival. If she dies, so do we all. So I'm going to ask some of you to come with Nina and me to rescue her—or to try. Of course, you might not return. Yet I won't judge anyone who chooses to stay behind. There are girls ranging in age here from five years old to eighteen and they need people to care for them while they heal."

Murmurs and whispers rippled through the people gathered in the room.

"I ask anyone willing to help us to come up here and stand with me by the fireplace."

Now everyone except one strawberry-blond novice with thick braids left their seats close to the fireplace. She stood and walked to Sophia's side, joining the male student with his thick glasses, two more female students, and a male novice who kept his gaze fixed on the floor, as if he'd found his fate there.

Sophia spoke in whispers to those who'd gathered near her. Then she turned back to everyone else again. "Thank you. I sincerely hope you feel in your heart that you made the choice you feel is best. Good luck, and pray for our success."

Nina walked over to join them and heard Sophia whisper to her little crowd, "Follow me . . ."

They trudged up the staircase nearby as a group.

Darkness overtook them. Nina slid her hand against the florid wallpaper that ran the length of the staircase up into the upper hall. Only one candle glowed in its sconce at the top of the stairs. Oddly, Sophia paused to blow it out.

A deep silence overtook everyone as they walked down the long hallway to a narrow door at the far end. Dust lay heavily everywhere. Their shoes tapped with uncomfortable loudness against the wooden floors.

Nina was last in line, but she swore she heard a heavy trotting sound behind her.

She turned in time to spot phosphorescent yellow eyes, a mane, and long bestial legs traveling within the shadows as if they were a living part of them. An echoing snort reached her, though no one else seemed to hear or notice. Nina paused for a moment and watched in dumbstruck amazement as the winged Kirin Angela had ridden out of Hell emerged into full view only to disappear into a pocket of black and empty space again, as if it had jumped from one dimension to another. If she hadn't been looking in the right direction, she might have missed the beast entirely. It was following their group, and Nina had the strong sense she spotted the creature only because she was a Vapor.

Nina folded her arms and shivered a little anyway, stopping with everyone else at the narrow door.

She looked back into the darkness again.

The Kirin's great eyes flashed once and disappeared.

"Before we enter this room," Sophia said to their group, "I want everyone to promise me that they will stay silent about what they're going to see. Please don't say a word, and let me and Nina do all the talking—otherwise you can be certain you might find yourself in real trouble."

Sophia's gaze met Nina's.

She set her petite hand on the knob and turned it with a nasty creaking noise.

The door seemed to swing open on its own. In reality, Sophia was pushing it with the edge of her slipper. She peeked inside, and then gestured for their little group to file in one by one. Nina noted, though, that Sophia was careful to be the first to actually step over the threshold.

To the more ordinary humans among them, the room was probably pitch-black. But Nina's new eyes could make out most of its hidden features. It was a spare bedroom with a thick queen-size bed, a set of wooden dressers, and heavy drapery that blocked out almost all the light from the angelic city on Luz's skyline. Nothing seemed unusual—until she noted the wiry shadow in the room's farthest, darkest corner. It moved slightly, revealing a single sickle-shaped wing. Yellow eyes like the Kirin's flashed from the darkness.

The male novice balked. He grabbed Nina because she happened to be standing closest to him, and his fingers felt like claws.

"A Jinn," he whispered.

The yellow eyes rested their gaze right upon him. He stiffened with terror.

"Then . . . you've found her," a voice hissed from the direction of the deep darkness, and the gaze attached to it left the novice and returned to Sophia.

"Yes," Sophia said tersely. "It's time to get Angela back."

Chilling laughter nailed them all to wherever they stood. "I've been waiting for this," Troy said, as she slunk nearer to their group. She licked her nails, as if relishing what they were about to do. Nina could make out the cold flash of Troy's teeth as she grinned. "Those angels laugh at death as they inflict it on others," Troy said.

Her voice held a dire prophecy.

"That's because they never met me."

PART THREE

Regret

Two Days until the Great Silence

*Demons equate love with foolishness, and thus
they are fools themselves.*

Twenty-two

◇ LUZ ～ THE ALTAR OF THE BLOODLETTERS ◇

Angela's journey to her execution began with nightmarish cold, escalated with the frenzy of a mob as she was paraded through the streets surrounding Westwood Academy, and ended only when she and Kim arrived at the great iron-clad doors of the institution that Luz's most-feared witch, Stephanie Walsh, had eventually called home.

They were at the edge of the highest sea cliff in Luz, and though the waves had died long ago to an eerie and glassy calm, dampness still seeped into the many-armed tower and oozed from every pore of its mortared stone and bricks. Its windows resembled blank eyes. Angela tried to imagine how many students had already lost their lives behind these unforgiving walls.

She looked up at the stars and noticed the silhouettes of angels perched like birds on the Luz Institution's turrets.

One or two of the angels rustled their wings and shifted position.

She and Kim looked at each other. They were close enough to whisper at least.

"So this is how it ends," he said bitterly. But Kim gritted his teeth, and a spark of his old mischief brightened his eyes. Maybe he had a plan.

"Not if I have anything to say about it," Angela muttered. "We'll find a way out of this."

Kim sighed and didn't reply this time. His expression dropped its confidence and took on a haunted aspect.

Most of the crowd around them had started to disperse. The bone-chilling cold chased away all but the staunchest individuals after a while. Angela's fingers and toes were already numb, though her captors had made sure she was warm enough to stay alive and for her blood to flow freely. Before she could say another word, rough hands took her by the shoulder and guided her up and into the forbidding building. Kim followed behind her, suddenly wordless and deadly again. Their footsteps met the stone with ominous clicks. Angela sniffed, recoiling at the stench of mildew.

Even if the women imprisoned here managed to survive the bloodletting, the cold and dampness were sure to kill them anyway.

Maybe I can at least get a glance at the other people . . . I want to engrave their faces in my mind. How dare these officials and administrators take their lives so easily . . . These are people, not objects—

"Faster, blood head," a gruff voice said in Angela's ear.

She turned to regard her newest tormentor, but met with a harsh shove up the next stairwell instead. Their group spilled out into a wet hallway lined with cells crosshatched by barred windows. Unlike Stephanie's portion of the institution, which had boasted some degree of civilization and whitewashing, this section of the building could have been constructed during the Middle Ages. Black crosses had been tacked above each cell, though very few of the blood heads trapped inside happened to be praying. Some clung to the barred windows available to them, staring at Angela with large forlorn eyes.

A deep shudder of outrage and anguish moved through every inch of her being.

She scanned the row of cells to her left as her captors pushed her toward one of the doors marked by a pitted brass lock.

A woman with thick, deep red hair watched Angela from her position on a worm-eaten wooden bench. A young red-haired girl clung to her voluminous skirt and had hidden her face deep in her mother's colorful shawl. It was Gloriana Cassel and her daughter, Tress.

Angela had almost forgotten about the feather Tress had given her. Thank God, Angela had remembered to hide it in a safe dry spot no matter what clothes she wore. It lay against the skin near her leg right now, safe and sound.

A nasty push sent Angela reeling into the cell. Kim followed shortly behind. He was a man with dark hair, but he was also obviously her accomplice and their murderers seemed to want them together for a reason. Angela couldn't help breathing a sigh of relief that they hadn't been separated, but something within her sounded a sharp warning anyway. She looked at Kim, trying to speak to him with her eyes, but he refused to meet her gaze.

Instead Kim immediately walked to a corner of the cell, where he crouched and sat with his head buried in his knees.

"So we meet again, Archon," Gloriana whispered the second the cell door slammed shut and the lock turned. "But our reunion will be brief. They've only put you here while they prepare the altar. This is the cell reserved for their next victims."

"How long have you been here?" Angela choked out.

Tress shifted in her mother's arms, and she turned slightly, revealing that she was in fact asleep. Dark circles ringed her young eyes.

"Two weeks," Gloriana said sadly. "I managed to keep myself and my daughter safe by bargaining and making myself useful to these monsters. But servants of the Devil are hard to please. Eventually, we were slated for removal to the towers here. By coincidence—or perhaps fate—we were moved to this cell only yesterday. And now you're here."

"I won't let them take you," Angela snapped.

Gloriana sighed and shook her head. "Unless you open the Book of Raziel, our deaths will be soon to come regardless."

Angela had nothing to say to that.

"But don't blame yourself," Gloriana added. "I know that if you could open the Book, you would. That much was clear after I spoke to you. And though I'm not sure what obstacles you are encountering—I'm firm in the belief that you will overcome them."

Angela couldn't say that her roadblock was her love for Sophia. So she lowered her head, and a tight pain tore through her chest and heart.

"The Cherubim below Luz . . ." Angela began hesitantly.

Gloriana straightened, and her face became even more serious. "You found her, then? Kheshmar?"

Angela nodded. She glanced at Kim, who still sat unresponsive. "Yes . . . we both did. We learned that if the Book of Raziel can't be opened, there is still a way to save everyone. I would need to create new stanzas and notes for a song called the Angelus . . ."

Angela trailed off as Gloriana shook her head.

"What?" Angela said. "What's wrong?"

"That's impossible," Gloriana continued. "The Angelus is the song of creation. Changing the notes would mean a new order to things—a—a revolution of some kind."

Angela felt her eyes widen. Sophia had mentioned a revolution once before, shortly before Lucifel nearly beat Angela to death while they were trapped in Hell. She'd mentioned it in connection to the dire prophecy that Angela's choices were long supposed by so many to be the ruin of humanity and of all living things. But—Sophia had added—perhaps it would not be so much a matter of ruin, as it would be a revolution of the established order to the universe.

"It doesn't matter," Angela said softly, though her mind had started to race. "I wouldn't even know how to go about doing such a thing."

"It wouldn't be possible here, certainly," Gloriana said. "To do that, you would have to approach the foot of God's throne, just like Raziel did."

That meant going to Heaven, the home of the angels. Angela didn't see how that was even remotely possible at this point.

"Kim," she ventured, looking right at him.

He and Gloriana were now in the same room, and Angela still didn't have it in herself to tell him the truth: that he wasn't the only half-Jinn in existence.

If only he would look at her, and somehow see everything for himself.

Kim still didn't answer her. His face remained on his knees and half hidden by his arms. Angela tiptoed closer to him and he didn't stir. She reached out and brushed the long bangs from his eyes. He was asleep, just like Tress.

"Who is he?" Gloriana said, studying Kim keenly. If she noticed anything unusual about him, she didn't seem about to mention it.

"He's . . . a friend," Angela said.

She turned to the barred window and its view of the dark and mirrorlike ocean. An eerie glow danced across the water as the angelic city shone down like a gigantic moon on Luz. Angela stared and stared at the placid expanse before her. She thought of the Mirror Pools and their salty taste. The ocean was said to taste salty, though she'd never actually swallowed a mouthful, even accidentally. Angela had never been allowed to play on the shore or mingle with other children when her parents were alive.

"Do you know what some religions have said about the ocean?" Gloriana said. She stood by Angela's side, sighing and gazing with her out over the star-speckled scene. "They say," Gloriana continued, "that water is the blood of the gods. Sometimes, they took it one step further and mentioned the earth as the corpse of a god."

Blood is salty too, Angela thought in spite of herself.

But Angela looked at her and said, "That sounds ridiculous."

"Does it?" Gloriana said. "Yet the ocean is the source of all life on Earth, and who knows where else water might be found throughout the universe, waiting to give life to creatures? Not too long ago, people stopped believing in angels and demons too. They called such notions superstitious nonsense. Now they know better. In the end, there is so little we know about why we exist and where we are going after death. I once asked an angel what happens to their kind at death. He told me that an angel's spirit returns to its original home. He had no answers for me beyond that. Honestly, I don't think he knew the truth either."

Angela pondered Gloriana's words. The more she stared into the stars, the more she seemed to see. Her left eye burned, and suddenly she felt like she had crossed space again to stand before the Father's bleeding corpse.

They looked so much alike. It could have been her, winged and dead, streaming endless rivers of blue blood.

"Do you ever get the feeling," Angela said, "that you've experienced something before? That perhaps you've made certain choices in—well, let's say in a past life, for instance—and now you've been given one more chance to set everything right?"

Gloriana's gaze burned into her. "No," she said after a while. "But if I did, the first thing I would ask myself is 'what went wrong?'"

Gloriana returned to her daughter and unfolded her shawl, laying it over Tress's sleeping form. Angela continued to stare out at the sea and the stars, entranced by their peacefulness until her eyes began to feel heavy. Then, with a final glance at Kim resting serenely in his corner, she allowed herself a moment to relax.

And that was when she fell asleep.

Morning soon arrived, and though Angela had awakened, she wondered if this was all just one long and endless nightmare. But the scene before her never changed.

For a second, she wished for the relative comfort of their jail cell all over again.

The altar to Lucifel used by the bloodletters had been hastily constructed from any available materials, but Angela shivered at the eerie likeness of the Supernal in the statue erected above the long stone table that might be Angela's deathbed. The proud angel's arms outstretched in an almost merciful gesture, yet her marble-smooth face and apathetic expression emphasized her otherworldly loveliness to devastating effect. Her great wings had been reconstructed with black crow feathers. Some kind of red stone had been used for her crimson irises.

The bloodletters had chosen the pinnacle of the Luz Institution's highest tower to commit their murders, and besides the cold altar, there was nothing but mortared stone composing the walls and ceiling, flickering candles set high in the eaves to stay out of the reach of any possible wind, and large windows without bars or glass of any kind.

This must have been a bell tower for the Institution at one time. That alone explained the openness of this room to the elements.

The two priests who'd dragged Angela and Kim from their cell now forced them to kneel on the unforgiving stone. Angela struggled, but the combined strength of two pairs of hands was enough to make her collapse. She skinned her left knee, wincing with the pain.

Footsteps approached them from across the room.

Father Schrader emerged from the shadows, dressed in a long woolen black coat. His eyes shone a terrifying shade of red.

Kim's face twisted with shock. His tone became furious. "It's *you*?" he spat indignantly.

"Unless you want things to move faster, you'll stay silent from this point on," Father Schrader said with dangerous softness. Yet his speech was uncharacteristically lilting. Angela recognized it: this was the angel Mikel's sweet musical voice. She'd possessed Father Schrader, as if confirming the worst of Nina's fears about him.

Visions of pain and sorrow raced through Angela's mind.

She'd suspected Mikel had betrayed them all, and she'd been correct. Yet the reality of it was infinitely more horrible with the angel here in front of them.

"Mikel," Angela whispered back. "Why?"

Mikel knelt in front of them. "You ask me 'why,' yet your eyes are judging me," she said with a hint of real pain in her voice.

Angela let out an ironic and pained laugh. Though she couldn't move, inwardly she recoiled from Mikel in disgust. "What choice do I have? You're a traitor. You told me when we first met that you wanted to help your father, Raziel, and here you are, doing the Devil's dirty work. Do you realize how much blood you have on your hands?"

"This would never have been necessary if Israfel hadn't conspired with my brother to imprison me. I . . . I could have found another way to end my life."

"End your life?" Angela shouted. "That's what this is all about? You want to commit suicide?"

"As if it makes me any different than you were once upon a time," Mikel shouted back. "As if you of all people can't understand what it is to be born in an unfair world. I didn't ask to be what I am—and I'm not like the other angels, Archon. I can't die like they can, whether from illness or accident. My mother alone—only Lucifel—can end my misery. If that means an end to this universe, so be it. But I'll be damned if you try to stop me like Zion and Israfel did."

"You are already damned," Angela hissed at her. "Do you hear yourself? How selfish can you be?"

This was unbelievable. Angela felt like any at second she'd

wake up from this nightmare, and yet she knew with equal conviction that it was never going to happen.

"It doesn't matter," Mikel shot back. "I don't need lectures from a human who caught the fancy of my dead father. You don't know the real truth. We—all of us—have been down this road before. It's time to put a stop to it once and for all. The world no longer needs to suffer for the sake of your redemption, Angela Mathers."

"I have no idea what the hell you're talking about," Angela snapped. "You're just as insane as Lucifel."

"Wrong," Mikel said, breathing into her face. "*You* are the real source of our misery. *You* are the very reason my father died. *You* are the reason the cycle of death refuses to end. Well—my mother is determined to put a stop to it, and I've decided to help her. My final wish to end my pathetic existence is only a bonus."

"There's no way I can be the cause of everyone's misery," Angela shouted. "How can you blame one person for everyone else's fates and circumstances?"

"You tell me," Mikel said. "You helped set the wheels in motion eons ago. You don't remember? How convenient. But that doesn't change the facts. Even if you're the only god this world has, it's better that it doesn't exist at all."

"That makes no sense!" Angela said. A painful quiet took hold of her. Once again, she was on the verge, ready to tip over into something that frightened her more than she ever thought possible.

"I'd be a fool to give you any more to work with," Mikel said. "It's enough for you to know that at least these other girls won't have to bleed to death now that we have the blood necessary to open the Book."

Mikel stepped away from them, gesturing for the priests

to come closer. They grabbed Angela by the shoulders and dragged her toward the stone table. She struggled violently while Kim remained eerily still and silent. His gaze had riveted on Mikel and a frankly contemptuous smirk touched his lips.

"And you, half-breed," Mikel said too sweetly to him. "You should be happy I'm allowing you to stay by the Archon's side in Her final moments."

A priest with long and tangled dark hair quickly set a knife to Kim's neck.

"Yes, I should thank you, Mikel," Kim said to her gently. "This was an entertaining game to play, after all. But I think there's another hand that has you in checkmate."

Mikel—though residing in Father Schrader's body—paused, with the look of a frightened child on her face. She glanced at the drained hourglass pendant resting near Kim's chest.

Suddenly, Angela could barely see. Her head slammed against the table and stars pinpricked her vision. Hands fought with her as more hands gripped her ankles. Angela kicked and squirmed as her captors tried to wrap ropes around her limbs.

A deathly hissing sound echoed through the air.

Everyone froze. Hands lifted from Angela's body. She lay on the table for a second, breathing hard. The hissing sound continued to echo, and a chill shuddered through her.

A creaking, crumbling sound took over. Stones now tumbled from the ceiling and clattered onto the floor. Angela shot up onto her elbows, and the ropes wrapped around her waist and wrists slid to the rock. The priests who'd been hard at work tying her down stared at an enormous shadow circling the round chamber outside. It resembled living smoke, but the more Angela focused, the more it condensed into a solid mass of muscle and glittering black and violet scales. A gigantic serpent was busy encircling the tower. It hissed again, sending a fiery dart of fear right through her.

Two of the priests tripped over metal urns at the foot of the table in their effort to get away. Sluices ran from the table to their dull iron insides, probably the most efficient means they had right now to collect Angela's blood.

The tower groaned, as if in pain. More stones dropped and smashed against the floor.

The priests ran for the doors that were the only safe exit available.

Instantly, the snake's coils smashed through the far wall. Rocks sprayed everywhere. Angela screamed and ducked, using her arms to protect her head and face. She rolled and found herself close to Kim. The eerie smile was still on his face, but then he saw Angela and he shook his head, as if clearing it. He'd been in a trance.

He turned and glanced around in horror. The tower was now close to collapsing.

Angela looked at the exit. It was open, but the priests had been crushed to death like mice pressed in a vise. She clapped a hand over her mouth, trying to contain her nausea. Mikel remained in Father Schrader's body, staring defiantly at a gigantic snake's head that slipped through an open window and swayed dangerously above her.

Python had arrived in his true form as a feathered serpent. The plumes on his head fluttered majestically and he yawned, displaying his enormous teeth.

"What are you doing here?" Mikel shouted at him.

I've merely come to collect what belongs to me, Python said. His voice shivered through the walls and floor that remained. *It's just unfortunate you happen to be standing in the way. So please step aside. I would hate to see your little mortal worshippers suffer any more casualties.*

"You have no claim on anyone here, serpent."

On the contrary, I happen to have the only valid claim left. Let's face it, you're not exactly in a position to argue. I wouldn't have traveled out of Hell, biding my time, if it weren't for a very good reason, little chick. Taking control of Luz is a bonus on its own. I think it's high time for you and the other angels to soar back home for now.

As if to emphasize the point, Python coughed up two mangled, severed wings. Mikel jumped back as they landed at her feet in bloody lumps. She looked up at him with a nasty expression.

"Why is Python doing this?" Angela asked Kim.

Kim shook his head, and then he grabbed his pendant. "He's come to claim my soul," he whispered. "And God knows what else . . ."

"What do you mean he's here to claim your soul—"

Kim clasped Angela's face. "Because I sold it for your sake."

"*That was the deal you made with Python? Are you insane?* No, that can't be—" Angela felt herself shaking.

"It is. It's true."

"*Kim!*" she screamed at him.

"I won't let him hurt you, Angela. If he tries to make me harm you in any way, I—I'll—"

But how in the world could you stop Python from doing anything? Angela wanted to scream back at him. But she only stared at him in horror, suddenly aware that Mikel and Python were still talking.

"I'll make sure Lucifel sends an entire army after you, snake," Mikel was saying to him.

Python laughed.

Now Mikel turned away. *Thud*. With that sickening sound, Father Schrader's body dropped to the cold hard floor.

Angela broke away from Kim and ran over to Father Schrader. She shoved back one of his long black sleeves, trying to feel for a pulse. There it was. Thank God, he was alive. But for how long?

Well, now that we're alone, we can get down to business, Python whispered. His serpentine body condensed amid a blinding violet smoke. When it cleared, he stood in his more human-looking demonic form, gazing curiously at Angela with his intense orange eyes. "Now if you'd be so kind as to get back on that altar," he said to her, gesturing impatiently at the stone table and the urns.

"Over my dead body," Angela muttered.

Python smirked. "Yes, that is entirely the point." He looked to his left.

Two angels had landed outside the tower. They notched their bows, aiming for Python's head.

He flicked his wrist and a wave of crackling red energy blasted toward them. They opened their wings and soared out of reach, becoming silhouettes amid a deep night sky, their forms only visible far over the ocean.

"Something tells me those sparrows will be back again before long," Python muttered. "So come now. I have more to do today besides bleeding you to death, Archon."

"So sorry," Angela said, gritting her teeth, "but I enjoy making things difficult for you."

"Fair enough," Python said. He winked at her. "I suppose I deserve your contempt by now." He folded his arms, wandering dangerously close to her. "I must say, you've exceeded all my expectations, Angela. It was my fault to think I had you cornered in Hell. I should have known it wouldn't be so easy to use you. This was one instance where my mother—much as I hate to admit it—had a clear advantage." His eyes narrowed. "And you have no idea how much it cost me to escape her and come here. I doubt I can ever return, so I might as well settle down on Earth for a little while. Until the Book of Raziel is opened anyway. Then—I dare say I'll aim a bit higher. It's been a long time since I walked the crystal pathways of Malakhim."

"Lucifel wouldn't let you get that far," Angela said breathlessly. "How stupid do you think she is? I guarantee she'll kill you the moment you enter Heaven."

Python smiled. "Oh, you should have more faith in me than that by now. I'll make sure the Book is opened first, remember? And at that moment, I'll have much more power than Lucifel. She'll be nothing then but a toy dog snapping at my heels."

"First you need the Book," Angela said. She allowed a note of triumph in her voice. "And I don't see Sophia, so—"

"But you see, the Book will always return to you as long as you're alive, Angela. That's the way of things. She found you first, I'm sure. And she is about to find you again. In fact, she'll do anything to reunite with you. You're her child, after all."

Angela felt her soul bottom out.

"No, I'm not," she said weakly. Her breath came in shallow gasps. "That's impossible . . ."

"Really?" Python arched an eyebrow. "You don't know the truth? Oh, that's right. You never did get a chance to speak to the Cherubim. I made certain of that. How disappointing for you, but it looks like I have the upper hand right now, Archon. Perhaps if you play nice, I'll whisper the truth in your ears before you die. You're likely to find it as fascinating as I did." Python paused and looked across the half-destroyed room to where the staircase opened onto a landing. "Well, speak of the devil . . ."

Angela whipped her head around. Sophia stood there, all alone, staring at Python like he'd already drained Angela of all her blood.

"Sophia?" Angela croaked painfully. "But—but how did you—"

Sophia glanced at her, her face sapped of every last ounce of color. She turned back to Python. "How dare you, *you wicked serpent*," she shouted at him, her voice resounding like thunder.

Python smiled at Angela. "See," he said sweetly. "Just like I said—she'll always find you, Angela."

"What are you doing here?" Angela shrieked.

She didn't know what to feel. Of course, Angela was beyond ecstatic that Sophia was safe. But why in the world had she endangered herself by trying to rescue Angela? And—worst of all—why had Sophia been keeping secrets from her that Angela now had to learn from a demon's lips?

Sophia balked at Angela's tone. "I came to help you," she said.

"*Run!*" Angela screamed back at her. "*Go!*" Now she felt hot tears running down her face.

But Sophia didn't budge. She gazed steadily at Python, her head held high.

"Well," Python said. "Shall I enlighten the Archon about things? I'm sure She'd much prefer hearing the truth from you. It's just a pity it's under these circumstances, isn't it? Imagine how nice everything would have been if you'd been honest with Her from the start."

Sophia clasped the lifeless pendant at her chest. "Angela . . ."

"Tell her," Python whispered. A wicked gleam lit his reptilian eyes. "Come on now. This is just too entertaining to pass up."

Sophia shot him a murderous glare but regarded Angela again, walking over to her. Angela still knelt by Father Schrader. She was vaguely aware of Kim watching them, yet his attention still seemed somewhere else, as if he'd focused on a point far beyond whatever lay in front of him.

"What is the truth?" Angela whispered to Sophia, and she felt a million needles of pain drive through her heart.

Sophia knelt in front of her. She didn't say anything at first. And then she reached up to Angela's face and stroked her cheek.

"Python said you're my mother," Angela said. "But that doesn't make sense—"

But at that very second, she thought of her terrible visions where she'd been born to the stars.

"And yet," Sophia said, her voice achingly proud but still overwhelmed by sorrow, "it's the truth."

Twenty-three

"It's not possible for you to be my mother," Angela said. She could barely speak. "I had a mother—Erianna. And a father—Marcus. I had a brother—"

"You *did*," Sophia said softly. "But only because Raziel made it so. You're human *now*, Angela, but once upon a time you were my child. Your soul is still mine. It isn't human or angelic. It is beyond all those things because you are above them. Remember, I died in childbirth . . ."

"Because of me?" Angela said. Dizziness gripped her. She struggled to hold herself upright. "No, no, that's ridiculous . . ."

"I brought you to this universe," Sophia said, clasping Angela's hands. "And it was my fault you've become what you are now. I am—"

"A goddess," Python said, his eyes blazing as he smiled.

Sophia glared at him again. "I died, and my true body fell into the Abyss. But bits of my flesh became matter, and my blood became the water that brings life and reflects all things."

"Enough," Angela muttered. She clenched her fists and ripped away from Sophia. She thought of the Mirror Pools, and considered how ancient they were, and how they tasted salty, like blood. The ocean on Earth tasted like blood. Sophia's blood. Angela was talking to a replica of the real Sophia. A memory made by Raziel using what remained of her corpse. Now she could put all the pieces together, and she hated it. "Enough!" Angela screamed. "*ENOUGH!*"

She pushed Sophia aside and pointed at Python. "You," Angela hissed between her teeth. "Your game is over, *snake*."

"And that's it?" Python said, regarding her with surprise. "You don't want to know why you're standing here? There isn't a speck of consciousness in you that wants to know why that green eye sits so neatly in your head? Or why you look like the Father himself? It's now all about punishing me? Interesting."

He laughed, and the cruel sound drove Angela mad.

"It no longer matters," Angela screamed. "My past has no bearing on what's happening right now—"

"Oh, but it does," Python suddenly hissed back. He bared his teeth. "But if you want to remain ignorant about why I'm ready to bleed you to death, *so be it*." He gestured at Kim. "Get up, boy. It's your time to shine again."

Kim grabbed for the floor, but Python's gesture jerked him roughly to his knees. Slowly, Kim stood, clasping his hands over his knees and breathing hard. Tears dripped from his face to the stone.

"Now," Python began. "Your first order of business is to bleed your girlfriend dry."

"Not on your life," Kim seethed, glaring at Python through a screen of ratty black bangs.

"How right you are. It's *your life* I'm betting on," Python said. He curled his fingers as if tugging Kim forward. "You remember the deal, half-breed. Once that last grain of sand touched the bottom of the hourglass, your time was through." Python snapped his fingers, and the large hourglass appeared in his right hand, empty at the top and blood red at the bottom. Python tossed it at Kim, and the hourglass exploded in a burst of brilliant light. "And that time—from what I can see—is officially over."

Kim struggled, but faint strings of light seemed to pinch through his clothes. He screamed as the strings cut into his skin.

"Look," Sophia gasped by Angela's side again. "If you watch carefully you can see them!"

"But if I cut them, will he die?" Angela said heatedly.

Sophia seemed to think. Her face became dark. "Most likely. Wait a moment—" Sophia whispered, holding Angela back. But her hands shook just as much.

"I don't understand the resistance you're putting up," Python said to Kim. "Is this about love, boy? All right, fine . . ." Python relaxed his hands. "I do have a heart, whether you wish to believe it or not."

Kim sank to his knees, breathing painfully. He grabbed at his bleeding arms.

"I'll let you choose," the demon said too kindly. "Do what I say—or die."

"And what would I get for murdering Angela?" Kim muttered. "An eternity of slavery by your side?"

"Far from it," Python said. "I plan on ruling like an emperor once everything is over. My servants will prosper, and you can take anything you desire, enjoy all that you wish."

"Except the one thing I want most," Kim ended for him.

Python's mouth set to a solid line.

Kim lifted his head wearily and looked at Angela. The same haunted expression crossed over his face as it had in the Academy and during their time in the cell. She opened her mouth to say something, though she really had no idea what to say. If Kim killed her, all was lost. If he didn't, he would die—and Angela would lose him forever. The one person besides Sophia who understood her inside and out would be gone.

"I . . ." Kim said.

Python folded his arms, waiting. "Yes?" he snapped.

"I . . ." Kim closed his eyes, seemingly unable to look at Angela anymore. "I refuse."

The words fell like drops of death and poison onto Angela's heart. Everything froze, and she stopped breathing, and something within her screamed. She expected the world to end and shatter like a glass ball dropped over a ravine, yet what happened next felt just as terrible.

"All right," Python said, shrugging. He made a tugging motion with his hand.

In that split second, a terrible *snap* rang through every inch of Angela's body, soul, and brain.

Kim collapsed to the ground with his neck bent unnaturally.

Sophia screamed his name and then covered her mouth. Angela stared at Kim wide-eyed. Disbelief riveted her to the spot.

He couldn't be dead. He couldn't be. Yet it was obvious Kim wasn't breathing.

"It looks like time's up for you as well, Archon," Python said. He sauntered slowly down to meet her.

Angela still couldn't stop staring at Kim. Something black

and awful welled up inside of her. The world hazed over. It was like all her senses had ceased to function.

"This little play is now running too long for my taste," Python continued.

Sophia shot in front of Angela. "Don't you dare come a step closer to her—"

Python waved his hand and a powerful bolt of purple lightning hit Sophia and thrust her halfway across the room. She shrieked and slammed against the floor.

Angela wasn't aware she'd started edging closer to one of the enormous openings in the walls until she was only a few feet away. All the while, Python came closer and closer. But Angela saw only Kim, dead and pale and lost to her forever.

"Where do you think you're going, dear?" Python said. "Ready to jump off a cliff to reunite with your love? Maybe you and Lucifel aren't so different. Although she jumped off the cliff called sanity long before you."

Angela froze. She turned, and the glassy ocean seemed to beckon far below.

In her mind, she'd already summoned the Glaive and cut Python's head clean off. In reality, summoning the Glaive would leave her too weak to defend herself against anyone else. It would be even more foolish than usual, because all Angela would have to do is falter by a second, giving Python a chance to use the weapon against Sophia. The only thing she could do now was get far from the demon's grasp. But there was nowhere to go—except down.

Sophia was already running for Angela, but it was too late. They both knew what had to happen next.

Angela gave her one last lingering look—and jumped out of the tall window.

Python's scream of rage followed her all the way down.

Angela clutched the pendant Sophia had given her, squeezing her eyes shut and praying for the best. It was a long way to fall. She knew the ocean waited for her like a glass plate ready to be smashed. The pendant felt shockingly warm, Angela's left eye burned like mad, and then it was all over that quickly.

The last thing Angela saw were two angels with enormous wings swerving away from her just as she plunged into the unforgiving water.

Light exploded around her. The same whispering voices that had beckoned her through the Mirror Pool to Luz echoed in her ears. She couldn't breathe. She couldn't feel anything but the heart-stopping cold.

And soon after, she no longer felt, heard, or saw anything at all.

Twenty-four

Sophia dashed to the edge of the window ledge, roughly shoving Python out of her way. Light gleamed up at her, and then the waves Angela's splash had caused stilled. It was as though Angela had been no more than a pebble plummeting into the sea.

A larger group of angels now patrolled the horizon. Word of Python's presence must have been spreading fast. Even though Sophia knew she probably sounded insane, she started laughing anyway. *Angela was alive.* The ocean was one giant Mirror Pool, and Angela had unwittingly used it to travel somewhere else.

She must have had an object with her that still connected her to Hell—or Heaven.

But what?

Python gritted his teeth. Rage emanated from his body like smoke. "You irritating doll," he hissed, striking Sophia across the face.

She took the blow and glared at him. "So," she said. "You dare to strike a goddess, as you so ignorantly called me?"

"A goddess? No, I do stand corrected. You're more of a demon than I ever was," Python snarled. "Tell me now, where has the Archon gone?" he said, with each word more clipped and awful than the last.

He began to approach her again.

Sophia stepped backward, trying to put distance between them. His face was more dangerous-looking than ever. As if slapping her had given him even more courage.

"The Earth's ocean is made of my blood," Sophia said. "I had no idea Angela could use it like she did. But she *is* special. That's the whole point. It's why Lucifel fears her. It's why you wanted her blood and her power. You know her real nature, and I won't bother asking you how you've come across it."

Python paused briefly and crossed his arms, and though Sophia could see him as nothing more than a petulant child, she still didn't expect the next few words to leave his mouth. "Haven't you caused enough suffering?" he said softly. Then he began to stride toward her again, not even bothering to hide the murderous gleam in his eyes.

He couldn't kill her. They both knew that. But it wouldn't help Angela right now for Sophia to be torn into a hundred pieces either.

"If my actions have caused anyone to suffer, it's for the same reason your mother, Lilith, puts up with your existence, Python. Because you're her child. A mother's affection never changes. If I'd given up on Angela long ago, you wouldn't even be standing here. Now step away from me, before it's too late."

"You know so little about my mother," Python whispered dangerously. And he didn't stop moving.

"What I do know," Sophia shouted back, "is that my

hopes in Angela have been justified. Now this universe can continue as it should in a new and more peaceful direction, and you're too arrogant to realize that you're still helping Lucifel halt the process. *Now stop where you are, Python. This is my last warning. And that's a mercy infinitely more than you deserve considering all the evils you've caused. But you are all children of mine in a way . . .*"

Python halted right in front of her, and his whispers were low as hisses. "What makes you think this cycle of time is so different? What good reason can you give me for not grasping the reins of power myself?"

Sophia stared deep into his eyes. A shadow had settled around them both, and a presence. "Because this time, my prayers have finally been answered and Angela exists. Isn't it true that after a million cycles of time that one thing will change, and then another? One fluctuation can set destiny on another course entirely. This is the course I plan to see through to the absolute end. The very one that began when the Supernals came into existence, born from what remained of Angela's body the last time she failed to stop her twin from murdering her. The one that Raziel perpetuated when he found my corpse and Angela's soul. The one that Lucifel fears, because she sees Angela as a Ruin who can never die, and this existence as a mistake."

Python remained fixated on her, and Sophia wouldn't allow herself another moment where he'd have a chance to turn away. She had warned him, and he hadn't listened, and his face suggested that he wouldn't back down. As she spoke, galaxies reflected in his widening eyes. Stars erupted to life and died. The universe exploded into being and returned to nothingness again. Each and every time, something changed.

Python bared his teeth, revealing snake's fangs. His eyes

flashed. His handsome face contorted as he opened his jaws, as if to strike and force venom into her veins. "*What are you?*" he hissed.

Around her, she felt air waft from two great leathery wings.

Sophia felt her entire self burning and blazing. "You're about to find out."

The winged Kirin that had been circling them all the while burst from the ether where it had been hiding, rearing up over Python with its paws flailing.

He gazed up at it in shock. An expression of pure incredulous wrath touched every feature of his face.

And in that second, its great horn pierced right through his chest.

Python gasped, and blood bubbled up his throat as he grasped the horn. He stared at Sophia, and then the Kirin flung its head to the side, pitching him right into the wall. Rocks clattered to the floor with him and his body slumped. He tried to speak, but didn't seem capable of more than a croak.

Sophia gripped the Kirin, and as it lowered to the ground, set herself on its back between its enormous wings.

They flapped powerfully, scattering rocks beneath them in every direction.

If she wasn't quick, she would lose her chance to escape. Sophia's sole hope rested on the possibility that Nina, Troy, and the others had infiltrated the tower.

She glanced one last time at Python and set the Kirin into a gallop, leading them straight to the window.

Then she and the powerful beast soared right out into the deep dark sky.

Twenty-five

Sophia lied to me . . .

Angela still couldn't hear, or see, or even speak, but her mind hadn't stopped working since the moment it flickered to life after such shocking cold and darkness.

No . . . worse, Sophia didn't trust me enough to tell me the entire truth about our relationship from the beginning.

Angela felt herself struggling to awaken, but her eyes remained sealed shut. It felt like heavy stones weighed her eyelids down.

WAKE UP.

Angela jerked upright, gasping for breath and clutching her arms to her chest.

She felt the rough fabric of the Academy clothes she'd been wearing, and she patted her hands down to the skirt. Icy cold still worked its way through her, but Angela wasn't soaked at all anymore. How long had she been asleep? What was happening right now? It was so bright, she still couldn't see. Her eyes throbbed painfully, and her left eye also burned more than ever. She clapped a hand over it, trying to suck in the pain.

After another minute, she shifted onto her elbows, and a jangling noise erupted from the pocket of her skirt. Angela knelt and rubbed at her eyes again. They still hurt, but now she could probably see what was in her pocket. She reached inside, grasping an icy metal chain.

Angela lifted it in front of her face. It was Kim's necklace, complete with the filigreed hourglass pendant.

Strangely, the grains were now at the top again, filtering slowly to the hourglass's bottom.

Nausea overtook her. Kim was dead, and Angela's last moments with him had been far from ideal. Memories of their first kiss overtook her, and once again, she felt his warm lips and tasted their sweetness. Once more, she saw the hardness and coldness of his demeanor grow into warmth and protectiveness. Like her, Kim had built walls. Was this how he'd been repaid for sacrificing so much for her sake?

Hot tears slipped down Angela's cheeks. She swallowed hard and tried to calm down. Her entire body shook like a leaf anyway.

He's gone? I'll never accept that.

Angela studied the intricate hourglass. She couldn't remember how it had ended up in her pocket. She and Kim had been side by side at one point. Perhaps he'd slipped it into her skirt pocket while Angela was distracted.

Now his haunted face and silence made sense. Kim's anguished tears while in the mansion where he'd rescued her tore Angela apart all over again.

Kim had known he was going to die.

Maybe I'm not alive either right now. I don't know where

I am, after all. It's so quiet here. But I wonder . . . why is the hourglass working again? Does that mean anything?

Angela stared at the red grains one last time with a painful and illogical hope swelling her heart, and then she slipped Kim's necklace back into her pocket.

She glanced around. Her tear-blurred eyes had adjusted to the powerful light at last. She was in a wide-open space flanked by crystalline pillars that reached so high, there seemed to be no ceiling. It was actually darker than she'd realized, but still far brighter than Hell or Luz. She could have been surrounded by a garden of rainbow jewels. Space appeared through the gaps between the pillars, and the galaxies and stars shone so powerfully that Angela realized *they* were the reason her eyes hurt.

A low humming noise pervaded everything. It had been so subtle, she didn't even notice it after awakening.

But now Angela could make out a faint melody.

The pillars and portions of ceiling and wall she could see had been carved top to bottom in strange symbols that looked like constellation patterns. Those also glowed with a soft bluish light. Yet there was no Mirror Pool beside her.

So how had she ended up here—wherever "here" was?

A sound of murmurs and voices reached her, and she turned around. Three figures approached one another from opposite directions. Wings took shape before her and then familiar faces and forms. It was Raziel and Lucifel—*and Sophia*. Raziel wore his jewel-studded blue coat, and the four blood-red wings extending from his back looked more majestic than ever. Lucifel appeared spartan compared to her sibling. Her gray coat nearly blended with her smoke-colored wings and hair, and a thin coronet on her brow bore a single round green jewel. A strange emptiness hollowed out her already chalky complexion.

Sophia was in a scarlet dress decked with ribbons. She looked exactly like the Sophia Angela had always known, but her steps were more tentative, and her expression more uncertain. The second her gaze met the jewel on Lucifel's brow, she blanched frightfully.

Wait—they were coming closer.

What is this? I've seen Raziel's memories, but that was different. I still felt separate from all that I witnessed. But this is . . . the same as reality.

None of them seemed to see Angela. Angela smarted in pain, slapping a hand over her eye. She took deep breaths and waited for the angels and Sophia to come closer.

Soon, they were only a few feet away. Angela tried to look away from Lucifel's commanding presence, but it was impossible. Her lined and flashing red eyes demanded attention with every darting glance.

Sophia looked like a porcelain doll at Raziel's side.

He was the first to speak. "Why are you doing this?" he murmured to Lucifel. "Why this war? Is there nothing I can do to stop you from crusading against Israfel, against the Father—"

Lucifel held up her hand, signaling for him to stop. "I'm doing it, because I can win," Lucifel said.

"How? The angels working to see you on the Throne aren't numerous enough."

"That's not the victory I'm referring to," Lucifel retorted even more softly.

Raziel appeared to notice the deadly coldness all over her face. Now he also saw the gem on her brow. But it was no ordinary stone. It was unmistakably the Grail—the Eye that was now Angela's eye. Sophia hadn't taken her gaze off it once.

"Ah, so you've noticed my new trinket," Lucifel said.

Raziel's already large blue eyes widened. "You didn't," he began.

"Oh, but I did," Lucifel murmured. She crossed her arms. "Raziel, *brother,* do you know? The Father has revealed his feelings at last. He told me that if I ever stepped into his presence again, I would nevermore see the light of Malakhim. He has rejected me. In favor of Israfel. Forever."

"No, he wouldn't—"

"Yes," Lucifel spat with sudden viciousness. "And so I took the trinket he clutched to his heart so madly. Its power is mine now. So you can either join in my revolution or watch it unfold. Make your choice."

"We have two chicks between us—children who need a mother—"

"I am no mother," Lucifel said even more viciously. "And I refuse to raise them in the loneliness of this Realm. My place is on Israfel's Throne, seeing to it that his decadent regime no longer exists. The lie that those chicks have been executed can and should continue. The Father's influence over us must die once and for all. Because I'm certain he's lied to us about our identities, our origins, and our ultimate fate at his feet. Israfel is too in love with you to come to terms with any of this. He's so twisted, he doesn't even understand the danger he's carrying within himself. He's merely accepted it for the torment that it is—*for your sake.* His blind infatuation will be the death of us all."

"What are you talking about?" Raziel shouted back.

"He is carrying an infant within himself," Lucifel said,

her voice soft with danger. "All along he's refused to accept his true dual nature, and now the Father has forced him into a sick slavery."

Sophia lowered her head, her features shadowed and her mouth set in a tight line.

When she lifted her head again, she looked directly at Angela. She could see Angela—it was written all over her face.

Angela froze, unable to think for a moment. So many feelings warred within her.

She could only stare back at Sophia. Even when Sophia smiled upon noticing the white sapphire pendant at Angela's chest—and she certainly seemed to have guessed at its significance—Angela couldn't smile back. A strange and painful wedge had been driven between them.

Sophia lost her smile. Her eyes glazed over with tears.

"—and I can't understand why you bring this vapid doll wherever you go," Lucifel said to Raziel. She stood over Sophia, examining her up and down in a chill and calculating way. "What have you been looking at all this time?" Lucifel said to Sophia coolly. "Tell me now. I'm tired of guessing at what your vacant stares mean."

"Don't speak to her like that," Raziel said with surprising firmness.

Lucifel looked directly at where Angela remained on her knees and narrowed her burning red eyes.

Then she regarded Sophia again. "Well? What's so interesting?"

"I enjoy the stars," Sophia whispered, clearly swallowing back tears. She seemed to have a hard time lying.

Lucifel turned away from her, looking as uninterested as possible. She walked up to Raziel and touched his face, caressing his cheek. All too soon her face dropped into its studied coldness again. "If you care too much for Israfel, I'll make sure to do what you can't, and put him out of his dangerous misery. I was born as a shadow, after all. What's one more descent into the darkness?"

Then she walked away into the blackness that seemed to lead toward the stars.

Raziel watched her go. After a long and painful time, he spoke to Sophia. "Come. We should return to Malakhim."

But Sophia continued to examine the glittering stars. She sighed heavily. "Everything is my fault," she said with heart-rending sadness. "And I've waited for too many cycles of time to remedy the sin that has led us to this point. Promise me that you'll watch over the Archon when She appears. No matter what, Raziel. She'll need your protection. Because She will be so weak existing as a creature even lower than the angels, and subject to so much pain. Her destiny is a difficult one. We can't let this chance escape us to set things right. There might never be another . . ."

Raziel watched Sophia carefully, seeming to consider what she was saying. Then he smiled at her. "Of course," he murmured.

He walked up to her and stood by her side, both of them gazing out into the infinite sea of space beyond the pillars flanking their sides.

"Have you noticed that the Angelus's notes are changing?" Sophia said to him. "One of my children—your 'Father'—is now utterly beyond salvation. If you confront him, I fear—"

"No. Don't be afraid anymore," Raziel said. He took Sophia's hand.

Slowly, he knelt before her and kissed the back of it with reverence.

Tears rolled down Sophia's face.

"I believe that this change will be a good thing. Perhaps you should take it as a sign that the time has come to let go of your original purpose. As you said, you need to concentrate on finding the Archon when She arrives. I'll be certain to help you. I don't know how, but I promise, I will find the soul of your missing child and bring it back to you."

"Thank you," Sophia whispered between her tears. She turned away from him again, and her face became deeply solemn.

Raziel let go of her hand and walked away in the direction of Lucifel and the angelic city.

Sophia and Angela were now alone.

Angela got up onto her feet. Step by step, she walked over to Sophia. She felt like this was all a dream, knew it wasn't, and yet couldn't bring herself to speak or act like she would ordinarily. Angela replaced Raziel by Sophia's side and stared with her out at the numberless stars.

"Do you hate me?" Sophia whispered.

Angela hugged herself, rubbing her cold arms. "I don't know," she whispered back. "You've kept so much from me. How am I supposed to know what to do next? How should I feel? Go ahead and tell me if you can."

Sophia lowered her head. She spoke again after a while. "Aren't you curious why you're here and why I can see you?"

"Of course," Angela said. "But I don't know what good an explanation will do me at this moment."

Angela clenched her hands and shut her eyes, trying to think.

Sophia turned and looked at her keenly. "Tell me it all happens as I've hoped and prayed. Tell me that you are succeeding, because your face says otherwise. Yet I can't imagine how you've come to the past if at least some of your power has yet to return to you."

This is the past . . . I traveled back into time. No wonder the hourglass is working again. But how?

"I don't know if I'm succeeding," Angela said. "What I do know is that everything I thought was the truth about myself is some kind of lie. And you—the one person I trust above and beyond anyone else—fed me those lies."

"No, I would never lie to you to hurt you," Sophia said. She touched Angela's cheek, begging her to look Sophia in the face. "All I can possibly do is whatever it takes to keep you from despairing."

"Keep me from despairing?" Angela demanded angrily. She stepped away. "You told Raziel to protect me—"

"—and he did," Sophia said. "Your hair—"

She reached out to touch Angela's blood-red hair, but Angela shook her head and stayed at arm's length. "Well, Raziel's spirit within me was the sole reason I've suffered so much. Because of him I was born into a world that hated me before I ever existed."

Sophia's face paled even more. She bit her lip and squeezed her eyes shut. "I'm sorry. I never meant for you to suffer through such a life."

"Why am I here?" Angela said. "Who am I really? I want answers, and the Sophia I know right now refuses to give them to me."

"Because she certainly remembers this conversation," Sophia said, her voice breaking. "Because learning how many times you've existed only to die again in the same way would destroy your soul and drive you mad. So she kept that from you. Because she is your mother, and a mother does anything and everything for her children—until they are beyond all possible help."

How can I believe that? Is it a matter of not wanting to believe? My mother Erianna didn't do anything and everything for me, so how am I supposed to understand so easily?

"I want to know who you are. Right now," Angela said. She grasped Sophia by the wrist. "Now."

Sophia opened her mouth, but no sound came out. She turned away.

"*Now, Sophia.* You're not just the Book of Raziel. I've always guessed that much."

"You wouldn't understand where I come from," Sophia said, her fathomless eyes downcast. "But I can tell you that it was my choice to help life flourish and exist throughout the universe. Now, everything has gone wrong. Now I see that you and the other child I brought to this existence were never meant to live in it, and its currents tugged on your spirits too much and too soon. Your twin murdered you before I could bring you both into the world like you deserved. And in that moment, my material body perished. I fell into the Abyss, and my soul remained trapped there until every last star burned out and I was left alone to experience the cycle beginning anew. But something changed this time—Raziel is here. My prayers . . . have been answered . . ."

Angela breathed hard, feeling utterly lost. She tried to fathom how old Sophia must be and couldn't. She looked at her hands and still felt herself to be human. What Sophia said only seemed to skim the surface of the truth no matter what words were used.

"This time, Raziel found me in my prison of sorrows," Sophia continued. "But I fear it's too late. I fear what the enmity between Israfel and Lucifel means. They are unstable, and I truly believe that one of them will precipitate our ultimate ruin. I can't allow that to happen. Not when I am so close to redeeming this universe." Sophia's anguished voice now grew angry, and she gritted her teeth. "Yet—what can I do? I can't approach your twin—the Father. He must never know of my existence. Your soul is lost right now, and I speak to you only by special circumstances I can never hope to repeat. I am powerless—a doll, a replica of who I used to be. And I can no longer remember the final stanzas of the song that existed here even before I did, that I sang when you were still a burning light next to my heart, and that continues as it is only because of your twin's voice. Raziel has sealed those stanzas away—in anticipation of you."

"Raziel can't sing them?" Angela said, suddenly overwhelmed by the pain written all over Sophia's face. She held her hand again.

"No. He doesn't have that power."

"But surely the Father knows them? Isn't he the one singing right now?"

"He doesn't know the final part of the song. If he did, creation would start over."

"So that's what would happen if I created new stanzas to the Angelus myself? The laws of the universe would be rewritten?"

"Yes . . . a new cycle would begin, but all would be changed. It would be a great Revolution of what exists. It is what I can only hope for."

"Then how do I accomplish that?" Angela said, wanting to scream.

"You can't do it alone," Sophia said. She sighed heavily.

"Since it is the song of creation, it encompasses all things that live. Every soul remaining in a state of awareness and light would need to join with you."

"Souls?" Angela said. She thought quickly, and a searing fire went through her entire body. That's why Lucifel was gathering all the souls she could that were not alive anymore and trying to make them her own. That was why Mikel spoke in the Netherworld of how souls would help Angela fight in a final battle. Lucifel knew what it would mean if Angela created a new song, and she was determined to stop the possibility.

"You're right, I can't do it alone," Angela said. "And I shouldn't."

Sophia regarded her with surprise.

Angela swallowed painfully. "I've been alone most of my life—at least this human life that is real to me and that I remember. I've always tried to do everything myself. But this is a battle I can lead, not win alone, and I need to try and accept that. Now—I have friends. Sophia, on Earth right now, the Realm of Heaven is about to collide with Earth. Lucifel has taken over Heaven, and she's stealing all the human souls. She's preparing to battle me one-on-one."

Sophia's expression grew stricken. She put a finger to her lips. "But she no longer has the Grail," she said in a hopeful tone. "That much is clear from your eyes . . ."

"So what can I do? How can I stop her and free all those souls before it's too late?"

Sophia took a deep breath.

"Well?"

"I'm sorry. I don't have an answer for you."

"But you must!"

"I don't." Sophia smiled faintly. "But that's all right. You said it yourself. This time—you have friends to help you. Start from there."

Angela couldn't believe what she was hearing. Of all places, at the edge of the universe she should have found a solution to the most pressing problem of all.

"So you can't help me?" Angela said. She clasped Sophia's hand. It was cool and delicate as always. "Sophia . . ."

"Answer one question," Sophia said, and tears sprang to her eyes again. "What is your name? So that I can find you again someday."

"Angela. My mother gave me that name after she dreamed of Raziel before I was born."

"Angela . . . I can't help you sing the new Angelus or defeat Lucifel like you're hoping. But I can send you back to your time, where you belong. And that's exactly what I'm going to do."

Sophia placed a hand on Angela's heart. Angela pressed her hand over Sophia's and squeezed it, trying to see a mother in Sophia where once she'd seen only a friend. Maybe—just maybe—she could. It would take time, but anything was possible now. "You should thank the soul that brought you here, Angela." Sophia said. "It appears you and he are powerfully connected somehow. I hope that knowledge will give you strength."

She's talking about Kim! Somehow, he brought me to this place!

Was his soul with Angela right now? Wild hope plucked at her again.

"How can you send me back to my time?" Angela said to Sophia. "How can you have that kind of power even as the Book of Raziel?"

Angela tried to move, but couldn't. Suddenly, all she could see was a swirling darkness behind Sophia's eyes that grew and grew. Angela's left eye burned, yet she couldn't look away no matter how hard she tried.

Now she saw that deep within the Book of Raziel existed a sea of churning chaos.

Who was Sophia? Better still, *what* was she? If Sophia had truly given birth to the Father and the creature Angela used to be, then was Sophia divine? Or was she the embodied darkness from which so much life sprang? Angela remembered the writing all over Sophia's skin as the Book of Raziel, as if she were a blueprint for existence. Was she—perhaps in a shockingly literal sense—the universe itself? But with her own personality, thoughts, feelings.

Angela sensed some kind of answer in the latter, and she also sensed that perhaps she might never really know the entire truth.

Now, Stephanie Walsh's sudden insanity that fateful day she'd attempted to open the Book of Raziel without the proper means made sense. This is what she'd seen: galaxies, light, and endless darkness. Angela stared into Sophia eyes, which now seemed greater and more encompassing than the world. She heard the familiar lullaby of the Angelus before Angela's twin murdered her, and tore her apart, and she seemed to feel the rending pain all over again.

Over and over, she seemed to suffer without end.

"Good-bye, my sweet child," Sophia's voice echoed in Angela's ears. "Remember, I am always with you in one way or another."

Then a brilliant vision of stars and light swept over Angela and carried her away.

Twenty-six

Angela felt like she was descending through one layer of air after another, until suddenly she ascended instead, and a shocking cold seeped powerfully through to her bones again.

She splashed to the surface of eerily calm water and gasped for breath.

Salty water poured into her mouth and she coughed painfully. She had to shade her eyes to look at the glory of Malakhim, revolving in the sky like a brilliant galaxy above the dark crooked towers and leaning spires of Luz. From Angela's spot within the glassy ocean, a great part of the island city resembled a jagged heap of sticks and stones ready to collapse at any second. Silhouettes of angels swarmed like starlings out in the distance.

Angela glanced around and then up at the sky overloaded with stars. She pumped her legs and arms, trying to stay afloat. Already, a frightening numbness had started to take her over.

I'll never make it back into the city like this. If only it weren't so cold!

Angela's teeth chattered violently. She tried swimming, but even though the water looked placid, a current drove her back. The numbness made her limbs feel like iron weights. Every second that passed made it harder for her to stay afloat. More water found its way into Angela's mouth every time she breathed.

Boom. Boom. Wingbeats sounded overhead.

Fear coursed through her. Angela looked up, trying to spot whatever angel flew overhead. But there was only the darkness, the stars, and the intimidating shadow of the Luz Institution still sitting on the sea cliff high to her left. Angela searched the peak where she'd plummeted into the water. There was no sign of Python now, but he was certainly on the lookout for her. He had to be.

I wonder if Sophia is all right. And Kim . . . Is he with me? Or if not, what if his soul's already been found by the angels—or even taken to Lucifel?

Angela shuddered. She too would be taken if any of the angels spotted her. That couldn't happen before she found some way to reach the souls Lucifel had stolen.

The powerful wingbeats boomed high above her again.

This time the water grew choppy. Air blew down on her from above. Angela fought the urge to scream and began to swim as fast as she could. But her arms and legs were suddenly heavy as lead. She was so numb, the water no longer felt cold. Angela could barely even lift a finger by the time bony hands grasped her under the shoulders and lifted her clear from the water.

A thrilling sensation of weightlessness overtook her. She was flying toward the single part of Luz where the shadows still burned with candles in the windows and lights in lamps.

And then, Angela must have fainted, because the next thing she met and the last thing she remembered was utter darkness.

"Angela . . ."

Angela tossed and turned in the warmth that surrounded her. Tiredness had overwhelmed her spirit, and it had been so, so long since warmth like this embraced her body. Her face, though, felt oddly wet. Perhaps she'd been crying in her sleep.

Suddenly, the reality of all that had taken place struck her inside and out.

Kim was dead. Even a dream she was cursed never to remember couldn't summon him again.

She hoped to continue seeing his face when her eyes at last opened to the flickering of a hearth. Instead, her vision vanished and she couldn't recall it no matter how hard she tried. All she had now was the hope that he was indeed with her somehow, watching and praying.

She felt down for her skirt pocket, but of course her skirt wasn't there. She now wore warm, dry clothes—slim-fitting pants and a long shirt. Kim's necklace, if it hadn't been lost in the ocean, was probably gone.

Angela stared at the flames and their hypnotic dance, a million thoughts racing through her mind. Sophia's revelation should have floored Angela. So why did she feel so detached from the truth of her real identity? Was it because right now, she was only a human being? Someone who loved and feared, who grew hungry, tired, and thirsty like every other mortal creature?

Angela sat up from under a thick quilt and searched the room where she'd been set to rest. She recognized this place—the hearth, the open room with brocade furniture, the inset window where Sophia usually set her long candle at night. Filigree wallpaper covered the wall next to the window. Angela was in the den of the Emerald House, a mansion once owned by their pitifully tiny sorority at the Academy.

She hadn't been abducted by an angel after all.

But then—who had brought her here?

Angela slipped from the sheets and was about to stand up, when a shadow dashed toward her. She tensed, her left eye burning madly. But of all people, Nina stopped a foot away from her, staring back at Angela with a cautious expression. Without another word, Nina threw herself at Angela, embracing her tightly.

Angela fell back against the quilt again, but returned Nina's hug, forcing herself to let go only after a few long minutes.

"Angela . . . thank God, you're all right," Nina whispered.

"What's going on?" Angela whispered back frantically. "Who brought me here?"

"Shhhh. Quiet," Nina said, setting a finger to her lips for emphasis. "We can't be too loud or some of the girls upstairs will awaken. We managed to save some of them from the bloodletters. Now there are even more of them here because the institution has been emptied since you were thrown there. Everyone's targeting redheaded women your age now, but every time someone is brought to the authorities they're released, of course. They know it isn't you. Mikel must be watching for you like a hawk."

"Then we're not safe here," Angela said. "I can't believe no one has searched this house yet!"

"They did last night. But it was obvious you weren't here. Juno only rescued you from the ocean this morning. We wouldn't have had you in the open in front of the fire, but . . . you were so cold, Angela. Your skin was literally blue. We're lucky you're not dead. Sophia managed to stay by your side most of the night—"

"Where is she!" Angela said, gripping Nina's arms again. Angela was just as shocked hearing Juno's name mentioned, but somehow the possibility of seeing Sophia again overwhelmed her. Tears sprang to Angela's eyes.

Nina noticed them. Her tone became even more hushed. "She's not here right now. In fact, that's the trouble. We can't figure out where Sophia has disappeared since we left the institution. Not even Troy can search for her right now, because Sophia can be anywhere in the city."

"Troy! Then she's with you too? Did she help Juno find me?"

"Despite Troy's advice otherwise, Juno had been patrolling the water since Sophia told her what happened inside the institution. Juno's getting better at hiding. Most of the angels didn't spot her, and the one that did . . . well, Troy took care of him apparently. I'll admit Troy's vicious, but by God, she gets things done."

Angela sat back, resting her hands against the rug set before the hearth. "If Troy is here, I need to talk to her."

"That's probably not a good idea."

"Why?"

"She's eating right now," Nina said. She made a warning face.

Angela could only imagine exactly *what* Troy might be eating. Perhaps the same angel she'd killed. She shivered, trying to get the image out of her mind. "At least tell her I'm awake and I need to speak with her as soon as she's done."

"Sure," Nina said. She stepped away, but Angela stopped her.

"Nina! What about Fury? The angels captured her and . . ."

"She's upstairs, watching over the girls and resting. Fury's been through a lot—it's horrible. The angels looked into her soul, which is a very painful process for any Vapor. But thank goodness those winged menaces still know nothing about Troy. I'm not sure how Fury kept that information from them, but Troy said it's nothing short of a miracle that Fury is even alive. Most Vapors die after being forcefully examined like that."

"I see," Angela said. She allowed Nina to leave, watching her walk up the wooden staircase.

Angela stared into the fire again. It was already dying, getting down to embers and ashes. Finally, Angela sat alone in the dark room.

A rustle to her right brought her to attention again.

She turned to find Troy sitting right next to her, examining her closely. The Jinn's predatory eyes transfixed Angela. It seemed like forever since she'd been with either Troy or her niece and every time she came close to either of them again, the same instinctive fear of their teeth and nails and hypnotic eyes riveted her to the spot. Troy's wing had been folded tightly against her back.

"I wanted to wait until most of the fire burned out," Troy said as way of explanation. "The light . . ."

She didn't need to explain further. Angela tended to take it for granted that she was a being who didn't find light so painful.

"Are you done—eating?" Angela said, choking back the sour taste in her mouth.

Troy licked her bottom teeth and smirked. "Why? Feeling hungry?"

Angela made a sarcastic face. "No, thank you." She sighed. "Tell me what happened—Nina said you infiltrated the Luz Institution."

Troy's mouth settled into a tight line of what looked like pure and unfiltered wrath.

"What?" Angela said sharply. "What did I possibly say wrong?"

"Nothing," Troy snapped. "It's what you didn't do that's pissed me off. You allowed Sariel to die."

Angela's mouth hung open. "What! No, I didn't! Sophia told me if I cut the astral strings connecting Kim to Python, that would have killed him instantly!"

Troy grunted nastily. "Excuses."

Angela jumped to her feet. "What right do you have to be angry with me? I'm the one who should be angry. I'm the one who lost a friend! Not you!"

"Don't you understand?" Troy said, speaking through gritted teeth. "Now that he's dead, I can never hope to return to the embrace of my Clan. *That was my last chance.*"

"You had a chance to kill him in Hell. What you're saying makes no sense."

"He was connected to you. I couldn't risk it."

"That's bullshit and you know it," Angela muttered. "You're grasping at anything to justify your anger that he's actually dead! What were you going to do? Wait a million years for my connection to Kim to disintegrate? Look at you—I can tell by the expression on your face that you're sad. *Just admit it, damn it.*"

Troy slammed her lethal fist against the floor, and for a second, she looked quite ready to lunge for Angela's throat.

But the frightening moment passed just as quickly. Troy reclined on the floor with her head slumped against her pale arms. Then Troy squeezed her yellow eyes shut, and Angela could taste the frustration in her voice.

"We gathered a group to enter the institution and rescue you," Troy began. She sighed and a low growl left her. "Obviously, the attempt was only partly successful. Before the demon interrupted everything, we managed to free most of the captives there. Among them was a half-Jinn woman and her daughter. I couldn't believe an abomination like her had escaped notice for so long. And I would have put her out of her misery if she hadn't mentioned your name."

"That was Gloriana," Angela said quietly to herself.

"She had a little one," Troy said, watching Angela carefully. "I spared that one as well. Juno brought them back here personally before returning to search for you. She seemed fascinated by the human chick. It's typical of her naïveté to assume she has anything in common with a weak mortal girl, but I allowed it for the sheer relief of knowing Juno was safe. Until she revealed to me that as the new Jinn Queen she had officially forgiven Sariel his transgressions to our Clan. The proof was this," Troy said angrily again.

She dug into her rags and held out an iron crow's foot pendant.

There it was—the talisman Kim said Juno had given him. Now that he was gone, though, Juno's compassion seemed tragically wasted.

Troy sighed. "She'd given it to him before leaving Hell and joining with Nina in Luz. Juno had escaped using one of the last dimensional portals that were not the Mirror Pools before they disappeared entirely."

"If she forgave Kim," Angela said, "then why didn't you? She is your Queen now . . ."

Troy laughed. "Juno is a chick. Her sense of justice is impaired by her inexperience."

"And I would say yours is impaired by just the opposite," Angela murmured.

Troy looked at her sharply. Astonishingly, she didn't argue the point. "I never had the chance to take Sariel's body. Too many angels swept into the upper tower of the institution, forcing us to retreat. We took a dark and roundabout route back here, cursing our luck all the while that we might have lost both you and the Book in one blow. But Sophia returned after a while, and infuriatingly she offered us few answers besides the fact that you were safe for the moment, and we should keep a strict lookout for your return near the institution. The demon may or may not be dead. Sophia said that she 'had words' with him but left it at that. My fear is that now Lilith will come to Luz looking for her snake of a son."

Angela let all the information Troy had offered her sink in as much as it could. There was so much she wanted to say, and so much she had to hold in, because only Sophia would possibly understand.

Why isn't Sophia here? Is she trying to hide so that if I'm found again, she'll be far enough away that they can't open her with my blood?

Yet deep inside, Angela sensed another reason.

"Troy," Angela said. She took a deep breath, still trying to stay calm. "You have to find a way to get me to Lucifel. I need to free all the souls that she's captured. They must be in Malakhim somewhere."

"Impossible," Troy said. "You would need wings and the speed to fly into Malakhim without perishing. You're the Archon, but you're still a weak mortal creature."

Angela went silent.

There has to be a way.

"Besides," Troy continued. "It isn't necessary. Lucifel is already on her way."

"She's coming to Luz?" Angela said. "Why didn't Nina tell me that?"

"Because she knows you'll recklessly run out to meet the former Prince of Hell."

That cinches it. That's why Sophia separated herself from me. The farther apart we are right now, the better. But if only I knew she was safe.

"Then why did *you* tell me?" Angela said incredulously.

Troy smiled wickedly, and her eyes flashed in the darkness. "Because, Angela Mathers, I'm going to help you. You should be grateful. It seems Death is on your side."

Twenty-seven

Sophia rubbed the winged Kirin's neck and patted its enormous muzzle. The beast cantered against the flat shingles, its hot breath sending plumes through the icy air. Slowly, it lowered its body to the rooftop and Sophia slid off, still petting its flanks.

The Kirin's wings folded crisply against its sides, and it lowered its head for more caresses.

"Thank you," Sophia whispered. "Now I'm going to ask one more favor of you. Stay by my side just in case there's any danger. But don't act until I say the word. All right?"

The Kirin's intelligent eyes flashed in reply as it stepped into the ether and disappeared. The only sign of its presence was the unusual size and blackness of Sophia's own shadow, where the Kirin hid watching her and waiting. Sophia clutched her arms and wrapped her shawl tightly around her body, looking from the rooftop at the terrifying nearness of Malakhim. She was lucky she and the Kirin hadn't been spotted.

Troy was right. Every other night, the angels patrolling the city diminished considerably. Certainly, existing in Earth's

Realm taxed their strength over time just as it did to Troy.
They were wise to leave only stronger individuals behind
while they returned to Malakhim to recoup their health.

Sophia stared at the glorious city, her eyes watering.
There, to the north, was the white tower Israfel had called
home. In the city's center, the bridge to Ialdaboth glistened
like a string of diamonds leading step by step to a black hole.

Once again, she pictured the intricately carved balus-
trades and ledges.

Once again, she existed in a time when Israfel sat on a
crystal throne, wearing a great crown of spindled rays on
his head, his hair powdered a blue that matched his eyes, his
bronze wings surrounding his body so magnificently. Sophia
heard the lyres, she witnessed the decadence, the crystal gob-
lets, the nectar, the overwhelming perfection all over again.
Smells met her: spice, and something like lilac, and amaran-
thine.

It seemed like only yesterday that such a beautiful dream
ended in a haze of blood and violence. To Sophia, mere seconds could have passed since Lucifel's children were torn
from her lithe body, since she started her War, and then fell
to Hell with Sophia by her side.

That punishing fate for Sophia was ironically what Raziel
had wanted.

Back then, Sophia had been safer with the Devil than
living in an unstable Realm where the Father would have
destroyed her at the first opportunity. Yet what a nightmare
it had been to witness Lucifel's deathly majesty hanging in a
spider's web of chains for so many eons.

Sophia shuddered in spite of herself.

A brief flash of light signaled Mikel's arrival. So—she'd
been willing to speak to Sophia, after all.

Sophia knew that Mikel was nothing more than a child, even more so than Python. And children wanted nothing as much as attention. Surely the pain she saw behind Mikel's eyes could be healed. Mikel had done great evil, yet hers was the evil of an infant throwing a violent and prolonged tantrum that accidentally slapped others in the face. She didn't understand the value of a soul, because she'd never been taught.

If Sophia could somehow turn her against Lucifel, who Sophia knew cared for her daughter as much as a spider cared for a fly, then the odds stacked against Angela would change considerably.

Mikel didn't realize she and Angela were so much alike. Both of them had suffered from the beginning of their lives for their parents' sins. Israfel's solution of imprisoning Mikel in a flesh-and-blood body in Heaven—his attempt at keeping her dangerous power in check—had never been wise.

Sophia turned around. A tall person wrapped in a heavy hooded cloak stood opposite her on the rooftop.

"I'm glad you decided to come," Sophia said carefully. "If you'll just let me explain about Angela, I know we can come to a better understanding, Mikel."

The tall person let her hood fall back. Raven black hair fluffed around her shoulders, and Lilith's dark face and slim neck appeared. She scanned the rooftop, glanced at Malakhim, and then examined the stars with such a hungry expression she could have been starving for millennia. "How long it's been," Lilith said softly, "since I saw this beauty."

A spider peeked from underneath her hood and then escaped back into the warmth of the fabric.

Sophia's heart went cold.

"What are you doing here?" Sophia managed to croak.

But the answer was obvious. Lilith had used the Mirror Pool below Python's mansion to arrive in Luz.

The demon swept her gaze across the snow-covered city as if examining every soul that remained, claiming each for her own.

"As I'm sure you've guessed, Mikel isn't coming," Lilith said with her sweetly poisonous voice. "My son truly thinks I'm an idiot, but I've been observing his correspondence with that brat of an angel until it recently went sour. I actually came to Luz for him, but capturing Lucifel's child in the process was most certainly a welcome reward for my hard work."

"Capturing her?" Sophia said angrily. "Why would you do such an insane thing?"

"Insurance," Lilith said. "If I'm to oversee Hell while Lucifel sits on her new throne, I need some way to keep our former Prince from getting too greedy again. I guarantee dangling her daughter in front of her nose will keep Lucifel's relations with me friendly from this point on."

Sophia wanted to laugh. "Lucifel cares nothing for Mikel. She's using her and that's all."

"Oh, I know she cares little for her. But Mikel is dangerous. A loose cannon, as humans say. We both know it's in Lucifel's best interests to kill Mikel when her usefulness passes; otherwise, what other havoc will she instigate before the end? But now that I have the chick, the stakes in this drama have changed. I can always release her if I choose."

"Lilith," Sophia said, trying to control her rage. "Free Mikel and let her act while Lucifel has her somewhat under control; otherwise—"

"Now, now, not so fast," Lilith said.

She waved her hand and a very familiar hourglass appeared, hovering in the air beside her. Its insides shone a soft blue.

It was the hourglass Python had used to link Angela's and Kim's spirits.

"But . . . Python destroyed it," Sophia murmured. She clearly remembered Python smashing it to pieces in the institution as he told Kim his time was up.

Lilith granted Sophia a pitying look. "Well, he pretended to. My son can be quite irritating like that. But I suppose he didn't tell you that the half-breed's essence now resides in the glass, hmm? I guarantee Python left out that little detail when Kim made his deal to help the Archon."

The blue light . . . that was Kim's soul in the glass! So how had he been able to help Angela enter the past?

Sophia thought quickly. That was it—Kim must have slipped his hourglass pendant to Angela somehow. Since it connected to his soul, he'd been able to control its power when Angela entered the ocean. "You know what this means, then," Lilith said, her tone instantly scoffing and sharp. "Now Kim's soul is in my hands. And in a way, so is the Archon's."

Sophia's heart quaked. She didn't like where Lilith was going with this. *At all.*

"Angela isn't dead, certainly, but she could be. I wouldn't try anything rash," Lilith said. She let the hourglass hover before her. "Because it wouldn't take much to accidentally drop this hourglass and send the Archon's spirit irretrievably to the Abyss."

"You'd be a fool then," Sophia said, unable to hold back her angry tears anymore. They poured out of her as if she could cry another ocean into life. "Without Angela's intervention this universe will be silenced, Lilith. Forever. Or have you forgotten that overwhelmingly obvious fact?"

"But all we really need now is her blood to keep the universe intact. Well, that and you," Lilith said in her silken tone.

"In fact, I suppose there's no real reason to stall the more I think over the situation. Perhaps I would have thought differently if Kim were still alive. He was a sweet boy when he didn't irritate me terribly. I could also say the same for you, dear. How nice it was to speak to you again, Sophia. How much I've missed our chats during the time you still resided in Hell, standing like a statue beneath the spider's web of our Black Prince. Here's to our memories."

Lilith lowered her hand.

Now it was as if time continued after endless frozen moments. There was a hideous pause where nothing significant seemed to happen. Then the hourglass began to fall.

Sophia dashed for it with all her strength.

The hourglass tumbled end over end, its carved metal gleaming in Malakhim's light.

Sophia dove below it, and the hourglass dropped into her waiting arms.

Now! Sophia thought, sending all the power of her mind to the winged Kirin hiding in the ether.

The beast leaped from the space between the shadows and reared frighteningly on the rooftop. Its sides flickered with ghostly blue light, and it charged Lilith with its spiraling horn aimed right at her heart.

Lilith gritted her teeth angrily. "This horrid thing," she whispered. She kicked Sophia away with her foot and lifted her hand.

Sophia grunted painfully and tumbled, still clutching the hourglass. The shingles tore at her skin and dress and she stopped perilously near the edge of the roof, looking up in time to see green light pulse around Lilith's body.

Before Sophia could do or say anything, the energy shot toward the Kirin.

Sophia shielded her eyes from the blinding light. A terrible animal scream tore through her. The roof shuddered as an enormous weight dropped against it, and when Sophia opened her eyes, she knew even before looking that the winged Kirin was gravely wounded. Its legs and paws trembled and blood streamed from its flanks. Its leathery wings thrashed against the rooftop, and it screamed piercingly again.

The angels would definitely hear that.

Lilith lowered her hand. Her face was far from triumphant. Just like Sophia, she probably also knew that by defending herself, she'd given everything away.

She looked over her shoulder at Malakhim, her orange eyes burning. One of them flickered red for the briefest second.

Sophia blinked, hoping she'd imagined everything. But of course she hadn't.

That was how Lilith had chosen to capture Mikel? Then she'd sorely miscalculated. Lilith mustn't have known that Mikel could possess more than one person—that her spirit could split its essence. Lilith's means of capturing Mikel had clearly been offering herself to be possessed, as some kind of twisted bait. In the end, she was housing something too great even for an ancient angel like herself to control. Mikel was a child of the Supernals. Her powers would in some way always be above a creature's like Lilith.

"Mikel, listen to me," Sophia shouted at Lilith. "It isn't too late for you to help remedy at least a little of the evil you've caused. Mikel. *Please.*"

"It's no use," Lilith said, but her tone suggested it was another person speaking.

Lilith's eyes widened. She clutched her throat.

Sophia could only imagine what it must feel like to have

another soul within you controlling your voice and actions. Lilith's horrified face suggested she was fighting Mikel, but Sophia already knew the battle was a useless one. Even so, Sophia waited, holding in her breath, trying to balance on the roof's edge with the heavy hourglass still clutched protectively within her arms.

In a minute Mikel completely took control. Lilith's left eye deepened to a bloody crimson and her face calmed as her hand lowered back to her side. She turned and stared out at Malakhim again, but without any trace of the hunger and memory that had haunted her expression before.

Sophia watched with her.

Against the glory of the angelic city's crystalline bridges and spires, a swarm of dots of varying size appeared. They grew larger with every passing second. Soon, Sophia could faintly make out wings and serpentine forms scattered among a sea of angels.

"I appreciate your faith in my goodness, Sophia," Mikel said to her, still looking out at Malakhim and its approaching army. "But I can't turn back now. Israfel and my dead brother made sure of that. Besides, haven't you ever wondered whether you're on the right side in this battle? My mother only seeks to end a cycle that refuses to stop. Each and every turn at life has ended terribly for all of us. It's much better to allow a deep silence to take over. It will be so much better to rest for eternity."

"Except that what you're calling rest is merely a twisted way of saying 'eternal death,'" Sophia shouted at her. "Mikel. Please. For pity's sake, stop this madness while you can help."

"As I said, it's too late . . ." Mikel gazed proudly out at the horizon, her eyes blazing as the dreadful army approached.

"Mother is on her way, and no one will be able to stop her victory now. At last . . . the real Revolution can begin."

Lucifel was arriving on Earth in the flesh?

Sophia felt like all the blood had drained out of her at once. Where would she hide now? And with the precious hourglass? She clutched it harder and peered down at the cobblestone alley below. She would survive the fall, of course. But her legs would break. Then there would be no escape.

Mikel turned around and watched Sophia carefully before striding toward her. Using Lilith's long legs, she crossed the space between herself and Sophia all too quickly.

"That hourglass," Mikel whispered. "I know Mother would want it. I know if I give it to her . . ."

"What?" Sophia said frantically. "You believe it will make her love you? You heard what I said to Lilith, Mikel. Lucifel can't love. Or—she has only ever loved one person truly."

"Who?" Mikel snapped. "Herself? How trite and predictable of you to say such a thing. I expected better than that."

"No, not herself. *The Father.* Lucifel has loved and will always love only him. Everything she has ever done since he rejected her was solely to spite him. Everything."

"No," Mikel said, laughing though her face twisted with pain. "That's ridiculous. He tortured her—"

"She welcomed torture. But she couldn't bear being ignored. She couldn't stand rejection. She couldn't live knowing that the Father hated her simply for who she was— embodied darkness like himself. Even when she discovered the Father wasn't her true Creator, her feelings couldn't change. And for the sake of her rejected love, the entire universe has been suffering longer than it should.

"I am right," Sophia said. "I know her better than anyone, Mikel. She is no different from Israfel in her obsessions. The selfishness of my children has been the cause of endless pain, but Angela's soul is innocent, and it's utter foolishness to think destroying it will help in any way. The Supernals are parts of who she used to be, but she had no hand in their creation."

"Then who did?" Mikel demanded. Her voice dripped with rage and disbelief.

"*I did*. My spirit sought to amend the sin I had been unable to prevent when Angela's twin tore her apart. After so many painful cycles of time, I'd gathered enough of Angela's original mutilated body to bring the Supernals to life. I shared my essence to give them souls. And then I had to fall asleep for eons and eons. That was the ultimate price of my intervention, and I knew it would be a great sacrifice. By the time Raziel discovered the fragments that remained, there was so little left of me that this"—Sophia pointed at herself with a free hand—"this was the best he could replicate. If it weren't for me, Mikel—you would have never existed at all. Be sure of that."

"I don't believe you," Mikel said. Her face was terrible to look at. "It makes no sense to me, because then where did you come from? *Who are you?*"

Sophia allowed a stony silence to settle. She breathed hard, holding the hourglass.

The more Mikel stared into her eyes, the more pained her face became. She looked at the hourglass again, thinking.

Then she lunged for it with a cry of utter despair.

Sophia was too shocked to move at first.

She slammed back against the roof, her arms still locked around the hourglass even though Mikel desperately tried to wrench it from her grip. Sophia screamed, holding on as tight as she could. The wounded Kirin, which had been silent for so long, now brayed painfully again.

"*Mikel, stop it!*" Sophia screamed again, no longer caring how loud she might be.

But Mikel was in a frenzy. She wasn't about to let go either.

The thunder of wingbeats sounded beside them. Sophia could see nothing but Mikel's wrathful face hovering over her, until a pair of bony white hands grabbed Mikel by the shoulders and flung her to the side.

Mikel shrieked, tumbling to the edge of the roof.

She snagged an icicle-rimmed gutter with a pained grunt and hung on, her fingers—Lilith's fingers—now bruised and bloody from the sharp ice. Lilith could fly, but it appeared Mikel didn't have that much control over her host's body yet.

The same hands that had flung Mikel sideways helped Sophia stand again.

She turned to find her savior was Juno. Juno's ears pressed back into her hair, and she growled with a noise that rumbled through Sophia's entire body. She stalked over to Mikel, slamming a foot with sharp nails down on one of her hands.

Mikel howled and glared up at Juno murderously. "You ragged crow," she spat at her.

Juno cocked her head at her. "I know you. We've encountered you before. What a horrid nuisance . . ."

"If you let this body perish," Mikel hissed at her, "I'll just enter yours. So be careful what you do next."

Sophia straightened. That's right, Lilith had captured part of Mikel. Somehow she'd made it so that Mikel's spirit couldn't escape to another host freely.

Juno knelt down. She licked the blood from Mikel's fingers, and then her lips. "I don't think you'll possess me."

"What? Why not!"

"Because I'm not going to kill you," Juno said. She spread her wings and fanned them in the freezing air. "I'm just going to devour the parts of you that matter most."

Mikel's eyes widened. For the first time in a while, she appeared to be truly speechless.

Juno leaned down and snagged her nails into Mikel's hands. They bled profusely, and Mikel moaned and squirmed like a worm on a hook. Juno opened her small mouth, displaying two rows of orderly sharp teeth.

Sophia had no choice but to watch.

She couldn't intervene even if she wanted to. The second Mikel was free, Mikel would do anything to capture the hourglass again. And that couldn't happen. So Sophia huddled with the freezing cold hourglass against her chest, squeezing her eyes shut when the first bite came, and all the ones that followed.

Twenty-eight

Angela leaned against the ice-slicked brick wall of a mansion near St. Mary's Cathedral, trying not to retch. She could actually feel the Earth Realm starting to buckle and warp. Strange groans met her ears, as if the earth itself cried out in pain, and every so often objects before her twisted slightly or shivered like mirages. The spires of the cathedral seemed to ripple, as if in a breeze. Behind the great church, Malakhim resembled an enormous and forbidding moon rising over the horizon, but one that took up almost half the sky.

The stars surrounding the angelic city burned so gloriously, Angela's eyeballs pulsed.

She closed her eyes and pressed her hands against them. The roar of the crowd in the courtyard outside the cathedral was deafening. She could have sworn all of Luz worshipped Lucifel.

That certainly wasn't the case. When Angela dared to glimpse faces, there were too many frightened people. Certainly, a great majority of them were choosing to participate in these horrid sacrifices because they didn't want to become victims themselves.

I'd rather drown in the sea than behave like that. But I shouldn't judge . . . If only Kim were still here. If only everything had happened differently at the institution.

But Angela couldn't think of any way events would have followed another course. Kim seemed to have felt the same way. His face had been that of a man staring into death, and she'd never quite caught on until it was too late.

Where is his soul? I don't even feel him near me anymore.

She held out her hands and gazed at them, aware of sorrow splitting her heart in half.

He would have tried to stop me from doing this, especially after all that's happened. But now there's no other choice.

Angela would be practically offering herself on a silver platter to Lucifel to be bled dry. She couldn't screw this up, and the strategy would have been madness if it wasn't absolutely essential to everyone that Lucifel disappear, and this might be Angela's only chance to make sure it happened. Thank God, Troy was on Angela's side and willing to sacrifice her life so that Angela could destroy the Supernal once and for all. What Angela hadn't been telling Troy was that she planned to reach Heaven itself by abducting one of those feathered serpents.

Unlike Python, their scales shone like iridescent pearl, and the plumes on their heads had the ethereal quality of peacock feathers. Their blood-red eyes suggested great intelligence, but nothing that approached the demon who shared in their heritage.

Angela had been able to subdue the winged Kirin with the

Grail. Now that it was gone, she would have to find another means to fly.

But Troy couldn't know about that plan. She'd never agree to it.

Angela looked up at the sky again and watched the serpents against the silver backdrop of Malakhim, flying with a great army of angels. Two squadrons composed of thousands of angels had already arrived. Troy had killed at least one hundred angels on their way here. They'd been lucky so far, and the entire time, Angela had her eye on the feathered serpent that arrived with the last contingent.

It rested curled around one of the spires of the cathedral, testing the air with its enormous tongue.

A scraping sound caused Angela to jump.

She clapped a hand to her heart and adjusted the hood over her head again. No one could see her until it was time. This entire endeavor was insane enough.

Troy had returned. She crawled sideways on the opposite wall of the narrow alley, her face scrunched with irritation. She was also wearing a long cloak and hood, which would have made her look like a harmless human if it weren't for her bloody teeth and mouth. "Can you feel it?" she said. "It won't take much more for the Realms to collide." Troy's long ears swiveled as if to catch a specific sound. Angela listened with her, and the earth groaned again. "No wonder Lucifel is arriving now. She won't have much more time to reach you."

"You know . . . I still don't believe you," Angela whispered. She knew she had to enter the crowd in the Academy's courtyard, but every time she worked up the courage, she lost it again. "I still think there's a way I can get to Heaven to rescue all those souls."

Troy glanced at the feathered serpent and back at Angela again.

"Like what?" she snapped suspiciously.

Angela just sighed. It would be better to keep everything to herself, as she'd thought. "All right," she whispered. "I'm going to enter into the crowd now."

"Wait," Troy said. She grabbed Angela's arm, accidentally sliding back the sleeve and cutting into Angela's skin with her nails.

Angela winced at the pain. She watched the blue blood well up as she quickly pulled the sleeve back down and wrapped a hand against it.

"If you use the Glaive to its full potential and don't kill Lucifel in time, all will be lost," Troy said. "Remember that. And remember that I don't feel like dying without a good reason. So don't do anything as stupid as Sariel would have—"

Troy's voice cut off. Her ears flattened and she shook her head. She turned to melt back into the shadows again.

She's trying to say good-bye to me.

"Thank you, Troy," Angela said. "For everything. I know we never understood each other completely, but maybe respect is enough. We'll meet again someday. I promise."

Troy paused, and she actually looked startled. Her lips smiled ever so slightly. "Good luck, Archon. You'll need it." Her great eyes gleamed at Angela one last time. "So . . . until we meet again . . ." Then the Jinn's greatest hunter disappeared into the long shadows of the alley.

Angela stared after her.

A moment later, hysterical screams erupted from the courtyard.

It was a woman shouting someone's name. The horrid sacrifices must have started.

Without any more hesitation, Angela turned and entered the crowd. No one paid any attention to her, and she slipped ahead of one person and the next, weaving her way toward a platform erected especially for the occasion. The bitingly cold air was punishing enough. She couldn't imagine how most of these people could even stand it. Perhaps it was because they feared becoming victims themselves and had decided that joining the mob would save them, at least until the end. Curiosity and fear did strange things to good people.

Soon, Angela got her first real view of the platform. She willed the blood from Troy's accidental cut on her arm to collect in her hands and start forming the Glaive. She would have to keep it small like a knife for now, just in case.

Black pillars had been erected with red pentagrams carved upon them. A lone chair had been set between the pillars. At least two-thirds of Luz's priests, novices, and city officials had arranged themselves in a semicircle before it. They wore black robes, and the angels behind them presided over everything like crows perched on wires.

The woman screamed again. Someone had taken her child up to the platform. It was a little blond-haired boy who kicked and cried furiously.

Angela gasped along with the rest of the crowd.

As the boy shrieked, ice grew over the platform, spreading from a deep blackness that hazed over the air.

Lucifel's lithe figure appeared from amid the haze, her four gray wings like a terrible smoke fanning from her body. The two gray wings on her ears were elegant as a swan's. Her piercing eyes roved over the crowd with utter disdain. She'd dressed herself head to toe in black, without any ornamentation of any kind. The jewels of her eyes were apparently enough.

A chilling silence took over.

Even the chosen child's mother went utterly still and quiet.

Lucifel took a few steps forward, and ice actually spread from where her feet touched the platform.

Two men threw the boy at her feet.

He cried pitifully as Lucifel stared down at him without any emotion whatsoever.

Angela tensed. The moment Lucifel touched him, the boy would die. His energy would transfer to her completely. Angela trembled, trying to hold back from revealing the Glaive in all its fearsomeness. Her entire body ached from the effort, and her feet were already growing unsteady. It didn't feel like the right moment. This was all happening so fast. But then she noticed the blood head students being herded like cattle up to the platform. A few novices shoved them roughly onto their knees. Angela was sure she recognized some faces from her classes at the Academy.

All right. Let's do this.

Her left eye burned fiercely. Brilliant light surrounded her body. The Glaive appeared, forming from the blue blood that had dripped and still dripped from her arm.

It was like a bomb had been tossed into the courtyard.

Chaos erupted everywhere. The feathered serpent screeched so loudly, Angela thought her eardrums would burst. She could hear exorcisms being pronounced until harsh words from the angels forced the priests to be silent again.

Angela expected the crowd to rush upon her, but most people dashed far away and ran into the alleys or hid beside buildings.

Lucifel, though, had spotted Angela. Her gaze sliced the air between them like a knife.

Two angels landed beside Angela, but she swung the

Glaive right and left as swiftly as possible and they dropped to the ground wingless and flailing with pain, causing more screams and more panic. The other angels suddenly swerved, giving her a wide berth from every direction. A wild mob began, but the few people who ran up to Angela quickly changed their minds when they saw her weapon.

"It's her!" a priest's voice shouted from the platform. It was Bishop Kline. He pointed at Angela. "Get the Archon!" he shrieked wildly. Angela recognized his voice instantly. So he'd been the one who'd tried to capture her in Memorial Cemetery. "Do anything to take Her down! Now!"

But no one listened to him.

Almost everyone backed away as Lucifel turned from the boy on the makeshift altar and walked slowly in Angela's direction.

The boy scampered off the platform into the waiting arms of his mother. She then held him tightly, staring at Angela as if she and not Lucifel were the real Devil. But Lucifel continued walking toward Angela as if everything around her—the surging crowd, the screams, the panic—were nothing more than a whirlwind of dust easily fanned away by her wings.

Her gaze pierced through Angela like a twisting blade.

"What a shame," Lucifel said, her voice echoing powerfully through the air. "And here I thought you'd play hard to get again. But isn't it just like you, Angela Mathers, to play the hero now that you have no other role to adopt?" Her voice resounded until it was painful to hear.

Angela's brain screamed at her to turn away, to do anything besides look into Lucifel's crimson eyes. Instead, for some reason even Angela couldn't understand, she remained transfixed and nearly helpless.

What am I doing! She'll kill me!

Lucifel smiled coldly. She wasn't very far away now. If anything, she was far too close. "Angela," the Destroyer Supernal said, "your eye has healed nicely since I dug it out of your head. How lucky you had a spare waiting in the wings."

Flashes of pain, of Lucifel's fingers burrowing into Angela's face, erupted throughout Angela's mind. She could have screamed or fainted, but instead she only shivered and dared to stare down Lucifel with as much defiance as she could. She breathed shallowly, her heart pounding like a mouse's. Dizziness tugged at her, but she was getting better at fighting it off. For now. By God, she had to.

"I can't say I mind disappointing you," Angela murmured with the same coldness. Though she didn't sound confident at all.

Now her grand plan to get rid of Lucifel and travel to Heaven revealed itself for the impossibility that it was.

"Did you like being the new Prince of Hell?" Lucifel whispered. Somehow her voice still seemed louder than ever. "Did you enjoy sitting on my Throne, Archon? I suppose the prophecy came true after all. Judging by the pitiful state of the universe, Sophia is still alive. And I thought that *I* could be selfish—"

A heavy booming in the background interrupted Lucifel. The cathedral shivered and warped.

It seemed impossible for the situation to get any worse.

BOOM. BOOM.

Now Angela recognized this noise. It was exactly like the sound Troy's wings made when she flew, except amplified a million times over.

Angela glanced up at the cathedral's black turrets. Silhouettes of innumerable angels shot over the spires and into the city. The angels approached too fast and grew larger by the second. Hundreds of them were alighting in Luz. The next regiment had arrived in earnest and likely at Lucifel's direct decree. Now some of the priests actually tugged prayer wards out of their coats and pockets, though they trembled and shivered like leaves. Bishop Kline stood at their helm, stalwart, but his face deathly pale.

Angela refused to feel sorry for him now. He'd made his ultimate choice.

Wind barreled across the courtyard. The stained glass of the cathedral's windows exploded all at once with a deafening roar.

People ducked screaming beneath a hail of rainbow-colored shards.

Angela fell on her knees with them, half covering herself. Pieces of glass struck her skin and left cuts that burned in the icy air.

Two more angels touched down next to Angela, seeming to converge on her with determined eyes. Long coats covered their bodies and brushed the ground as they walked. They held up shining metal bows with arrows that sparked at the tips.

Angela still crouched, holding the Glaive. She wasn't fast enough to swing in time.

Two of their arrows whistled through the air above Angela's head. Painful cries and the cold thump of bodies hitting the stone ground echoed around her. Blue light flashed, and souls in the shape of spheres flew toward the angels.

The wind grew more violent. Another groan that rumbled through to Angela's soul shivered everywhere, as if reality itself screamed with her. Her blood-red hair whipped into her eyes, and she gritted her teeth. Her lips hurt so bad. She must have bitten them by accident. Blue blood dribbled like liquid salt into her mouth. The shouts and cries of the priests and novices and the swarming crowd mixed with the howling gale. Words in the Tongue of Souls were barely audible.

Suddenly, a male angel with chestnut-colored wings landed directly between Angela and Lucifel. He lifted his bow and arrow, notching it so swiftly and expertly his arms were like a blur. He pointed it straight at Angela's face.

She barely had a chance to duck this time.

With a lethal whirring sound, the arrow shot right into her left arm.

A sword could have been driven right through Angela's shoulder. She screamed even louder, sinking to her knees and clutching at her wounded arm manically. A burning sensation wormed its way through every inch of her skin. Fire exploded throughout her chest. Warmth gushed from her wounded skin. She clenched her jaw, fighting off the mind-melting agony as she broke off the arrow shaft sticking out of her arm.

Thump.

A man dropped beside her, right next to Angela's face, an arrow pierced straight through his chest. Blue light flashed around him, and his spirit materialized as a sphere and shot in the angel's direction.

Those revolting monsters, Angela's mind moaned. *They're not getting away with this.*

Angela still clasped the Glaive, but her left arm now felt dangerously weak and heavy as iron. Blue blood gushed through her fingers.

Another angel dashed in front of Lucifel and approached Angela quickly.

The arrow hadn't been enough to cripple her severely.

Certainly that was unusual enough to cause alarm even if she weren't the Archon.

She staggered to her feet, using the Glaive's pole end to help herself stand.

The pain in her arm and shoulder was excruciating.

Come on, Angela. You can do this. You have to do this. FOR EVERYBODY.

A shrill scream that sounded like an innocent child's rang through the air. Hot anger burned in Angela all at once. She cried out savagely, summoning her strength and bearing down on the angel. He dodged in time to avoid losing his head, but the Glaive caught the tips of his wings. He slammed to the ground, bleeding, his handsome face contorted with shock. Now at least ten other angels nearby whipped their gazes in Angela's direction. They circled her as one glittering, murderously beautiful cotillion. All the world turned into feathers and sparking arrows.

Angela ignored the pain and swung the Glaive over her head, finishing with its great blade pointed at one of the angel's throats. He glared at her, but glanced around in sudden fright and leaped into the air as if he sensed a different danger.

Another groan shivered up through the earth. All of Luz seemed to rock on its foundations.

The wind screamed and cried.

A noise like stones chewed by a giant erupted, and the bricks and cobblestones of one entire building peeled away. St. Mary's Cathedral buckled at its heights, and the spires cradling the feathered serpent began to collapse as if in slow motion. The creature flew up and into a blackness behind it that was absolute except for the enormous galaxy of buildings and spires of Malakhim, spinning so that the city now took up most of the sky. The angelic city seemed close enough to touch. Even windows in individual towers could be seen.

Angela fell to her knees again amid the piercingly bitter wind. She stared at the angelic city, disbelief overwhelming her.

Finally, weakness rushed upon her like a flood.

Angela gripped the stone beneath her as the Glaive collapsed in her hands into a puddle of blue blood. Droplets whipped away in the maelstrom. Angels fought against the gale around her and sought out whatever human survivors were left in the courtyard, their beating wings almost equal to the storm. Some of them lifted from the ground and flew like gigantic birds of light and perfection toward Malakhim, dipping and diving into the ruins with wanton abandon, lifting up again with snowy nets of bluish souls. This was the beginning of the end for Earth, and for Luz, and for all humanity. The crack of crumbling masonry and stone echoed through every inch of the air, reverberating out into the rest of the doomed city.

"*DAMN IT!*" Angela screamed so hard, her voice went hoarse in an instant.

Lucifel stood only a few feet away. Angela had no chance now.

"Are you really so sad that I'm taking everything away from you?" Lucifel said. "But that's your reward for being too weak to end the cycle that started with your death. This—all the destruction you see around you—*is entirely your doing.*"

"Listen to yourself," Angela screamed back. "But I suppose the old legends are true. You're just too proud to think clearly. If it weren't for me, Lucifel, you wouldn't even exist."

Lucifel flinched slightly, but in a second she returned to

her characteristic hardness. "You're delaying the inevitable, causing others to suffer more. As always."

"No," Angela said between her teeth.

"Yes. Raziel helped put your soul in this body because he must have believed that human beings were different. That there's something within your pathetically weak spirits that could grant this universe a spark of hope. But I can see the truth. Nothing there is any different from the angels, whether they live in Heaven or Hell. So now the long drama can finish at last. I will see to it that there're no more attempts to right wrongs that should have never occurred. If you're too weak to vanish, I can help. All you have to do is stand still."

This isn't working. I've lost the battle here. If I don't act quickly—

Lucifel halted. She must have noticed the fire burning behind Angela's left eye.

Angela shifted her gaze to the feathered serpent trying to latch itself on to other parts of the crumbling cathedral. *Come to me,* she thought. And now the pain felt like a fireball trying to work its way through her head. *Come to me. You belong to me now.*

The serpent looked directly at her with its enormous ruby eyes.

It screeched, and the powerful echo shuddered through to Angela's bones. In a minute it was descending toward her. Though the creature had no wings, it slithered through the ether as if the air were made of tree branches, and its enormous coils destroyed everything in its path once it hit the ground. The platform built for the horrendous sacrifices crumbled like sand. Angels parted before the creature in waves. Even Lucifel was forced to dash aside, though her face suggested she'd return.

Angela took her chance. She gripped the serpent's enormous platelike scales and climbed onto its sinewy back.

To Malakhim, she thought, making sure to catch the serpent's gaze again as it looked back at her.

And then they were off, and everything passed beneath her in a blinding blur.

Twenty-nine

The sudden powerful wind forced Angela to lay flat on her stomach, clinging to the serpent desperately. Its great body undulated, and fire and fierceness shot through her at the memories that started to come rushing back. The last time she'd seen these creatures had been during her vision of Raziel's death, as an endless rain of feathers and blood fell through the sky.

She hoped history wouldn't repeat itself. Clenching her jaw and tightening her grip, Angela prayed that they would make it to the city unnoticed.

The beast shot through the ether toward Malakhim like an iridescent comet. A shimmery haze in the air peeled back before them as the stars grew larger and the angelic city took up more and more of the sky.

Now she knew—there was no way they'd escape notice.

Angela could now make out individual buildings, including a white tower with innumerable balconies and strangely twisting spires. If she peered closely, she could see the glittering stairway—the bridge to Ialdaboth—where Raziel had fallen to his death. Above it, a swirling cauldron of energy and black mist signaled the entrance to the Realm of Ialdaboth itself.

Angela's heart raced. This was really happening. She was going to make it farther to Heaven than any human had ever dreamed or dared. Angels flying toward Luz began to appear in front of her on the horizon, not merely as black dots in the distance anymore, but so close that Angela could pick out the multicolored gems on their wings' cuffs. The city glittered behind them like a gigantic glowing planet, infinitely larger than the moon had ever appeared in Earth's sky. Only the upper hemisphere of Malakhim had been visible from Luz. Now Angela realized the city's lower half was just as enormous, and the entire metropolis was an artificial pinwheel galaxy of crystal and light. Angela gaped at how angels on the lower half seemed to fly upside down.

The city was like a planet in more ways than she'd ever guessed.

Suddenly, the serpent screeched as if in warning.

A flock of angels approached them fast now. Angela held her breath. Her hair whipped behind her like a great red flag. She stared unflinchingly at the angels in the lead, catching the gazes of more than a few.

They must not have expected to see a human on the serpent's back. Shock blanked over one face after the next. Some of the angels paused midflight and notched dreadful arrows to their bows, but it was too late.

Angela squeezed her eyes shut as the serpent collided with its former caretakers.

Something hot splashed back against her skin. The serpent screeched, and Angela was certain she heard it champing its jaws. Sickening snaps reverberated through her. Then the creature shuddered, and a weight seemed to hit its back behind her.

Angela opened her eyes. As she'd feared, blood rained from the sky. The corpses of angels fell like shooting stars into the ether. One passed by her with his wings in tatters, screaming as he plummeted to the Abyss.

The wind shrieked against her, and Angela knew the serpent was now ascending vertically.

Amazingly, three angels had managed to land on the serpent's back. They ran across the serpent's scales toward Angela, even with its body almost as straight as a tree trunk. Their sense of balance and grace was terrifying. Then the serpent twisted its body sharply in the opposite direction.

One of the angels lost his balance and fell off.

He spread his ebony wings and caught the ether, circling back to land next to Angela again.

In a second, the serpent plucked him from the air, shook its head, and flung him aside like a broken doll.

An angel streaked after him, yelling frightfully and obviously enraged and horrified.

The other angels remaining on the serpent's back looked at one another, nodded, and dropped off its body. Angela heaved a sigh of relief. Her heart now beat so fast and hard it felt like it might explode. Those angels had at least managed to escape with their lives—maybe because they'd chosen to plummet out of reach.

But where can I go once I'm in Malakhim? Where are the souls loyal to me that Lucifel imprisoned?

Angela thought of the souls also trapped within Luz where the Cherubim had died. They had wanted to help her but had been too afraid of Lucifel's power.

She had to try summoning them. But how?

Maybe it was too late.

Angela's body jolted on top of the serpent. She shouted in alarm. Quickly, she looked back over her shoulder, her hair whipping into her mouth. Fear coursed through every inch of her body like a spreading wildfire. Lucifel stood on the creature's back and stalked in Angela's direction, her wings great and gray as two storm clouds. Her balance and grace put the other angels to shame. The serpent rolled to the side, but Lucifel held her ground so easily, she didn't even crouch. Her stony face promised Angela all kinds of pain for the trouble she was causing.

Angela turned back to the city and peered at the vortex marking the entrance to Ialdaboth.

Maybe if I enter the portal, it will shake her off. I have to try. Otherwise—

Angela was already out of time. Lucifel sprinted for her and was going to be right on top of her any second.

Just in time, Angela remembered her wounded shoulder. She'd been so entranced by the city, and so overwhelmed battling the angels, that she'd forgotten her pain. She gritted her teeth, pressing her hand against the blood of the wound where the arrowhead remained embedded in her flesh. She didn't have enough energy for the Glaive. The pole and haft lengthened only halfway, and Angela was left with a jagged crystalline spear.

She grasped it with a hand tightly and turned around.

Angela grunted from the force of Lucifel bearing right down on her.

She lifted the spear lengthwise and pushed back at Lucifel.

It was enough to throw the angel off guard, and Lucifel's face twisted with rage. She grabbed the spear, trying to tug it from Angela's grip.

Perhaps because half of Lucifel's concentration focused on keeping steady, she couldn't quite seem to wrest the spear out of Angela's hands. Instead, they continued to fight each other, pushing and pulling for seconds that felt like an eternity.

Toward the vortex to Ialdaboth—hurry! Angela thought. Her left eye blazed like a flame and she sent her thoughts to the serpent with as much force and power as possible.

Now it began to bank to the left.

Lucifel's eyes went wide and she lost her footing. She rolled, her wings flapping thunderously as she flattened to the serpent's back and struggled to hold on to the creature's smooth scales.

Angela didn't have the option of fighting with her now. Instead both of them held on dearly as the serpent twisted backward. Angela felt her stomach rise in her throat. Her skull was ready to shatter from a million pounds of pressure. Rapidly and upside down, they were approaching the northern hemisphere of Malakhim.

The serpent was flying straight for the vortex at Ialdaboth's pinnacle, just as Angela had hoped. They were already nearing it, and the feel of the wind ripping at her flesh, and the burning pain of ether against her eyes, threatened to knock her unconscious. The bridge's glistening, spiraling steps led up, and up, and up until they stopped at the platform where Raziel had hurtled to his death, and a swirling mass of raging black cloud, and greenish ether, and flickers of lightning and starlight congealed.

Beyond, a portal as dark as starless space beckoned. It pulsed like a beating heart.

Angela squeezed her eyes shut again. She screamed as the wind tore at her with icy claws. She briefly reopened her eyes to the beginning of the giant glass stairway that matched the one that had appeared in Luz, all those terrible months ago when Angela had allowed the souls trapped in the Netherworld to escape to Heaven.

The serpent spiraled up and around the bridge.

The vortex at the peak waited as a disc of utter blackness. Clouds of purple and gray streaked by lightning surrounded its flashing mouth.

Angela had no more thought for what was going on with Lucifel. All she could see was the darkness about to swallow them. Her eyeballs pulsed and her entire body throbbed and hummed. For a brief moment, she felt like a million hands tore her into a million more pieces. And then what followed was a blackness so all-consuming it leached through to her soul and tore at it like the very teeth of death.

Thirty

How long had she been here, floating like this?

Angela felt herself curled into a ball, her knees tucked under her arms. That same beautiful song Sophia loved floated around her in muffled notes. Was she dreaming? But Angela knew she'd been in this place before, so very many times.

"Open your eyes, Angela," a gentle male voice echoed around her.

Angela obeyed.

She was nowhere, surrounded by darkness and silence. She couldn't even quite remember what had happened or how she'd come to this place again.

Yet as Angela thought and time seemed to pass with aching slowness, a blue light appeared in front of her. Was she imagining it? No—the light was now growing brighter and taking shape. The familiar contours of arms, legs, and wings appeared. A strange burning sensation filled Angela's chest. Her heart ached so punishingly. Then, Raziel's magnificence took form at last.

The Supernal angel's red hair dazzled her eyes and his midnight blue coat didn't just twinkle with gems now, but with real lights that cast their brilliance into the suffocating shadows around him and Angela. The four wings on his back and the two wings on his ears fanned gently in some mysterious breeze Angela couldn't feel.

The angel smiled graciously.

No wonder Israfel had fallen in love with him. He was so gentle and charming, and even at a confusing moment like this, his presence soothed and healed. Angela hesitated, then smiled back. But the uncertainty in her made it hard to be so hopeful so soon. Did she even have the right to hope anymore?

"You're doing well, Angela," Raziel said. "I've been watching over you for so long, unable to share my deepest thoughts. But now my spirit has its chance to speak to you within the shelter of your mind before the end. And what a journey it has been for us both . . ."

His voice shivered through her sweetly.

"I always knew," he continued, "that you would make the right choices. I believed in you . . . and now my belief has been justified. You have only one step left. Now it's time to bring about the end of a tragic cycle of misfortune. A Revolution that Lucifel could never have imagined is ready to begin. The Ruin of the old universe will be the foundation for the new. The time has arrived to retake the crown stolen from you so long ago."

"I've been told I need to create new stanzas to the Angelus to save this universe," Angela whispered. Now, all the horrors that had passed were returning to her little by little. As well as a sense of utter helplessness. "But what can I do? The souls that can help me—Lucifel stole them away. And *those who are still free remain beyond my reach. And even if they came to me, I wouldn't know what to do."*

Raziel leaned down and kissed Angela gently on one cheek, then the other. His lips were so soft and warm.

"You're speaking as if you are all alone, Angela. Think hard about what it means to have the friends you do. They're risking their lives for your sake. Believe in them, like I've always believed in you. Call to them, and they will come. Now . . . I must leave you. You no longer need my protection, Angela. It's time that you stand as your own person without the shadow of my spirit burning within you.

"But to see yourself clearly, you must have the strength to withstand the truth."

Raziel's body began to disintegrate into millions of azure sparks. From the hem of his coat up to his blood-red hair and wings, he disappeared. Soon, all Angela had left was the ghostly memory of his voice, still echoing in her head.

It's time to reclaim what is yours . . .

Without warning, the burning sensation in Angela's chest grew almost unbearable. It was like a sun threatened to burst from her and brighten everything a thousand shades of white. She closed her eyes and listened to her heartbeat and then deeper to the hum of blood in her veins.

There. She could hear it. A song.

As if a dream spread out before her, Angela seemed to stare at herself in a giant mirror, her eyes shining back wide and glassy. A strange pain cut through her like the blade of a jagged saw. Angela looked different, and yet without a doubt—this was her. She was taller in the reflection, with the same face, but her hair hung long and pure white. She wore a black robe with white jewels, and her large green *eyes flashed like emeralds in the sun. Wings in the colors of bronze, red, and gray trailed decorously from her back.*

She looked just like the Father. Like his twin.

Raziel's voice continued in pained whispers. "It was no mere coincidence that I chose you to be the Archon. Now, Angela, you have returned to where you belong. The Grail was always yours. The Eye was always your Eye. Now, you are becoming whole again. The blue blood in your veins is your true blood, returned to you. This is the TRUTH."

Now the mirror of her soul reflected other things as well. They were memories, erupting like forgotten nightmares. Where had they hidden within her for so long? Yet without a doubt, they'd always been there, buried, submerged. There was the glory of space and the sensation of warmth and protection. Then, Angela was being ripped away from some sheltering womb, crushed and mangled and torn to pieces. Every part of her screamed with agony as bones crunched and muscles shredded, and her eye—oh, the horrific pain in her eye—

She clasped it, moaning.

The memories continued, and in them her blood spattered. Her veins gaped open. Worst of all, her soul dropped into some deep and bottomless darkness. First there was the noise of rushing water, then nothing. Such horrible, horrible nothingness.

She was dead and still dying, and she continued dying in every cycle of time as if the tragedy could never end or change. But the Eye torn from her could still see. Finally, it watched the creation of Lucifel, Raziel, and Israfel from the mangled remains of her old body. It observed the deaths of countless angels as it swung on its chain from Lucifel's neck. It bled and the precious blood within it became the Glaive,

*slicing and destroying all that was lesser, which was every-
thing. Then Raziel stole it. He brought the Eye down into an
Underworld of gloom and misery, giving it to the Jinn as a
promise for hope. There, Angela's former Eye saw nothing
but pain and starvation. There, it absorbed more darkness,
until all it seemed to ever know was darkness.*

*Meanwhile her soul waited, and waited, and waited, and
waited in the measureless Abyss.*

*Until another cycle of tragedy was almost over—and it
was time to put an end to it once and for all.*

"*Eons, millennia, centuries of this cycle of time had
passed,*" Raziel's voice echoed faintly. "*Human beings
existed and continued to evolve as well. They were different than angels, however. Their spirits were more resilient,
more apt to adapt and survive the cruelest changes. I knew
that. So I chose one, to hold your ancient soul, and I—who
died so miserably for that truth—rested beside you in the
same body and protected you from harm until the end came
at last. And you were born again into the world, with a
new name, and the blood-red hair that sadly marked you
as cursed and wicked. You had to exist again, because you
were the only creature with the powerful soul that could
overturn a well-established cycle of pain.*"

*Sophia's face appeared before Angela now. But it was less
doll-like, and dazzlingly beautiful, and so unearthly that no
human word could describe it.*

Angela couldn't bear much more.

*But she had to open her real eyes. She had to continue on.
Angela's past was a horror to her—and a pain worse than
any before or since; but even though she no longer knew
herself, she did know her new family and friends. That was
enough to awaken her for the end that was now to come.*

They're ready to fight for you, *Raziel said in her mind.* They've always been a part of you . . . and so will I.

And with that thought, and the weapon that was her memory, more scintillating and sharp than the Glaive could ever be, Angela opened her eyes to the end.

PART FOUR

Ruin

One Hour until the Great Silence

Every possible life to be lived ends here,
in the place where silence was born.

Thirty-one

Israfel clutched at his head, trying to wish away the throbbing agony as Lucifel's shadow relentlessly worked and worked to destroy his body one cell at a time.

This was the end, and he would either survive it with the precious child within him intact, or he wouldn't. The syringes he'd used for so many centuries to help inject the Father's healing blue blood into his veins were no longer available. He now had to survive in a more animalistic and humiliating way.

How long had he been lying nearly broken to death in the middle of a bone-cold floor, drinking blood from a corpse, all to keep his dream of redemption for the universe alive?

This was all just one long nightmare, he had to tell himself. *Soon it will be over forever.* But he'd thought that way for millennia and it had gotten him nowhere. Ultimately, in the saddest irony, it had merely led him back to the painful past where he'd begun. Even so, Israfel had no strength to move and no more will to fight. There was only one throbbing thought in his soul: he had to stay alive for everyone else's sake.

He clutched his stomach, feeling the chick inside moving again.

The Nexus was darker than he remembered, even though Israfel had freed himself from both it and Ialdaboth's empty horrors only a year ago. There were no more stars to gaze upon. Those had probably faded and died by now in the approaching apocalypse. But a dull, reddish light threw itself from the crystal walls that made up the Nest of God. This place had familiar things, though perhaps only by an angel's or a demon's standards: a floor, darkness, walls, stone and crystal, and the faint, faint light of billions of souls floating out in dark nothingness, beyond the endless honeycomb of the matrix that now imprisoned him again. They could be seen as if through octagonal portholes, bobbing and dancing ceaselessly. But they were now home. There was nowhere better or worse to go than here, even though Israfel had tried finding a place and had, at the very least, been determined on making one.

Israfel's eyes bled again.

Warmth and redness blurred his vision. He reached up to wipe away the mess with trembling hands.

If only he could see or know what Angela was doing right now. If only he could know whether Angela was one step closer to opening the Book of Raziel at all.

A large and strong hand stroked Israfel's feathery hair. He froze, shaking violently, and his thoughts screeched to a halt. His wings stiffened and he gasped for breath. All he could hear was the Father's slow, echoing breath close by. He knew it was all an illusion brought on by his dying mind. Scenes from the past were replaying themselves, and Israfel could do nothing to stop them.

A great shadow loomed over him. Fabric rustled as someone sat down beside Israfel and a great robe slid across the floor.

"You thought that you'd killed me," the voice next to him said chidingly.

I did. I did kill you. You're nothing but a ghost now, Israfel's brain screamed. *Stop touching me. If you don't stop, I'll go mad again.*

But he said nothing, quietly listening to the phantom words in his terror.

Now it struck him—where was the Angelus song that had always echoed so faintly in the background of Ialdaboth and creation? Why couldn't Israfel hear it anymore?

In the world of the living, only the winged ears of the Supernals could hear it at all. That was why the wings existed there in the first place. On and on, that song had always continued like a gentle humming in the back of Israfel's brain. He'd always sensed that he was supposed to continue the song, to help spread its notes in his own special way. Instead, he'd nearly forgotten the true meaning of most of the lyrics.

Who had sung it first, though? Even he didn't have the answers.

All he knew was that the Father had nothing do with it. The Father had hated that song, and every time Israfel had dared part his lips to join in the refrain, he'd been punished for it cruelly. He shuddered, remembering his pain.

Now mad laughter thundered out of the Father who in reality lay dead beside Israfel.

It rang in all its darkness, as if it could spread more waves of disease farther out into the universe with every second that passed.

"Israfel," the Father said in his peerlessly perfect voice, plucked straight from Israfel's worst memories, "what will I do with you? How many cages does it take to tame a bird? How many times did I tell you that you're mine, and mine alone? You do understand you've left me so . . . so *disappointed*. I have so many wounds from the many times you stabbed me, Israfel. It seemed to take forever to drag myself to this spot while I bled so profusely and so much. That was your thanks for how I kept you alive for so long, even after Lucifel poisoned you, and the treasure inside of you . . ."

Don't touch me. Don't touch me, Israfel's mind screamed again. He breathed harder.

The unreal caress through his hair grew rougher.

"And my blood," the Father continued ominously, "was the only thing to keep you alive. You always used to try to spit it back at me, until I forced your mouth open. After that you knew what was good for you." There was a meaningful pause. "So much so, *that you murdered me for it to keep yourself and our child alive.*"

Israfel clenched his fingers. A terrible insanity began to well up within him.

His fingers shook. His heart quivered, and he repeated Raziel's name in his mind, trying to picture the Supernal's gentle face and deep blue eyes.

You are beautiful, Israfel, Raziel's voice said in his soul. The words echoed back from the past. *Remember . . . you know what must be done to redeem yourself . . .*

"Don't listen to him," the Father said. "You know that someone like yourself can't find salvation."

Now the hand that had been caressing Israfel switched

tactics, turning him so that he had no choice but to gaze back into his false Creator's terrible green eyes, and perfect androgynous face, lined by all its flawlessly symmetrical stripes.

Israfel closed his eyes, but when he opened them, the hallucination continued.

What insects did humans hate? Hornets? Wasps?

Israfel's Creator was like a wasp fading with autumn's approach, and the universe had been his hive. The Father's immense, seemingly innumerable wings fanned above Israfel like death in shades of bronze, crimson, and black. His wounded body was slender but immense, strong but delicate, and he was perfect but also so terrible to behold now that all his beauty was marred and disfigured by Israfel's frantic violence. His robe could have been made of night and ink, and he wore no adornments and didn't need any. His curtain of long, pin-straight dark hair was enough, and his face matched Angela's except for the all-consuming fire burning behind his eyes.

A twin . . . a twin . . . the Father had a twin?

Israfel's soul shuddered. Pain lanced through all his dying veins, and then his angelic mind grasped everything once again with a full and clear light. *That* was why Angela looked like the Father. *That* was why her soul had always been a mystery. *That* was what Raziel had known that led to his death . . . that led to . . .

It all crashed upon Israfel at once as if for the first time. Anger iced into a lump of hatred in his heart, he grew numb inside, and his life, and his choices, and all his sins blew back in his face like a burning wind that, even so, failed to melt that ice.

God was not God. The Father was just playing God, pretending to be God, acting as God. Whoever and wherever God happened to be, this rotting monstrosity wasn't Him. He was an imposter.

"You murdered Raziel," Israfel said with a slow coldness that surprised even him. He knew he was talking only to himself, to a dream, yet he dared to sit up a little and think of even more to say. His dirty coat hung dejectedly on his body, exposing one of his shoulders. His wings stiffened.

"I murdered who?" the Father whispered, stroking Israfel's death-white hair.

"Raziel . . ." Israfel said blankly, relishing the name and how it rekindled the spot of light left in his soul.

The Father's eyes narrowed. He drew his hand away. "No one needed his arrogance and meddling anymore," he said softly. "You least of all. I didn't need your eyes turning to Raziel instead of me, my Israfel. I didn't need you to know the truth. Even if Lucifel knew. Yes, yes, eventually she knew. But I grew to detest her long before that. I always enjoyed how you both grew to hate each other. I enjoyed the pain in Lucifel's eyes when I denied her love from the start. I always had wondered what would happen—you see, I had so much time to wonder—if a creature grew up without love. I found out with her horrid little Revolution, and when she took the Grail from me. You, Israfel, were all I had left after that . . ."

He turned back around and grabbed Israfel by the chin, gently but oh so menacingly at the same time.

"You never needed a family. You only needed me. I was your home. I was the source of everything. Why do you think you're back here with me after so long?"

Israfel couldn't even think. He could only adopt the cold, cold mask of so many eons. The one that hid pain and fear and held promises of justice.

Justice, justice, justice, his mind said over and over. Beyond those words, he could see Raziel's mangled wings and broken body as he plummeted to his death.

"And look what we've created together, you and I," the Father said silkenly. He brushed a finger across Israfel's stomach. "You thought you had no purpose in life, beautiful Israfel. So I gave it to you. You're not male or female. You're like me. You are the last piece of the twin I murdered, and the one that resembled him most. It's hardly fair you have your own soul. But such things are dealt with gently, one step at a time.

"I dare say, from the look on your face, you've almost lost the little bit of your spirit left to you. That was always the point. I promise that once every last shred is gone, you'll know what happiness is. The death of any dream is never easy. But you and so many other creatures are moths that I pinched between my fingers, holding you to the flame. You twisted and writhed, but eventually, always, you succumbed."

Footsteps broke the silence that rang after those final words.

Israfel paused. His heart hardly dared to beat.

The Father paused, his own winged ears stiff with what could only be disbelief as he turned to regard their unexpected visitor. From out of the dismal shadows of what had once been their Eden, Lucifel emerged into view like bleakness forming itself into a person. She looked ravaged. Her wings bled, and she breathed hard, clutching a gaping wound in her arm.

She'd clenched her teeth, baring them as she sucked back what must have been great pain.

She shared one quick pitiless glance with Israfel and then

regarded her God—who was not really anyone's God at all—with a face reflecting his death. Her crimson eyes flashed in the darkness.

"YOU," the Father growled at her with all the wickedness of a billion Jinn. Or was it Israfel who spoke? He no longer knew. His own anger was like a storm cloud seething on the horizon for far too long and as he drew closer to death, reality escaped. "I knew you would try to come back. Did you think I wouldn't foresee that?"

But Lucifel paid no attention because of course she wasn't sharing in Israfel's hallucination at all. She never moved, but continued staring at the Father's broken and bloodstained corpse like a lost lover or a bewildered child.

Israfel couldn't bear looking at her beseeching face.

It was the same face he remembered from his days as a chick, when the Father had shunned her so mercilessly. But just as quickly, Lucifel lost the fleeting innocent expression of her past. Her bloodless features hardened again and her jaw set. "You're still alive," she whispered to Israfel, though he heard her voice all too loudly. "Even after all your time by this corpse, Israfel, you still refuse to become one yourself. Why must you make me do this? Why must I put an end to that miserable child within you by myself?"

Israfel shifted his gaze to a spot in the darkness where a deeper blackness had appeared on top of it, like a hole overlaying reality. Someone else had crossed the Realm of Malakhim to enter Ialdaboth, even though no one should have been able to do so anymore.

His eyes widened. Israfel's breath caught.

Angela's face was unreadable as she stepped into the light, as she looked at what had become of Lucifel, and then Israfel, and last of all, the Father.

Her gaze met with Israfel's and he shuddered in spite of himself. She no longer looked like the Angela he'd known. Her hair was now as white as Israfel's and both her eyes had achieved the brilliant green of the Grail. Or at least it had seemed that way, because Israfel's vision warped again, and she quickly returned to the red-haired woman he'd always encountered. Angela already had the Glaive in her hands, fully formed. Her left shoulder bled. Her teeth chattered, perhaps from pain. Her expression spoke of nightmares and she barely seemed able to stand.

She held out the Glaive slowly and majestically anyway so that its deadly point aimed right at Lucifel.

"I'm here," Angela said resoundingly. Her body heaved for breath. *"And now I'm going to reclaim what's mine."*

Thirty-two

The words had barely escaped Angela's mouth when every-thing went wrong.

Every brave and noble scenario that went through her head devolved in one instant as an insane blackness that Angela knew to be Lucifel slammed her in agony to the ground.

She could no longer see Israfel or the terrible corpse of the creature that had once been her twin. She couldn't even rely on the feathered serpent for help anymore. It had left her and Lucifel shortly after they'd arrived and the force of entering this Realm drove them temporarily apart. The last Angela saw of it, the serpent had been weaving through the stars that remained hanging like dim lamps in the ether of space.

Help was impossible now anyway.

Angela knew she was about to die and everything was falling apart. Already, strange holes were appearing in the space where she and Lucifel and Israfel stood. Without a doubt, the Realms had started to disintegrate.

"This was all your fault!" Lucifel's voice thundered like murder in Angela's ears. *"All of it! Everything!"*

Angela could barely see. Even Israfel disappeared, and it was obvious he was in no position to rescue her. She was alone. The Glaive collapsed in her weak hands to a puddle that trickled down her arms.

Her entire body moaned with the pain of hitting the ground so hard. Her head spun. Lucifel's face was a blur and her eyes burned like embers. Her face had twisted to a horrific mask of grief. Was it because she'd seen the Father, the supposed Creator whom she loved, dead again? Was it because of Israfel's condition? Maybe no one would ever know. With lightning-quick ferocity, the angel's fingers clutched at Angela's skin, and wherever bare skin happened to be Lucifel tore at it, screaming.

Angela screamed with her. There had never been a pain within her like this one. Fire shot through every inch of her nerves. Warmth gushed from every split and gash in her skin.

This pain, this pain. She was being torn apart again and could do nothing to stop it.

Still, Lucifel hovered overhead, her eyes bright with ferocity. As the Devil's wings beat the air powerfully, the blue souls danced out in space, some of them suddenly descending to swarm down around Lucifel as if to stop her. She took as much heed of them as dust in the air.

Angela's sight threatened to leave her. Lucifel shrieked something else at her, but she couldn't hear it for a while— there was just too much pain. She could make out the words *Father* and *love* but nothing else of meaning.

Then, it was all over. The tornado of terror and blood ceased.

Lucifel stood up over Angela, her lips trembling with more grief and rage. She kicked Angela savagely in the chest.

Ripples of pain exploded through Angela again.

She gasped. Her brain fogged and churned. Everything was agony and torment. Was Angela bleeding to death at last? She lifted a trembling hand and found it covered in rivers of azure liquid. She tried to move her legs, but couldn't.

Her bones must have broken. Certainly the odd sensation in her arms was because even more splinters of bone poked through her skin. A dull crackling signaled her efforts to move.

"Now," Lucifel whispered, her voice sounding so far away. "Time to finish everything."

She knelt down by Angela and plunged her hands into a gaping wound in Angela's leg, emerging with blue blood cupped in her palms. It streaked Lucifel's skin like paint. "All I need now," she whispered more, "is Sophia. The Archon is such a waste, a joke. Raziel was wrong." Her voice choked away with more grief. "This is the best and only path. No more pain, sadness, or worry to come. Existence will simply be existence. Nothing more. We don't *need* anything but silence from this point on, and an end to the cycle of sorrows."

Angela tried to remonstrate with her.

That was impossible. Her voice no longer worked. She croaked, sensing warm blood bubbling up her throat.

Lucifel examined her coldly and then turned, letting the blue blood in her hands solidify with sparks of her own aura. A brilliant red glow outlined her entire body as a weapon resembling the Glaive took shape and glittered. "Oh, Raziel, Raziel," Lucifel whispered. "It was all such a mistake. Your gentleness blinded you. Why didn't you listen to me? Well . . ." Lucifel closed her unbearable eyes for a moment. "Now, I will be the new God. In memory of Him. I know what's best. Yes . . . no more rot, love, and death."

Lucifel advanced on Angela, though the rifts in space around them were growing wider. Most shone a beautiful pearlescent color, as if suggesting worlds of beauty and light existed behind them. Around them, the shining souls danced and dived in whirlwinds of beauty.

Angela, Angela, a warm, concerned, male voice seemed to say from somewhere nearby. Angela struggled to keep her eyes open.

Kim's handsome face appeared above her like a dream. His amber eyes reflected back all the light she was sure she'd lost forever. His ghost took her hand, pressing it to his cheek. Tears poured down his transparent but beautiful face. An hourglass pendant hanging from his neck had run out of sand. *Yes,* he whispered. He kissed her tenderly on the forehead. *That's it. Look at me. You can't give up now.*

"Where are you?" Angela tried to say, but only a croak actually left her. "Why . . . can I see you now?"

I've been by your side since I died. Now all you have to do is call me. Call the people who care about you and who are on your side. And we will help you, Angela. You don't have to do this alone. You're not meant to save everyone alone, remember? The Angelus must be sung by more mouths than yours now if anything is to change.

"Call you. I just have to call you," Angela whispered back brokenly. Angela's heart struggled to keep beating. She couldn't die. She couldn't.

But Kim couldn't really be here. She was dreaming him *because* she was dying.

Yet if that was true—why wasn't she seeing Sophia? Perhaps it was best she wasn't here to watch Angela perish so miserably, to see all their shared dreams die in a messy sea of

Angela's blood. Angela was so close to failing. But instead of her death instigating a new cycle of time as it had in the past, Lucifel would silence existence.

Call me, Kim's voice reminded her. *Call us . . .*

Angela's mind fuzzed over. "Where are you?" she whispered. "All the souls . . . who want to live in this world? Where are you?"

Now she knew for certain—Lucifel had never meant for Angela to get this far. It had never been part of the plan, and she was scared and on edge. She stood over Angela like a living shadow, eyeing Angela cautiously, and then something caught Lucifel's attention.

She looked up.

Souls were erupting into the ether of the Nexus in a sheer flood, even compared to the souls who had already broken through the barrier of the walls. The souls streaked for Lucifel and Angela, swirling around them in a twister of pulsing bluish light.

They danced and swarmed around Angela like a trillion azure fireflies, melding into her veins and skin, becoming one with her blood, healing her from the inside out. The Nexus brightened and burned to a pulsing whiteness. A galaxy of souls spread their arms out into the vastness of the voids, shining like newborn stars. They avoided the rifts growing around them, but they never stopped dancing.

Angela's limbs could move again. She sat up, suddenly able to feel her legs.

Angela broke from her trance as life returned to her.

Lucifel drew back. She narrowed her eyes, examining the glowing sphere-shaped souls that drifted and bobbed around them in a whirl of stars and glowing snow. And all around them, the other dimensional rifts, like holes between the space of creation, widened. There were so many, yet none were as pulsing, horrid, and dark as the Nexus had become. Instead, they shone softly like a full moon. The light exuded an overwhelming aura of peace.

Different songs erupted through the holes, as sweet as the Angelus.

Then, one strange hole appeared near the Father's dead body. It held no song. It held no light. There was nothingness beyond it, as dreadful and absolute as what their own universe might become if Angela didn't do something fast.

Abruptly, Israfel's wings stiffened and he leaned forward as if listening. His lined sea-blue eyes turned toward Angela, and an endless grief and longing broke his androgynous beauty. He clutched his stomach, sighing in horror.

What was he thinking?

I know what he's thinking. I can hear his heartbeat. I know that look. THAT LOOK THAT MEANS HE'S GOING TO DIE.

"*Angela!*" a familiar voice said.

A soul hovered near Angela and took shape. It was Camdon Willis, Nina's dead half brother who'd lost his life to Python. Stephanie Walsh, the blood head witch of Luz who had tormented Angela, stood next to him, staring at Lucifel resolutely. More souls took shape, gazing at the Supernal angrily. They were all set on the Devil. They were all of one purpose. They sided with Angela. No one wanted to have their minds, feelings, and hearts erased.

Lucifel searched them.

She turned to Angela now, but didn't bother to smile. "You irritating bitch," she hissed.

Lucifel's own Glaive hadn't disappeared, and now she swung it lethally right at Angela's head.

❧

Angela had no time to stop Israfel from shoving her aside.

He flew toward her, his great wings like white banners, and their weight connected.

Angela hit the floor hard, crying out with the pain, sliding dangerously close to the Father's corpse and the black and ugly rift that had manifested like a disease among the others.

Israfel collapsed beside her, a gruesome slash blossoming right across his chest and his left wing. Blood poured out of him. He tried to stand up, slipped, and tried again. He clutched at his stomach, gritted his teeth, and seemed to suck up all the hellish pain that must have overwhelmed him, and this time he actually stood for a second before crumpling to the ground in a heap.

Lucifel's mouth gaped open in shock. Her weapon collapsed, running down her arms.

She looked at her hands in surprise, and rage twisted her face. Without more of Angela's blood, she couldn't make another weapon.

Lucifel cursed viciously under her breath. She thrust out her hand, and a blast of crackling red energy flew straight for Angela.

Angela ducked, and that was all the distraction Lucifel needed to be upon her again. But this time something had changed. Angela didn't need her blood to make the Glaive anymore. Energy thrummed through her entire body. Voices whispered to her as they had from the Mirror Pools—the voices of innumerable souls crying out to her, to save her.

Help me, she thought frantically. *Let's do this together!*

Hundreds of souls converged on Angela again. Their brilliant blue light solidified into a new Glaive that Angela clasped quickly between her aching hands. She caught Lucifel's chest with the pointed edge, pierced halfway through the angel's muscle and bone, and twisted around, thrusting Lucifel backward into the empty rift behind them.

Lucifel snagged the blade with her hands at the last moment. She held on, anything to stop what they both knew was her fate.

But the souls that made the Glaive decided to disperse. Light exploded around Angela and Lucifel in a sea of blinding silver.

Angela flew backward onto the ground. Lucifel also fell backward out of reach.

Angela jumped to her feet, and her eyes cleared in time to see the Destroyer Supernal staring at her in disbelief from where Lucifel floated in the frightening void beyond the rift. Lucifel gave one last lingering look at the Father's dead body before a throbbing but silent blackness took her. Tendrils of smokelike ether smothered her and grasped at her like the tentacles of some terrifying octopus.

Her hand escaped the void a final time, grasping for Angela maniacally.

Then, with one final and horrific cry, the Devil disappeared, sucked away into a universe of death and nothingness, just like the one she'd worked so hard to create.

Thirty-three

Angela stared at the rift where Lucifel had vanished.

Quickly, she backed away from it to a safe distance, still horrified by the throbbing darkness. Her ankles brushed against one of Israfel's half-broken wings.

"Oh no, oh no," Angela whispered. She knelt by Israfel's side and looked him over hastily. One of his four large wings had nearly been sliced in half. His chest was one big wound, and his eyes bled steadily.

He's dying. There's no way he can lose so much blood and still live.

With tears blurring her vision, Angela grabbed Israfel's wings and, despite feeling as weak as a gnat, dragged him away from the Father's dreadful corpse to the center of the room, directly underneath an octagonal opening to the bleak space outside. Israfel gasped with pain and stared up into the opening, his face paling as he seemed to remember something. "This was where I was," he whispered, "when I first opened my eyes to the stars . . ."

Angela knelt beside him again and grabbed his creamy-white hand.

Israfel turned to her, and his gaze, so vacant since she first saw him again, cleared. He looked at Angela as if seeing her for the first and only time. "I was wrong about everything," he said, his voice still enchanting and musical despite growing weaker and fainter. "I thought I could save this universe myself. I thought you and I—together—could be its new deity. But now I see . . . I only wanted to believe there was a reason for what I suffered." Israfel pressed a hand against his stomach. "You can understand what kind of creature I am, right? You've lived your life in a world that doesn't allow for difference." Israfel lifted a shaking hand and touched Angela's red hair. "Now . . . I will take the child within me into death. It is much better for me to pass away . . . as my siblings have done. The old order must come to an end . . ."

"You . . ." Angela tried to wish away the tears in her eyes. All she could remember was dancing with Israfel in Luz, in that decaying old church, with feathers falling around them like snow. "You can bear children . . . so you're not just a male?"

That explained his strange beauty. Every time Angela had looked at Israfel, he appeared different. Perhaps he merely reflected the desires of whoever set their eyes on him.

"The Father did this to me . . ." Israfel whispered, indicating the infant inside him. His voice was almost inaudible. "And I killed him. It was my last chance at escape. And at the time, I truly believed . . . it was the only way to reach you and save what was left of this broken universe. And as I said . . . I now know I was wrong."

Angela didn't know what to say. She thought of the kiss

Israfel had shared with her so long ago. He'd been tasting her soul, and she'd wondered at the odd attraction between them.

Now it all made sense.

It's because he's a part of me—of the old me that no longer exists.

He's all that's left of what Heaven used to be. And he's dying.

"I deserved the cruelest justice for my sins," Israfel said so softly. "Have I paid enough? Tell me . . . have I now been redeemed?"

He looked at Angela beseechingly.

Angela closed her eyes. She couldn't talk. It even took a while to realize she was crying.

"Raziel," Israfel said. His voice was now faint as a dream. His fingers slid slowly—so slowly—out of Angela's red hair. "Do you see? There is no more pain. My heart no longer bleeds anymore . . ."

Silence descended. Angela opened her eyes, ready for the worst.

Israfel no longer moved or breathed. His eyes had glazed over.

Angela shook him by his slender shoulders, and Israfel's body jostled. Feathers dropped from his wings. But he was dead, and Angela let out a low moan, shaking him harder as if that could change the truth. "Wake up," she said, all the pain in her pouring out at once. "*Wake up*! You can't die— you can't—"

Angela let out a wild cry and flung herself off him. She collapsed sobbing into her arms, embraced by the ice-cold floor. The rifts continued to widen around her. Everything had now tipped into utter destruction. The time she had left to change the outcome of the recurring tragedy was vanishing fast.

This is my chance to bring about a revolution. What am I waiting for?

But Angela knew what she was waiting for. There was a good chance she would never leave this place, and the idea had suddenly paralyzed her.

It was very clear she'd survived the way in, and would never survive the way out even if she cured the world of all its ills, and she'd never considered that possibility until now.

Did Angela want to be alone forever?

She pushed up on her elbows, watching the rifts grow and grow.

No. This is what I came for. Besides, I'm not alone.

Angela clasped the glittering white sapphire Sophia had given her and looked up and around at the beautiful souls dancing. Angela's eyes burned and she reached out with all the power within her own soul, calling to those who would listen. Fear worked against her like a relentless current, tugging her back to shore. What if she really never saw Sophia ever again? Nina and Troy and Juno would never know what had happened to her either. But as Angela thought this, more souls and light raced toward her in countless glorious streaks, and she finally made her choice—she welcomed them with uplifted arms.

An infinite number of suns could have exploded in her chest.

All the heat and light in the universe condensed within her, down into something small enough to be the most brilliant star.

Her human life passed before her in every shade of happiness and sadness, and behind every memory Sophia's face seemed to shine as if she'd been watching Angela all along.

All I've ever wanted was to be a normal human girl. All I can imagine is being with Sophia and Kim and Nina. Everyone deserves the happiness they've earned. I can't take that away from them, allowing the home that is our universe to disappear. I can't push aside the dream of countless souls burning within me. The new Angelus is there, warming my blood, right now. I guess all I have to do is share it for the first time.

The burning sensation in Angela's chest grew almost unbearable.

She closed her eyes and listened to her heartbeat and then deeper to the hum of blood in her veins. There. She could hear it. A song.

Help me, everyone. This isn't Ruin. This is change. It's Revolution. Let's work with what we have. Let's make the choice together.

At last, the words of the new Angelus found their way to her lips. Angela couldn't bring herself to open her mouth. The final remnants of fear held her back, and then she opened her eyes a final time and saw Kim's soul reaching for hers with a confident smile. He leaned down and embraced her as the light took over and swallowed them completely.

Hoping for the best, she sang.

PART FIVE

Revolution

The Cycle of Time Has Ended

Every last promise must be kept.

Thirty-four

Python awakened to a place so unlike the one where he'd fallen asleep, the two were barely comparable.

The Luz Institution's meagerly civilized surroundings had still been miles away from the oppressive, echoing space he found himself in now. Python caught sight of thousands of skulls set in the stone walls and didn't move another muscle for a long, long time. Then he tried to move and found he couldn't. His body was paralyzed, and the stone beneath him bit any exposed skin with jagged pebbles.

He was back in the catacombs beneath Luz? How? What had happened to him?

A strange heaviness had taken over his limbs and his thoughts.

As Python's eyes adjusted to the strange light in the cavern, he remembered Sophia's frightening face and the winged Kirin's horn as it pierced through his chest. It had missed his heart, thankfully. In another stroke of good fortune, his demonic blood had healed him rather quickly.

That still hadn't prevented him from being poisoned.

Python had always longed for a winged Kirin as part of his personal menagerie. The very idea that their horns were tipped with slow-acting venom fascinated him. How irritating that the same poison that enthralled him now coursed through his own veins.

Fear rippled through him all at once. Python breathed, turning his head slightly.

He could hear someone else breathing beside him. Certainly it was whoever had brought him to this rank little den again.

"Awake, finally?" a familiar voice said with a low and throaty hiss.

It was *her*. Python went rigid. His heart threatened to stop beating. It was *her* of all creatures, and here he lay, weak as a trapped rat.

Troy appeared above him, her chalk-white face and phosphorescent eyes mesmerizing in the odd light of the catacombs. Her single wing tested the air gently. She bared her teeth, exposing their reddish stains. She'd fed on something recently. Python could only guess at what, considering her appetite was large. He remembered that well enough from her time as his pet.

"You brought me here?" Python said to her groggily.

Troy sat beside him. She licked her bottom teeth before speaking. "Yes . . . I dragged your body from the institution myself and brought it here. For safekeeping."

Python laughed. "And what do you plan to do? Cage me in the darkness below Luz? Turn me into a new Lucifel? The second you drop your guard, I'll crush all your bones with one snap of my jaws—"

Now it was Troy's turn to smile—and in that awful Jinn way that wasn't a real smile at all.

"Really?" she said. "Will you? But I don't think you're in any kind of position anymore to make threats."

Python clenched his jaw. His let his voice turn murderous. "Let me go NOW."

"Oh, I don't think so," Troy said. She settled down beside him. "I'm not giving you up anytime soon. I made a promise to you, Python. Do you remember it? I told you I would destroy you—and I promised myself that I would then destroy Babylon afterward. I warned you fairly, and you made your choice when I became your slave. It's as if you wanted me to devour your heart someday. I'm flattered."

Python's heart raced. "Listen to you," he hissed back. "You speak madness. Release me, and I will give you Babylon myself. You can rule as the new Queen of the Jinn, just as I always planned."

"Why?" Troy said, her ears pressing back into her hair. "So that I can be a puppet lorded over by you? A pawn and an eternal slave to a serpent? No deal, snake. I like you here just fine, and here you'll stay. I'm not done with you anyway. Once I'm done, we can figure out what to do with the rest of you."

Now Python felt fear sink its knifelike teeth into his nerves. He would have shivered if his body wasn't so unresponsive and numb. "What are you saying?" he muttered.

"I'm saying that your game is officially over," Troy said so softly. "Babylon is already being emptied as we speak. Juno is the new Jinn Queen and we're gathering what's left of the loyal Clans to re-create the city that used to be my namesake, just as we'd always dreamed."

Python let out an incredulous laugh. "Lies. Utter nonsense. As if my mother would allow such a thing—"

"Oh, she's never said a word. In fact, I doubt she ever will again," Troy said.

For Python's benefit, she lifted a dark arm from a body resting next to him.

Python's insides turned to ice. He gritted his teeth and shut his eyes, burying the pain of the fact that his mother was very likely dead deep inside and not succeeding. It tormented him instead. It swallowed his soul and colored the world. But, oh, he refused to scream like he wanted to. "What did you do to her, you feathered rat?" he spat at Troy, though in reality his voice now sounded so weak.

"Ah, not me," Troy corrected him gently. "This—" She held up the arm again. It was clearly ravaged. "This is Juno's work. Far too messy and unfocused for a seasoned veteran like myself, yes?"

Now, as if out of nowhere, Juno appeared beside Troy and stared down at Python curiously.

"I told you once upon a time," Troy said to Python, "that I would devour your heart first. However, I'm sorry to say I had to work from the bottom up. In the meantime, I've been enjoying my hours spent here, because as you can see, the souls that used to swarm the catacombs have gone. They all left Luz, flying into Malakhim like a flock of glowing jewels. I wonder . . . Angela must have called them. So, as you can imagine, your stay would be quite lonely if I hadn't thought of delivering your mother to you."

Python wanted to say so many things. Instead he said nothing. Because it was obvious nothing good could come out of trying.

So—she'd been eating him piece by piece. Python hadn't felt any pain because of the Kirin's venom numbing his flesh.

He was about to open his mouth to say something witty and profound. But he chose in the end not to say a word. Troy didn't look disappointed in the slightest. Python knew their kind well enough to understand Troy was enjoying this dark little pocket of existence beneath Luz. He also knew now that he should have never helped destroy *only* Troy's namesake city in the past. He should have spread his campaign against the Jinn to encompass all of Hell, never stopping until every last one of the lethal vermin was dead or caged.

Yet that no longer mattered, because Python had chosen differently.

He'd gambled with Troy and Juno and the Archon in a vicious bid for power, trampling over everyone and everything. And he'd ultimately lost.

Troy stretched her wing and regarded him with clear irritation. "Now if you'll excuse me, I'm going to return to my meal," she said. "It's been a few days and I'm rather hungry."

Troy dipped down out of sight.

Juno turned and stalked away, appearing supremely bored with the grand spectacle that was the slow end of Python's life. He winced as he felt a dull tugging on his body.

He thought of the Archon, and his mother, and how he'd wasted so much of his life on hating, and wanting, and hurting. Where had it all gone wrong? Python wanted to blame somebody—perhaps his mother, Lilith, as usual. Yet he couldn't bring himself to do it this time when faced with the truth of what he'd done and how many lives he'd crushed. And then, mercifully, enough time passed that Troy was practically kissing him—though of course it wasn't kissing. Instead it was teeth carving the last of him to pieces.

And that was when Python at last let his tenacious hold on life go, and with it any idea of repentance, and choosing to be arrogant to the end, no longer thought of anything at all.

PART SIX

Return

The Eternal Year Has Begun

I'm home.

Thirty-five

Sophia clasped the hourglass tightly to her chest, trying to protect it from the pouring rain.

Slowly, she looked up at an old brick-and-mortar mansion sitting at the edge of the university's grounds and watched as the windows in the upper floor lit to a cheerful golden color. Sunset was approaching, though the gray sky meant that what had been a reasonable gloom during the day now shifted to a velvety night. It hadn't been her intention to get caught in the rain like this, but all those days she'd spent in Luz's typical gloom had gotten her used to being soaked to the skin.

Sophia continued to watch the window and think, allowing the water to drip off her hood and slightly into her eyes.

Then, she made up her mind.

She walked up the sidewalk and past the well-manicured landscaping, then climbed the steps onto the porch, stretching out her free hand to use the brass knocker. Sophia's heart quaked inside of her. It threatened to leap from her chest as the door swung open.

Angela stood within the door frame. She scanned Sophia up and down, lifting an eyebrow. "Can I help you?"

"Yes, I—"

Sophia paused. Angela looked the same, except that her eyes were now a brilliant green. "Yes," Sophia said again, "I'm here about the request for a portrait model? I've modeled before . . ."

Was it possible Angela didn't remember anything again? That she had no idea who she really was anymore? The idea seemed too ironic and cruel after all they had been through. Sophia couldn't even use Luz to back up her case once she started talking. Luz had finally collapsed into the sea, and though the innocent souls within the city had been saved, the city itself had not. It was nothing now but a legend long gone, rotting away beneath the ocean, with only a few of its levels still connected to the Underworld the Jinn had claimed. It had taken Sophia three long years, but she'd managed to travel from one country to the next across the Earth, searching for Angela.

She'd long suspected Angela had willed a reversal of many misfortunes and fates.

However, the laws that applied to souls themselves could not change. Those who'd died remained dead. Those who lived remained in their current state.

Hurry, a voice said, breaking into Sophia's thoughts. *Before she changes her mind.*

Sophia glanced back over her shoulder at a leafy oak. Nina rested as a large crow-shaped shadow in its branches, croaking impatiently.

"Well, are you coming in out of the rain?" Angela said to Sophia. She gestured for her to enter. "Besides, I'd like to ask a question or two, if you don't mind. I've seen you on campus a few times. I could swear I know you from somewhere."

Sophia took a deep breath and stepped over the threshold.

She followed Angela into the foyer, where Angela graciously took Sophia's wet coat and hid it inside a closet. Then they entered the living room, and Sophia gasped. One painting of the Supernals after the next decorated every available easel. There was Raziel's midnight-blue coat, Israfel's bronze wings from his youth, and even Lucifel's burning eyes. Finally, there was a lone painting of Luz as seen from the sea.

Sophia walked up to it, fighting the urge to start talking too much.

"Oh, I hope those pictures don't give you the wrong impression," Angela added hastily. "They're just a hobby of mine. I'm in serious classes for art, but I like to think outside the box sometimes. I guess you could say angels are a bit of an obsession."

"And this city?" Sophia whispered, pointing at Luz.

Angela smiled. "I have weird dreams . . ." She sat down on a leather armchair and signaled for Sophia to sit also. Sophia smoothed down her skirt and settled into a velvet loveseat. She set the hourglass down beside her. Its metal caught the light of the lamps and threw it back in rays.

Now Angela noticed it. Her brow scrunched in confusion and she pointed at the little oak sapling nestled in its mound of dirt behind the glass. "The hourglass is broken," she said, pointing at a jagged hole in the glass as if Sophia hadn't noticed. "And there's a tree inside? Is this a prop of some kind for the picture?"

Sophia smiled. "I suppose you could say that. My name is Sophia, by the way."

Angela paled a little. "You know—you really are so familiar for some reason . . ."

"Am I?" Sophia said, acting nonchalant. "Well, would you mind if I tell you a story before we begin the session? I'm an artistic type as well, and I'd like your opinion on certain elements of the plot."

Angela shrugged. "Sure, as long as we're quick. I'm kind of on a clock with my latest project. Time waits for no one, as they say."

"Well, for almost no one," Sophia clarified gently. And she began the long story they had lived through, careful to change names where appropriate. And all the while, Angela listened more and more intently, her expression rapt with concentration. And very soon time had raced by them, and the clock on the wall spoke of the earliest possible hours in the morning.

But Sophia still had to end with the song—the new Angelus. She sang it quietly, focusing on Angela's emerald green eyes.

The light always casts a shadow,
The fire of life is the same that burns,
Nectar nourishes but one still perishes,
Fate's wheel obeys only its turn.
Better to dream as life's tender pains happen
Better the future than to break the soul's wings
In the Garden of Stars you will always find me,
From the Beginning to the End, I now sing.

"I remember," Angela whispered when the last notes of the song faded. She had been staring at the hourglass and its little sapling. "I remember everything. The old laws have been overturned, and . . ." Angela regarded Sophia with a mixture of shock and elation on her face.

"Welcome back, my child," Sophia said gently. "I'm so happy I found you again."

She sat next to Angela and ran some fingers through her deep red hair.

Angela stiffened, but relaxed just as soon. A dazzling smile appeared on her face, and her eyes shone with a mysterious inner light. "Tell me," she whispered. "Does the story end like I think it does? With two friends reunited forever?"

And Sophia was about to explain, until she realized Angela was merely stating what she knew.

Sophia brushed away sudden tears. She reached into her skirt pocket and took out Tress's feather, the same feather the girl had handed Angela in Memorial Cemetery in Luz that cold and fateful night.

"Where is everyone?" Angela said breathlessly, taking Israfel's wing feather and cradling it in her hands.

"Many places," Sophia said. "Yet only one soul is truly beyond your reach. Mikel remains trapped in the body given to her by Israfel and Zion in Ialdaboth. It seems she's taken on her mother's old role as the universe's troublemaker with enthusiasm."

"I see . . . and what about Troy and Juno? And Nina and Fury? And—and Kim!"

"Perhaps you should find out for yourself. We have all the time in the world now, Angela. You made it so." Sophia stretched out her hand. She felt herself growing taller and the mysterious fiery words of the Book appearing on her skin. "Your old Throne in the Nexus is waiting for you. Your authority is now resoundingly acknowledged. But like the universe you've saved, you are now free to live as you choose. Now it is the hopes, wishes, and dreams of countless souls that define this world. It can afford to be without you for a time."

A black rift in the air appeared beside them. A warm breeze blustered from it, tossing around Sophia's hair.

The winged Kirin jumped through the gap in the ether the second it became wide enough, his great paws slamming powerfully into the hardwood floor. Thunder seemed to follow his footsteps. He trotted up to Angela and lowered his nose to be petted. His great ribbed horn resembled a spike of obsidian in the lamplight.

Angela gaped in spite of herself.

Sophia waited for an answer, watching her.

"Let's go," Angela said, smiling, "and find our friends."

Sophia grinned and took Angela's hand, using it to hoist herself onto the Kirin's shimmering flanks and between its wings, carefully grasping the hourglass as it was passed to her again. All that remained of Luz rested in this fragile container that had once held Kim's soul. Angela soon followed, stroking the creature's dark mane. She rubbed the base of its horn and the beast began to nicker, eager to escape back to what for him was the blissful darkness between the Realms.

Angela glanced behind her one more time at the ordinary room and her paintings that filled every inch of space. Sophia waited more, allowing her to say her necessary good-byes to her possessions again.

"Until next time," Angela whispered.

Then, as Sophia steeled herself, Angela kicked the Kirin's flanks and with one powerful leap into the air, they both entered the space between worlds, and the notes that now held creation followed them, singing once again of a Garden of Shadows forever lit by the souls that are stars.

Glossary of Terms, Places, People, and Things

Abyss: the lowest dimension of Hell. Raziel was the first creature to explore the Abyss; shortly after he returned to Heaven, he created Sophia.

Angel: intelligent beings that reside in the upper dimensions of the universe known as Heaven; beautiful and powerful, they are thought of as the pinnacle of creation. Angels are known for having striking eyes, feathery hair, and abilities ranging from flight to telekinesis.

Angela Mathers: a human girl discovered to be the Archon, she is known for her striking red hair, blue eyes, and preternatural skill at painting. Angela's family abused her from a young age, and her arms and legs bear numerous scars from an attempt to kill herself that backfired, killing her parents instead. From childhood, she has had visions of Lucifel and Israfel that have since revealed themselves as the angel Raziel's memories. Recently Angela has been trapped in Hell, forced to reign in Lucifel's stead as Prince of Hell.

Archangel: formal title for the angel whose authority is below God alone. Israfel was the first Archangel; the current Archangel is Zion, one of Lucifel's children.

Archon: arcane name for the human protected by the deceased angel Raziel's spirit, now known to be Angela Mathers. Since the Archon is a messiah figure with the ability to ultimately save or destroy the universe, her power is wanted by various factions of Heaven and Hell for their own purposes; she is the only being who can open Raziel's Book (Sophia).

Azrael: name of the Angel of Death who guarded deceased human souls. He was destroyed by Angela Mathers after she entered the Netherworld for the first time.

Babylon: a dimension of Hell; the city of the demons. Babylon is known for its pyramids, obelisks, and mansions that are home to some of the most powerful demons.

Binding: name for a contract linking a human soul with a Jinn's, this contract ends only with the human's death, usually at the hands of the very same Jinn protecting them.

Blood head: a derogatory name for any human with red hair, which is thought to be one of the Archon's distinguishing features; it refers to a prophecy wherein the Archon will "have blood on Her head, and blood on Her hands."

Book of Raziel: a mythical book created by the angel Raziel that contains all the secrets of the universe and an immense power. It can only be opened by the Archon with a special Key, which is a weapon the Archon alone can wield correctly called the Glaive; those who try to open the Book otherwise are fated to go insane. Surprisingly, to most, the Book of Raziel's true form is a doll-like girl named Sophia, and her body is the Lock, or seal, upon the Book; this means that to open the Book, Sophia must be killed by the Glaive.

Brendan Mathers: Angela's deceased brother and the witch Stephanie Walsh's informal boyfriend. He became infatuated with Israfel and treated his sister cruelly. He was killed by the demon Naamah in St. Mary's Cathedral and now exists as a soul forever in service to Israfel.

Camdon Willis: Nina's half-brother; he showed a strange interest in Angela, but later revealed himself as a servant of the demon Python, working to deliver both Angela and Sophia into Python's power in exchange for resurrecting Nina from the dead. Camdon is killed by Python after outliving his usefulness and his soul then becomes Lilith's property.

Catacombs: a series of canals in the lowest levels of Luz leading to a hidden network of caverns stockpiled with human bones and skeletons.

Celestial Revolution: Lucifel's failed rebellion against Heaven, also known as "the War"; the end result of which was that a third of the angels followed her to Hell to start their own regime and imprisoned her. It is commonly believed that Lucifel instigated this war because she wished to be ruler of Heaven instead of Israfel.

Cherubim: an order of angels that guards the highest dimension of Heaven, although many escaped into the lower dimensions when given the opportunity. The Cherubim are the Throne angels' original form and they have an animalistic appearance that resembles a winged sphinx; their fallen counterparts are the Hounds in Hell. Cherubim have the ability to eat time and can devour a person's remaining lifespan.

Chick: term for a young angel, demon, or Jinn.

Clan: in the realm of the Jinn there are six tribes, or clans; the Sixth Clan was the most powerful until an insurrection in its ranks led to the death of the Jinn Queen Hecate and forced Troy, who is the High Assassin of the Clans, and her niece, Juno, to become fugitives. The Sixth Clan's symbol is a crow's foot.

Covenant: refers to Raziel's ancient promises to the Jinn that he would free them someday from their harsh existence; the Archon has long been expected by the Jinn to fulfill this promise. Lucifel also used this term to describe the strong and indefinable bond between Angela and Sophia.

Crow: derogatory term for an angel, demon, or Jinn, often used among their kind as an insult; many Jinn familiars take the shape of a black crow.

Dead Tunnels: a feared part of Babylon that acts as a direct route to Lucifel's Altar; here, hundreds of angels, demons, and other creatures have been melded into the stone walls in a state of suspended animation.

Demon: intelligent beings that reside in the lower dimensions of the universe known as Hell. Beautiful and powerful, they are either former angels or direct descendants of those who have fallen and share many characteristics with angels, though they often wear tattoos signifying their rank, and their wings are in varying states of decay from Hell's acidic mists. Most demons worship Lucifel, but there are some who wish the Archon to rule in her place.

Devil: the formal name for Lucifel among most humans; in its plural form it refers to the Jinn.

Dominions: the angelic term for the dimensions that make up the universe.

Emerald House: formerly the home of the cult headed by Stephanie Walsh called the Pentacle Sorority, it has now been renamed by Angela Mathers; it is named after Lucifel's Grail, which resembles an emerald in color, and its symbol is a green eye.

Ether: the substance that composes much of the universe, it can be manipulated by angels and demons to perform feats of telekinesis; it is believed that angels and demons use etheric currents to fly, even without the use of their wings.

Exorcism: a method that can be used to injure or banish an angel, a demon, or a Jinn to another dimension; very powerful exorcisms can kill creatures like Jinn or their familiars.

Eye: another name for Lucifel's Grail, as it resembles a large emerald eye and sometimes even blinks or weeps; it looks remarkably like the eyes of the Father.

Fae: former angels who left Heaven to dwell on Earth and live in symbiosis with host plants; most Fae are believed to be extinct. Tileaf, a Fae dwelling in an ancient oak tree, had been abused by Luz's Vatican officials for her powers; she managed to show Angela Mathers part of Raziel's mysterious past before dying. A portal to Hell could be found beneath her tree and is occasionally opened by creatures moving between the Underworld and Earth.

Father: the angelic name for God; Angela strongly suspects that Raziel did not commit suicide out of despair, but that the Father—a powerful being with qualities much like the Supernals—murdered him deliberately.

Feathered serpent: intelligent, serpentine dragons with feathered plumes crowning their heads, they live in the high dimensions of Heaven. The most infamous of these creatures sided with Lucifel during the Celestial Revolution and became the demon Leviathan.

Fury: Troy's familiar in the body of a crow; she was once a human girl, but remembers little of her previous life.

Glaive: Lucifel's fabled weapon used in the Celestial Revolution; it is a pole arm made entirely of crystallized blue blood with a sharp blade at its tip; the Glaive is the mysterious Key that opens the Book of Raziel by destroying it.

Gloriana Cassel: a blood head fortune-teller who makes her home in Luz; she practices in secret, as her profession is outlawed by the Vatican; she owns a mirror claimed to have mysterious powers. Gloriana and her daughter saved Israfel's life when he found himself trapped on Earth.

Grail: see *Lucifel's Grail.*

Grand Mansion: the building in Luz where some of Westwood Academy's most formal affairs are celebrated; enormous angel statues line the steps to its entrance.

Half-breed: derogatory name for half-human, half-Jinn offspring; most are killed at birth. Kim (Sariel) is the only one known to exist at the present time.

Heaven: the highest dimensions of the universe; home of the angels.

Hecate: the deceased Jinn Queen and Troy's sister; she believed in the Archon and was murdered by rival Jinn, who feared she had become delusional in her hopes to rule. Juno is her only surviving child.

Hell: the lowest dimensions of the universe; home of the Jinn and demons; its uppermost levels are known as the Underworld.

High Assassin: Jinn term for their most illustrious and deadly hunter, second only to their Queen in respect; Troy is the current High Assassin and is a legend throughout Hell for her lethal skills.

Hounds: voracious predators of Hell that share characteristics with sphinxes; they are thought to be fallen Cherubim and are one of the only creatures Jinn fear.

Ialdaboth: the highest dimension of Heaven, accessible only to the ruling Archangel by a spiraling bridge. Ialdaboth was the first Realm to be inhabited by the angels but has been abandoned for millennia. Israfel was imprisoned here against his will by the Father.

Israfel: the Creator Supernal and Heaven's first ruling Archangel, legendary for his beauty and charisma. His once-defining bronze-colored hair and wings have since bleached to a shocking white; he disappeared into Ialdaboth at the end of the Celestial Revolution and had been presumed dead for ages. Angela Mathers was infatuated with Israfel but found him shockingly changed from the person he used to be; he has been slowly dying since Lucifel infected him with her shadow during the Celestial Revolution.

Luz Institution: a mental asylum in Luz; it is a forbidding medieval-looking tower perched on a sea cliff; Stephanie Walsh was sequestered behind its walls after she went insane; later, it was used as the base of operations for Lucifel's bloodletters.

Jinn: intelligent beings who live in the dimensions of Hell known collectively as the Underworld. With a society structured into six ruling Clans, they are descendants of angelic offspring judged to be imperfect and thrown into Hell to fend for themselves or die. Beautiful but savage, they are known by humans as devils. Out of all the angelic races, they have had the most contact with humans.

Juno: the only surviving heir to the Jinn throne, she is Hecate's daughter and Troy's niece.

Key: the object that can open the Lock sealing Raziel's Book; its identity and whereabouts were initially a mystery; it has since been revealed as the Glaive.

Kheshmar: a Cherubim living in the catacombs beneath Luz; she is Azrael's female twin but unlike him was never given a new and more human-looking body.

Kim: a half-Jinn who pretended to be a novice in Luz to get close to the Archon (Angela Mathers); his Jinn cousin Troy is hunting him out of revenge for killing her uncle, who was Kim's father. He is also known by the Jinn name of Sariel, given to him by his father. After killing his father, Kim was protected and raised by the demon Mastema, who hoped to use him in the future to free Lucifel from her chains, which could not be unlocked by any other human, angel, or demon of pure blood.

Kirin: creatures of Hell that vaguely resemble horses but have sharp horns, paws, and bioluminescent eyes and markings on their bodies. They are often hunted by the Jinn and their horns are used in Jinn headdresses. The winged males of the species are exceedingly rare.

Lilith: the most powerful female demon in Hell after Lucifel; Python's mother, whom she created with the feathered serpent Leviathan.

Lock: the seal on the Book of Raziel; it can only be opened by the Archon. Though the Key's whereabouts were initially a mystery, the Lock has since been revealed to be Sophia's physical body; it is unsealed by cutting into her lethally with the Glaive, which acts as the Key.

Lucifel: the Destroyer Supernal responsible for the Celestial Revolution at the dawn of time, Lucifel fled to Hell with the demons but ruled her regime as a god imprisoned by her own worshippers. Her ultimate goal is to use Raziel's Book to silence the universe, but why she wishes to do so remains a mystery; most believe she has gone insane from her long imprisonment. Lucifel sent her shadow to confront Angela Mathers in Luz, but Angela destroyed it, weakening her. Lucifel has the ability to drain a person's energy or kill them with a touch. She has recently been freed from her imprisonment in Hell by Kim, leaving Angela trapped in her place and forced to reign as the new Prince of Hell.

Lucifel's Grail: a mysterious eye-like pendant in the possession of the Jinn, first embedded in the hand, and now in the left eye of Angela Mathers; it was initially worn by Lucifel and has fearsome powers; most who look into its depths go mad. Its origins are a complete mystery; the Grail must bleed for the Glaive to be formed.

Luz: an island city off the American continent, officially under the jurisdiction of the Vatican. Luz's most well-known feature is Westwood Academy, the school that has become a haven for gifted students as well as blood heads; it has been besieged by increasingly foul weather for at least one hundred years. Technology and the occult are outlawed in Luz. Angela Mathers has learned that Luz is the connecting point between Earth and the other dimensions and is thus a portal for the supernatural.

Malakhim: a dimension of Heaven and the city of the angels. Malakhim is incredibly large and revolves in space in the shape of a galaxy-like disc.

Mastema: the most powerful male demon in Hell, and Arch-demon under Lucifel. Kim's foster father, he wanted Kim to destroy the Archon when She appeared. He is now suspended in eternal punishment in the Dead Tunnels of Babylon.

Memorial Cemetery: a large grove near Luz's western coast that was once a park. It was originally famous for the enormous oak tree at its center—Tileaf's tree—but is now a graveyard dedicated to those who died in one of Luz's greatest storms.

Mikel: a female angel who claims to be Lucifel and Raziel's daughter and sister to Archangel Zion, she has been presumed dead for millennia. Mikel is a spirit and has no real body, so she must possess a host in order to communicate. She was responsible for letting the demons know the Archon existed, effectively setting events in motion. Mikel possessed Nina Willis after Angela accidentally summoned her to Earth; Angela then brought her to Tileaf. Once Angela's ally, Mikel's true allegiances are now shrouded in suspicion; she harbors an immense grudge against Israfel and her brother Zion for imprisoning her in Heaven, and has more than once expressed a desire to die by Lucifel's hand.

Naamah: demon and foster mother of Stephanie Walsh, now deceased.

Netherworld: a dark and forgotten dimension where human souls used to gather after death, it was emptied by Angela Mathers, and the souls within, who claimed allegiance to the Archon and went to a higher dimension to await her rise to power.

Nexus: the highest existing dimension, known to be the dwelling place of God and where all souls, whether human or angelic, must eventually return after death.

Nina Willis: human girl who, during her mortal life, was ostracized by others for her psychic abilities. Nina developed a friendship with Angela, but unintentionally became possessed by Mikel in a séance gone wrong; she was murdered by Naamah shortly afterward and allowed herself to descend to Hell in exchange for Angela's freedom. A year later, Nina was resurrected by Python in a deal made with her half-brother Camdon Willis, but ended up dying again trying to save Troy and Juno from a possessed Stephanie Walsh. Nina is now a Vapor in the shape of a crow, with the unique ability to shape-shift back to her human form at will.

Python: one of the most feared demons in Hell; the son of Lilith and Leviathan, he can take on the form of a feathered serpent like his father. Python eventually lured Angela into his deadly maze in Hell, hoping to use her to confront Lucifel and claim Lucifel's empty Throne for himself. He is known to be capricious and cruel.

Raziel: the Preserver Supernal and creator of the Book of Raziel (Sophia); well known for his wisdom and gentle disposition; he was thought to have committed suicide after his lover Lucifel failed in her rebellion against Heaven. He is believed to be the Archon's guardian spirit, and his presence near her soul has given her his distinctive red hair and blue eyes; recently, it has been strongly implied that Raziel did not commit suicide but was murdered by the Father.

Ruin: the most common term for the dark messiah known more secretly as the Archon; many prophecies predict the Archon will choose the side of evil and destroy humanity. Angela seemingly fulfills this prophecy when she is forced to reign as the new Prince of Hell in Lucifel's stead.

Sariel: Kim's Jinn name, given to him by his deceased Jinn father; Troy always refers to him by this name.

Sophia: the human form of the Book of Raziel; though commonly regarded by others as a "thing," Sophia has a strong personality that belies her delicate appearance. She told Angela Mathers that her body was created as a Revenant, with the ability to be destroyed and resurrected by Lucifel as long as Sophia is in her power. She said she originally died in childbirth, which Angela suspects is a lie.

St. Matthias Church: an old church in Luz no longer in use; it is the place where Angela and Israfel first met.

St. Mary's Cathedral: an enormous church in Luz that has been the scene of numerous supernatural occurrences. The demon Naamah murdered many people behind its walls, though the Archon is solely to blame in the memories of most citizens in Luz.

Stephanie Walsh: a blood head witch who was once imprisoned in Luz's sanatorium, the institution; at one time, she was suspected of being the Archon. She is the demon Naamah's adopted daughter and is indirectly responsible for Brendan Mathers's death, as well as the deaths of many other individuals in Luz. Stephanie went insane after Lucifel possessed her, forcing her to try to open Sophia against her will. She was in love with Kim (Sariel).

Supernals: the highest-ranking angels of all, they are three siblings, Israfel, Raziel, and Lucifel, known collectively as the Angelic Trinity. Unlike most angels, the Supernals have six wings, but they rarely reveal them all; they are immortal and have immense power. The Father claims to be responsible for their creation, although Lucifel has long suspected this is not the case.

Theban: the demonic tongue; in its written form it resembles a scripting of curves and sharp lines.

Thrones: the angelic rank acting as bodyguards for higher-ranking angels; most Thrones have a deformity of one kind or another. They are direct but artificial derivatives of the sphinxlike Cherubim.

Tongue of Souls: otherwise known as Latin, it has the power to harm or bind angels, demons, and Jinn.

Troy: the greatest Jinn city in the Underworld, destroyed millennia ago by an alliance Python formed between the angels and demons; it is often used among the Jinn as a given name and is the name of the current High Assassin of the Jinn.

Underworld: name for the dimensions in Hell that are home to the Jinn.

Vapor: the term for a Jinn familiar; they are a human soul within an animal body, usually that of a crow, cat, or dog; Vapors communicate with their masters through telepathy.

Vermillion Order: a coalition of blood head students at Westwood Academy who have segregated themselves from the remaining student population.

Westwood Academy: an illustrious school that is the only haven for blood heads in the world; maintained and run by Vatican officials, Westwood derived its name from the enormous oak tree (Tileaf's tree) that could be found in Memorial Park, near the western coast of Luz.

Witch: a female human who can conjure angels or demons.

Zion: the currently reigning Archangel of Heaven; one of Lucifel's legendary children, presumed to have been executed long ago.

About the Author

Sabrina Benulis lives in the Pocono Mountains of Pennsylvania with her husband, daughter, and a spoiled but sweet cockatiel. When she isn't writing or cooking up another story to tell, she's learning to be Supermom.